Dear Reader,

Welcome to another month of exciting romances from
Scarlet. From your letters to date, for which I thank
you, it seems as though you are enjoying my monthly
choice of new novels.

I wonder, have *you* ever thought of writing a romance?
We are always looking for talented new authors here at
Scarlet. Do you think you could produce 100,000
words of page-turning storytelling which readers such
as yourself would enjoy? Don't worry if you're not a
professional author, as we're happy to help and advise
you if your work shows promise. If you *are* interested in
trying your hand at writing for *Scarlet*, why not write
to me at Robinson Publishing (enclosing a stamped
addressed envelope) and I shall be happy to send you
a set of our guidelines?

Keep those letters (and manuscripts!) pouring in!

Till next month,
All best wishes,

Sally Cooper

SALLY COOPER,
Editor-in-Chief – *Scarlet*

About the author

Andrea Young started writing because it was a wonderful excuse for not doing any housework! She has lived in Cyprus, Abu Dhabi and Oman and has variously been a model, an air stewardess and a teacher of English as a foreign language.

Andrea now lives in Surrey with her husband, two teenage daughters, and, as she says, 'a barmy spaniel and the fattest cat in the Home Counties!'

Other *Scarlet* titles available this month:

MASTER OF THE HOUSE – Margaret Callaghan
SATIN AND LACE – Danielle Shaw
NOBODY'S BABY – Elizabeth Smith

ANDREA YOUNG

NO GENTLEMAN

Enquiries to:
Robinson Publishing Ltd
7 Kensington Church Court
London W8 4SP

First published in the UK by Scarlet, 1997

A copy of the British Library Cataloguing in
Publication data is available from the British Library

ISBN 1-85487-929-4

Printed and bound in the EC

10 9 8 7 6 5 4 3 2 1

Part One

PROLOGUE

'It's that agony aunt,' said Tara. 'The smug one you can't stand.'

Daisy had no time for breakfast television. With half a slice of toast in her mouth, she was hunting for her car keys. 'Some of us have to go to work, you know. Where the hell . . .'

Tara was enjoying a twenty-four hour virus, also known as the after-effects of the heavy weekend she'd only just crawled in from. Still dressed for London's wilder clubland, she was sprawled on the sofa. 'She could do with some advice herself, if you ask me. On her non-existent dress sense. Just look at that gruesome sweater!'

Pausing in her key hunt, Daisy cast a glance at the screen.

'Of course, some people don't actually want a reply,' the agony aunt was saying. 'Some of them actually say so. Sometimes the very fact of putting a problem on paper and sending it to somebody sympathetic can help enormously. Sort of exorcise a ghost, if you know what I mean. Literally hundreds of people begin by saying, 'I've never told anybody this before, but – '

'Die, you boring woman.' Tara pointed the remote control at the television and flipped to children's cartoons.

About to say, 'I was watching that!' Daisy stopped herself. She unearthed her keys from under a magazine and grabbed her bag. 'Got to go – see you later.'

But three hours later, during a lull at work, she found her mind wandering back to that agony aunt.

'*I've never told anybody this before, but . . .*'

Idly, she began writing a letter in her head.

'*Dear Smug Agony Aunt,*

I saw you today on breakfast television – I didn't like your sweater, by the way – dayglo colours are a bit much first thing in the morning. However . . .'

That night, propped up on navy striped pillows, she wrote it by the light of her bedside lamp.

'*However, I'm going to test your little theory and see whether telling a total stranger will exorcise my ghost. Once upon a time (four years ago, actually) I had a Brief Encounter. We were only together for about three hours and in that time he managed to make me feel I had taken some lethal aphrodisiac. I never even told him my name and yet – shock horror – we nearly Did It. I should perhaps add here that I had never actually Done It before, so I suppose it would have been a total disaster anyway, because when I actually did Do It a few months later it was a bit of an anti-climax, if you'll pardon the pun. The thing is, even after all this time, I still can't quite get him out of my mind. I'm not languishing non-stop – I do have a life – but occasionally I wonder whether I will ever forget him completely. Sometimes I have this ghastly feeling that when I'm thirty-eight and married with two point four*' kids and a labrador I'll suddenly see him again, and that will be it. I'll have a raging affair, he'll disappear again, and I'll still be be yearning for him for ever more.'

She thought a while, and wrote her own reply.

'Dear Yearning,

Because I am such an extraordinarily caring human being (I will pretend you didn't call me smug), I'm just the sort of person who knows exactly what is best for everybody else. I can't help being perfect – that's the way I was made, and by the way that sweater cost a bomb. If you want my candid opinion, you are what your friend Tara would call a dippy cow. Firstly, you'll probably never see him again, and even if you did, by the time you're thirty-eight with two point four kids he'll be forty-two or so with a fat wobbly gut and probably a receding hairline, too. If you ever bump into him, it'll very likely be at the DIY superstore where he'll be buying non-drip gloss and saying to his wife, "Yes, dear, I think primrose'd be perfect for the kitchen." With every appearance of enthusiasm, too.'

Lying back on her pillow, she re-read the whole thing.

Why ever didn't I do this before?

She ripped the pages out, screwed them up and tossed them into the bin.

Bye bye, O haunter of my dreams.

CHAPTER 1

Just occasionally Daisy wondered what it would be like to have a normal mother.

'I don't think you quite understand, Mum,' she said patiently. 'I'm not talking Guide Camp here. I'm talking four days in London with Tara. Days *and* nights. At Tara's brother's student flat. You're supposed to be throwing a fit and going on about sex, drugs, and general depravity.'

'You're nearly eighteen, darling. I'm sure you'll be sensible.'

Maybe I don't want to be. 'Tara's going up tomorrow, but I'm babysitting so I can't go with her. I'll have to go on the train.'

'No need for that.' Her mother looked up from the roses she was dead-heading. 'Why not take the car?'

'But I only passed my test three weeks ago! I haven't even been on a motorway yet!'

'Motorways are nothing, darling. You'll have to do it sometime.'

Thunderstorms were forecast when Daisy finally set off, but that was the least of her worries. Since she had never driven more than fifteen miles from home before, her main concerns were to make it to the murky suburbs of south-west London without a) getting lost, or b) her mother's eleven-year-old banger breaking down.

Banger had recently been serviced, but that was no guarantee of good behaviour. Banger resented having his innards poked about by oily-fingered mechanics who made insensitive jokes about scrap heaps. He frequently reacted by sulking; conking out at roundabouts or flashing ominous red lights when you were miles from a garage.

Daisy had accordingly armed herself with a spare fan belt and four orange squash bottles full of water. On a hot day Banger could gulp more water than a Sahara-crossing camel.

She passed five roundabouts before hitting the M4 and, amazingly, Banger went round them all like a lamb. He didn't so much as cough at a crossroads, and by the time she was half a mile from the motor-way, Daisy had begun to relax.

This was her fatal mistake, of course. Banger loved doing this – lulling you into a sense of false security before launching his offensive.

There were no red lights as she hit the slip road. Banger was more subtle than that. He just seemed to be pulling the wrong way, like a horse that's made up its mind to ignore an inexperienced rider. In fact, Daisy sometimes wondered whether Banger had been just such a horse in a previous life. He knew perfectly well that his 'rider' was only pretending to be experienced and he was going to show her up if it killed him.

She barely saw the hitchhiker thumbing a lift at the side of the slip road, even when he stopped thumbing and waved at her, instead. She was too busy having forty-eight kittens all at once at Banger's eccentric behaviour.

Just on the motorway, she pulled into the hard shoulder and got out.

Banger was laughing at her. She could swear it. His radiator looked suspiciously like a malicious grin, and his headlamp-eyes had a positively wicked glint.

'You useless apology for a car!' Nearly in tears of rage and misery, she kicked the flat tyre at his left front end. 'Couldn't you have done it yesterday, while I was just nipping into the village?'

Banger made no reply, so she kicked him again.

'If you do that again,' said a lazy voice behind her, 'I shall have to report you to the Royal Society for the Prevention of Cruelty to Geriatric Cars.'

Daisy jerked around and saw the hitchhiker strolling towards her.

Her first impression was of a Centre Court tennis player in the wrong kit. He wore denim shorts and a denim shirt with rolled-up sleeves, completely unbuttoned. His chest was as nut-brown as his legs and arms, and fuzzed likewise with dark hair. He wore sunglasses and a sweat band over his brow. His hair was dark conker-brown and just long and untidy enough to make her think of beach bums.

'It's not funny,' she said crossly, passing the back of her hand across a brow that was rapidly becoming very hot and bothered. Which was not perhaps surprising. It was eighty-odd degrees, the air so thick with humidity you could practically swim in it.

He stopped about four feet away and dumped the bag which had been slung over his shoulder on the tarmac.

'You should have stopped back there, when I waved. Driving on a flat wrecks it.'

'It was only a hundred yards!'

'That's enough to wreck it.'

'I thought you were just trying to get a lift! I didn't realize it was flat! I knew something was wrong, but . . .'

'You didn't know what. And now you do, alas.'

Oh, do shut up. Daisy cast a wretched eye at Banger's wheel, wondering how much new tyres cost. Twenty pounds? Forty? A lot, anyway. Enough to make a big hole in the spending money she'd worked so hard for, babysitting and stacking supermarket shelves.

'It's an unfortunate fact of life,' observed the hitch-hiker, 'that merely gazing dolefully at flat tyres doesn't get them fixed. The usual procedure is to whack the spare out of the boot and whack it on.'

'Do you specialize in stating the obvious?'

'Now and then,' he mused. 'And if you'll bear with me, I'll do a bit more. Right this minute, two thoughts are going through your head. The first is roughly, "Oh, sod it, I've never changed a wheel before," and the second is, roughly, "This scruffy guy could probably do the honours, but then I'd have to give him a lift and that would be asking for trouble."' He added a smile as if to say, '*Right*?'

He oozed a laid-back confidence that went perfectly with the dusty grubbiness of his shorts and shirt. It went perfectly with his voice, too. It was dark and deep and warm as melted chocolate. There was a faint burr, too, which she couldn't quite place, but it made her think of warm, lazy days by the sea.

He was older than the boys she hung around with, but not by many years. He wasn't a boy any more. He

8

wasn't quite a man, either. He was sort of poised between the two.

Daisy, on the other hand, had only binned her school blazer two weeks back. 'Wrong,' she retorted, pushing a few tendrils of hair from her forehead. 'I know perfectly well how to change a wheel so you might as well just toddle back to the slip road.'

Of course, he'd been partly right. She had never changed a wheel before, but three doors away at home there lived a retired policeman who had not only taught her to drive, but had also impressed upon her the dangers of being female, stranded and clueless, and had gone through the routines of wheels and fan belts with her.

Returning to Banger's other side, she took the keys out, unlocked the boot and removed the spare and tools.

Hitchhiker folded his arms across his chest. 'How about a deal? I'll do it, if you'll give me a lift to London.'

'I don't pick up hitchhikers. And what makes you think I'm going all the way to London?'

'The *A to Z* on the front seat?'

'Brilliant, Monsieur Poirot, but I repeat, I don't pick up hitchhikers.'

'I don't bite,' he said. 'I don't even back-seat drive. Just look on me as your Knight of the Road, who's temporarily without a charger.'

Was there no limit to the bull some of them dished out? For once in her life, she thought of a smart remark in time. 'You're so full of you-know-what, I bet even your eyes are brown.' *Blast it, why didn't I do it properly and say 'shit'? Trust me to be polite and spoil the effect.*

The hitchhiker tried to looked pained and shook his head sadly, but his mouth gave him away. Unlike his nose and chin, which were lean and rather stone-carven, his mouth looked as if it were always just about to smile. Just now, it looked very much as if it were trying hard not to laugh. 'It grieves me to hear a girl of obviously tender years use such a coarse expression. And they're not brown, as it happens.' But he didn't take his sunglasses off to prove it.

Daisy gave him a pitying look. It didn't work quite as well as she'd have liked, partly because of his grossly unfair height advantage. He made her five foot four and a half feel positively titchy, especially with the flat, skimpy-strap sandals she'd teamed with an equally skimpy-strap sundress.

'I don't need any knights, thank you, with or without chargers. I should get back to that slip road if I were you, before we get that thunderstorm the weathermen have been promising.'

But the hitchhiker did not trot off back to the slip road. He removed himself to the verge, where poppies grew in the long grass and a thousand grasshoppers buzzed. He sat back, leaning on his elbows with the general air of a man about to enjoy a good laugh. 'Got the handbrake on?' he enquired.

She didn't even bother replying. Did he think she was completely clueless?

Trying another tack, he picked a scarlet poppy and gazed at it. At least, she thought he was gazing at it, but it was difficult to be sure, partly because she was only watching out of the corner of her eye while trying to pretend she wasn't, and partly because of his sunglasses.

'Now I've offended her,' he remarked sadly to the poppy. 'She thinks I'm one of those appallingly patronizing males who assume The Little Woman doesn't know one end of a spanner from another. Whereas I was only thinking of her breaking her nails and getting in a muck sweat. The thing is, Poppy, just because you can do something doesn't mean you have to. You conserve your energy and get some willing mug like me to do it for you.'

Cornish, Daisy thought, with satisfaction. It had been bugging her. *West Country, anyway*. No wonder he reminded her of the sea. She'd spent masses of summer holidays in Cornwall when she was younger.

He yanked his bag behind him, and lay back, using it as a pillow. 'My name's Nick, by the way,' he went on to the poppy. 'I know I don't look exactly like the Archbishop of Canterbury, but I'm reasonably harmless, not that it's any good telling her that. She reads the papers, you see, and all these horror stories about men who look like your Nice Lawnmowing Mr Average, but are actually raging psychopaths.'

Although she was intent on leafing through the manual for instructions, Daisy managed a retort. 'Anybody who talks to poppies has to be a raging nutter.'

'Whatever next?' he said wonderingly to the poppy. 'She was listening to our private conversation. A bit of a nerve, don't you think? As for calling me a nutter, I'll have you know our esteemed heir to the throne supposedly talks to flowers. You'll know him if he ever pulls in for a chat, because he's got sticky-out ears and walks with his hands behind his back.'

11

Daisy was doing her best to ignore him, but it wasn't easy, since he was only about six feet away and obviously watching her every move behind those sunglasses. Cars whizzed past incessantly, the heat and fumes and humidity making her crosser and more irritable than she was already.

Just ignore him, she told herself firmly.

Everything was ready. Spare, instructions, jack, spanner. First you levered the hubcap off, then you loosened the nuts, then you jacked it up and took the flat wheel off, then you put the spare on and did everything in reverse.

A doddle, in other words.

The only real problem had nothing to do with mechanicals. Her dress, a clingy navy item with tiny white flowers, had not been the shortest on the rail but it wasn't long enough to ensure modesty if she was bending over wielding spanners. Not with him sprawled on the grass right behind her.

What do you care? You can bet he's seen plenty of knickers before. Both on and off.

Yes, but not like mine. They're those titchy black ones Mum put in my Christmas stocking and half my bottom hangs out the sides.

Just be thankful it's not a big fat flolloppy one, then. Tara wouldn't care if half a dozen men were gawping up her skirt. She'd think it was all a huge giggle.

Tara wouldn't be changing wheels in the first place. She wouldn't even have considered changing wheels. She'd have given him a dazzling smile before he'd uttered one word and said, 'Oh, gosh, I suppose you couldn't possibly help me, could you?' And she'd have sat back like Lady Muck instead of getting all hot and bothered. She'd have given him another dazzler when he'd finished and very possibly a kiss too. She'd have given him a lift and flirted outrageously all the way. Because even you must admit that he is decidedly flirt-worthy.

If you were the flirting type, that is. Tara had made flirting into an art form. But Tara would never have got a flat in the first place, because she had a brand new Suzuki Jeep, bought by Daddy for her eighteenth birthday, not some old heap with tyres that would surely be condemned to death at their next MOT.

Tara was Daisy's best friend, but there was no denying she sometimes made her sick with envy.

Forget Tara, and get spannering.

Levering the hubcap off was such a piece of cake, her confidence soared.

Loosen the nuts before jacking up. This was less cakey, but no big deal. With a bit of effort, the first three gave way quite easily.

It was the fourth that defeated her. No matter how she heaved and grunted, it refused to budge.

Hitchhiker was really enjoying himself now. Lying in the grass, propped on his elbow, he issued helpful advice. 'Probably just needs a good squirt of lubri-cant. Got a can of lubricant in the boot?'

Shut – up! She heaved and grunted some more.

'Get down a bit more,' he advised. 'Really put that little back into it.'

You'd love that, wouldn't you? A really good eyeful.

But what the hell. She got down a bit further and put every ounce of strength into it.

13

The bastard still wouldn't shift.

'Seized-up nuts can be a trifle stubborn,' remarked the bastard behind her. 'Sometimes the heads snap off and then you're really up the proverbial creek.'

That did it. Red-faced with exertion and fury, Daisy straightened up and approached him, brandishing the spanner. 'How would you like your nuts snapped off, you pain-in-the-neck wretched – '

With a swift, fluid movement he rose to his feet. 'Oh, give it to me,' he said, with infuriating male tolerance, taking the spanner from her hand.

God, it was so galling to see the easy, confident way he applied spanner to nut, expecting it to shift with only a modicum of his massive strength.

Except that it didn't.

Being only human, Daisy enjoyed a silent but sweetly triumphant laugh as a frown appeared on his brow. However, the gloat-impulse quickly died. He tried again, with more show of effort this time, and failed again.

'Hmm,' he frowned, straightening up. 'It would seem that we are in a stuck-nut situation.'

From early childhood Daisy had been forming the impression that most men were pretty useless at the best of times and this had not changed it one whit. 'You can't shift it, you mean. After you thought it would be such a doddle.'

As she'd fully expected, he rose to this. 'I was hardly giving it all I've got. If you want me to force it and possibly snap the head off, I will.'

'Then what would I do?'

He shrugged and pushed his flopping hair back with his forearm. 'Ring the AA. There'll be a phone box not far up the road.'

Thank heaven, belonging to an emergency service had never come under her mother's list of Urgent Economies. With a car like Banger, failure to pay your AA sub was a very false economy indeed.

But she'd be messing about for ages. Whereas if he could shift it . . . 'Give it all you've got, then. Please,' she added hastily, just in case he decided to sulk and disappear up the slip road after all.

He got stuck in again, and this time she really thought it was going to snap. His muscles bulged under the shirt and his face positively contorted with effort. And suddenly, the nut gave up the unequal struggle.

'Phew,' he breathed, straightening up. 'Stubborn little devil. Almost as stubborn as you.'

Daisy was almost sick with relief.

Almost at once, he bent down again and began fitting the jack.

'No! I will give you a lift,' she added hastily, as he glanced up, 'but I'd really rather do it myself. I've never done it before and I'd rather know.'

He straightened up and gazed down at her. 'I knew you hadn't.'

And I just knew you were going to say that. 'But somebody showed me. So if you'll kindly just shift yourself . . .'

He stood back and managed to refrain from giving advice, restricting himself to holding the nuts.

When it was done, she was hotter and sweatier than she'd been in years, her hands filthy and her hair

15

escaping in wonderful disorder from its hastily twisted knot.

'Get in then,' she said shortly, after loading everything back into the boot.

He dumped his bag on the back seat and took the front passenger seat, adjusting it to its longest-leg position.

Phew. Daisy banged her own door. *And if you dare play up any more*, she threatened Banger silently, *I swear I'll drive you into the nearest river*.

She'd have given anything for some wet wipes, but there were only tissues to wipe her filthy hands on. 'Your face needs a lick,' observed Hitchhiker with mild amusement. 'You've wiped your mucky little mitts on your face.'

A glance in the rear view mirror told her he was right. There were smudges on her nose and cheeks, making her look like little Tom, the chimney sweep.

A lick on a tissue shifted them, and before moving off she adjusted her hair, letting it cascade in a golden-brown tumble down her back, before re-twisting it up in a scrunchie.

'My God,' said Hitchhiker. 'You could do a Lady Godiva with that hair!'

'It's not that long.'

'It's nearly to your waist! You could strangle yourself with hair like that!'

'I could also strangle irritating men.' With a glance over her shoulder, she pulled out.

This cutting remark had the effect of keeping Hitchhiker quiet for the first few miles, but he wasn't exactly ignoring her. On the contrary, she was all too conscious that under those dark lenses, a certain pair of eyes was giving her a pretty thorough going-over. And gradually, her relief at being on the road again wore off. She wished to heaven the radio wasn't broken. The silence, coupled with his evident scrutiny, began to make her feel acutely uncomfortable. Banger was not exactly large, and Hitchhiker seemed to be taking up more than his fair share of space. His brown, powerful thigh seemed almost indecently close to her own, and about twice the girth.

Everything about him seemed as strong and brown as that thigh. Even his warm, muskily male scent and his very air of relaxation began to unnerve her. She began to think of tigers, sleeping in the sun.

She glanced down at that thigh again, and her stomach suddenly contracted. He must be thirteen stone. And what was she? Barely eight.

An uneasy chill prickled her spine. Ever since she was five or six, she'd had it drummed into her. Strange men. Cars. '*He might seem as nice as pie, darling, but . . .*'

He could be absolutely anybody. What if . . .?

Don't be stupid!

Her fingers had tightened on the steering wheel. Consciously she relaxed them.

As if he sensed it, he glanced across at her. 'I dare say I'm not the best person to say this, but I'm glad you're not in the habit of picking up hitchhikers.'

Some minute nuance in his tone made her fingers tense again. 'I do assure you, I never will again.'

'I'll bet your sweet life you won't.'

The tiny lump of ice that had started forming in her stomach suddenly grew to iceberg proportions. Why would he bet her 'sweet life'? And what was that he had said about her getting strangled with her own hair?

Don't be stupid!

Who's being stupid? This is what nutters do – get you terrified bit by bit, in tiny little doses. It's how they get their kicks.

Keep calm. She had moved into the middle lane, but there was a space in the slow one. With a quick glance in the rear view mirror she swerved into it and on to the hard shoulder where she braked sharply. 'Get out,' she said, her voice as rigid as her fingers on the wheel. 'Get out right this minute, or I swear to God . . .'

She did it, anyway. Put her hand on the horn and kept it there.

'What the – '

'Get out!' she screamed.

'Shut up! Shut – *up!*' He yanked her hand off the horn.

Before she could say or do anything, he held up both hands at chest level, almost as if warding off evil. 'Don't scream. I'm going, OK?' His voice was terse and wary, as if he were dealing with somebody seriously deranged. 'I'm going to get out, and then I'm going to open the back door and get my bag off the back seat. And then you can drive away. OK?'

And in precisely five seconds, he had done just that. 'Now get going.' Savagely he banged Banger's flank. 'To a shrink, for preference. Get yourself straightened out.'

He turned and strode off in the opposite direction. Fast.

18

Daisy had not moved a muscle. In a few seconds, the iced fear in her stomach had melted, and something else had replaced it. That ghastly, complete-and-utter-prat feeling.

In the rear view mirror she saw him stop fifty yards back, and start thumbing again. And just then the first, spattering drop hit the windscreen.

Whatever have I done?

Feeling sick, she reversed slowly back to where he stood.

He ignored her.

She wound the window down. 'I'm sorry – I just got scared.'

'You don't say . . .'

The sarcasm in his voice brought tears to her eyes.

The raindrops were coming thicker now, several spattering the windscreen at once. In moments they would turn into semi-tropical sheets.

He was still thumbing, as if she wasn't there.

'I'm really sorry,' she faltered, leaning over to speak to him. 'Please, get in. It's going to pour any second. You'll never get a lift here.'

'I'd rather drown, thanks all the same.'

She thought of how soaked she'd have got if he hadn't shifted that nut, walking miles to the emergency phone and sitting wet and miserable in Banger till the mechanic showed up.

'*Please* get in,' she pleaded. 'I'm not really hysterical. It was that strangling remark that set me off, and . . .'

As her voice tailed off, he looked at her at last. And slowly, she saw his mouth soften. Slowly he walked the three steps to the car, opened the rear door and slung his bag in.

The rain was already turning to sheets, and his hair was glistening wet when he resumed his place beside her. 'Of all the bloody stupid things to say,' he said ruefully, turning to her. 'I didn't think. I'm sorry.'

'So am I,' she said unsteadily.

The corners of his mouth lifted. 'Peace?' he said, extending a hand. 'But just in case you still think I'm full of fertilizer . . .' He removed his sunglasses. 'See? Not brown at all.'

Daisy's heart gave a violent twist.

It was a bit like *The Wizard of Oz*, when the black and white bit suddenly changes to glorious Technicolor. His eyes were certainly not brown. They were dark onyx-green, rimmed with the kind of thick dark lashes no wretched man has a right to and glinting with something you couldn't quite put your finger on – something wild and sweet and wicked . . .

And for the next couple of hours, he was going to be sitting beside her. In rusty old Banger.

If only Tara could see her! She'd be sick as a pig. But Tara would not feel like this, all fluttery and worrying about saying something stupid and making a prat of herself all over again.

'Peace,' she said, taking his hand.

'I'm Nick,' he said. 'As you may have gathered.'

His hand was warm and firm and delicious, and held her own rather longer than necessary. And all the while, those devastating eyes melted the remaining shreds of her cool.

20

She hesitated only a millisecond. She had never liked the name Daisy much – it made her sound like something munching buttercups, with a brain to match. Her real name wasn't much better – it always provoked comments, if not downright incredulity.

'Hi, Nick,' she said carelessly, just as her best friend would. 'I'm Tara.'

CHAPTER 2

It was unbelievably liberating being Tara, once she'd started. And oh, how easily the lies came!

'Is this your car?' he asked, as she finally pulled out into the traffic.

'Oh, yes,' she said carelessly. 'I know it's a bit of an old heap, but I only passed my test three weeks ago and Daddy thought it'd be better to learn on something that wouldn't mind the odd scrape. He's getting me a Suzuki Jeep for Christmas.'

'Very nice,' he murmured.

'I'm just going to London for a long weekend,' she went on. 'My friend went up last night. We're staying at her brother's flat in Wandsworth.'

'Then maybe you can drop me at Putney tube station,' he said. 'I'm on my way to Fulham.'

'Is that far from Wandsworth?'

'It's just across the river.'

Dammit, why couldn't I have known? Now he'll think I'm some dozy country bumpkin who doesn't know one end of the Metropolis from the other.

'Are you on holiday?' she asked, changing the subject.

'More or less. I've just been catching up with friends I haven't seen in ages.'

'And now you're going home?'

'No, just back to some other friends I've been dossing down with for the past couple of weeks.'

Dossing, hitching . . . Is he unemployed, or just a bum?

'I start work on Monday,' he added, as if reading her thoughts. 'After three years as a student and another year travelling, I finally have to join the ranks of the grey suits. Find somewhere to live and buy a season ticket for the seven-fifteen.' He did not sound in the least enthralled at the prospect.

Four post-school years would make him twenty-two-ish – more or less what she'd thought. 'Where did you go on your travels?'

'All over. Greece, India, Oz . . .' With a rueful smile, he glanced across at her. 'That's why I need a job. I've run out of money. I've got just about enough to buy a grey suit and get a haircut before Monday morning.'

'What sort of job?'

'I don't want to talk about it,' he said. 'The mere thought depresses me intensely. A month ago I was diving off the Great Barrier Reef.' His voice lifted a little. 'What about you?'

'Oh, I'm off to Jamaica with my parents for a few weeks,' she said, trying to sound suitably blasé about it as she daringly pulled out into the fast lane. 'And then it's a boring course in French and Business Studies for three years.' That bit was true, anyway. 'Still, I don't suppose I'll have to do much work. It's all pubbing and clubbing and wild nights out at the place I'm going.'

She had a horrible feeling he was trying not to laugh. 'Delicious student decadence,' he murmured. 'I remember it well.'

Maybe he wasn't laughing, after all. She could just imagine him at the kind of parties Tara had already enjoyed several times at her brother's flat; everybody stoned out of their heads and hardly even knowing who they'd been to bed with. Tara's brother Tom never came home for the holidays because he was having far too good a time in London. He'd only been to two lectures all term. But as Tara often said, he was so incredibly brilliant, he didn't have to. All the lecturers were thick as planks – he should be teaching *them*.

'This rain's awful,' Hitchhiker murmured, as the wipers went hell for leather in vain. 'Slow down a bit, will you?'

She'd hardly noticed that her speed had crept up to seventy-five. 'I thought you said you didn't back-seat drive!' she said, slowing down anyway.

'I make a partial exception for very new drivers who don't seem to understand about torrential rain and stopping distances.'

Great. Now she felt about one and a half worms high. As if to rub it in, the person behind flashed impatiently, to make her move over.

'Are you sulking?' he asked, eventually.

'No.'

'I think you are.'

The mild amusement in his tone only made her crosser. 'I'm not!'

'I have three younger sisters,' he said. 'And I think I know when a girl's sulking.'

24

I wasn't sulking. I just feel too stupid to open my mouth.

'Where are you going in Jamaica?' he asked.

Oh, help. 'How should I know? Some hotel. My parents booked it.'

It was all going horribly wrong. He had sussed her out, she could swear it. He was thinking that the kind of father who could afford a few weeks in Jamaica would not buy a clapped-out old rustbucket for his daughter to drive. He was eyeing her dress and thinking it was pretty cheap; not the kind of thing a girl who was about to swan off to Jamaica would buy. She could feel those onyx-eyes on the skimpy skirt that only came halfway down her thighs.

Maybe it's not your dress. Maybe it's your legs.

Oh, yeah?

Why not? You know you've got nice legs.

Yes, and he's already seen enough of the backs of them, right up to my bottom. Including my bottom, most of it.

Maybe he's recalling that very image. It's one of your best bits, after all. The one thing Tara really envies you is your bottom.

Yes, but she's bound to have a big bottom, with a cleavage like hers. I'd give anything for a cleavage. All I've got is two pathetic little apples. A pair of Cox's Orange Pippins.

Well, you know what they say. Any more than a handful's a waste.

Dammit, was this wretched Nick a mind-reader? She could swear his gaze had slowly travelled upwards to the very area in question. And what was he thinking? '*Distinctly lacking in that department*', no doubt.

25

She couldn't help it; she coloured. Not a lot, but she felt a faint pinkness washing her cheeks.

Please, please don't notice. And if you do, don't comment.

If he did, he kept it to himself. What he did say, eventually, sent quite a different wash to her cheeks.

'That was a crazy remark to make, about your hair. But if I'd told you what I was really thinking, you might have got the wrong idea.'

Heaven help me, what? 'What?'

'I'd rather not say, or you might sling me out again.'

It didn't take too much imagination, after his Lady Godiva remark. '*I saw you naked, with all that beautiful hair cascading to your waist . . .*'

Oh, help. She knew she ought to be thinking, 'How dare you?' in a primly feminist way, but all she felt was a delicious, naughty little thrill. It died pretty fast. *Talk about wishful thinking. I bet he wasn't thinking any such thing. I bet he was thinking, 'Just as well you've got long hair, to cover up your Cox's Orange Pippins.'*

'Now I've made you blush,' he said. 'I knew I should have kept my mouth shut.'

This time, his gently teasing tone did not upset her at all. Even if he was just having a bit of fun with her, it'd be something to tell Tara. The trouble was, Tara would never believe how incredibly gorgeous he was. She'd say, 'Gosh, really?' but she'd think, '*I bet he wasn't that startling.*'

It was always Tara who got the gorgeous boys. Not because she was incredibly beautiful, but because she was so sickeningly bubbly and confident.

Daisy's confidence varied. Sometimes she was bursting with it; sometimes she felt as awkward and embarrassed as a six-year-old who's just wet the bed at a friend's house. And the one could change to the other with no trouble at all.

Her confidence started deserting her once they approached London. It was still raining, though not as hard, and the lorries threw up blinding dirty spray. Looking for signs was a nightmare.

Whether he sensed it and was just being tactful, or whether he just had the usual male attitude she didn't know, but he directed her without being asked. He navigated her over a horrendous flyover and into traffic-snarled streets where everybody but her seemed to know exactly where they were going.

He picked up the *A to Z*. 'If you tell me the address in Wandsworth, I'll direct you.'

She had just realized they were already in Fulham. Trying hard to look as if all these aggressive London drivers hadn't turned her into a nervous wreck, she said airily, 'I'll be fine. If you tell me the way, I'll drop you off at your friends' house.'

'Tara, it's right out of your way. You'll get lost trying to find the main road again.'

She gave what she hoped was a woman-of-the-world shrug. 'I've got a tongue in my head. If I get lost, I'll ask. You'll get soaked, walking in the rain.'

'It won't kill me.' As they paused at the traffic lights, he turned to her and smiled.

Those devastating onyx eyes wilted her completely. *Oh, Lord. For another smile like that, I'd get lost for a week.* 'You did me a favour. Tit for tat . . .'

He paused. 'If you're sure . . .'

'Quite sure,' she smiled.

His smile did a funny little twist. 'You know something? You're very pretty when you smile. You should do it more often.'

Oh, crumbs. How she got away from the lights without stalling, Daisy would never know. She was fluttering like a whole nest of baby sparrows.

For a mile or two he directed her down several streets and into a road of wall-to-wall parked cars and the smarter kind of little terraced house, with estate agents' signs at every other one. 'Here,' he said, outside a house where the front garden had been razed to provide parking space.

Suddenly, she couldn't bear to see him go. To see him just get out of Banger and walk away . . .

'Bye, then,' she said brightly. 'Good luck for Monday morning.'

But he didn't get out. His eyes dropped to her hands, and he removed one from the steering wheel. 'Still mucky,' he observed. 'Why don't you come in and wash them and I'll make you a coffee?'

Never had a prayer been answered so quickly. 'I'd love to,' she said unsteadily. 'But where do I . . .'

'In the front garden. They won't be back for hours.'

Thank heavens she didn't have to reverse park into a titchy space and mess it up and have him laugh at her. Banger slotted neatly into the front garden, and they went inside.

The house was Victorian, a large hall, two large rooms knocked into one, and all floored in bare blond wood. It had the bare look of somebody just moving in or out, with hardly any bits and pieces, and boxes everywhere. 'They're moving soon,' he said. 'You'll find the hand-washing facilities in there.'

He indicated a door that was obviously converted from an understairs cupboard. As downstairs loos go, it was minute, but Daisy didn't care. Her mind was racing into overdrive. *Why ever did you call yourself Tara? What if . . .*

What nothing, so don't start going all fluttery. He merely felt obliged to offer you a coffee.

But her heart was still racing when she came out. The kitchen was an open-plan part of the living room, and done in the same colour wood as the floor. He already had coffee on, the aroma wafting as it dripped through the filter. He had removed the sweatband and replaced the damp denim shirt with a navy heavy cotton sweater. She stood near him, about two feet away, watching the rain on a patio garden full of flowers.

After the earlier torrid heat, she felt suddenly chilly. Shivering, she folded her arms.

'You're cold,' he said, and casually ran a finger down one of her shivery arms. 'Like one of my sweaters?'

That touch electrified her. 'No, I'm fine.'

I don't want a sweater. I was thinking more of you standing just behind me and putting your arms round me and warming me up like that.

Fat chance.

He returned to the coffee maker. 'It's ready. Take a seat.'

She sat on a blue and lemon checked sofa and wished she'd accepted that sweater, after all.

'How do you like it?' he called.

'Milk, no sugar.'

Bearing two mugs, he came to sit beside her.

She sipped, and shivered again.

'You are cold,' he said. 'Maybe you should let that hair down. It's as good as a fur coat.'

Something in his tone sent an entirely different shiver through her. Well, why not? Her hair *was* warm. Putting her mug down, she lifted her arms, undid the scrunchie and let it cascade like a silky golden-brown curtain that fell way past her shoulders.

She knew he was watching every second, and it gave her an odd little thrill, as if he'd been watching something intimate.

For a moment, neither of them spoke. And suddenly, unbelievably, he reached a hand up and touched the hair that shimmered on her bare shoulder.

She froze. Not with fear, but with unbearable trembling anticipation.

His hand melted away. 'Tara, relax. When I said coffee, I meant coffee. Nothing else.'

She gave him a pitying look, like Tara would. 'I'm not *nervous*, if that's what you're thinking.'

'I'm glad about that.' He paused. 'You've got fantastically beautiful hair.'

Oh, help. Tara's never going to believe this. She shrugged carelessly. 'It's not that special.'

'I think it is.'

Oh, crumbs. I'm going all funny inside. His eyes are making me go all woozy.

For several seconds, his eyes held her fast. 'You know what?' he said softly. 'I think you'd better drink up that coffee and go, before I forget I'm supposed to be behaving myself.'

In that moment, Daisy knew she was at a crossroads. Tara would have giggled and said something like, 'Did I say I wanted you to behave yourself?'

She wasn't taking the act that far. She could go all tart and say, 'You'd jolly well better behave yourself.' Or she could do an eyes-to-heaven 'Oh, please.'

But somehow, she couldn't bring herself to do any of them. She looked away from those eyes, but they were drawing her like superpowered magnets, and they drew her back.

And held her.

It happened in the most trembling slow motion, first his hand, brushing her hair again like a whisper, then his finger, tracing a line from her cheek to the corner of her mouth, then his fingers, lifting her chin so delicately towards him.

From the first, shattering contact with his lips, Daisy was lost. She felt as if somebody had injected her with some wild intravenous drug. She trembled like a baby bird as the first softness of his kiss grew stronger, more demanding. His arms came around her, his hands caressing her back, the back of her head, as his lips and tongue possessed her.

Oh, Lord. This is what they mean when they talk about your legs going to jelly. If I were standing up . . .

The kisses went on long enough to turn the rest of her to jelly, and the way he touched perfectly innocent bits of her anatomy, such as the side of her neck, practically made her dissolve. Until he applied his magic fingers to it, she'd had no idea that the side of her neck could be an erogenous zone.

But it was nothing to what came next. With a touch like a butterfly's wing, he stroked the bare skin of her shoulder, and her heart stood still as he slipped the shoestring strap so gently off it.

She wore no bra. It wasn't possible, with a dress like that, tiny straps criss-crossing the back. Besides, her little Cox's scarcely needed one.

This was a stage Daisy had dreaded on previous such occasions. She always felt they were thinking, '*Blimey, is that it?*' and felt she ought to apologize. But this time, as he folded the material down and exposed her little round breast, she felt no such thing. Delicately he traced its curve with his finger, as if it were priceless alabaster. 'Like a little angel,' he whispered. 'Did anyone ever tell you you have the breasts of an angel?'

Oh, help. Why am I saving up for silicone implants? How she found a voice at all was a miracle. 'No,' she croaked. 'I can't say they have.'

Equally delicately, he touched its little pink peak, teasing it between finger and thumb.

If anything remained of her self-control that melted it for ever. It was as if he had sent shock waves to the V of her thighs. Heat and moisture flooded her instantly, her lips parted and her cheeks flushed. And when he bent his head and covered her nipple with his lips, she found out that overwhelming desire was not just something you read about in *Cosmopolitan*.

It flooded her, overpowered her. Gently he laid her back on the sofa, slipped off her shoes. His mouth on her nipple was like some exquisite torture, bringing tiny moans from her lips.

32

There wasn't room for both of them on the sofa. There was barely room for her to lie. He slithered to the floor, kneeling as his mouth caressed her breast. Her legs were bent up, her dress flopping back, not that she knew or cared. And when he gently parted her knees and his hand stole gently up the inside of the thigh, she thought she would die of agony.

But he made her wait. Like a whisper-torture, he brushed first the inside of one thigh, then the other. Time and again they brushed within a whisper, and left her crying out.

When at last he brushed the tiny slip of pink, she actually shuddered. And when he eased her pants over her hips and tossed them on the floor, she felt only a wild, stomach-lurching thrill.

After that, it was almost too much ecstasy for one girl to cope with. While his tongue created liquid fire in her mouth, his fingers fanned another fire. Her thighs melted apart as he found and stroked and teased her almost beyond endurance.

Until then, the thought of the actual act had always worried her. She'd never believed all that stuff about fireworks. It would hurt like hell. How could something so big and hard tearing into you not hurt?

But now . . .

Her hand fell to his shorts. Even under the thick denim, the feel of him made her gasp.

'*Damn!*' As if he'd been scalded, he jerked away.

For about half a second, Daisy thought she'd committed some terrible breach of sexual etiquette. Until she realized why he'd done it.

Frantically he was picking up her pants from the floor. 'I'm sorry, quick, get dressed . . .'

She'd already heard the key in the front door and there was no time to feel anything but panic.

Two seconds later she was outwardly respectable, her heart pounding as if she'd overdosed on adrenalin.

'Nick!' yelled a furious female voice from the hall.

'Yes?' he yelled back.

The door burst open and the furious female fumed on the threshold. 'If that's your ghastly, prehistoric old heap of metal in the garden, for crying out loud move it! I'm double parked!'

Despite the vocabulary, the voice was pure, cut-glass Sloane.

How she produced such self-possession, Daisy would never know. 'I'm terribly sorry, it's mine,' she said. 'I dropped Nick off and came in for a coffee. But I was just leaving.'

'Oh.' The woman, who was dark, strikingly attractive, and about his age or a little older, looked her up and down with a considerably less aggression. 'Sorry, but it really browns me off when people park in my space. It's my house, after all.'

'Hello, Juliet.' With his coffee mug, Nick stood behind the breakfast bar that divided kitchen from living area; just at the right height for concealing hard evidence. 'You're early. Fancy a coffee?'

'No, but you can bring me up a large vodka while I run a bath. Henry was driving me so mad, I walked out. I swear he's menopausal. God save us from temperamental, middle-aged old queens.' She slung her bag on a chair.

'Juliet works in an art gallery,' Nick said, as if that explained everything.

Certain that her recent activity must show on her face, Daisy marvelled at his aplomb. Anyone would think he was caught in the act on a weekly basis. How long would he have to stand there? Did sudden shock have an instantly deflating effect?

'This is Tara,' he added.

'Well, hi and bye, I'm off upstairs. Shift my car, will you?' She tossed her keys to Nick. 'And don't forget my vodka.' At the door she paused and looked directly at Daisy as if seeing her properly for the first time. 'A bit young for you, isn't she?'

Without waiting for a reply, she turned back to Daisy. 'Whatever he's been telling you, do take it with a couple of barrels of salt. Nick's a dear sweet boy but he's got gold medals for knicker-shedding charm. And I should know. They were Janet Reger, too. Red silk French knickers, and I never found the damn things again.' With a sweet smile, she departed.

By some heaven-sent grace, Daisy was sufficiently in control not to gape as the door shut behind her. She grabbed her bag and made for the door.

'Tara . . .'

It was as if she'd been under hypnosis and the hypnotist had suddenly snapped his fingers. 'I've got to go.' She didn't even look at him as she fled through the hall.

As she grabbed the door handle, he took her arm. 'Tara, wait!'

'I can't.' She shook him off and opened the door. 'I'm late already, and – '

'You don't know the way!'

'I'll find it. Thanks for the coffee.' She wrenched Banger's door open.

'Tara . . .'

She didn't even look at him. She reversed out so fast, she nearly hit what was obviously Juliet's car, double-parked on the other side of the road.

Her last sight of him was a perplexed, exasperated expression on his face as he watched her drive away.

She drove for several streets before even thinking of finding a place to park and consult her *A to Z*. When she finally found one, she hadn't a clue where she was and had to ask a passing pensioner. Her heart was still racing erratically but her voice came out more or less normally.

Even when she'd found herself on the map, she got lost several times more before finding the house with Tara's Jeep outside. She found a space about ten cars down the road, and managed to reverse park in only seven manoeuvres. When she got out, she did a double take. On the other side of the road was a sleek blue Jaguar that looked oddly familiar.

The house was both larger and shabbier than the one she'd just left, which did not surprise her. She hadn't expected luxury in a house chopped up into student flats. She never expected luxury at the best of times, which was just as well, since she never got it.

By the time she knocked on the door of flat 6B, her various systems were outwardly back to normal. 'Where have you been?' Tara demanded. 'I was expecting you a good hour ago!'

Daisy opened her mouth, but Tara cut her off. 'Our weekend's right up the spout.' Shutting the door behind her, she grabbed Daisy's arm. 'Quick, down the road.' Surreptitiously she took a packet of cigarettes from her pocket, lit one, and puffed furiously. Glancing back at the house, she groaned. 'The shit's really hit the fan. Tom's failed all his exams and they're probably going to kick him out and Daddy's only just found out. He came up half an hour ago and Tom was still stoned out of his head from last night, and Daddy went absolutely mental. He says he's not letting me stay here another night.' A few minutes and endless bewailings later, she said, 'Where *were* you, anyway?'

Sometimes, nothing ever sounds quite so fantastic as the truth. 'You'll never believe it, but I picked up a gorgeous green-eyed hitchhiker on the M4 and went back to his place and nearly had wild sex on the sofa, only some woman came home and wrecked it all.'

'Yeah, right.' Disconsolately Tara stubbed out her cigarette in the gutter. 'I suppose it was Banger playing up again. It's high time he was put down.' She gave a deep, browned-off sigh. 'Tom had a really wild party planned and now we'll be back to Bore-shire before the ten o'clock news. It's just not fair.'

Ten minutes later, against a noisy background of Tara's pleadings and a firm putting down of paternal feet, Daisy escaped. Gazing at her own clear grey eyes in the bathroom mirror, she wondered how she had ever come to nearly Do It with a total stranger.

It wasn't the Nearly Doing It that bothered her. She had been meaning to Do It pretty soon, only she had never quite fancied anybody enough. Well, she'd fancied Rob Carter enough, but she'd had a feeling he was the type to go and tell all his friends how he'd been the first to get Daisy Rose's knickers off, never mind telling them all about her Cox's Orange Pippins and the entire football team having a good laugh.

It was the total stranger bit that bothered her. She had never intended it to be like that. When she finally Did It, it was going to be after several dates, with a man she felt really comfortable with. Above all, she was going to be Properly Prepared.

Still, at least she knew now how these things happened. At least she knew how *she'd* happened.

In her mother's case it had been three days, not three hours. And here she was to prove it: Loveday Florence Rose. Loveday because that was when she had 'happened', according to her mother. On a lovely day of love. Florence, because that was where she had 'happened'. And Rose, because that was her mother's maiden name. She didn't have a married one and probably never would.

Some masochistic impulse made her slip the straps from her shoulders and peel her dress down.

That was what did it. Him telling you that pathetic pair of Coxes were the breasts of an angel. All he needed was those eyes and half an ounce of bull and he was nearly there.

Part of her was still trembling as she replaced the straps, the other part was more cynically employed.

Maybe she should be grateful to green-eyed Nick. From now on she would be immune to Fatally

Attractive Bastards. OK, so she'd feel rough for a few days, like after her BCG jab, but most inoculations were like that. Something you just had to get over and done with. But he had inoculated her, well and truly.

If only she could say the same for her mother.

Part Two

CHAPTER 3

The New Year's Eve Ball was proving something of a disappointment, even in a swish London hotel complete with chandeliers and gold-plated ballroom.

The supper had been lovely; flown-in strawberries and truffly bits on the terrines, but now it was over, Daisy was horribly bored. She was dying to dance. Everybody else was dancing – just about everybody, anyway.

But not Simon. Simon was still sitting at their table, discussing his investments with some overweight Hugh person he knew vaguely from the squash club which had organized the ball.

The couple they'd come with had disappeared; Jane, one of the girls who shared a flat with her, and Ian, her other half. They were probably dancing, but the floor was so packed, it was difficult to see.

'. . . and this new European fund looks very promising, but I'd have to sell some of my Far East holdings,' Simon was saying.

Restlessly Daisy stood up and scanned the floor. The band was taking a break and a DJ had taken over. He was playing an old Beatles number and people

43

were getting drunk or mellow enough to be in the mood.

Suddenly Jane appeared at her elbow. 'You still haven't managed to drag him up, then?' she asked, nodding towards Simon.

'No such luck. Discussing his investments on New Year's Eve, for heaven's sake . . .'

'They're hopeless,' Jane sighed, flicking back her blonde hair. 'I managed to get Ian up for two dances, but now he's sloped off to the bar.'

The music changed, to an even older Elvis rock and roll. 'He'd never dance to this, anyway,' Jane went on glumly. 'Won't make a prat of himself.'

They scanned the floor together. It had thinned out a bit. 'There's one man who doesn't mind making a prat of himself,' Jane observed. 'But maybe that's because he isn't.'

A little space had cleared as less adept dancers admired a couple who were putting everybody else to shame. In a sea of immaculate dinner jackets, the man stood out like a nun at an orgy. His jacket was discarded, his black tie likewise, his shirt just open at the neck. With the flair of a demon gypsy baron, he was whirling some redhead off her feet.

'That's at least the fifth woman I've seen him dancing with,' Jane went on. 'He's going through them like nobody's business.'

As she watched, an odd little prickle ran up the back of Daisy's neck. He was moving so continuously, it was impossible to be sure, but something in the set of his head, something in the way his hair flopped wildly over his forehead . . .

44

'You know what he puts me in mind of?' Jane went on. 'A wild Edwardian aristocrat, going to the dogs, as they used to say. Before the night is out he'll gamble away his inheritance, gallop a horse through the ballroom and shoot down all the chandeliers.'

Just as she said it, the man seemed to pause in his whirling. For half a second, over twenty feet of dance floor, he caught Daisy's gaze.

The prickle turned to an odd numbness. The noise around her turned to a faraway buzz as a massive penny hit her like a meteorite.

And bounced.

It's impossible.

Why? It's a pretty small world.

And how many years was it? Nine? Even if it was him, it was impossible to be sure.

If only he'd keep still! And if only those wretched people who'd just moved into the space in front of him would get out of the way!

But for a second or two, enough of a gap formed for her to see him again. And in that tiny moment, his eyes caught her again.

Heaven help me, it is him.

Or is it?

'Looks like you'll be next,' Jane giggled. 'He's giving you the eye.'

Daisy turned away from the floor, but her voice came out nearly normal, considering. 'I'll wait for Simon, thanks. I'm not that desperate.'

'Yes you are. And Simon'll be only too pleased to be relieved of his duties, if you ask me.'

Simon was topping up Hugh's glass with Chardonnay. '. . . thirty per cent last year,' Hugh was saying. 'Can't guarantee it in the future, of course, but the fund has out-performed all the others on the Footsie for the past two years.'

'I'm off to the ladies,' Jane announced. Lowering her voice she added, 'I don't know why they can't invent knickers that don't ride up into your bum-cleavage after a mere two dances.' Raising it again she directed it pointedly at Simon. 'And then I'm going to the bar to prop up Ian. Do come and join us, hon, before you die of terminal boredom.'

Simon looked up with an apologetic expression. 'Sorry, darling, I'm neglecting you. I promise I'll dance once this idiot DJ puts something slower on.'

The confusion in Daisy's stomach began to settle. Whenever she was in a state, Simon settled her. That was what she loved about him. His reassuring, anchor-like, always there-ness. What the hell did it matter if he had two left feet? He was better-looking than ninety per cent of the men in the room and his dinner jacket made him look like an advertisement for Armani evening wear.

She took his hand and gave it a squeeze. 'I'm not desperate. It's too hot in here for anything very energetic, anyway.'

Jane raised her eyes to heaven. 'Fibber,' she mouthed. 'See you, then. I'm off.'

Keeping her back to the floor, Daisy sat next to Simon at the round, white-clothed table. The flowers in a tiny vase were beginning to wilt, so she topped them up from a bottle of mineral water. She then refilled her

46

glass with Chardonnay and took a fair-sized swig, to drown the remaining squirms in her stomach. *It can't be him, can it?*

So what if it is? You put him out of your mind aeons ago. Don't look. However much you're dying to.

Restlessly she tapped her feet on the floor, her fingers on the table. It was Elton John's *Crocodile Rock* now, one of her all-time favourites. If Simon would only get off his backside! He might not be John Travolta, but he wasn't much worse than most of the other men making valiant efforts on the dance floor. At least it would take her mind off anything else.

'. . . and the Japanese market's bound to rise again,' the Hugh person was saying, 'but if you're looking for a short-to-medium term investment . . .'

Daisy's restlessness suddenly snapped. 'I tell you what would be a really good investment, if only some-body would invent it. Women's knickers that don't ride up into your bum-cleavage the minute you do anything energetic. They'd sell like hot cakes.'

They both stared at her. Simon's expression was vaguely startled; the overweight Hugh person's even more so. But a second later Hugh's face creased up, his ample, white-shirted gut wobbling merrily. 'Lord, that's a good one. How to test the product, that's the question. You'd need – '

'*Scusi.*' The satin-Latin voice came from nowhere. 'All night I die for just one dance wiz you.'

Daisy looked round and found herself looking up into two, onyx-green –

Without so much as a 'May I?' he took her wrist and pulled her to her feet.

47

She was too flabbergasted to even think about resisting. That firm hand threaded her through the crush and within two seconds she was being whirled off her feet.

Her brain was in a whirl of its own. *He's got an Italian double. A flaming, smooth-talking Italiano doppelganger. I got all in a stew for nothing.*

She hadn't danced like this in ages. With a man who really knew what he was about, who never twizzled her the wrong way or looked vaguely embarrassed as if dancing were really a cissy thing to do, or trampled her toes with his size elevens.

The dance was too fast and furious for her to look at him properly. But when it was over . . .

My God, he must have had Italian relations. The hair's shorter and there's no tan, but he's got that olivey skin that goes mahogany in two seconds. And the eyes are the same. Wild and sweet and —

'Hello, Tara,' he said.

For the first time in her life, Daisy found out what it was to be well and truly gobsmacked. But somewhere her brain was still working, even if only on one cylinder. 'I beg your pardon?'

The confident smile disappeared and a crashing disbelief replaced it. For about two seconds. Then an apologetic charm replaced that, with a smile to match. 'Forgive me. You look uncannily like someone else.'

That voice was like an arrow from the past, hitting the bullseye dead centre. The Cornish burr was fainter, but still there. The eyes were going full blast, but she was twenty-seven now, and immune. Folding her arms, she gave him a pitying look. 'Why did you put on that stupid Italian voice?'

'Because . . .' Lowering his voice, he bent down and whispered, 'I thought that guy whose leash you were on would tolerate such monstrous behaviour from some dashed Johnny-foreigner who didn't know any better.'

Who needs Italian smoothies, with home-grown ones like this? 'I was not on any *leash*. And if you think he'd have made the slightest fuss just because I danced with somebody else . . .'

'I can see that now.'

Over her shoulder, he nodded towards the table where Simon was still engrossed.

Daisy felt a pang of perverse irritation. Normally she numbered Simon's thoroughly civilized lack of cave-man jealousy among his many virtues. Now it rather felt as if he were taking her fidelity for granted.

'Another dance?' murmured the man at her side. 'Or shall I abduct you to the bar?'

The DJ was prattling on again. '. . . and now, to let all you lovers get your breath back, a nice, slow smoochy-feely one, to get you in the mood for . . .'

'Neither, thanks.' The floor was filling up again, and he was close enough for assorted male scents to waft into her nostrils. Warm male body mixed with clean shirt and shaving stuff . . .

'You don't get away that easily.' With an easy confidence that shattered her he put a hand on her waist and nodded over her shoulder again. 'He hasn't even missed you.'

Even if she'd never laid eyes on him before, that easy confidence would have made her bristle. He was just too certain of his own irresistibility. But quite apart from that, his very nearness and that light hand on her waist were opening various dusty files in her brain. Files she hadn't opened for ages.

Removing his hand, she put on her coolest smile. 'Thank you so much for the dance, but you can go and try your Latin smoothie act on somebody else now.'

But she didn't go back to Simon. She made for the only place a girl can repair her composure in peace – the Powder Room.

How fortuitous to have called myself Tara. At least I could look gobsmacked with some sort of conviction.

But even if you'd called yourself Daisy, it wouldn't have mattered. You'd have smiled – maybe a trifle sheepishly – and said, 'I wasn't sure it was you' and he'd have said, 'Me too, I had to get a bit closer to be sure', and then you'd have chatted for half a minute, like any other two adolescent ships that had passed in the night ages ago, and then you'd have said, 'Well, bye then, nice to see you again,' and gone your separate ways. You'd have been thoroughly grown-up about it.

But Daisy was uncomfortably conscious that she hadn't quite been grown-up about it. If she had, she'd have smiled – maybe a trifle sheepishly – and said, 'It's Daisy, actually. I was pretending be my best friend because she was so much more together than I was.' And then they'd have chatted for half a minute and gone their separate ways.

Still, too late now. Mechanically she adjusted her hair, tucking various bits back into the jewelled snood that contained its coiled masses.

It was nothing like as long as it had been, but it still fell to just below the bra area. Cutting it short had never appealed to her. Long hair was so versatile; loose and seductive, a neat French plait, or elegantly upswept, like tonight.

She re-applied her dusky rose lipstick, which was meant to stay on all night but obviously hadn't read the advertisements, and inspected the end product.

Do I really bear much resemblance to that dope in poor old Banger?

The skirt was almost as short, but the dress could hardly be more different. For a start, it had cost an arm and a leg. The top of the bodice and sleeves were of black, transparent material, almost as sheer as her ten denier stockings. Fitted to the waist, the black velvet then fell in soft folds that swirled gently when she moved.

The fact that he'd remembered her alias surprised her not at all. Smooth men always did. It was part of the *spiel*, to make you feel warm and special. '*And do you know, he actually remembered my name after all this time, even though we only had a quickie behind the filing cabinet.*'

She added a squirt of Jean-Paul Gaultier and headed for the bar. She needed her mind taken off a certain person, and Jane and Ian were always good for a laugh.

The queue at the bar was three deep, but Jane wasn't in it. She was nattering in a corner with a couple of friends of Ian's, from the squash club. For ten minutes it was welcome light relief. Everybody was swapping horror stories about family Christmases; Auntie So-and-So refusing to speak to Auntie Whatsit and what a pain their sister's kids were.

'Di and I had enough last year,' boomed a tanned, bearded chap whose name was Roger. 'This year we

51

rebelled. Buggered off to the Grenadines for some sailing.'

Ian turned up bearing a massive tray of drinks and an apologetic grin. 'The barman was going off his head and I couldn't remember what everybody wanted, so I just got beers and Buck's Fizz. And if anybody doesn't like it, tough.'

He had got extras to save going back, so Daisy helped herself to a Buck's Fizz. The orange juice was freshly squeezed and the champagne was real, giving her a proper New Year's Eve fizz.

'Bloody small world,' Ian went on. 'I bumped into an old friend at the bar. Haven't seen him for years. Cheers.' He winked at Daisy. 'Simon still talking money?'

'Afraid so,' she sighed. 'Balls really aren't his thing. He only came because it was for charity.'

'Simon's got his priorities right,' Ian said. 'By the time you finally get hitched, he'll have a portfolio fat enough to retire on.'

He winked again and Daisy smiled. Ian was one of her favourite men; tall, jolly and very slightly over-weight.

Jane linked her arm through his. She was five foot nine and as fond of her food as Ian, only on her it just looked voluptuous. 'Cheers, darling,' she said, raising her glass. 'Here's to our little Caribbean jolly. I can't wait to get out of this diabolical weather.'

'I'll second that,' Daisy said. 'I'm counting the days.'

The winter had been vile; so cold and miserable the four of them had decided they couldn't possibly wait for summer. A week before Christmas they had booked a thoroughly self-indulgent and horrendously expensive February fortnight in Barbados.

'Sun,' Jane sighed. 'Lovely hot sun.'

'And cricket,' Ian grinned.

Jane didn't even groan. 'You and Simon can watch all the cricket you like. Daisy and I'll be lying on the beach getting utterly worn out with trying to decide whether to fall into the sea or merely fall asleep.'

'While plugged into the intravenous rum punch,' Daisy reminded her. She could almost feel the sand between her toes already. She could almost hear the steel band, feel the sun on her –

'Coming to join us, me old son?' Ian was looking over the top of her head, his face breaking into a broad grin.

Glancing over her shoulder, Daisy thought, 'Oh, hell.' But she managed to keep a smile glued on.

Ian accomplished the introductions with informal speed. 'This is Nick Trevelyan, an old mate from college. This is Jane and she's mine, so keep your thieving hands off, the beard is Roger and that's his other half, Di. And this is Daisy.'

He was very good at hiding it, but the fleeting disbelief on his face told her he'd not been so easily taken in. He had come over in order to be introduced and prove himself right, after all.

For a moment she was wretchedly cross with herself for not having come clean before. It was impossible to do it now, in front of all these people. She would just have to continue the ridiculous lie. He'd probably disappear in five minutes, anyway.

'We've met,' she said, with a cool smile. 'We've danced, anyway.'

'I knew you were going to dance with her,' Jane said mischievously. 'I saw you giving her the eye, but I think I should warn you she's practically married. Still, she was dying to dance so maybe Simon won't beat you to a pulp. And her real name's Loveday, but she hates it.'

The bar was getting so packed, they were crammed together like commuters on the Tokyo underground. Nick was facing her, at a distance of about two feet. He was still minus jacket and black tie, the top button of a pristine dress shirt undone and his hair still wildly dance-tossed. She'd have liked to say he looked scruffy, but he didn't. He just looked, well, devastatingly dishevelled.

The evening trousers fitted perfectly, and he had obviously not put on any flab in the intervening years. The greatest difference in him was something more subtle than flab or hair-length. The Nick she had almost made love with had been a youth – not quite a callow one, perhaps – but a youth. This was a man.

While she was giving him a covert once-over, he was returning the compliment – a meticulous green going-over, like an antique dealer trying to prove your granny's priceless Sheraton is a fake.

Not that anybody else would have noticed. He was too subtle to gawp. 'Loveday's Cornish, isn't it?'

'Originally, but I'm not. And I don't hate it. I used to. They called me Lovedaisy at school.' She said it all quite coolly, and then wished she hadn't. Coolness would indicate that she was on her guard, and that would make him think he was right, after all.

54

Jane's mouth curved with typical mischief. 'You haven't come all on your own, have you? I've seen you dancing with positively scores of women.'

He raised a wry, dark eyebrow. 'I did come with someone but we had a tiff on the way and she's sulking somewhere.'

Jane just loved anything like this and didn't care who knew. 'You'll be having another tiff on the way home, I shouldn't wonder,' she said mischievously. 'Personally, I'd bash your head in, the number of other women you've been dancing with.'

Daisy thought a little more winding up wouldn't go amiss. 'Go and find her and make up,' she said reprovingly. 'This is no way to start the New Year.'

'If she wants to sulk, that's her problem,' he said. 'New Year's Eve's the perfect time for catching up with old friends. *Auld acquaintance*, and all that . . .'

As he raised a glass to his lips, his eyes never left her face. 'So here's to *Auld acquaintance*.'

'Here's to mud in your eye.' She added an airy smile intended to confuse him, but still had a horrible feeling it wasn't working. The lazy quality to his scrutiny did not fool her in the least. It made her feel as if her every thought was coming up in a liquid crystal display on her forehead.

It was a positive relief when Simon slipped an arm around her waist. 'Sorry, darling,' he said, dropping a kiss on her cheek. 'I just couldn't resist picking Hugh's brains. He works for one of the top stockbrokers and you don't often get advice like that for nothing.'

Ian did the honours again. 'Simon, this is Nick, an old friend of mine.'

There was a brief handshake. 'You're the fellow who dragged my girlfriend from right under my nose,' said Simon, with no noticeable rancour.

'Afraid so,' said Nick lazily. 'But I hadn't realized she belonged to anybody. She was tapping her foot and looking so wistful, I took pity on her.'

He said it casually enough, but Daisy's antennae were sensitive enough to pick up a sudden, minute antipathy between them. Very subtly, Nick was winding Simon up, and equally subtly, Simon reacted with a minute stiffening of the arm around her waist. But his reply was equable enough. 'Well, I'm no Fred Astaire, so I can't complain.'

Roger started saying something about squash and the minute tension eased. It quickly transpired that Nick had recently joined the club but had not got round to playing yet, and Simon invited him for a game the following week. Nick accepted, and Daisy sensed instantly that this was not quite going to be a 'friendly'. Still, Simon would very likely beat him and honour would be satisfied. Simon beat just about everybody except the coach.

They were very alike in some respects. Simon was six foot one and Nick only fractionally taller. They had exactly the same strong, athletic build, but there the resemblance ended. There was never anything remotely dishevelled about Simon. His black tie was just as geometrically perfect as when he'd picked her up, and his hair never flopped. It wasn't the flopping type. It was short and curly mid-brown, and there was nothing wicked about his eyes, although they could twinkle very nicely when he smiled. They were blue – the kind of what-you-see-is-what-you-get blue that inspires confidence. As her mother had said more than once, he looked like the kind of nice young hospital doctor that student nurses fall in love with and old ladies go gooey about.

'. . . of course, when I say he was a mate of mine, that's not strictly true,' Ian was saying in jovial tones. 'Sometimes I hated the bastard's guts. He was one of those sickening sods who divide their time between the bar, the sports hall and fighting off women, and still manage to come out with a First.'

'A First in what?' Simon asked, but never got a reply.

A striking girl in a midnight blue dress that looked like Thai silk had appeared from nowhere and taken Nick's arm. 'Hello, darling,' she said sweetly. 'I thought I might find you here.'

Daisy had noticed her before, dancing with somebody who was not Nick. Her hair was the kind of silky black that looks almost blue; her skin very white and her eyes the kind of mid-blue that makes such a striking contrast. She also had a cleavage that would have made a younger Daisy sick.

'Hello, Amanda,' he said, without much enthusiasm. 'Are you speaking to me again?'

'Of course.' She tipped what looked like a whole gin and tonic down his dress shirt. 'Happy New Year, asshole.'

Five pairs of eyes widened in shock as she stalked off. Only Nick did not seem particularly surprised.

Jane broke the silence first. 'Dear me,' she said wickedly. 'It would seem that your lady friend's just the teeniest bit miffed about something.'

57

His mouth gave a lazy, almost imperceptible twitch. 'I'd have preferred a bit more ice with it. I needed cooling off.'

Daisy shivered as they waited for the valet-parking-person to bring the car round.

'I'd have thought you'd want to stay a bit longer,' Simon said. 'Not that I'm complaining. I'd had enough.'

It was only ten to one, but for once, Daisy had been glad of an excuse to get home. There had been rather too much lazy, green-eyed scrutiny in the past hour or so. 'We'd be fit for nothing in the morning. They're going to make a real night of it. First some club or other, and then descending on some poor, unsuspecting hotel for breakfast . . .'

She and Simon could not afford to be too hungover, not that Simon would be hungover since he was driving and therefore drinking very little. He would be merely shattered and in eleven and a half hours they were due for lunch with his parents – twelve-thirty for one precisely. Which meant leaving by twelve, which meant waking by ten-thirty to get with it, shower and make themselves presentable.

'What is that fellow *doing*?' Simon was a trifle twitchy in case the valet-parker scraped his new BMW. The car appeared; he breathed again and opened the door for her. He always did, just as he always opened every door and walked on the traffic side of the pavement.

There were still revellers in the streets, singing and staggering and generally looking as if they'd had a wild time. 'I didn't care for that friend of Ian's,' Simon said, as they hit Knightsbridge. 'One of those irritating fellows who has to look scruffy to make some sort of point.'

Once again, Daisy felt that faint antipathy coming off him. 'He wasn't exactly scruffy,' she said, wondering why on earth she was defending him. 'He was dancing practically all night. A jacket and tie's too hot if you're dancing the way he was.'

'It wasn't just that. His behaviour was very telling, if you ask me. Dumping the girl he'd come with and dancing with everybody else's women . . . Cracking girl, too. Pity it was only a gin she slung over him. Should have been a pint of Guinness.'

Daisy was vaguely irritated. She had thought more or less the same herself, but hearing Simon say it was perversely different. And she didn't quite like hearing him refer to Nick's girlfriend as 'cracking'. Simon never went on about other women. It was one of his numerous good points. 'You don't know what preceded it,' she pointed out. 'They'd had a row. She might have started it for all you know.'

'I bet she didn't.'

Her tiny seed of irritation sprouted shoots. 'How do you know? Why do you have to take her side?'

'It's obvious. You can tell what sort of fellow he is, just to look at him.'

'You hardly know him!'

'I don't have to.'

For only about the sixth time in their two-year relationship, Daisy got cross. 'You're only taking her side because she's "cracking".'

59

'Don't be silly.'

'You are.'

Simon made no reply. She'd known he wouldn't. There would be no row. Simon refused to row. He just retreated into I'm-not-going-to-argue-about-it silence, she seethed for a bit, and after a while it wore off.

Somehow, she didn't feel like seething tonight. She felt like arguing. 'While we're on "cracking", he was a pretty "cracking" dancer. I don't suppose you even noticed, but his rock and roll had my skirt twirling out like nobody's business. Gave me a chance to show off that suspender belt you bought me.'

'Of course I noticed. Hugh's eyes were out on stalks. I wondered what the hell he was gawping at.'

But you hadn't been looking until then. 'At least I gave him a treat, then,' she retorted.

He changed down hard, to overtake a dithering vehicle. 'And while we're on Hugh, I wish you hadn't made that bum-cleavage remark. It wasn't, well . . .'

'What?' she demanded, really irritated now. 'Lady-like, for heaven's sake?'

'If you put it like that, yes.'

My God, he really takes the cake sometimes. 'How can you have a go at *me*? What about the "cracking" Amanda and her "asshole"?'

He had the grace to hesitate. 'That was different. She was provoked.'

'*I* was provoked! By you sitting talking about shares at a New Year's Eve Ball! And you're only upset because it was Nick I was dancing with. If it was Ian you wouldn't have cared. You just don't like him.

You've taken a totally irrational dislike to him. You only asked him for a game of squash because you don't like him and you think you're going to beat him. It's pathetic.'

'I'm not going to beat him,' Simon said grimly. 'I'm going to thrash him.'

Daisy was almost ashamed of the tiny, warm glow that trickled through her crossness and melted it like a lolly in the sun. Bless him, he really was just a teensy bit jealous, after all. And off to fight a duel on the squash court. *Take that, thou varlet. No lets will be given. With my trusty racket and slow balls I will give thee the thrashing thou deservest.*

By the time they pulled up outside her Richmond flat, she was back in a reasonably good mood. Any residual irritation had been mellowed by all the Buck's Fizz still circulating in her system, never mind winning a voucher for a free facial in the charity raffle.

But Simon didn't hunt for a parking space, as she'd expected. He pulled up near the door and said, 'I won't come in tonight, if you don't mind. I forgot to bring a change of clothes so I'd only have to go home in the morning and it'll delay us.'

Daisy could hardly believe it. She had assumed he'd stay the night and they'd have a lovely lazy morning in bed with the odd joke about his mother's inevitable roast.

'Great,' she said, more crossly than she'd intended. 'Why can't we just get up a bit earlier? We could stop on the way.'

'It's not on the way,' he pointed out. 'And to be honest, I'm a bit tired.'

'I can't think why. You hardly danced at all.'

'I know,' he said, with reproachful patience. 'But in case you hadn't noticed, I've been working all the hours God sends.'

If he meant her to feel bad, he succeeded. 'I'm sorry,' she said, leaning over to kiss him. 'I'll see you in the morning.'

His return kiss made her feel even worse. Soft and loving, tender and forgiving . . .

As usual, he came with her to the door. He always did, just in case of lurking muggers.

But as she shut the door behind her, Daisy couldn't prevent a tiny thread of disgruntledness returning. *New Year's Eve, and I'm going to bed all on my own. He's never too tired for squash, blast him.*

It was ages before she fell asleep. Vaguely cross and dissatisfied, she wriggled endlessly under the duvet. A certain pair of green eyes were refusing to be banished from her mind. And the more she tried to banish them, the more they intruded, along with a certain face. And the more she tried to banish the face, the more it was right there, like a wretched unpaid bill that just won't go away.

And like an unpaid bill – the kind that had given her mother so many sleepless nights – it kept coming back, with nasty red writing that said, 'You're going to have to face up to me sooner or later. It's no use sticking me in the kitchen drawer and hoping I'll go away.'

By the time she finally fell asleep, it wasn't just the eyes she was trying to stick in that drawer. It was the whole wretched package: the hand that had dragged her from Simon, the arms that had caught her in that wild rock and roll, open-necked dress shirt and all. Never mind a nine-year-old seductive whisper that said, '. . . like a little angel . . .'

Her last cross thought, just before she fell asleep, was, *Full of it, like ninety-nine per cent of them. If his wretched eyes aren't brown, they jolly well ought to be.*

The alarm woke her at a quarter past ten, but it might have been seven, the way she felt. She turned it off and snuggled back under the duvet, wishing to heaven she could slob for the rest of the day and not have to get all dressed up for Simon's parents.

They were terribly nice, of course; faultlessly polite, but it was all so horribly predictable. 'Gin and tonic or sherry, my dear? How's your mother? You really must bring her to meet us soon.'

And she must. But Daisy had been putting it off. She just could not see her mother's slightly faded, wild-child charm in the golf-clubby environs of Weybridge.

Or rather, she could see it. Only too well. They would be terribly nice, of course. 'Gin and tonic or sherry, Isabel? Daisy tells us you do people's gardens and are terribly original with flowers and things. Must be lovely to be so creative.'

And her mother would be terribly nice, too, because she couldn't help being anything else. She would wear some long floaty skirt and various musliny, beady bits and pieces garnered from various ethnically-inclined charity shops that would just look a mess on anybody else but on her would look merely like the essence of faintly bohemian style. She would say how delicious the food was and listen to Colonel Forster (retired) banging on about politics and not disagree once, because she'd be trying so hard to make a good impression for Daisy's sake.

And Colonel Forster would be captivated, as most men were. And Mrs Forster's smile would slowly frost very slightly at the edges, because she was pushing sixty and looked it, with hair like an old Brillo pad, and her mother was forty-five and looked thirty-nine, with natural blonde hair that was still naturally blonde.

She got out of bed, feeling vaguely rough but not exactly hungover. Her head felt foggy and out of focus, her mouth horribly dry, as it always was after more than three glasses of wine.

A shower and rapid fluid intake would restore her, however. She padded on bare feet to the bathroom in a pair of slinky, cream satin pyjamas she'd splashed out on in the sales.

The flat was deathly quiet. Vaguely she'd heard muffled laughter as Jane and Ian had come home and she had glanced through fogged eyes at her bed-side clock. It had said ten past five. Jane's door bore a sign she'd nicked ages ago from some hotel or other. As usual, it said, 'Do Not Disturb.'

As if I would.

She opened the bathroom door and felt as if some-body had hit her over the head with a mallet.

Somebody was standing at the basin.

Except for a face half covered with shaving foam which he was scraping off with her ladies' razor, he looked rather like Michelangelo's David, breathed into glorious, green-eyed life. His hair was wet from the shower and drops of water still clung to his skin.

And just like Michelangelo's David, he seemed to have mislaid his fig leaf.

CHAPTER 4

If anyone was embarrassed, it wasn't him.

'Morning, Daisy,' he said, just as if he'd bumped into her in the ready-meals aisle at the supermarket. He had the grace to grab a towel, however, and wrap it round his waist.

Daisy had grown roots. Somewhere between brain and mouth her *'What the hell are you doing here?'* changed to an unsteady, 'Sorry – I didn't realize – ' She fled on auto-pilot to the kitchen.

Heaven help me. What the hell is he doing here?

The hands that opened the coffee cupboard seemed to have a bad case of the DTs. It hadn't exactly been a full-frontal; more a full-side-al, but the effect was more than enough to cope with first thing.

Damn it. No coffee!

There had been plenty yesterday afternoon, but no doubt they'd all staggered back in the early hours and sobered up on best, freshly ground Kenyan.

And I bet they used all the milk, too.

Of course. One carton with about two drips in it. *Thanks a lot.*

She slung it in the bin, her hands still DT-ing and her pulse coming out in sympathy.

But by the time he strolled in she had made a mug of emergency instant with emergency whitener, and her emergency wobbles had settled.

On the surface.

He was still clad only in the towel, his hair damp and tousled from a quick towel-dry. He smelt rather incongruously of her soft-and-gentle lady-shave foam. A scrap of red-soaked tissue clung to his chin. 'If that was your razor I used, it's blunt,' he said. 'You should treat your underarms with a little more respect.'

'I'm terribly sorry,' she said tartly. 'If I'd known you were coming I'd have got a super-duper Macho Smoothie-Shave and some of that gel that makes all men irresistible.'

He perched on the pine kitchen table and helped himself to a satsuma from a pottery dish. 'Look, I'm sorry if you were embarrassed . . .'

'I wasn't embarrassed. Just put off my breakfast with the shock. Why didn't you lock the door? And what on earth are you doing here, anyway?'

He was peeling the satsuma and depositing the peel on the kitchen table. 'The thing you slide the bolt into was hanging by a one-screw thread. It finally parted company with the door when I tried to lock it.'

Damn it. She closed her eyes in delayed-action recall. That bolt had been on the list for a couple of weeks.

'I found the other screw on the shelf,' he went on. 'Which suggested that somebody had picked it up and put it there, intending to do something about it. Either she suffers from "putting off till tomorrow", or she's intending to leave it and Get A Man In.'

67

'We forgot,' she said testily. 'Jane and I have very demanding jobs. We've got more important things to do.'

'Ah,' he said. 'In that case, your luck's in. I'm currently unemployed with nothing better to do. So give me a screwdriver and I'll fix it.'

Unemployed? She gave him a sharp glance. Still, one never knew. 'For heaven's sake, I can do it myself.' She very nearly added, '*If I can change a wheel, I think I can manage a couple of screws.*'

Thank heaven, her brain was working well enough to slam the mouth-brakes on in time.

For a moment she wondered whether now was the time to come clean, after all. With nobody else around it'd be relatively easy. In theory.

'Could have been worse,' he remarked. 'I could have burst in on you.'

'No, you couldn't. If the bolt was that bad, I'd have fixed it.' She hesitated. Since she was hiding under a big fat fib, a little white truth might be appropriate. 'Well, maybe not. But at least I'd have pinched the Do Not Disturb sign from Jane's door.'

She hated to admit what would have happened later. Simon would have come round, gone to the loo and said, 'Your bolt's falling off. Where's the screwdriver?' If Ian hadn't done it first.

In the two years since they'd been sharing, Jane's attitudes had been rubbing off where household repairs were concerned. 'You have to let them feel useful,' she'd said, more than once. 'Men suffer from such low self-esteem these days. They feel emasculated, poor lambs. Surrounded by women with more balls than any of them . . .'

It had been her usual mickey-take, of course, since neither Simon nor Ian suffered from either low self-esteem or lack of balls.

Nick appeared to suffer from an overdose of both. 'Any chance of a coffee?' he asked, eyeing the mug in her hand.

'Help yourself.'

His eyes shot to the jar on the worktop, and he made a very slight grimace. 'Not instant, is it?'

'I'm terribly sorry, that's all there is,' she said tartly. 'If I'd known you were coming I'd have ordered some freshly ground glass.'

Your twitches are showing. Don't overdo it.

If he hadn't been perched upon it, she'd have been sitting at the table leafing through the *Marie Claire* that lay there, instead of leaning against the worktop and trying to pretend it was nothing unusual to entertain a man you once nearly lost your virginity to and pretending he wasn't.

It would have been easier if he'd been dressed. The kitchen was done in farmhouse antique pine, with Delfty-blue tiles, but wasn't exactly of farmhouse proportions, which wasn't perhaps surprising in a fourth floor flat. And all that obvious maleness didn't exactly blend into the woodwork.

If anything, his build was slightly heavier than she remembered. The last traces of stripling were gone for ever, but the muscles that fitted so neatly under his skin were not of the super-bulgy, iron-pumped variety.

Evidently not in any hurry for instant coffee, he helped himself to another satsuma. His eyes were elsewhere, however. 'I like your hair like that,' he mused, popping a couple of segments into his mouth. 'All softly pillow-mussed from sleep . . .'

He said it almost like a poem, and the effect on her – a disconcerting mix of tingle and wooze – made her wonder whether that long-ago FAB jab might be wearing off. Even Yellow Fever only lasted ten years

She very nearly put her size fives right in it again with a tart, '*Are you a hair-fetishist or what*?' but stopped herself just in time. 'Never mind my hair. What are you doing here? Haven't you got a home to go to?'

'Ah.' He consumed the rest of the satsuma and took another. 'Remember Amanda?'

'How could I forget her?'

'Not easily forgettable,' he agreed. 'Amanda's petulant six-year-old act was not confined to gin-slinging. Some time after that little episode, she decided she'd had enough.' He paused and took another satsuma from the rapidly emptying dish.

'Help yourself,' she said tartly.

He put it back at once, which make her crosser with him than she already was, for making her feel stingy.

'You can have it,' she said, more grudgingly than she intended. 'Just don't eat them all.'

'Thank you.' Apparently quite unabashed, he took another. 'As I was saying, Amanda took herself off. She also took my jacket, complete with wallet and keys. She then helped herself to my car and disappeared.'

Amanda had just shot up about five trillion points in her estimation. 'I bet that wiped the grin off your face.' She turned away, partly to make another coffee, partly because she needed a break from his scrutiny. 'She's probably parked it in a towaway zone,' she added helpfully. 'Or a wheel-clamp zone. It's really good fun getting clamped. They stick a huge thing over your windscreen that takes about forty-eight hours to get off.'

'Clamping's the least of my worries,' he said. 'She could have parked it in a nicking zone. I'll have a coffee, if you're making,' he added.

She grabbed another mug. 'There's no milk, only whitener.'

'That's fine. Two sugars.'

She poured, stirred, handed him the mug and retreated to her lean-to on the worktop.

'Thank you.' His eyes were doing another idle twice-over. They travelled lazily from her face to her bare feet and back again, flickered over her satin pyjamas (thankfully loose enough to reveal next to nothing) and back to her face. 'So where's this guy you're "practically married" to? Still snoring his head off?'

This gave her a little jolt. If Simon had still been in her bed, she'd hardly be standing here. In any case, he wouldn't have been in bed. *She'd* have been in bed and he'd have been in here making the coffee and probably toast, too. 'He doesn't snore and we're not "practically married". We've been going out a long time, that's all. And he went home last night.'

He took a sip from his mug, winced at the heat of it, and put it down. 'Shame,' he mused. 'I was looking forward to winding him up a bit more before we hit the squash court.'

My God, they're as bad as each other.

No, they're not. He started winding up first. Simon was only reacting to it.

71

She felt a sudden, protective loyalty for Simon. 'He'll beat you. He beats everybody. He's top of the ladder.'

'Top of the ladder's a dangerous place to be,' he mused. 'Only one place to go from the top . . .'

'He'll beat you, and I've got a good mind to come and watch.' With a withering look, she put her mug down. 'I'm going for a shower.' Remembering the bolt, she hunted in the drawer for the screwdriver. It was in there somewhere, along with spare plugs, batteries, fuses, and countless other bits of junk.

It was a big one, the kind that could make a lethal weapon in the wrong hands. As she straightened up, he said, 'I can see you mean business with that thing, so I won't offer again. Could be dangerous.' He paused, sipping his coffee. 'I once tried to help a very stubborn girl change a wheel. She wasn't having it. She threatened me with very drastic action involving nuts and spanners.'

He looked her directly in the eye; a shrewd, amused look that put her insides through the mincer. 'It was years ago,' he went on lazily. 'I wonder why it came back to me just now?'

'Search me.' With faintly unsteady hands she picked up his pile of satsuma peel and dropped it in the bin. 'If you want any breakfast there should be some eggs in the fridge and don't leave a flaming mess everywhere.'

She escaped to the bathroom. Fixing the bolt should have been a doddle, only her fingers had the DTs again, fumbling and fiddling and making her curse.

He knows, damn him.

Of course he knows. Why ever didn't you come clean in the first place?

72

Because I'm a silly cow, that's why.

You said it. Go back now, before anybody else is up, and say, 'Look, I know it was daft, but . . .'

I can't.

Slowly she calmed herself. He'd be gone soon and she'd hardly be bumping into him every five minutes.

When she emerged from the bathroom fifteen minutes later he was still in the kitchen, making toast, from the smell of it. She walked right past to her bedroom and locked the door.

Gazing at herself in the antique pine dressing table mirror, she despaired.

Whatever was I afraid of? He'd hardly have told everybody in graphic detail about our 'previous'. I'm behaving like one of those wallyettes in an old-fashioned romance.

She could just see her. One of those irritating girls you wanted to slap because despite 'huge violet eyes that stared wistfully from a heart-shaped little face', she'd always thought she was ugly.

'*. . . she would fain have died rather than face the handsome Sir Torquil again. For was it not he who had so nearly stolen her virtue? She, who had been as driven snow! And yet Sir Torquil had needed but a look, but a touch, to turn her into a . . . a wanton!*

O, the memory of her sinful lust! Arabella blushed for shame, for her virgin soul had not trembled, even as the lusty spear of manhood had burst forth from his breeches! Had not the tempestuous Lady Juliet interrupted them . . .'

That's quite enough, thank you. Wincing at both Arabella and tangles, she attacked her wet hair with a comb. *You were getting a bit carried away. Nick's lusty spear never burst forth. We didn't get quite that far.*

Stop thinking about lusty spears, for heaven's sake.

But once her mind had turned to lusty spears, 'twas but a step to a certain scene not half an hour back. A firm, olive-skinned body; firm curves of a lighter olive the sun had never touched. A flat, hard stomach; the kind you knew could withstand a hefty punch. A tapering of dark hair, and then . . .

Well, what? Just a non-lusty spear, minding its own business. Neither the shrivelled-acorn variety, nor one of those whoppers you see in top-shelf girls' mags. She and Jane had bought one of those once, and Ian had demanded to see what they were giggling about. 'They're all semi-erect,' he'd said scathingly. 'Normal at-ease dicks are nothing like that size.'

They had nearly wet themselves laughing. 'You're just jealous,' Jane had giggled.

He had retreated huffily behind the sports page. 'I'm not. Anyway, those blokes all look gay to me.'

Jane had nobly repressed her mirth. 'Sweetie, we didn't buy this to get turned on. We bought it for a bloody good laugh.'

First I'm a wallyette, now I've got spears on the brain. Am I going schizo or what?

It's him. He's unsettling you.

Understatement of the century.

Suddenly she longed for Simon. Simon would settle her. He always did.

She'd been right off men, just before meeting Simon. She'd been sick of men who took her out for a not particularly good dinner with only the final course in mind: *'One dish of the day, please: hot, no dressing, and tell the chef I'll stuff it myself.'*

She had begun to wonder whether it was her; whether something about her just attracted that sort of man. She had even begun to wonder whether any other sort of man existed. She had known they did, of course, only they were always somebody else's. Or else they were the wimpy, desperate-to-please type she never fancied anyway.

And then, enter Simon. Tall. Confident. No previous wives or kids in the closet. No drink problem. No violence. No weird inclinations. Reliable. Not only employed, but well paid.

And mad about her.

Simon had wooed her. He had made her feel special. He had wooed her with flowers and phone calls when she'd never expected them, like half an hour after he'd taken her home, just to say goodnight again. There had even been a surprise trip on Eurostar and a supper in Paris to follow. It had been a full three weeks before they'd made love. He'd been a gentle and considerate lover, and still was.

And fairly soon, she felt sure, he was going to ask her to marry him. She had a feeling it was going to be Valentine's Day, when they were in Barbados. Simon would do it properly. In style, with romance aforethought.

When she emerged from her room dressed in a soft grey wool skirt and pink sweater, her hair in a neat French plait, Jane was up at last. In tracksuit bottoms (Ian's) and a shirt (Ian's) she was putting the kettle on.

'Oh, hi,' she yawned. 'Hope we didn't wake you up last night.'

75

'Not for more than a second. I zonked out again straightaway.'

Jane yawned again. 'Nick just left. Off to get his car. The lovely Amanda had parked it on double yellow lines near her flat, but mercifully it was still there.'

She started giggling. 'He was so laid-back about it last night, we couldn't believe it. Ian couldn't, anyway. Frankly I was a bit ratso and laughing my head off. Ian said if a girl did that to him, he'd give in to his repressed cave-man instincts and give her bottom the best tanning it was ever going to get outside a nudist beach. And Nick said he wouldn't waste the energy, she'd probably enjoy it.' She started giggling again.

Daisy raised an eyebrow. 'Nothing repressed about his cave-man instincts, then.'

'Oh, come on. It was just a laugh. He was stranded, poor lamb. No car, no keys, no money – not even a bit of plastic for the cash machine.'

Anything less like a lamb is hard to imagine, Daisy thought. *Unless it's a wolf in fancy dress.*

'And you should have heard him on the phone to her just now!' she went on. 'No frosty just-you-wait, like I'd expected. But of course, that would only have made her bang the phone down. I could tell she was still livid.'

'You weren't listening on purpose?'

'Of course,' Jane giggled. 'It was an education, hearing him in action. That voice would have melted stone. And by the time he'd finished, she'd gone the other way, into tearful penitence, and he was doing the "don't cry, sweetheart" bit.'

I bet he was. Smooth bastard.

'And then he called a cab and went,' Jane went on. 'I had to lend him the money, of course. He'd only got forty-five pee in his trouser pocket' Her lips curved wickedly as she poured boiling water on to a teabag. 'He's lethally attractive, don't you think? If it weren't for Ian, I'd be seriously tempted.'

Daisy swallowed her automatic, '*I wouldn't.*' 'Lethal,' she agreed. 'It's the eyes.'

'He said to say goodbye to you,' Jane went on, and started giggling again. 'He told me about the bathroom door. Said you'd got a bit of a shock.'

Daisy managed a shrug. 'A minor one. I wasn't expecting to find a lodger.'

Jane's hazel eyes gave a passable spark, considering the amount of sleep she'd had. 'Did you get a good old eyeful?'

'I tried not to look.'

'Bet you did, though.'

'Well, a bit. Nothing to write home about. They all look the same, if you ask me.'

'True,' Jane sighed. 'Unless they've had the operation, of course.'

That was enough to start Daisy off. They were erupting together as Ian walked in. Unshaven, wrapped in Jane's knee-length pink dressing gown, he looked comical enough to send them off into another wave of fits.

'God, I feel rough,' he said, groping for the kettle. 'Morning, Daisy. Nick gone?'

'You just missed him,' Jane said. 'He's gone to make it up with Amanda.'

'Not sure I'd make it up with her,' he grunted.

With Simon's 'cracking' remark still rankling just a little, Daisy was glad he'd said that. But he hadn't known then that she'd pinched his car. If anybody had pinched Simon's BMW, there'd have been hell to pay.

Still, he'd deserved it. Even if they'd rowed, it just wasn't on to ignore her and dance with scores of other women. Looking back, she felt sorry for Amanda. Probably they were making up right this minute. Making up in the time-honoured way . . .

A tiny, uncomfortable cramp seized her stomach.

That wasn't jealousy, was it?'

It's hunger. Have a piece of toast.

Jane yawned again. 'I put him in Tara's room. I knew she wouldn't mind.'

Tara was ski-ing in Austria and wouldn't be back till the weekend. She'd moved in six months back, after being out of Daisy's immediate circle for a while. Tara had surprised everybody by marrying a man she'd only known four months and going to live in Brussels. It had lasted eighteen months and she'd come back to England more abjectly miserable than Daisy would ever have believed possible.

'We were telling Nick about poor old Tara and how you got her through her bad patch,' Jane went on.

'She's still in her "bad patch",' Daisy reminded her. 'Only in a different form.'

'Yes, but you know what I mean.' Jane frowned. 'Nick said something funny when I told him about Tara.' Her brow cleared. 'Oh, yes. He said he knew a Tara once, ages ago, but she looked just like you. Isn't that weird?'

'Not really.' *Just the little piece of evidence he needed to be sure he was right. No wonder he was so sure of himself this morning.*

'I gather he and Simon are having a game on Wednesday,' Ian said. 'I told him Simon'd probably thrash him, but he didn't seem bothered.'

'He said, "We'll see",' Jane put in. 'With a certain gleam in his eye. I've got a feeling he's one of those men who are deceptively laid-back about everything, just to fool people into thinking they're not a threat. If Simon thinks he's going to be a pushover, I think he might be in for a bit of a shock.'

Daisy didn't watch the match, after all, but not because she was afraid of Simon getting beaten. Even if he did, there'd be none of the brattish racket-throwing she'd occasionally seen from his opponents. He'd shake hands in a thoroughly civilized manner, buy him a beer at the bar, and pretend he wasn't burning up inside.

It was the bar bit that put her off. She didn't want to sit up at the bar with a certain pair of green eyes lazily licking over her whenever he thought Simon wasn't looking. Or even when he was looking, on purpose.

But even if she'd wanted to go, she'd been late home after a terrible panic at work. She had just about slung the dinner in the oven and grabbed a quick shower when her mother had phoned, and made her heart sink. She had only hung up two minutes before Simon arrived. 'How did it go?' she asked.

Daft question. It was obvious, from his thoroughly pleased-with-himself expression.

'We played best of five,' he said, giving her a kiss. 'And I beat him three-two.' He dumped his sports bag on the floor and flopped into an armchair. 'I have to say, he's a damn good player. Made me fight for every point.'

With faint astonishment, she saw that his previous antipathy had changed to respect for a worthy opponent.

'Actually, he's not a bad bloke,' he went on. 'We got chatting at the bar. Did you know he was working on Wall Street till a couple of weeks ago? Looking for something in the City now. I rather got the impression he can pick and choose.'

Perversely, she was irritated at his fickleness. 'So that makes him a good bloke, does it? Just because you beat him and he's possibly going to be a City big shot who might give you the odd tip?'

'It was you who said I'd taken a totally irrational dislike to him! God, I can't do anything right.'

His hurt expression made her feel instantly guilty. 'I'm sorry,' she said unsteadily. 'My mother just phoned. She was in a bit of a state.'

He looked up, saw her face, and frowned. 'What?'

'That wretched Miles.' Her voice trembled slightly. 'I knew there was something wrong when I phoned on New Year's Eve. He's dumped her.'

'Oh, strewth.' With a faintly resigned sigh, he got up and put his arms around her. 'But you were half expecting it, weren't you?'

'She wasn't.' They sat on the sofa, and she wiped her eyes on the sleeve of her shirt. 'It was no good saying anything. She'd never have listened. Why does she always get involved with these bastards? What is it about her that only attracts bastards?'

'I don't know. But nothing's going to change until she starts letting her head rule her heart a bit more.'

'She can't,' Daisy despaired. 'She always falls for the wrong sort of man. They see her coming.' She sighed, and pushed her hair back. 'You'll have to go on your own to that do, I'm afraid. I'm going down at the weekend to try to cheer her up.'

'I can cancel. Make some excuse.' He squeezed her hand. 'I'll come with you. We could take her out somewhere nice.'

'Oh, Simon.' She put her arms round him and gave him a massive hug. 'It's sweet of you, but you must go to the Parkers. It's important.' Mr Parker was the senior partner in the lucrative solicitor's practice where Simon worked, and Simon was hoping for a partnership.

She leaned over and kissed him. 'I'll go and check on the dinner.' Jane and Ian were out, she had a lasagne in the oven, and it would have been a nice, relaxed evening – if not for the ongoing panic waiting for her next morning and her mother on her mind.

'Nick's dropping in later,' he called, as she headed for the kitchen. 'Left something here the other night.'

This is all I need. She glanced back. He was already unfolding a paper to the financial pages. 'A scarf,' she said. 'Jane put it away somewhere.'

'Maybe. He didn't say.' He was already engrossed in the paper.

Daisy went into the kitchen, her stomach suddenly squirming. The lasagne was nowhere near ready, which was just as well, since she still had salad to prepare.

Calm down. Find the scarf, and then he'll be off in two minutes. Unless he stays for a drink.

She fought the instinctive desire to inspect her face and tart it up a bit.

She had a quick look in the hall mirror anyway. Naked, after that hurried shower. Well, not quite naked. A slick of the kind of transparent lipstick that's supposed to look as if you aren't wearing any. Nothing else. How lovely to have thick dark eyelashes that didn't need any mascara. Having them dyed had been the best investment ever, making her quite passable grey eyes into something special. Put-in-with-a-smutty-finger eyes, just like she'd always wanted.

As for the rest of her, she was glad she was only wearing her second-best Levi's and one of Simon's rugby shirts, her hair twisted up in a common or garden knot. She could hardly have dressed less enticingly if she'd tried.

'Want a hand?' Simon called.

'No, I'm fine.'

She found the scarf in the first place she looked – a drawer in the little chest in the hall. It was an evening scarf, the kind that goes with immaculate dinner jackets: soft, expensive white silk, with fringed ends. A faint scent still clung to it; the scent he'd worn on New Year's Eve, something tangy and elusive . . .

She shoved it back in the drawer, returned to the kitchen, poured herself a glass of wine from an already open bottle of Frascati, and shoved some frozen garlic bread in the oven.

When the doorbell rang only minutes later, an odd nervous tension seized her stomach. She let Simon answer it and he really dropped her in it.

After half a minute of talk she couldn't quite hear from the kitchen, he called, 'Daisy? OK if Nick stays to supper?'

What? She went into instant-panic mode.

Say there's not enough.

But there is. Why do I always make too much?

Because recipes are always for four. And Simon'll only come in, check the oven and say, 'What are you on about? There's masses.'

'Of course,' she called. 'As long as he's not expecting Michel Roux.'

Mechanically she carried on chopping cucumber, spring onions, green peppers . . .

Simon came in, opened the fridge and tutted mildly. 'No beers. I'll nip to the off-licence.'

'No!' Hastily she covered up with a bright smile. 'I'll go. You stay and chat.'

'Darling, you've got your hands full.' With a peck on her cheek, he left her. And four seconds after the front door had shut behind him, Nick wandered in.

'Hi,' she said brightly, her back to him.

'Hi.'

He was perched on the table again; she knew even without looking. Slice, chop, sling into the bowl, slice, chop . . .

'It's a nice enough back view,' he mused at last, 'A face would be even better.'

Brace yourself and do it. He must think you're utterly screwed up, the way you've been carrying on.

She put her knife down and turned around.

He was indeed perched on the table, in jeans and a winter-green tracksuit top, the sleeves pushed up over his forearms. His hair was still damp from the locker room showers, but his eyes were the same as ever, his mouth hovering on the edge of a smile. 'Much better.'

That smile was a killer. Not a big, gleaming cheesy one, to show off all his lovely white teeth, although they were. Not a smirky, aren't-I-gorgeous one, although he was. It hovered lazily, just as his eyes hovered lazily over your face, as if he were thinking it might be rather nice to kiss you.

He did kiss you, dope. And the rest.

She folded her arms defensively. 'It *was* me, OK?'

'I know.'

'I know you know. That's why I'm telling you. If you didn't, I wouldn't bother.'

Even to her own ears her logic sounded daft, and the hovering turned to a twitch that decimated the remains of her cool.

Returning to the chopping board, she attacked the tomatoes viciously. 'I'd have said before, but I was too shocked on New Year's Eve, never mind the morning after. And before you ask, I called myself Tara because she was my best friend and so much more together than I was. OK?'

It seemed ages till he spoke. 'I didn't plan it, you know. To be honest, it was the last thing I was expecting. You didn't look the type.'

'That didn't stop you, did it?' Viciously she opened the cupboard for the olive oil.

'Daisy, I was twenty-two. Even your boyfriend will tell you the average twenty-two-year-old is a mass of testosterone on legs. And if you'll forgive me for saying so, I didn't force you into anything you didn't appear to want.'

84

Calm down, Daisy. 'OK, so you didn't. I apologize. Now can we please drop the subject?'

God, I hope he's not recalling every lurid detail.

By some Superwoman effort, she managed not to flush. Mechanically she poured oil and vinegar into a jar, added salt and pepper. 'Simon tells me you're looking for a job in the City.'

'Yes, but I'm not in any hurry. I'm taking a break. I've taken scarcely any time off, the past two years.'

'On Wall Street, I gather.'

'Yes. The pace is stressed to say the least.'

Daisy still had her back to him as she shook the dressing, but was beginning to feel controlled enough to turn round again.

'Simon tells me you're in marketing,' he said.

'Yes. Beauty and "personal" products, as they call them.'

'And very demanding, I gather. Simon said you had a bad day.'

It's even worse, now. 'You could say that. We're running a promotion on a new moisturiser and it's proving rather too wildly successful.'

He frowned. 'How can it be "too" successful?'

'Because we're giving away a make-up bag with it,' she explained. 'The campaign is supposed to run for three weeks and after only six days we're running out of make-up bags and having a teensy little problem in locating replacements.'

'Then someone wants their backside kicked,' he said. 'I trust it's not yours.'

'No, thank heaven. I just have to cope with the fall-out.' She opened the oven and folded back the foil from the garlic bread, to let it brown. *Phew. It's going to be perfectly civilized, now the nitty-gritty's over.*

'Did you find my scarf?' he asked. 'I've got another flash function to go to.'

'It's in a drawer. Jane put it away.' She managed a casual smile. 'A Burns Night do?'

He shook his head. 'I've been given a couple of tickets for some charity gala at the Royal Opera House. The Kirov Ballet. I'm not sure it's my scene. I might give it a miss.'

His casual attitude scandalised her. 'Free tickets for the Kirov? It'd be criminal not to go!'

'You reckon?'

'Criminal,' she repeated. 'Could you get off the table, please? I want to lay it.'

He slid off and strolled to the worktop, where he helped himself to a piece of green pepper from the salad bowl. 'Maybe you're right,' he mused.

'You might even enjoy it.' She opened the drawer for knives and forks, serving spoons . . .

'I might.' He helped himself to more morsels of salad. 'A couple of hours of pure escapism, an intimate little dinner afterwards . . .'

'Don't forget a taxi,' she said. 'There and back. Just in case you have a row in the interval and Amanda zooms off in your car again.'

He took another piece of green pepper. 'Women who sulk give me a pain. I had someone else in mind.'

Off with the old . . . He's working out exactly true to type. 'I'm sure she'll be over the moon,' she said, more tartly than she'd intended.

'I'm not so sure about that,' he mused. 'I haven't even asked her yet.'

Jane's remark came winging back. '*It was an education, hearing him in action.*' Daisy was all for education. With a suitably offhand manner, she indicated the phone on the kitchen wall. 'Why don't you give her a ring?'

He shook his head. 'I can't phone her from here.'

Why not? Are you afraid she'll tell you to get lost and I'll laugh? 'Please yourself,'

'On the other hand, I can't leave it much longer,' he mused. 'Mind if I go and use my mobile in the car?'

'Feel free.' Damn. It would have been interesting to hear a really practised operator in action. Even more interesting if she'd turned him down.

'I'll be a while,' he added. 'I had to park right down the road.'

'It'll give you an appetite,' she said sweetly. Only when the door closed behind him did she realize just how wound up she'd been.

Phew. She lined a basket with a napkin for the garlic bread, dressed the salad and poured herself another glass of wine. It hadn't gone too badly. She'd been wonderfully grown up about it and he hadn't laughed or made any crude, embarrassing comments. Maybe he wasn't so bad after all, despite his doubtless crumpet-hopping tendencies. Only Simon had better not ask him for supper again. He had a way of looking at her that made her go decidedly wobbly, but no doubt he made Jane go wobbly too. Lethally attractive men do, that's why you avoid them like the plague.

Imagine going out with one! She shuddered. With every other woman giving him the eye, you'd never feel safe. It was bad enough with Simon. Quite a few women gave him the eye but if he noticed, he never showed it. He didn't preen or smirk and think what a Jack-the-lad he was.

It was another of his multiple good points. He had so many, she sometimes lost count. He hadn't even moaned when she'd forgotten to buy beers, for heaven's sake. Ian would at least have said, 'Oh, *damn*, no beers *again*.' And as for offering to skip the Parkers' do and come down to her mother's . . .

Bless his little heart.

Feeling relatively mellow and relatively hungry, too, she opened a packet of cheese and onion crisps and had her mouth full when the phone rang.

'Hello?' she said, and half-choked. 'Sorry, I've got a mouthful of crisps.'

'Hello, Daisy. Have a good swallow.'

That voice jolted her like a cattle prod.

'I could hardly phone you from your own phone,' he went on lazily. 'I'd have got the "engaged" tone. Or at least the "practically married" tone.'

It took a moment to find her voice but it was a pretty good one at short notice, like snapped-off icicles. 'How about the "bugger off" tone?' And she banged the phone down. Hard.

CHAPTER 5

It was a complete waste of icicles, because about six minutes later the front door opened and in he came, with Simon.

'Beautiful Nick,' Simon was saying.

Daisy nearly dropped her glass.

'Bit of a liability, though,' he went on, as they came through. 'Joyriders, and so on. The insurance must be astronomical.'

Her heart failure subsided. They were talking *cars*. *In* beautiful *nick!*

'Did you know Nick had an E-type?' Simon came in and dumped a six-pack on the table. 'Classic, soft top, British racing green. Beautiful condition.'

It would be green. For the classic, British-roving-green-eyed devil who'd practically asked her out behind Simon's back. After Simon had invited him to supper! Just how low could you get?

'Really?' she said casually. 'I once read that cars like E-types – you know, with great long bonnets – are thought by psychologists to be phallic substitutes.'

Simon shot her an askance frown. 'She laps up all this

psychological tripe,' he said apologetically. 'I don't know why women fall for it.'

It was infuriating, having him go all loftily male on her when she was fighting his corner. But he wasn't to know. 'Plenty of men are psychologists,' she pointed out.

'Plenty of men are astrologists too, and that's another load of tripe women lap up by the bucket-load. Take a seat,' he added to Nick. 'Like a beer?'

'Yes, please.' For once, he sat at the table instead of on it.

'Astrology's not tripe,' Daisy said testily, arming herself with oven gloves. 'You're a typical Taurus, for a start.' Even without looking, she would have bet about ten million pounds that they had just exchanged wry, eyes to ceiling *'women'* looks. She turned and looked Nick straight in the eye. 'And I bet you're a Scorpio.'

'Daisy, for heaven's sake,' Simon said, with a good-natured tolerance she ignored.

'Well?' she demanded.

Nick's eyes had a glint she didn't quite care for. 'Dare I ask how you knew?'

It was a minor satisfaction to see Simon's male loftiness temporarily shattered. 'Intuition,' she said sweetly. *Strewth, what a lucky guess. Still, with those eyes . . . Scorpios are supposed to be the most sexually magnetic of all the signs.*

'All right, I grovel. Abjectly.' Simon gave her a peace-making squeeze. 'Is that food ready? I'm starving.'

She dished up and spent the first five minutes of the meal rehearsing what she would say to Nick if and when she got him alone for two minutes.

'I'm afraid there's no pudding,' she said, with enough earnest apology to cover up the sparking grey eyes she fixed on her guest. 'I found a lovely recipe but it involved crushing nuts in the blender, and I couldn't get hold of any in time.'

Sitting opposite her, he actually dared to let his mouth twitch. 'Please, don't apologize. I'm not much into puddings.'

'You'd like Daisy's,' said poor, innocent Simon. 'Her "Death By Chocolate" is to die for.' He then returned to another subject dear to his heart. 'That car's a collector's item. You were phenomenally lucky it didn't get stolen the other night.'

'If it does, it does,' Nick shrugged. 'I bought it on a whim – the indulgence of a dream, if you like. I had a little model E-type when I was a kid and I told myself one day I'd have a real one. I'll probably sell it once the novelty's worn off. This is delicious,' he added to Daisy, and took another piece of garlic bread.

'Thank you.' While Simon's eyes were safely on his plate, she mouthed, '*I hope it chokes you*' and prayed he could lip-read.

His mouth hovered so minutely, nobody else would have noticed. 'That car was responsible for Amanda's sulks the other night,' he went on. 'She was itching to drive it.'

'And I suppose you thought she couldn't handle it,' Daisy said, with honeyed acid.

'Not after three gins. I had this quaint, old-fashioned desire to see another sunrise. Not to mention a quaint, old-fashioned aversion to putting innocent third parties in the morgue with me.'

Trust him to have some unarguable excuse to make him sound like a responsible citizen. 'You still shouldn't have ignored her all evening.'

'It wasn't my choice. She sulked and went off. She knew plenty of other people.'

'And the general idea, I suppose,' Simon put in, 'was for you to run after her and try to win her round.'

'I guess so.'

But you didn't. Oh, no. You let her get on with it, which was why she got so mad.

It was Nick who changed the subject. 'Ian tells me you're all off to Barbados next month.'

'I can't wait,' said Daisy.

'Have you been before?' he asked.

'No,' said Simon, for both of them. 'Have you?'

'Once. I escaped the New York winter for a week, but it wasn't long enough.'

He started telling them about things that had stuck in his memory. 'There was an old church overlooking the Atlantic – the most unbelievable view with the breakers crashing in. And tucked in the twisty old graves I found an old devil by the name of Ferdinand. According to his epitaph, he was "ye last in ye line of ye Christian Emperors of Greece, churchwarden of this parish".'

Daisy forgot she was trying not to be interested. 'Whatever was he doing there?'

'I didn't have time to find out.'

By the time the meal was over, there was not enough lasagne to provide a decent lick-out for a mouse, and Nick polished off the last of the garlic bread. After coffee and twenty minutes' chat, he announced that he must go. Daisy said a cool goodbye and let Simon show him out, but just as they left the kitchen, the phone rang.

'Simon!' she called. 'It's Steve Chandler from the club.'

He came at once. 'What does he want?'

'He didn't say.' Silently thanking Steve Chandler for his perfect timing, she disappeared to the hall, where Nick was waiting by the door.

'Don't forget this.' She yanked his scarf from the hall drawer. 'And may I suggest you strangle yourself with it?'

He did not seem in the least put out. 'Your eyes were sparking like a welder's blowtorch,' he said, in lazily amused tones. 'If you'd left the gas on we'd have had a major explosion.'

'What did you expect?' she hissed, folding her arms. 'He invited you for supper and you asked me out behind his back!'

'No, I didn't. You assumed I was going to.'

This threw her for only a second. 'Well, weren't you?'

'Would you have preferred me to ask you in front of him?' He slung the scarf around his neck, where it looked oddly at home with the tracksuit top.

She could hardly believe he had the audacity to say it. 'I've met some low, brass-necked men in my time, but you really scrape the barrel.'

He was holding the ends of the scarf halfway up, pulling on them as if testing for strength. 'You're not married to him. You're not even engaged.'

'That is not the point!' With a glance over her shoulder towards the kitchen, she lowered her voice again. 'We've been going out for two years!'

For several seconds he said nothing. There was just the endless lazy flicker of his eyes. 'I saw you long before you saw me, on New Year's Eve,' he said at last. 'I saw you sitting there, bored out of your mind. And I asked myself a question. I asked myself what sort of guy takes out a beautiful girl who's gone to all the trouble of getting dressed up to kill, and then ignores her. And I said to myself, a guy who doesn't deserve her.'

God, you smooth bastard. Even with minimum volume, she managed to score an A in withering contempt. 'If I was fed up for ten minutes because he doesn't like dancing, that's my affair. When Simon talks to me, at least it's not a load of soft-soap smoothie flannel. He has principles. He'd never ask out somebody else's girlfriend behind his back. I couldn't give a toss if he can't dance. He's worth fifty of you.'

Again, he did not seem in the least put out. 'Maybe. But that doesn't alter the fact that you're bored with him.'

His audacity took her breath away. 'If it weren't for the fact that he might hear,' she hissed, 'I'd slap your face from here into next week!'

'He won't hear, so feel free. If it'll make you feel better.'

'I will, if you don't get your despicable carcass out of here!'

For several seconds, he just gazed down at her. 'If I'm really so despicable, why haven't you flounced back to Simon and left me to see myself out?'

'Because,' she said tightly, enunciating every syllable, 'given your current form, you'd probably nick something on the way out!'

'That's not a bad idea,' he mused. With a quick, deft movement he flipped the scarf from around his neck. Like a silken trap it went over her head and tightened at her waist.

'Nicked,' he said softly.

She was too dumbstruck to take evasive action before he drew her in for the kill.

His mouth was warm and hungry, rough and fierce and tender, and as abruptly as he'd caught her, he let her go. Daisy was trembling with speechless shock.

'Bye,' he said lightly, and dropped a little pat on her waist. 'That was even better than your special nutty pudding.'

'Get out!' she trembled.

'I'm going.' But just after opening the door, he paused. 'And just for the record, I'm a Libra.'

For shock tactics, it was almost more effective than the kiss. 'Then why –?'

'Why do you think? I didn't want to see you look an idiot any more than you did.'

She was not taken in for a second. 'You wanted to make Simon look an idiot, instead.'

'That wasn't my prime motive, even if his patronising manner was rather asking for it' From his pocket he took a scrap of paper and tucked it into the pocket of her jeans. 'The Kirov's next Tuesday. Give me a ring if you change your mind.'

For several minutes after he'd left, she sat in the living room, gazing at the Nine O'clock News but hearing and seeing nothing. Somewhere her brain registered Simon on the phone; somewhere it registered when he stopped talking and started clearing up the kitchen, instead. He would never just leave it, expecting her to do it. He whistled as he did it, the theme from *Match of the Day*.

Her heart twisted. She got up from the armchair, and went to help him.

She lay in the crook of Simon's arm, gazing into the dark. He had already drifted into a contented, post-coital sleep.

Daisy was far from sleeping.

How could you do it? Think of that green-eyed devil while Simon was making love to you and pretend it was only him who turned you on? How would you feel if he got turned on by the cracking Amanda and came to you to scratch his itch?

That voice in her head was unbearable. She moved closer to Simon, as if his warmth could banish it. He was all she'd ever wanted. He was the rock she'd never had. Not a male rock, anyway. Her mother had always been there, but it wasn't quite the same.

It was only the thought of her mother that finally banished that voice from her head. She had known it would happen, only it had taken a bit longer than she'd thought. After eleven months smooth, charming Miles had told her mother he needed his 'personal space'. 'Personal space' had turned out to be Portugal – back to the woman who'd kicked him out fifteen months before.

And now she was going to have to pick up the pieces. Again.

Simon phoned on Friday night. 'I've cancelled the Parkers. I'll come with you tomorrow.'

'What did you tell them?'

'Oh, just some story about your mother not being very well and you wanted me to – '

'Simon! How could you?'

'Daisy, for heaven's sake, it was just – '

'Phone them right now and tell them she's OK and you're coming! Right this minute!'

'Daisy, you're being ridiculous!'

'It's tempting fate!'

'Now you're really being ridiculous. I only said she wasn't very well, not on her last – '

'I – don't – care! Phone and say she's better and you're coming!'

There was a long, resigned pause. 'All right. But I wish you wouldn't be so ridiculously superstitious.'

'And I wish you wouldn't tell fibs like that! I can't believe you did it!'

She hung up, more upset than she cared to admit. He came round half an hour later, armed with two bunches of flowers. 'One for you, one for your mother,' he said apologetically. 'I'm sorry, darling. I didn't mean to upset you.'

It was no use arguing. They belonged to diametrically-opposed schools of thought where superstition was concerned. Daisy had inherited hers from her mother, who'd had an Irish grandmother, who'd been full of them. A bird in the house meant death, a picture falling off the wall meant death, just about everything meant death.

Simon belonged to the no-nonsense, walking-under-ladders-on-purpose school, inherited from a very military father and a mother who'd have made a wonderful

Empire Wife. The type who'd have called, '*Would you mind awfully keeping the noise down? I've got a little bridge party in the drawing room,*' to half a million natives brandishing spears outside.

But they made up, and the next morning she went down to Gloucestershire alone.

The village was very quiet, not a bit like it would be in the summer, with scores of tourists. Katie's Kitchen – the café her mother had once co-run with a friend – was closed, but its gingham curtains were still bright and tubs of winter pansies smiled outside. Her mother would have done those. She did everybody's tubs.

Home was a mile and a half outside the village – an old farm cottage, with more tubs of pansies outside. Inside it was very small, but as pretty as paint, a sewing machine and a lot of flair could make it.

After the first hugs, she handed Simon's flowers over. 'He was going to come, but he had to go to the Parkers.'

'It's so sweet of him.' Isabel Rose buried her face in them. 'Scented narcissi. Freesias, too. They're terribly expensive at the moment.'

She was wearing a long red skirt with one of the jumpers she knitted herself – the kind that looked as if they'd cost a bomb in some classy little shop. And she was doing her best, but the cracks were showing. 'I know you didn't like him, but please don't say "I told you so",' she said, with a forced smile.

'Oh, Mum. As if I would.'

'Still, you'd be right. But it could be worse.' She poured boiling water into a delicate china teapot she'd picked up in a sale. Just about everything in the cottage had been picked up in a sale. Nothing ever matched, but that only seemed to add to the haphazard charm. 'He asked me to lend him some money a month or so ago.'

'*What*?'

'So he could go and research his book in Berlin.'

'My God. You didn't give him any?'

Isabel Rose shook her head. 'I know you think I'm daft, but I'm not that daft. I told him I couldn't afford it. He didn't say much, but I could see the writing on the wall then.'

Miles had been an 'incomer' to the village. He had occupied a picturesque but very run-down rented cottage half a mile down the road. A year younger than her mother, he'd looked a lot younger, just like her. He'd possessed the darkly romantic looks of a Byron and a lot of vaguely bohemian charm. Tara had fancied him when she'd dropped in for a visit, but then, Tara fancied a lot of people. 'Him and his wretched book. I bet it's arty-farty tripe.'

'It's not, darling. It's very good, so far. I'm sure he'll get published in the end.'

'After he's gone through all his redundancy money and sponged off a few more women.' She wished at once she hadn't said it. 'I'm sorry, Mum. But he did.'

'I know,' her mother sighed. 'But it was good while it lasted.' She put on a smile that tried to be airy, but ended up merely forlorn. 'For a few months, anyway. Maybe I'll get a dog. At least they mean it when they look into your eyes and tell you they love you.'

Almost for the first time, her mother was beginning to look her age. She had shadows under her eyes, and no amount of plaster could hide the sadness of a woman who had never got it right, and was beginning to think she never would.

She's lonely. Almost in tears, Daisy put her arms around her.

Next morning, while her mother was in the bath, she flicked through the Yellow Pages and made a couple of phone calls.

Telling her mother she'd booked lunch in a pub they'd never tried before, she drove seven miles and stopped by the village church to consult her map.

'I'm sure it's not this way, darling,' said her mother patiently. 'We should have turned at that little cross-roads.'

'No, we're right.' She drove another mile and a half and stopped outside a rather rambling bungalow that could have done with a coat of paint.

Beginning to wonder whether this was such a good idea after all, she turned to her mother. 'We are going for lunch, but I've made a little detour. It's probably a completely crazy idea and we don't have to go in but this is an animal rescue – they've got a seven-year-old dog called Barney who's desperate for a good home. He belonged to an old man who died, and everybody wants younger dogs or puppies. He looks like a rather scruffy hearthrug and he's not very beautiful, but the woman says he's good as gold.'

'I suppose he'd have loved anybody, but it really did look like love at first sight,' Daisy sighed. 'And he was so good! As if he was worried about being taken back, poor thing. We took him for a pub lunch, and he sat quietly and didn't ask for anything. Of course, Mum gave him half her roast beef anyway. He'll be sleeping on her bed tonight, you mark my words.'

Jane gave a rather double-edged sigh. 'Dogs are so much better than men. At least they don't swan off and play squash every other night.'

It was a sore point, Ian at the club again.

'It's no use moaning like some boring housewife in a pinny,' Tara said. 'You should be out on the tiles, getting your own back. I would.'

'I can't,' Jane pointed out. 'He's coming round later.'

Tara pushed back her gleaming dark hair and raised her eyes to heaven. 'Exactly. All the more reason for you to be out.'

She was looking a lot better than when she'd left; her face wore that unmistakable Alpine glow. Daisy tactfully changed the subject. 'So how was Obergurgl? Lots of lovely snow?'

'The snow was brilliant. The only fly in the ointment was our bitch instructor – bloody Claudia Schiffer lookalike, too. I mean, what's the use of ski school if you don't get some gorgeous *Klaus* to flirt with? I swear my parallel turns got worse.'

'No extra-curricular activities, then?' Jane asked wickedly. 'No *après-après* ski?'

'Not even a snog. There was a chap called Anton I really fancied till I found out he was gay. Makes you laugh, doesn't it?'

Daisy pointedly avoided Jane's eye, because Tara would notice immediately.

Tara went to the kitchen to top up everybody's *glühwein*. She had brought some of the sachets that

101

you just slung in a saucepan with a bottle of wine: as easy as teabags.

And just as she returned, Ian arrived. 'Hi,' he called from the hall. 'Anything for dinner?'

'I've done a lovely sod-all casserole,' Jane called. 'With *pommes a la* 'bugger off and don't come to me for your dinner when you're down that club every night.'

'Just what I fancied,' called Ian cheerfully. 'And just as well, because I've got Nick with me and he hasn't eaten either. I thought we'd go for a curry.'

Daisy's stomach contracted. It contracted even more when Nick and Ian walked in, just as Tara emerged from the kitchen with her tray of *glühwein*.

Tara didn't overdo it, but there was no mistaking the '*Well, what have we here?*' look in her eye.

My God. Those two will be a recipe for disaster.

Why? She'll sleep with him and dump him, and he won't give a damn. In case you hadn't noticed, men like that don't usually mind being dumped. It saves them all the bother of tearful bust-ups.

Nick didn't exactly ignore her, but it wasn't far off. He said, 'Hello, Daisy,' quite casually, before getting chatting to Tara. Nobody would ever have imagined the little scene in the hall only four days back. Jane would have had a fit if she'd told her.

Within minutes everybody but Daisy was on their feet, looking for coats and car keys.

'Aren't you coming, Daisy?' said Ian.

'No, I'll just have a sandwich.'

'Don't be so boring,' Jane scoffed. 'You need something to soak up all that *glühwein*.'

102

'Yes, but look at me! Manky old jeans and this old jumper . . .' She pushed her hair back. It was loose and she hadn't brushed it since leaving her mother's four hours back.

For a moment, Nick's unsettling eyes fell on her. And for a moment, she thought he was going to say something like, 'You look fine, to me.' But they returned almost immediately to Tara, who evidently thought the evening was looking unusually promising.

'For heaven's sake, we're not going to *Simply Nico*, Jane pointed out.

Daisy gave in. After so much *glühwein* she was quite unfit to drive and went with Ian and Jane. Tara was even more unfit, and went with Nick in the E-type.

'Good fun, but a bloody headache, a car like that,' Ian said, as they followed. 'And I bet the servicing costs a bomb. Still, I suppose it has pulling power.'

'I don't think he needs a flash car to pull the birds,' Jane objected. 'I hope Tara's behaving herself,' she added over her shoulder, to Daisy.

'I doubt it,' Ian said drily. 'She looked a bit pissed to me.'

Tara was, but she kept it under control for most of the meal. It was one of the classier Indians, with delicate dishes as well as burning ones, lovely just-cooked nan bread that you could eat all night.

Daisy found herself at the end of the table, like mother. Nick caught her eye several times. Once or twice it lingered, but she looked away. Tara did most of the talking, as usual, but by the coffee stage, after two beers on top of a lot of *glühwein*, she was getting noisy, giggly, and decidedly flirty.

103

She wobbled very slightly as she rose from the table and as they went out into the freezing air, Ian said, 'Christ, just look at her. We'd better get her in with us. The state she's in, she might make a dive for Nick's zip and he'll crash.'

So it was Jane who took Tara's arm and manipulated her towards the Audi, and Daisy who found herself pushed in with Nick, to stop Tara getting there first.

'That wasn't very subtle,' he said drily, as he pulled away. 'I hope they weren't afraid I'd take advantage.'

She knew from his tone he wasn't remotely serious. 'Tara can get very out of control after a few drinks.'

'She wasn't that bad.' After half a mile or so, he gave her a sideways glance. 'I suppose you haven't changed your mind about Tuesday night?'

Having thought he'd written her off as a don't-bother zone, this was a minor shock.

'No.' She kept her eyes resolutely ahead. It was the last thing she'd wanted, being crammed into this little space with him. It was too intimate, with the smell of leather seats and the heater going full blast. And the gear lever was far too close to her thigh, and he seemed to be changing gear rather more often than necessary.

'It was just the ballet and a meal,' he said mildly. 'I wasn't suggesting anything else.'

Oh, of course not. 'It's still "no".'

It was a moment before he spoke. 'Would you have come if not for Simon?'

She closed her eyes briefly. 'I hate to wound your poor little ego, but you're really not my type.'

He stopped at a red light. 'I seemed to be "your type" a few years ago.'

104

'I've grown up a bit since then.'

'So have I.' He pulled away and added, 'Will you tell me something?'

'Probably not.'

'Were you "*virgo intacta*"?'

She gasped. 'It's none of your business!'

'All right – I withdraw the question.'

Daisy felt acutely uncomfortable, because of what was evidently going through his mind. Maybe he didn't recall it in minute detail like she did, but he'd recalled quite enough.

'I thought about you a lot,' he said.

Something inside her stirred, drew breath, and was killed instantly by the voice of mature reason. *Watch it. He's trying different tactics now. The last lot didn't work, so he's using a more subtle approach. He's one of those men who love a challenge.*

'I only asked,' he went on mildly, 'because it was a possible explanation for you charging off like that.'

She took a deep breath. 'OK, so I was. Satisfied? Now can we drop the subject?'

He stopped at another red light. 'Then I'm glad we got interrupted. I'd have hurt you and felt terrible afterwards.'

That stirring 'something' was rapidly coming back to life. *Be careful, Daisy. This is precisely what he's aiming for.* 'I think you've got the wrong script,' she said casually. 'What you're supposed to say in such cases is, "*I wish it had been me. I'd have made it so wonderful for you.*"'

He gave her a glance that even felt sardonic. 'Have you been to evening classes in being a cynical bitch?'

'No more than you've been to evening classes in chat-up scripts.'

'Even if I had, I'd never have used a line like that. It probably wouldn't have been wonderful, as I'm sure you found out. Not for you.'

'Well, you should know. I'm sure you've made plenty of *virgos* non-*intacta*.'

It was another mile through the backwoods of Richmond and he said nothing till he pulled up outside the thirties block where she lived.

'You can relax,' he said sardonically, putting the handbrake on. 'I'm not going to make any more advances, verbal or otherwise.'

'Thank you so much.'

'Not until I hear you've bust up with Simon.'

His nerve still had the power to amaze her. 'I'm not going to bust up with him!'

'Never? You mean you're going to marry him?'

'Yes! If he asks me.'

Even in the dim light, she could see the sardonic glint in his eyes. 'Why don't you ask him? It's allowed nowadays.'

'Maybe I will.'

'It's a sinful waste.'

She gasped. 'You are the most unbelievably arrogant, conceited – '

'He'll bore you. He'll stifle you with boring, sub-urban predictability till you want to scream.'

'How dare you?' Her voice was unsteady with disbelief. 'You know nothing about me! How the hell do you know what I'd like?'

Unbelievably, he put up a hand and touched a wisping strand of hair. 'Because,' he said softly, 'un-

106

der that rather proper little exterior, I think there's a free spirit trying to get out.'

'*What*?' She could almost have laughed, if not for the shiver that touch produced. 'I suppose that's a smoothie-euphemism for sleeping around. Only it sounds better, doesn't it? For chat-up purposes, that is. When you're trying to persuade someone who's in a stable, loving relationship to jack it in and sleep with you, instead. And don't tell me, you've never even *mentioned* sleeping with me. All you want is a nice platonic night out because your Auntie Mabel's busy at her upholstery class and can't make it.'

'What do you expect me to say? That I don't want to sleep with you?' He paused, and his eyes held her in the dark. 'Of course I do. I want you like mad.'

That something that had stirred and quivered was suddenly so alive, it frightened her. It was growing like a Triffid, sending warm liquid fingers to every crevice she possessed.

Get out of the car, quick. He knows exactly what he's doing. He's got it down to a fine art.

'Then I'm terribly sorry, you'll have to want,' she said unsteadily, groped for the door handle and couldn't find it.

'Let me.' Reaching across her, he opened the door. She held her breath as his arm nearly brushed her body.

'Thank you.'

'Don't mention it,' he said drily. 'I won't come up. Tell Ian I had to go.'

'Forgive me if I don't try to change your mind. Thanks for the lift.' She got out and didn't look back.

107

All the way up in the lift, she was trying to compose herself so she'd look normal when she got in.

'Nick said sorry, he had to go,' she said, casually tossing her jacket on to a chair.

'You've been ages!' Jane said.

'We were chatting in the car.'

'What about?'

Oh, help. Think. 'Barbados,' she said casually. 'He's been, a couple of years ago.'

'Yes, he told me tonight,' Ian said. 'Said it was beautiful and he wouldn't mind going back. And since he'd said he hadn't had a proper break in ages, I said, why not come with us?'

'*What?*' Daisy was too shocked to control her reactions.

'I'm sorry.' Ian looked distinctly hurt. 'Only I didn't think anybody'd mind. The thing is, he's been working overseas nearly four years, first Singapore, then Wall Street, and he's lost touch with a lot of his old UK friends and I thought – '

'It was sweet of you, darling,' Jane said stoutly. 'Of course he can come.' She gave Daisy a Look. 'Daisy didn't mean anything. Did you?'

I damn-well did. I'm not surprised he's lost touch with his friends. I'm surprised he's got any, if he makes passes at people's girlfriends behind their backs. 'I was just a bit startled,' she shrugged. 'I mean, you only met up with him again ten days ago.'

'I know, but he used to be a good mate of mine. He probably won't come,' he added. 'Said he'd think about it.'

'That's a polite way of saying no,' Tara put in, slurring her words very slightly. 'It's not much fun for a single, tagging along with two couples. He ought to go on a Club Med. That Club Med in Greece was the best holiday I've ever had.' She paused, hiccupped, and started giggling.

'Not everybody wants non-stop booze and nookie,' Jane pointed out, a trifle acidly. 'Maybe he just wants to relax.'

'God, how boring. You might as well go and hike round the Lake District with a load of sad – ' she hiccupped again '– anoraks.'

'Even if he did want to come, it's probably booked up,' Daisy pointed out. 'The flights were practically booked solid when we booked.'

'There's always room for one,' Jane said.

'On a plane, maybe. I bet the hotel's booked. The travel agent said February's high season in the Caribbean, if you remember.'

'You sound almost as if you don't want him to come!' Jane said accusingly.

Daisy's tension came out as irritability. 'Don't be ridiculous – I'm just being realistic.' She picked up her bag. ''Night, everybody. I'm going to bed.'

She hardly saw Nick for the next few weeks, although he dropped in now and then with Ian. On one occasion Simon was there and they were just going out, on the other, she was just going for a bath.

They were leaving for Barbados on the ninth of February, and it was on January the twenty-first that Jane told her Nick was coming, after all.

'The hotel had a cancellation,' she said. 'A double, of course. He'll have to pay a bomb for it, but I don't suppose he's bothered. Ian reckons he's been earning telephone numbers the past few years and apparently he's recently landed a plum job with some investment bank.'

Having got used to the possibility, Daisy accepted it with barely a squirm in her stomach. She wasn't going to let anything spoil this holiday. Simon was working far too hard; she hardly saw him except at weekends and even then he found it difficult to unwind. She had taken him down to her mother's, hoping the rural atmosphere would relax him, but even there he had worked, fixing a blown-down fence and calling an aggressive person at the garage that had tried to rip her mother off. His terse, legal threats had produced an instant reduction in their bill, and Isabel had been over the moon with gratitude. Barney had loved him too, though that might have had something to do with the packet of doggy chews he'd so thoughtfully presented him with.

Barney had settled in wonderfully. Between mistress and mutt there existed a mutual adoration society, and Daisy's mother said she felt so much safer at night with a woof-alarm at the end of the bed.

So what with Simon and the vile weather, wet and windy with flurries of sleet, Daisy was thoroughly looking forward to the holiday. She bought sun cream, mozzie repellent and two new bikinis with matching sarongs.

And on the second of February, Simon dropped his bombshell.

CHAPTER 6

The check-in queue shuffled forward like a centipede with corns. Daisy pushed two trolleys forwards six inches and slid Jane's flight bag across the floor with her foot. She was minding everybody else's luggage because they had all nipped to the shop for last minute panic-buys.

Nick was not in their immediate party. Ten yards away he was at the front of the Club Class queue.

The woman in front of her laughed for about the sixteenth time. Daisy was getting really annoyed with that woman. Apart from that annoying laugh, which she exercised non-stop, she wore horrible green trousers and had really annoying hair.

The woman glanced over her shoulder and caught Daisy's eye. With a really inane, annoying grin, she said, 'Cheer up! It might never happen!'

God, I just knew you were the kind of really annoying person who says things like that. 'It already has, actually.'

The woman's grin faded to a tittery awkwardness. 'Oh, well. Can't be that bad, can it?' she said, and turned back to her husband.

Daisy felt crosser than ever; with herself, for being such a miserable bitch. Her eyes drifted crossly to the

Club Class desk, where the check-in girl was bestowing a dazzling smile on a certain passenger as she handed over his boarding card.

Surprise, surprise.

To make her crosser still, the certain passenger turned at that precise moment and saw her staring crossly. And of course, with a certain little smile, he came over.

He was wearing some sort of beigy cotton trousers with an olive polo shirt and one of those lineny summer jackets with his boarding card tucked in the breast pocket. His hair was very clean and shiny and flopped slightly over his right eyebrow, and the olive of the polo shirt seemed to intensify the colour of his eyes.

He looked so horribly, devastatingly attractive, he made her tense right up inside, which only made her cross with him, too, for adding to her woes.

'I'm sorry about Simon,' he said.

Tell me another. 'So am I.'

He was standing unnecessarily close – about eighteen inches – doubtless because he knew he made her feel uncomfortably titchy and therefore even more vulnerable. She almost wished she'd worn high heels, however ridiculous they looked with Levi's. She had long ago stopped dressing up when going on holiday, let alone a ten hour flight. With them she wore a pale pink shirt and a navy cotton sweater slung around her shoulders.

'I gather one of the partners had an accident,' he went on.

'Yes. A bad one. He's going to be in hospital for weeks and Simon felt he couldn't possibly leave them in the lurch.'

'Very unfortunate,' he murmured. 'Lousy timing.'

If there was irony there, it was very faint.

'But maybe not such a disaster for Simon,' he went on. 'Ian tells me he's up for a partnership and this will give him an edge.'

He said it casually enough, but she still felt he was implying that Simon was turning someone else's misfortune to his own advantage. 'That's not why he's doing it.'

'Oh, no,' he murmured. 'It's very good of him to give up his holiday. Especially since he couldn't claim on the insurance.'

'It doesn't matter. Tara was only too happy to step into the breach.'

Eventually. Her arguments with Simon had been like bashing her head against a brick wall. He could not let his colleagues down, but she must go. She could take her mother in his place; it would make him feel a good deal better to think of somebody he was fond of enjoying it, instead.

Daisy had been divided between tears at his stubbornness, and more tears at his unselfish thoughtfulness.

But her mother had refused point blank. First, she couldn't afford it. In vain had Daisy explained that they would only lose the money anyway, so she wouldn't have to pay. Next she had come up with the old, '. . . and you don't want your mother tagging along' bit. Third, she couldn't possibly leave Barney when he'd just settled in so well. The poor little boy would think she was abandoning him.

Since this argument had proved unshiftable, enter Tara.

'Just as well Tara could get time off at short notice,' he said.

'It's easier for Tara to get time off than the rest of us. She temps for an agency.' The agency specialized in emergency PAs and Tara could be surprisingly efficient in an office situation. Such employment also provided her with an endless fresh supply of men. And at least Tara was paying. She had not really been able to afford it either, but a quick phone call to Daddy had solved that one.

But Daisy had not wanted Tara to come, which was why she felt so crossly guilty. Not so long ago, Tara would have been her first choice for a holiday partner. She had been thoroughly good fun; a real party animal. But lately . . .

She would drink too much, flirt with everything in sight, and probably be a ghastly embarrassment. Daisy had confessed her misgivings to Jane, who'd just said soothingly, 'She'll be OK. We'll keep her under control.'

Even before it started, she knew her holiday was wrecked. She gave Nick a resentful glance. 'So you won't be slumming it in Economy with the peasants.'

The woman in front turned indignantly. 'Speak for yourself, love.'

Oh, help. 'It was just a manner of speaking,' Daisy said hastily. 'I didn't mean . . .'

'Then don't say it.' The woman turned her eyes on Nick. 'Is she with you?'

'Not exactly,' he said drily. 'I'm not her type.'

'I should count myself lucky, if I were you.' The woman turned back to her husband with a triumphant, 'well, that told *her*,' expression.

114

At that moment, Daisy could almost have sat down on the floor like a three-year-old and wailed that she wasn't playing any more, she wanted to go home.

Just to make matters worse, Nick appeared lazily amused by the episode. 'Look on the bright side,' he soothed. 'Maybe there'll be a hurricane warning *en route*, and we'll have to turn back.'

'It's not the hurricane season. I checked.'

She was saved the effort of further conversation by the others coming back. For the next ten minutes Tara did enough talking for all of them. 'I call it very unsociable of you to go Club,' she pouted, as they finally departed for Passport Control.

'It was all I could get.'

'Fibber.' Tara gave him an arch look. 'Don't worry, I'd go Club if I could. I'm surprised you didn't go Concorde. Ian said you could easily afford it. After all, it's only about four grand extra.'

Daisy winced for Ian and exchanged an eyes-to-heaven look with Jane.

'If you dare say "I told you so", I'll kill you,' Jane muttered.

'That was nothing,' Daisy muttered back. 'She hasn't even had a drink yet.'

'Just look at her,' Jane said drily.

'I am.'

It was their second full day. They were lying in the shade of the feathery casuarinas that fringed the beach. Ian was asleep beside Jane. Nick and Tara were standing at the edge of the water, chatting to a beach vendor. There was a lot of noisy giggling from Tara, who had the remains of drink in her hand. When the vendor strolled on and Nick started walking back up the beach, Tara's face lit in a wicked grin and she tipped the ice from her glass down the back of his shorts.

His reaction made them both groan. He swept her up in his arms, carried her into the sea, and dumped her in waist-deep water.

'Just listen to her,' Jane groaned. 'Talk about "Stop it, I like it". I bet they can hear her in St Lucia.'

Nick emerged from the sea, still half-laughing as he shook the ice from his shorts. Still giggling, Tara ran up behind him and gave him a massive shove intended to push him over in the sand.

He reacted with a lightning grab and a swift but harmless slap to Tara's pink bikini bottoms. Her giggly shrieks practically drowned the noise of the speedboat whizzing past.

'Maybe it's a case of "Stop it, I like it" with him too,' Daisy said drily. 'Coming for a swim?'

'No, hon. I'm too chilled out to move.'

Daisy strolled down to the edge of the turquoise water. The sand shelved steeply, and seconds later she was doing a lazy crawl to the raft.

It was anchored about fifty yards from the beach; a perfect, gently-rocking place to top up your tan. Nobody else was there. Daisy climbed up the little ladder and sat down, wondering why she had ever said the holiday was ridiculously expensive and couldn't possibly be worth it.

The beach stretched for miles; endless, little curving bays, each fringed with casuarinas or palms that dipped lazy fronds towards the water. The hotel was almost

116

buried in its lush gardens, the little blocks of rooms nestling among the greenery as if they'd grown there. There was no high-rise concrete to be seen and although it was high season, the beach could hardly be called crowded.

She turned over and lay on her stomach, looking over the edge of the raft. The water was about twenty feet deep and so clear, she could see sunlit ripples playing on the bottom. Tiny, blue and yellow fish pecked and darted, nibbling at the algae-covered ropes that held the raft in place.

It rocked gently as a speedboat passed twenty yards away. It was like a cradle and a water-bed combined. She rested her head on folded arms, and closed her eyes. The sun on her back was bliss.

Minutes later, the raft rocked again, as somebody else clambered up the ladder. 'I hope you're not falling asleep,' he said.

'I'm not that stupid.'

He had just taken the edge off her bliss. Of course, the edge was off it already since she constantly felt guilty for basking in idleness while Simon was working his socks off, but that was different.

The raft was maybe six feet by ten. He was sitting about three feet away, his arms clasped around his knees. Already he had gone ripe-hazelnut brown and the sunlit drops on his skin only emphasized the taut muscles underneath.

Whatever he'd said about backing off, Daisy was cynical enough not to believe it. Accordingly, along with her travel iron and personal CD player, she had packed a DIY wall-of-ice kit, just in case.

The kit was still in its box. There had not been so much as a glint in his eye; not at her, anyway. To say she was startled was not quite correct. Warily suspicious was more like it.

'I get the impression,' he mused, 'that you've been avoiding me.'

This shook her more than a little. She'd been very subtle about it, since Jane had eagle eyes for such things. She had not been avoiding him because of what he might do, since it had seemed that she was not, after all, on his agenda. It was because that FAB jab seemed to be wearing off. Every time he was within crackling distance, she felt the ominous little shiverings that herald a nasty case of FAB infection. Keeping him at a distance was just a sensible precaution. 'Don't be ridiculous.'

'I wouldn't altogether blame you if you did.'

'Neither would I.' The sun was getting rather too blissfully hot on her back, so she turned over and sat up, her legs stretched out in front of her.

'So I came to tell you not to worry,' he went on. 'You were – how shall I put it? A passing fancy that has passed.'

Her first reaction produced almost enough guilt to require therapy.

How dare he just go off me like that?

Wasn't that what you wanted?

Yes, but that's not the point.

'I'm delighted to hear it,' she said coolly. *I get it. Once you realized I wasn't up for it, I might as well be that old Auntie Mabel.*

With mock apology he added, 'In the circumstances, I hope you didn't mind my slightly ungallant turn of phrase.'

118

Don't make me laugh. 'Not in the least. It just confirms what I already knew.'

'Enlighten me.'

'I'll leave it to your imagination. I wouldn't want to frighten the fish.'

He did not seem at all put out, which didn't surprise her. Even if she'd said 'Crumpet-hopping bastard, if you really want to know', she had a feeling his mouth would only have quivered in that infuriating manner.

'You're going a nice colour,' he observed, glancing at her stretched-out legs. 'I thought you'd go painful, blistered pink and look like nothing on earth for ten days.'

Damn cheek. One thing Daisy did not possess was the kind of milk-and-roses skin that goes painful pink. She had cream-and-honey, which doesn't, unless you're really stupid. 'Any more compliments, while you're at it?'

'Can't think of any,' he mused. His eyes were on the beach, where Tara was playing beach bats with one of the watersports boys.

Daisy's mind was elsewhere, up Guilt Mountain. *How dare I care if the so-and-so's lost interest?*

Tara's giggles floated across the water, and even from fifty yards she could see her curves bouncing.

'Quite a girl, your friend Tara,' he mused.

Your fancy wouldn't have passed to her, would it? Because if anyone's sending out 'available' signals . . .

Ever since they'd arrived, Tara's behaviour had been bordering on the frankly embarrassing. She was noisy, drinking rather more than anybody needed to just to relax, and flirting with just about

119

everything. With Nick it would soon be getting beyond a joke, and she didn't want him lazily thinking she'd be the easiest pull in creation. Tara might not give a stuff what anybody thought, but she cared for her. 'She wasn't always like this,' she said. 'Not this bad, anyway.'

He turned to her. 'What do you mean, "bad"? She's just having fun.'

'Oh, for heaven's sake. You know what I mean. Flirting. All that stop-it-I-like-it horseplay.' She paused. 'And you're encouraging her.'

'What do you want me to do? Act like some pompous misery and tell her to cut it out?'

Exactly. It was almost too delicate to put into words, but however much of a pain Tara could be lately, they went back a long way. 'Look, Nick, there's something I want you to know about Tara. You knew her marriage broke up?'

'I gathered as much.'

She hesitated. 'Did you know why?'

'No.'

She hesitated again. It really wasn't her business, but if it would make him understand . . .

'She was mad about him. He was quite a bit older, very successful, good-looking, you name it. And one day she came back early from a visit home and found him *in flagrante*. With another man.'

He raised his eyebrows. 'Strewth. Bit of a shock.'

'It's more than a bit of a shock to find out your husband's bisexual. It destroyed her confidence for ages. She was terrified of HIV at first – waiting months for the test nearly killed her – but she was clear. But

120

she'd changed. Ever since, she seems to need to prove to herself that she can still attract men. She's always been a flirt, but this is different.' She paused. 'I'm sure I don't need to spell it out.'

He turned to her. 'Why are you telling me this?'

'I just wanted you to understand why she's behaving like this.'

'I don't think so. I think you're trying to tell me – very unsubtly, I might add – to keep off. If I were equally unsubtle, I might add that you're sounding remarkably like a sanctimonious little prig who thinks she's got her own love life perfectly ordered and thinks that gives her the right to order other people's.'

His lazy, melted-chocolate voice had hardened very sharply round the edges. She'd always suspected there might be steel in that laid-back sheath, but seeing it flash for the first time shocked her. 'She's my friend. I hate seeing her like this.'

'People have to make their own mistakes,' he said. 'People do the wrong things all the time. They mess up relationships. They have relationships with the wrong people.'

'And what's that supposed to mean?'

'Exactly what it says.'

'If you're having a go at Simon again . . .'

'I'm not.'

When he turned to her again, the glint was conspicuous by its absence. 'Whatever I said before, I withdraw it. It was an error of judgement.'

'Judgement?' she echoed. 'What judgement? You had nothing to base it on!'

'All right, not judgement. Intuition. The same intuition you used when you were arguing the toss about astrology with Simon.'

And got it wrong. OK, touché. 'I still can't believe you had the gall to say it. You saw me with him for a total of about four hours!'

A couple of snorkellers surfaced near the raft and she wondered whether they were going to climb up for a breather. She also wondered whether she wanted them to, as the current conversation would surely be cut short. 'Anyway, men aren't supposed to have intuition.'

'Instinct, then. I use my instincts all the time at work. Something either feels right or it doesn't.'

'Keep them for work, then, and your mega-buck deals. They're obviously more successful there.'

Part of her was beginning to feel it was high time she left him; the other part was wondering why on earth she should. 'Ian would never have asked you on this holiday if he'd known what you did behind Simon's back. He'd be horrified.'

'So why didn't you tell him? You didn't want me to come.'

'I really didn't care a hoot whether you came or not.'

'I think you did.' He rolled on to his side, propped on his elbow, where he could conduct his scrutiny more easily. 'I think you were nurturing the idea that I was going to be thoroughly ungentlemanly all over again and take dreadful liberties.'

His softly mocking tone made her more uncomfortable than she already was. 'Let's just say I wouldn't exactly have died of shock.' She added a mocking tone to match his own. 'But since your fancy has now passed, I can presumably breathe again.'

Closing her eyes, she turned her face up to the sun, and waited for his next move.

It came more quickly than she expected. The raft rocked again as he rose to his feet. 'I'm going for a beer. See you later.'

She opened her eyes and just caught the splash as he dived in. And as she watched his arms cutting the water in a powerful crawl, an uncomfortable truth dawned in her head.

You know the real reason you don't like him larking around with Tara? You're jealous.

I am not!

Yes, you are.

She thought of Tara after a few drinks at night, getting even more flirty. She thought of her contriving a walk on the beach with him at night. She thought of her getting even more physical; tickling him or saying something so deliberately outrageous he'd grab her and pretend to be mad, which was exactly what she'd want. With a lazy glint in his eye he'd say something like, '*Now what am I going to do with you?*' And Tara would put on that wicked-innocent look she did so well and say something like, '*Are you asking for suggestions?*' And before you could say 'lusty spears' . . .

Stop it!

She dived abruptly into the water and swam back a good deal faster than she'd swum out.

They were all up at the beach bar, except for Tara. Ian instantly vacated the stool he was occupying, which was next to Nick's. 'Have a seat, love. What can I get you?'

Passed fancy or not, she didn't want to sit next to Nick, but she didn't want to hurt Ian's feelings, either. 'Fresh lime squash, thanks.'

Calypso was playing from a cassette behind the bar, the barman half-dancing as he mixed coconut punch. Jane was on the other side of Ian, so it was easy to half-turn from him without being obvious. 'Where's Tara?'

'Gone to the shop. She's craving chocolate.'

Turning her back on Nick misfired badly. 'You're underestimating the local solar power,' he observed. 'You've got a pretty little pink stripe where your strap's shifted.'

He adjusted it. He did it oh-so-casually, sliding one finger between strap and skin and running it horizontally across her back as he eased it over the pink bit. Very casually he added, 'I wouldn't want you in agony tonight because your bra-strap's killing you.'

The effect on her was anything but casual. It felt like the prelude to something else altogether.

'With Jane, it's her pants,' said Ian. 'She lies there falling asleep with the lovely squidgy bits popping out and by evening she's got two bright pink crescents that make her scream in agony when she sits down. But if I try a tweaky little adjustment, she yells at me to get off.'

'That's because you make such a meal of it,' Jane said. 'You have a good old squeeze while you're at it and say "Phwoor, what a bum", and people think you're a perve.'

With her shivers driven away by laughter, Daisy managed to give Nick the kind of smile she'd give

Ian in such circumstances. 'The service in this place is wonderful. You don't even have to lift a finger to adjust your own bikini strap.'

The glint in his eyes resembled the sun on a warm, green river. 'That's what I'm here for. Fetching drinks, lugging sunbeds about, any minor little service . . .'

I hate to tell you this, my dear, but I have a horrible feeling he knows exactly what he's doing to you.

He will, if you let him. 'Fetch another stool then,' she said sweetly. 'Tara's coming.'

Tara was sickeningly brown already, partly because of her UV sessions at the gym. By a whisker, her curves just missed the 'overweight' category and fell into the 'voluptuous' instead, bouncing healthily in a bright pink bikini that made the most of them. She parked herself on the stool next to Daisy – which Nick had just vacated for her.

'What a gentleman,' she purred, and gave his bottom a little pat. 'Have some chocolate.' She broke off a bit of Fruit and Nut and popped it in his mouth. 'Did you know it's supposed to be an aphrodisiac?'

'Of course,' he said lazily. 'That's why I always have a nice cup of cocoa at bedtime.'

She gave an explosive giggle. 'I wouldn't have thought you'd need any extra lead in your pencil.'

Jane and Daisy exchanged 'Oh, my God.' glances.

He received the remark with a twitching smile. 'Like a drink?'

'You bet. I'll have a rum punch.'

'Tara, they're terribly strong,' Jane said hesitantly.

'I know, darling. I'm on holiday.'

Ian nodded out to sea. 'There's the Jolly Roger,' The famous pirate schooner was passing a couple of hundred yards out, red sails fluttering and rhythmic calypso belting from its decks.

Tara swivelled on her stool. 'I've absolutely *got* to go on the Jolly Roger. Who's coming with me?'

'No way,' Jane shuddered. 'Look how packed it is! I bet it's full of yobs from the cheap end of the island.'

Nick raised an eyebrow and even Daisy, who knew Jane well, was distinctly startled.

'God, you're such a snob,' Tara scoffed.

'Yes, hon, but at least I'm honest about it.'

'Even the cheap end's hardly "cheap",' Daisy pointed out. 'And just because people can't afford something doesn't mean they're – '

'Never mind all that, who's coming?' Tara demanded.

'It's just an excuse for a lot of booze and deafening music,' Ian said. 'You need ear plugs.'

'You're nothing but a load of boring old farts,' Tara announced. 'I shall go by myself and be a pirate's moll for the day.'

Oh, Lord, Daisy thought. *Havoc will be wreaked. Diplomatic relations will be broken off.*

But she braced herself nonetheless. A noble, self-sacrificing offer would do something to assuage the guilt she still felt for not wanting Tara there in the first place.

'I'll come with you,' said Nick.

Daisy gaped at him, almost angry that he had pre-empted her.

'Really?' Tara gave a delighted squeak, put her arm around his waist and gave him a flirty squeeze. 'We'll have a brilliant laugh.'

He did not look in the least daunted by the prospect of a 'brilliant laugh' with Tara. 'Someone has to come and keep you in order,' he said lazily. 'And if you call me a boring old fart again, I'll wallop you with my surgical truss.'

'Promises, promises,' Tara giggled.

Jane and Daisy exchanged glances again.

By the time they sat down for lunch on the pool terrace, Tara was on her third rum punch, and showing it. Still, it was a relaxed enough atmosphere for it to matter little. The sun glinted silver on the sea, and doves cooed softly in the trees.

Daisy tucked into a tropical fruit plate and flying fish, and tossed crumbs to the beady-eyed black birds that lurked nearby, waiting for pickings.

When Tara disappeared to the loo, Ian said, 'Sooner you than me, Nick. If the pirate punch is as lethal as they say, she'll fall overboard.'

He only raised an eyebrow. 'I think I can handle Tara.'

'That's precisely what she wants him to do,' Jane whispered to Daisy. 'Handle her.'

Exactly. The more she thought about it, the more Daisy didn't like the idea of Tara being alone with Nick all day in an atmosphere of non-stop booze and total lack of inhibition. It wasn't exactly that she thought anything would 'happen'. Somehow, she was beginning to think Nick's attitude to Tara was more good-natured tolerance than anything else. She just didn't like to think of all the body-contact horseplay that would undoubtedly go on. And she felt horribly guilty for not being quicker with her offer to go with her, instead.

Tara returned and the conversation was relatively decorous until Jane gave Ian a nudge. 'Put your eyes back, darling. They're out on stalks.'

'I can't help it, love.' Ian was still gaping incredulously at a woman walking past. She was about forty-five, very well-preserved, very tanned, in a thong and a minute gold bikini top that she might as well have left off for all it covered. 'I've never seen anything like it. Her boobs defy all the laws of gravity.'

With a faintly amused expression, Nick was watching, too. 'Silicone,' he pronounced, with the air of a connoisseur. 'It bounces differently from the genuine article.'

Tara and Jane exploded, and despite herself, Daisy joined in.

'There you are, Daisy,' Tara said, when she'd recovered. 'I told you, they can always tell. Daisy was going to have implants once,' she added, loud enough for the people at nearby tables to hear.

'Tara, for heaven's sake!' Jane hissed.

If Tara heard, she heeded not. 'She was saving up for them,' she giggled. 'Until some chap told her she had angelic little boobs or something. She said it was all cobblers, of course, as he was only trying to get her knickers off, but she stopped saving up anyway.'

By some miracle, Daisy managed neither to flush nor look embarrassed. 'I started saving up for a car, instead,' she said lightly, and carried on with her flying fish.

'And she never would tell me who it was,' Tara went on, regardless of Jane trying to kick her under the table. 'Daisy could be so damned cagey about her love life.'

'We're not all like you,' Jane said pointedly.

Daisy just smiled and pretended to be wryly amused. She stayed till the bitter end of the meal, lingering over mango sorbet and coffee.

More than once, she met Nick's eye across the table. And each time she met it with a cool, '*So what?*'.

When Tara departed to cool off with a walk by the sea, Ian gave a deep sigh. 'Talk about motor-mouth.'

Daisy shrugged. 'It didn't bother me.'

'It'd bother me,' Jane said, with feeling. 'We'll have to bribe that barman to give her more ice with her drinks.'

Their first two sunsets had been rather disappointing; fizzling out into wishy-washy pink.

Hoping for third time lucky, Daisy sat on the beach with Jane and a rum collins with a straw.

Other people were on the beach, many with cameras. The sun was like molten gold on the water. There was hardly any wind, and a boat drifted past, its sail silhouetted black against the water. In the gardens behind them, the tree frogs were beginning the chirping chorus that would go on till dawn.

'I dread to think what'll happen on that Jolly Roger,' Jane said. 'She's got ten times worse since we've been here. Whatever discretion she possessed, she's left it at home.'

'She'll be OK,' Daisy said, with a good deal more conviction than she felt. 'Nick doesn't seem in the least worried.'

'Exactly.' Jane lowered her voice, quite unnecessarily, since there was nobody within earshot. 'Between you and me, Ian says he can't see him holding out for two weeks. Not if it's dished up on a plate. She's not exactly the back end of a hippopotamus. Not that it's any of our business, of course.'

Daisy tried to ignore the uncomfortable little cramp in her stomach. 'I don't think he actually *fancies* her.'

'Oh, come on, Daisy. He's a man. He wouldn't be human.'

She managed an offhand shrug. 'I really don't care. At least he's got his own room so I won't be barging in on an energetic siesta.'

'If it's not him, it'll be somebody else,' Jane went on glumly. 'It's like a tan, with Tara. If you don't get one, the holiday's a dead loss. I hate to say it, but I'm ashamed to be with her sometimes.'

'Oh, Jane. She's not quite that bad.'

'She's not far off. I suppose you couldn't have a word with her?'

'It's no earthly use saying anything. It only makes her worse.'

The sun slid gently beyond the sea, and suddenly the display was over. Only a wash of gold remained.

Jane rose to her feet. 'Ian's probably crashed out on the bed. I'd better go and wake him up.'

'See you later.' Daisy glanced at her watch. Soon she would go and ring Simon, but not yet. Tara was there and she was still mad over the lunchtime incident. It would take only one more remark for a row to start, and that was the last thing she wanted.

Tara had always been outrageous. It had been funny once, often hilarious. It still was, now and then. More often, it was simply over the top.

Suddenly Tara was put right out of her head. Just as everybody had drifted off, the sun delivered a finale. Huge, burning rays burst from below the horizon, like the spokes of a gigantic wheel. They filled the sky.

Daisy had never seen anything like it, ever. She wanted to run after Jane, but knew it would be gone by the time she found her. All she could do was imprint it on her brain for ever.

Even after it had faded, she still sat in the sand. A young couple were swimming back from the raft, their laughter mingling with the lap of tiny waves. It was all absolutely perfect, except that she had nobody to share it with.

Until someone sat in the sand beside her. He came so quietly, so softly barefoot, she was taken completely by surprise.

'I was watching from my balcony,' he said. 'Jane should have waited a little longer.'

Of course, he would have seen her there. His room was one of the best; practically on the beach, palm trees almost brushing his balcony rails.

He was sitting a couple of feet away, gazing not at her, but out at the sea. He had obviously showered – she could smell the tang of shaving things and his hair was still damp, but he wasn't dressed for dinner. He wore white shorts and a T shirt that looked black in the nearly-night.

'It's good of you to go Jolly Rogering with Tara,' she said.

'It's not "good" of me. I like her.'

His tone left her in no doubt as to what he had left unsaid. Something on the lines of, '*Whereas it seems that the rest of you are only tolerating her.*'

It stung viciously, because it was true. 'I would have gone with her,' she said unsteadily. 'I was just about to offer, when you did.'

He half turned to her. 'There's nothing to stop you coming too.'

Now I've really dropped myself in it. He was right, of course. There was absolutely nothing to stop her. Except . . .

'I'll pass, thanks.'

He shot her a fleeting sideways glance. More than ever, she felt he knew exactly what was going on in her head.

For over half a minute, he didn't speak. There was just the lap of waves, the faint rustle of leaves, and wafting calypso from the little bar down the beach. The very fact that he was so near, without talking to her or even looking at her, aroused an odd, nervous confusion in her stomach. It was as if something was just trembling on the brink.

'I must go,' she said unsteadily.

Just as she rose to her feet, he caught her wrist. 'Stay a minute. I want to talk to you.'

'I must go. I have to shower, wash my hair . . .'

'They can wait.'

Making a ridiculous fuss was out of the question.

Slowly she sank back to the sand beside him, and he released her. 'Talk, then,' she said unsteadily. 'It takes me hours to dry my hair.'

He still wasn't looking at her. 'I know it's a long time ago and you probably don't give a toss anyway, but I'd just like to put the record straight.'

'What about?' She knew perfectly well.

132

'You know "what about". What Tara was shooting her mouth off about, over lunch.'

She took a deep, steadying breath. 'It was my own fault. I should never have told her.'

'That's not the issue now. I just want you to know it wasn't "cobblers", that's all.'

Something deep inside her lurched and twisted, but she covered it magnificently. 'You would say that, wouldn't you? Not that it matters a hoot now.'

'No.' He picked up a little stone and tossed it towards the water. 'Not a hoot.' With a swift, fluid movement he stood up. 'You can go and wash your hair now. Sorry I held you up.'

And he strolled back to his super-deluxe, ocean view room, leaving her alone on the sand.

CHAPTER 7

She went back to her room in a state of odd, irritable confusion. Tara was in the shower. She tried to ring Simon but the only reply she got was from the wretched answerphone.

She sat on the balcony, wondering why on earth she felt she'd been a bitch to Nick. Even if she had, his previous behaviour deserved it.

Their room was on the first floor of the little block, near the pool. It was surrounded by trees, its underwater lights shimmering, and two young couples were still swimming. Or rather, larking around *a la* Nick and Tara, laughing their heads off.

She resented them bitterly for being so carefree.

Wrapped in a towel, Tara emerged from the shower. Running a comb through her hair, she took the other rattan armchair.

'I hope you haven't used all the dry towels,' Daisy said. She didn't mean to sound irritated, but that was how it came out.

'You're mad with me, aren't you?' Tara's voice lacked its usual bounce. 'Jane said you were. She was having a go at me about what I said at lunchtime; you know,

134

about your boobs.' Her voice cracked slightly. 'I didn't mean to embarrass you. I thought it was just a laugh.'

However much she wanted to 'have a go' at her, Daisy just couldn't do it. 'Tara, for heaven's sake. It'd take more than that to embarrass me.'

'Are you sure?'

'Of course,' she scoffed. 'Forget it.'

'Thank heaven for that. Because I'd feel really awful, after Simon not coming and everything.'

Not as awful as I feel, for not wanting you to come. 'Tara, forget it. I really couldn't give a stuff.'

It was worth all the lies in creation to see the relief on Tara's face. And as usual, she bounced back pretty fast. 'I went to the tour desk and booked the Jolly Roger. For the day after tomorrow. One of the watersports boys was telling me all about it. They have walking the plank and everything and on the way back they have a pirate wedding. And guess what?' She started giggling helplessly. 'They send the happy couple below to consummate it.'

It was late afternoon by the time Nick and Tara returned from the Jolly Roger, two days later.

Daisy and Jane were lying on sunbeds by the water's edge with books and their first rum cocktail of the day.

Tara's giggles arrived before she did. 'It was a *brilliant* laugh,' she announced, plonking herself in the sand beside Daisy. 'The music was fantastic. You should have come.' She stripped off the frayed white cut-offs she wore over the titchy, bright pink bikini. 'Gosh, I can't wait to get in that sea.'

135

Nick had sat next to Jane, in the sand. As Tara ran into the water she said, 'Don't tell me – it was a complete nightmare.'

'I wasn't expecting high culture. I was expecting thoroughly unpretentious fun, and that's exactly what it was.' He rose to his feet again. 'I'm going for a beer.'

'Well!' Jane said crossly, as he went. 'Was he trying to imply that we're "pretentious" or something?'

'Of course not.' Daisy sipped her collins. 'But I don't think your "yob" and "cheap end" remarks went down too well the other day.'

'I didn't mean it!' Jane flushed slightly. 'OK, so I did. Oh, stuff it. I feel awful now.' She threw her book down and stood up crossly. 'Where's Ian? He's never here when I want him.'

Daisy watched her go, knowing Ian would soothe her wounded feelings in five minutes. She returned to her book but two minutes later Nick came back, with a beer. He stripped off his shorts and T shirt and sat on the sunbed Jane had just vacated. She wondered whether to tell him he'd upset Jane and thought better of it. 'Was the pirate punch as lethal as they say?'

'Pretty lethal. They had to pour a few of them off when we got back to Bridgetown. Tara had a few but she seems to hold it pretty well. She was dancing most of the time.'

Since the evening on the beach, their conversation had been more or less confined to 'Morning' or 'Hi'. Daisy was still harbouring the uncomfortable feeling that she'd been a bitch, and wondering why she cared.

She wanted to say something but it was horribly difficult. 'I didn't mean to sound like a cow the other night.'

'I shouldn't have brought it up.' His tone had an end-of-conversation crispness to it.

Why ever did I bring it up again? What if he thinks I want him to tell me it wasn't 'cobblers' all over again?

She glanced down. Her bikini was white, teeny and well cut, but the bandeau top did not exactly have a Wonderbra effect.

Not that he was looking. He was gazing at the sea, where a little catamaran was zooming into the bay on one hull. 'Have you heard from Simon?'

Given the previous topic, it was the last thing she'd expected. 'He phoned this morning. He phones nearly every morning, early. That way he catches me before I go to the beach.' She paused. 'I feel awful being here when he's working.'

'He didn't have to stay behind.'

'He felt obliged!'

'They'd have managed. Nobody's indispensable.'

'He doesn't think he's "indispensable"! He thought he was doing the right thing! Not that I'd expect you to understand that.' Crossly she flung her book aside and stalked into the sea. She would have gone anyway; the afternoon sun was getting too hot for comfort.

The water was warm and silky, but not so warm that it wasn't refreshing. She made for the raft, where Tara was flaked out.

'Hi,' she said sleepily, as Daisy climbed the steps. 'I'm about to crash out.'

'Don't you dare.' Daisy squeezed her hair out on Tara's brown stomach, making her squeal. 'I don't want to be rushing you to hospital with sunstroke.'

Tara sat up and yawned. 'Maybe I should go for a siesta.'

'Then you'll never sleep tonight.'

'I will. I was dancing for hours, never mind all that rum punch.' Her lips curved mischievously. 'Now there's somebody I wouldn't mind a siesta with.'

Nick was just wading in. Once up to his waist, he dived underwater and surfaced ten yards further out.

Daisy kept quiet. Any sniffy remark would only provoke Tara into something really outrageous, such as speculations about his 'equipment', and she didn't think she could handle it.

Since he was obviously coming to join them she wondered whether to abandon raft, but decided it would be too obvious. So she sat back on her elbows, apparently quite indifferent, as he climbed the steps.

'Get off!' Tara squealed, as he quite unintentionally dripped over her.

Here we go. Any second she'll start something and get him to throw her in.

'I suppose I should go for a swim and get some of my fat off,' Tara said, as he sat down on her other side.

'Excellent idea,' he said lazily. 'I heard the Jolly Roger crew complaining that they'd had to throw half a ton of ballast overboard the minute you got on.'

No prizes for guessing what's coming now.

'How dare you?' Tara pouted, but not quite well enough to hide her glee at perfectly-taken bait. 'I've got a good mind to chuck you in.'

'No chance.' He lay back lazily, propped on his elbows. 'You've got too much fat and not enough muscle.'

My God, he's a gift to her.

'Bloody cheek! You've got an incipient beer-gut, if you ask me.' She poked his decidedly gut-less stomach in a half-tickling way that would have made anybody jump, and he did. He made a grab for her and before you could say 'flirt of the year' the raft was rocking wildly.

'Daisy, help me!' Tara squealed, as he edged her towards the water.

Her first reaction was, '*No way.*' On the other hand, prim avoidance of potentially electric body contact might only confirm what he suspected. If he did suspect.

Oh, hell. This was getting so tortuous.

So she put on a mischievous tone to equal Tara's. 'Hold on, Tara, I'm coming.' She got behind him and started shoving at his back. 'You rat, how dare you call my friend fat? You're the kind of wretch who makes women anorexic.' She braced her feet and pushed harder, but it didn't seem to have much effect, probably because Tara was giggling too much to be any earthly use. Suddenly he half turned, caught her against him with one arm, and tipped Tara over the side with the other.

There was a screech and a massive splash.

'One down.' With glinting relish, Nick turned to his second victim. 'And one to go.'

Now she'd started, Daisy could hardly admit wimpette-ish defeat. Accordingly she kicked and struggled womanfully as he swept her into his arms.

And just as he was about to chuck her in, Tara's voice wailed up from the water. 'My top's come off!'

Daisy stopped struggling, and Nick's grip relaxed. And in the same moment, they started laughing together. Suppressed shakings quickly evolved into the full-blown variety. She melted against him as her whole body shook helplessly.

'It's not funny!' Tara wailed. 'It's my best one!'

As quickly as they'd started, Daisy's giggles ceased. *My God, whatever am I doing?*

For an instant, as he gazed down at her, various supercharged sensations reduced her to hot, erogenous jelly. 'Put me down, please,' she said unsteadily.

He plonked her down like a sack of hot, erogenous potatoes and they gazed over the side together.

Tara was treading water, peering into the clear depths. 'It's right down there! Look!' Her top had drifted gently to the bottom.

'I'll get it,' Nick said.

'No, I will.' *I need to cool off.* Taking a breath *en route*, Daisy dived in. Even without a mask it was easy to see the bright pink thing against the white sand. Seconds later she surfaced with it in her hand.

'Gosh, thanks,' Tara said.

'Well done.' Nick extended a hand and since the steps were round the other side, it would have been churlish to refuse. With one swift yank, he had her sitting on the side.

Still treading water, Tara was quite unconcerned about her unclothed bouncy bits. 'The catch is broken!' she wailed. 'Bloody rip-off shop! I've hardly worn it!'

'Put it on and I'll tie the ends,' Daisy offered.

'Stuff that. I'll swim back like this.'

'Tara, you can't,' Daisy reminded her. 'They don't like people going topless here.'

'It's ridiculous,' Tara grumbled but she slipped the top on anyway and turned around to let Daisy tie the ends. 'It's like the dark ages.'

'A lot of the locals are very religious,' Nick pointed out. 'It makes them uncomfortable.'

'A lot of Greeks are religious too, but nobody gives a stuff in Greece,' Tara grumbled. 'And now it's too tight. I'll have to go and change, damn it.'

Sitting on the edge of the raft, her legs dangling in the water, Daisy watched Tara go and fought the impulse to go straight after her.

Quite casually, Nick sat beside her, his legs dangling inches from her own. 'I shouldn't have said that, about her being fat.'

What a relief to have a neutral topic. 'No, you shouldn't.'

'If I'd actually thought she was fat I wouldn't have said it,' he went on. 'Maybe I should have a word with her.'

She was oddly touched that he took it so seriously. 'I wouldn't bother. She might think you're over compensating because you actually did mean it.'

'Well, I didn't. She looks great the way she is.'

Daisy couldn't help it; she felt slighted and hated herself for caring. Tara's hour-glass curves could still occasionally make her feel like a particularly sexless stick-insect.

'One of my sisters was anorexic,' he went on. 'She's fine now, but it was touch and go for a bit.'

No wonder you're feeling bad. 'Don't worry about it,' she added lightly. 'I can't see Tara getting anorexic. She's far too fond of chocolate. Anyway, she started it. You were only playing along.' She paused, hesitated, and said, 'I know you think we're not being very nice to Tara, but – '

'She can be a bit over the top.' He half-turned to her. 'I do see that, but it doesn't bother me personally. I don't give a toss what people think.'

No, I can imagine.

'She told me you'd originally asked your mother to take Simon's place.' he went on.

Oh, help. 'It wasn't that I didn't want Tara. I just thought it'd be lovely for my mother. She's had a bit of a rough time lately and she's never been anywhere like this.'

She didn't elaborate and he didn't ask.

'She was telling me you go back a long way,' he went on. 'Since Brownies and ballet-lesson days.'

For a moment Daisy wondered uneasily what else Tara had been telling him. She was quite indiscreet enough to have said, 'Of course, her mother never got married. She hardly even knew her dad.' But she wouldn't have said it bitchily. She'd have added, 'Daisy's mum's really nice – I love her to bits.'

But even if she had, Nick was hardly the type to give a toss. She'd been nervous of telling Simon. Everything about his family was so terribly proper. At first she'd told him her father had left them when she was small. But Simon had taken her in his arms and said, 'Darling, do you really think I care?'

'Her parents moved into the village when we were seven,' she said. 'I met her at school first – our teacher asked me to 'look after' her, not that Tara needed looking after. Her first words were, 'I've got a rabbit at my house. He's called Loppylugs 'cos of his ears.'

His lazy chuckle made her feel considerably more at ease. 'Her mother sent her to ballet lessons in a vain attempt to tone down her tomboyishness,' she went on. 'And when I saw her little leotard and ballet shoes, I just had to go, too.'

She could still remember it: the first proper guilt of her life. Even at seven she'd been vaguely aware of money being tight, but she'd been just dying for a little pink leotard and dainty pink ballet shoes. Satin ones. With ribbons, not elastic. She'd been dying to have her hair done in a ballerina bun with a pink headband. Her mother had never said she couldn't afford it; she'd had everything, just like Tara.

'My sister was heavily into ballet,' he said. 'The anorexic one. That was what started it. She wanted to make a career of it and thought she was too fat. In fact she just wasn't quite good enough, but she didn't want to see it.'

'What a shame.' She hesitated, almost ashamed of her curiosity. 'What's her name?'

'Karolinka. My mother named her after a Polish friend.'

'It's really pretty.'

'It's a bit of a mouthful. Most of her friends call her Klink. But even that's better than what I used to call her.'

143

'What's that?' she asked, idly kicking her feet in the water.

'Squirt,' he confessed. 'She's the baby, eleven years younger than me. I used to change her nappies now and then and I'm afraid that's where the name came from.'

Daisy couldn't help laughing. 'I bet she just loved that when she got a bit older.'

'It had to go, eventually. The showdown came when she was fifteen or so. She'd brought a boyfriend home and was putting on that intensely cool act, flicking her hair non-stop, as they do. I made some crack about shampoo commercials and she went right over the top. Put on a terminally bored look and said to the boyfriend, "Isn't he a pain? Shall I tell him to go and screw himself?"'

His perfect mimicry of a fifteen-year-old trying to sound cool made her laugh again. 'And you were not amused, I take it.'

'I was, actually,' he confessed. 'Trying not to crack up, if you want the truth. I said, 'Watch it, Squirt. I used to change your nappies.'

Daisy erupted into fits. 'That must have gone down like a lead balloon.'

'She nearly killed me, afterwards.' He turned to her with a very wry expression. 'I bore the bruises for weeks.'

Through her laughter, Daisy recalled another elder brother who had made her profoundly thankful that she was not so blest. Tara's brother Tom had been a nightmare when they were little. He'd called them stinky brats and delighted in decapitating their Sindy dolls or pretending he'd just crucified the rabbit.

Somehow, she doubted whether Nick would have been quite so gruesome, but it was impossible to tell. Even Tom was quite civilized nowadays.

Quite suddenly she realized that they were sitting on the raft having a perfectly normal conversation and that for a minute or two he had seemed like a perfectly normal human being.

And the instant she thought that, he stopped being a normal human being and reverted to a raging mass of fanciability who did dangerous things to her insides.

All that ballet talk had provoked a question she'd been trying to ignore for weeks. 'Did you go to the Kirov, in the end?'

'Yes,' he said. 'And you were right. I did enjoy it.'

Instantly she wondered who he'd gone with and what she looked like. She imagined him in evening dress again – immaculate, this time – with that silken evening scarf around his neck and some ravishing silken cow beside him . . .

Suddenly he stood up. 'I've got to make a phone call. See you later.' He dived in and was gone.

For the next five minutes, Daisy's thoughts consumed her with guilt. She swam back and immersed herself in her book. That didn't work, so she wandered to the shop, bought three post-cards; two normal size and one super-deluxe, with an incredible sunset. She wrote one to her mother (the second) one to the girls at work, and the super-deluxe sunset to Simon. She wrote, '*The one I told you about was even better than this. I miss you so much, it hurts. All my love, Daisy XXXXXX*' She posted them straight away, and wished to heaven

145

she could have stuck her guilt in an envelope and posted it to Outer Mongolia.

Jane's humour was fully restored by the time they went for dinner and she was making a special effort to be nice to everybody, specially Tara.

Tara was in an even better humour. She'd had two very exotic cocktails in the bar beforehand and a couple of glasses of wine with the meal, but her conversation managed to be merely hilarious.

Even Daisy was feeling relatively mellow. She'd phoned Simon, who'd just gone to bed, and five minutes' loving chat had finally banished that guilt.

After all, she told herself, *just because you love somebody doesn't mean you'll never fancy anybody else.*

Simon had obviously fancied gin-slinging Amanda, and if he'd been thrown together with her for two weeks and she'd started the kind of horseplay Tara was enjoying with Nick, he'd possibly have fancied her quite a bit more. But it still wouldn't mean he didn't love Daisy.

The dining room was practically open air, with just a roof to keep the odd tropical shower off. A huge tree grew right through the roof and lush shrubs planted round the edges blended it in with the surrounding gardens. Nearby, under the stars, a steel band played soft calypso.

After the meal they transplanted themselves to the tables surrounding the dance floor and Tara immediately dragged Nick up to dance.

'Go on.' Daisy gave Jane a little nudge. 'I know you're dying to dance. I shall get very put out if you feel you have to sit and babysit me.'

'Daisy, my love, I was just about to ask you,' said the gallant Ian.

'Later,' she smiled. 'Dance with Jane first.'

She really didn't mind a bit. She was too busy enjoying the soft, tropical night. And as she sat alone, drinking it in, two other guests sat at the next table and started chatting. They were from Lincolnshire; a thirty-ish male and a fifty-five-ish female who looked forty-five-ish until you got close up.

It was a moment before Daisy realized she was talking to the possessor of Ian's gravity-defying boobs.

'I was coming with a girlfriend but she was taken ill so Blair stepped in,' the woman explained. 'And since he works for me, the boss was only too happy to give him time off at short notice. He's my son.' She added an arch little wink. 'Just in case you were thinking he's my toy boy.'

'Oh, Mum.' Blair's face was twenty per cent amusement, eighty per cent embarrassment, making Daisy feel for him acutely.

'And I'm Marion,' the woman added brightly. 'Pleased to meet you.'

Daisy told them about Simon and how Tara had stepped in, and by the time Jane and Ian returned they were nattering like old friends.

Half an hour later she had danced with Ian (once) and Blair (once). Tara had danced more than once with Blair. He was Nick's height but more lightly built, with a sensitive face and dark, liquid eyes that put Daisy in mind of a Renaissance angel. *Too sensitive*, she thought. *And very much overshadowed by a rather relentlessly vivacious mother.*

She could not help feeling vaguely slighted when Nick led the relentlessly vivacious Marion on to the dance floor.

He hasn't asked me.

Of course not, you dope. He thinks you'll see it as making a move, and get all prickly.

Trying not to feel put out, she let her eyes drift now and then to a certain pair on the dance floor.

Marion danced with a manic, youthful exuberance that didn't quite come off. Casting a glance at Blair, she saw him cringing and trying not to show it. Still, Tara was in hilarious if rather noisy form, and distracting him nicely. His eyes darted from his mother to Tara's eyes and thence to her cleavage and back again.

Nick, however, showed no signs of cringing. He danced with every appearance of enjoyment, brought Marion back to her seat, and ordered a round of drinks.

The gentle breeze had dropped, and it was very humid. Tara ordered a Bailey's on the rocks, but before it was half drunk she went rather quiet. 'I'm feeling a bit yuck,' she whispered to Daisy. 'I think I'd better go to bed.'

I'm not surprised you're feeling a bit yuck. I'd be feeling extremely yuck if I'd put away the amount of booze you've had today.

'I'll come with you, for the key,' she said. As they slipped off, Tara was wobbling very slightly.

'Is she all right?' Nick murmured in an aside, when she got back.

'More or less, but she'll probably have a terrible hangover tomorrow.'

148

Ian covered a huge yawn. 'I've got to hit the sack. All this relaxing's wearing me out.'

He wasn't the only one. Although it was only just gone eleven, most of the guests had drifted off and the steel band was packing up.

Jane went with him, and Daisy and Nick were left with Blair and Marion, who showed no signs of wilting. 'Why don't we go up the road to Mullins Bar?' she suggested. 'It's a lovely little bar by the beach, and keeps going half the night.'

Nick raised an enquiring brow at Daisy. 'Fancy a change of scene?'

She hesitated, but it wasn't as though they were going on their own. 'If you like,' she said lightly.

Nick drove, in the mini moke he'd hired that morning. The bar was only a few miles away, up the narrow coast road, and overlooked what looked like a magnificent beach. It was packed and lively, and the music made you itch to dance. And this time, Nick did ask her. However, it was all fast and furious at-a-distance stuff; no smooching whatever, and by the time they left an hour later she was congratulating herself on having got through it with barely a shiver.

When they got back, everybody said, 'Goodnight' cheerfully, and they departed for their various rooms.

Beginning to wilt at last, Daisy was looking forward to her nice clean sheets. She walked round the back of their little block and up the wooden steps to the first floor, and put her key in the door.

For a moment she thought she'd got the wrong room. She glanced at the number, frowned, and tried again.

Damn. Damn and blast. Softly she tapped on the door. 'Tara, it's me. Open the door.'

There was no reply, so she tapped harder. 'Tara!'

There was no reply.

'*Tara!*'

Nothing.

She banged on the door as hard as she dared, given the other people sleeping either side, but that didn't work either, so she walked quickly towards the super-deluxe, ocean-view rooms. Nick was not only still up, but on the balcony, reading.

'Nick!' she hissed.

He stood up at once. 'What is it?'

'Tara's locked me out. She must have put the security catch on so the key won't work. I've banged like mad but she won't wake up. Can I use your phone? That might wake her.'

'Come up.'

She ran round the back and up the wooden steps. His door was already open. His room was rather larger than theirs, which was huge enough. The curtains and bedspreads were plusher too, real *Homes and Gardens* stuff. The two king-size beds were both turned down.

She sat on a bed-edge and dialled the number impatiently. 'I'd have gone to Jane and Ian but I didn't like to wake them,' she explained.

'Obviously not.'

The phone rang and rang, and she was beginning to get uneasy as well as mad. 'She said she was feeling sick. What if she's thrown up and choked? Or slipped on the bathroom floor?'

150

'It's highly unlikely. But if she's left the balcony door unlocked maybe we could get in there and check on her.'

'It's on the first floor!'

'They'll have a ladder somewhere.'

Daisy shook her head. 'I locked it before we went for dinner and she wouldn't have unlocked it again. She'll have fallen straight into bed, if I know Tara.'

She dialled again, tapping her foot restlessly. 'Come on, Tara. Wake up, for heaven's sake.'

For a moment, her prayers seemed to have been answered. The ringing stopped and a sleepy voice said, 'Go away, I told you, I don't want any.' A clatter followed, as the phone evidently fell from Tara's hand.

Daisy gaped at Nick. 'She burbled something in her sleep and dropped the phone!'

Arms folded, he was watching her with an expression of dry amusement. 'At least you know she hasn't choked to death.'

'It's not funny! Now what am I going to do? I can't even ring her now!'

He sat on the other bed, appearing to consider. 'You can ask the hotel if they've got a spare room. Or you can borrow a pillow and kip on the beach.'

'Very funny!'

'Or you can use the bed you're sitting on,' he went on. 'Seems a shame to waste it. Especially since I'm paying for both of them.'

Daisy closed her eyes.

You don't have much choice, do you? Unless you'd prefer to sleep on the beach.

151

He rose suddenly to his feet. 'Make your mind up – the offer expires in two minutes.'

As he headed for the bathroom, her fretfulness erupted. 'It's partly your fault she's in a drunken stupor! You shouldn't have let her drink all that pirate punch!'

He stopped dead, *en route*. 'Any more remarks like that, and you will be sleeping on the beach. What was I supposed to do? Forbid her to touch it, for God's sake?'

His tone was very curt. 'I'm sorry,' she said unsteadily.

It was a moment before he answered. 'Apology accepted.'

'I haven't even got a toothbrush,' she faltered.

He turned back from the bathroom route, and opened a drawer. 'Airline freebie,' he said, tossing her a little bag. 'I haven't touched it.'

'Thank you.' As the bathroom door closed behind him, she opened the Club Class offering. Since it was aimed at men, there was no cleanser or moisturiser, but at least there was a toothbrush.

He returned from the bathroom shirtless. 'All yours.'

Daisy glanced down at her little black camisole and white cotton trousers. 'I suppose you haven't got a spare T shirt I could sleep in?'

He yanked another drawer open and tossed her a black one. 'Try that.'

'Thank you.' She departed for the bathroom, locked the door, and wondered why on earth she was feeling so ridiculously wound up. He'd hardly pounce on her in the night.

She splashed her face, attacked her hair with the mini brush from her bag, brushed her teeth and stripped off top and trousers. Horizontally the T shirt swam on her, but was only just long enough if she remained absolutely vertical. Turning around for a mirror-check, she cursed herself for wearing a thong instead of proper knickers, because she hadn't wanted a line under the trousers. Even when upright, what Ian called the 'squidgy bits' were showing.

Oh, to hell. What does it matter?

She hung her things on a hook behind the door and returned to the bedroom, feeling ludicrously self-conscious. Naked to the waist, he was already in bed, sitting up with the bedside light on, reading. He cast her not a glance, but even so she walked past his bed poker-stiff, because of the squidgy bits. She slipped into bed and turned away from him immediately. 'Goodnight.'

'Goodnight.' He said it in an almost offhand manner and turned a page.

She heard him turning another page, and then another, and after a minute or two, he turned the light off. She heard the soft rustlings as he got comfortable, and then there was silence.

Daisy was still far from sleeping. No matter how she tried to shut them out, images were flashing through her brain. His hand, dragging her from Simon on New Year's Eve. A softly wicked voice saying, 'Nicked', and the fierce, melting kiss that had followed. The way she'd felt on the raft that afternoon. His arms, holding her so firmly against her struggles. The way he'd gazed down at her for just that moment, and the way her stomach had lurched so violently . . .

153

She felt so guilty, so terribly disloyal to Simon, she could have cried.

She was dreaming of someone shaking her shoulder, saying, 'Daisy, you're dreaming.'

She wasn't dreaming. It was real. She tried to tell the person shaking her shoulder it was real, but her mouth didn't seem to be working.

'Daisy!'

She awoke with a violent start.

It was pitch dark, and Nick was beside her. 'You were having a bad dream.'

Suddenly aware of the tears on her cheeks, she wiped them away, feeling a perfect prat. 'Did I wake you up?'

'It doesn't matter.'

The digital bedside clock said twenty to five. 'I'm terribly sorry.'

'What were you dreaming about?'

Her eyes were adjusting to the nearly-dark. He was sitting on the edge of the bed, his eyes dark and unfathomable. 'I can't remember,' she said unsteadily. 'Something stupid, I expect.'

'Go back to sleep.' His voice softened round the edges. With a little pat on her shoulder, he went back to bed.

He was wearing something that looked like white boxer shorts. She turned over and cursed that wretched, recurrent dream. It always started with her wandering blithely down some busy street or through some equally busy shop, minding her own business, when she'd suddenly glance down and realize that she had not a stitch on.

154

This time she'd been in the supermarket and just to make it worse her hair had been shorn to about half an inch all over. She was right by the fruit and vegetable section, and over the tannoy a bright voice was saying, 'And in our fresh fruit section today, we have a special offer on Cox's Orange Pippins.' And the entire shop was rushing towards her, bursting out laughing.

She could not get back to sleep. Whether he was asleep or not she couldn't be sure. If he was, it was a very restless sleep. Gradually, the darkness in the room was replaced by the grey shadowy light that said it was dawn.

His tossings became more restless. Very quietly, she turned her head and watched him through nearly closed eyes.

Suddenly, his head turned on the pillow. His eyes were open. Without quite knowing why she did it, she gave a little whimper and tossed her head restlessly, as if she were dreaming again.

Keeping her eyelids tight shut, she lay on her back, and for a moment there was silence. Then she she heard a swishy rustle as he got out of bed. She heard him open the curtains a little, letting more light into the room. She opened her eyes a tiny fraction, so that she could just see though her lashes.

He turned his head and watched her a moment, as if checking that she was asleep. Then he crossed to the chest of drawers, quietly pulled a drawer open, took out something that looked like beach shorts. Although he had his back to her, she could see him in the mirror, stripping off his white boxer shorts.

Her breath caught in her throat. Although she made no noise, he seemed to sense it. He froze, his eyes seeming to focus on her reflection in the mirror.

Acting for her life, Daisy whimpered, turning her head restlessly on the pillow as if she were back in that supermarket nightmare. She heard him shut the drawer quietly, pad softly to the bathroom and shut the door very quietly. She heard the sound of running water, first the taps, and then the shower. When he emerged, five minutes later, she kept her eyes tight shut. She heard him pad softly to the dressing table and pick up his key. He left the room, shutting the door almost silently behind him.

Only then did she open her eyes.

Heavens. Peeping Tom's got nothing on you.

She had seen him gloriously un-clad before, of course. Only this time there had been a teensy little difference. Well, maybe not teensy. Largish.

Whopping, even.

CHAPTER 8

She dismissed her first reaction instantly.

It had nothing to do with you. Sometimes they just wake up with an erection. Even Simon does.

What do you mean, even Simon?

Guilt washed her again. She began to feel she was standing under a non-stop power-shower of guilt, but it didn't wash her thoughts away.

He was probably dreaming about somebody.

Obviously. Spears do not get so whoppingly lusty from dreaming about tax returns.

Yes, but who?

How should I know? Maybe it wasn't anybody in particular. Maybe he was having a 'blue' dream about being ravished by three Kim Basinger lookalikes at once. That's the kind of thing they dream about. Being ravished by hordes of rampant women with massive boobs.

She turned and buried her face in the pillow, and the next thing she knew, somebody was saying, 'Daisy, wake up.'

She came to with a start. Nick was pulling the curtains right back and light flooded the room. Just beyond his balcony she could see blue sky behind the waving palm fronds.

The clock said seven-forty and her brain was rapidly getting back into gear.

Act dozy. She stretched sleepily. 'Where have you been? I woke a little while ago and you were gone.'

'I went for a walk on the beach.' He walked back towards his bed. Or rather, limped.

Daisy sat up sharply. 'What's wrong?'

'I stepped on an urchin.' He was sitting with one ankle crossed over his knee, examining the underside of his foot. 'Damn thing,' he added, in a mutter.

'However did you do that?'

'I didn't see it,' he said testily. 'If I'd seen it, I wouldn't have stepped on it.'

Having seen the spiny black things littering the coral, and sometimes the beach too, Daisy winced. She slipped out of bed and went to look.

Several black spines had penetrated his heel. 'Oh, Lord.' She winced again. 'Does it hurt?'

'No, Daisy,' he said, even more testily. 'It feels like I stepped on a little baby bunny.'

Since it had been a daft question, she ignored the answer. 'What are you going to do?'

'There's some local remedy,' he said, picking at his heel.

'Stop it! You'll make it worse!' With one hand she held back the hair that was falling over his face and chest. With the other, she took his hand away. 'You ought to see a doctor.'

'Daisy, please don't fuss.'

'But it might get infected!'

'I said, don't – fuss!' With gritted patience, he looked up. 'It's check-out time. If Tara's awake she'll be wondering where the hell you are.'

'I was only trying to help!'

'Maybe, but women who fuss get on my nerves.' Suddenly he stood up. 'I'd like my room to myself, if you don't mind.' He turned her smartly towards the door. 'Off you go. Vamoose.' He underlined the message with a slap that connected smartly with her squidgy bits.

She gasped. 'What was that for?'

'Target practice. Now hit that door, will you?'

'Pig! I hope it does get infected! I hope your damned foot drops off!' Within ten seconds, she had pulled her skirt on, grabbed everything, and slammed the door. Blinking back hurt, furious tears, she half ran through the early morning gardens to her room.

Bastard. And I bet he was having some disgusting porno dream, the filthy beast. I wish I'd told him I'd seen. I wish I'd said, 'Oh, and by the way, I've seen better erections on a hamster.'

Tara was up, but only just. 'Where have you been?' she demanded. 'Simon just phoned!'

'What?' Nick was banished instantly from her head. 'What did you say?'

'What could I say? I said I didn't know where you were, and your bed hadn't been slept in.'

'*What?*'

'I'm sorry, but I was half asleep and . . .' Her bewildered voice tailed off. 'Where have you been, anyway?'

159

Daisy was far too wound up to answer. She dialled Simon's office number at once. 'Simon, it's me.'

'Darling, where were you?'

If she'd thought a second longer . . . 'Tara locked me out by mistake and I couldn't wake her up so I had to share with Jane and Ian – '

'I just spoke to Ian! He hadn't a clue where you were, either!'

Oh, damn. Damn and poo and bum. She took a deep, steadying, breath. 'OK, I'm sorry, darling, it wasn't Jane and Ian – they were asleep when I got locked out – Nick and I went out with some people from Lincolnshire, you see – a mother and son – she's a bit of a pain and we felt a bit sorry for the son so we went for a quick drink with them and when we got back I couldn't get in my room so I went to Nick's to phone because Jane and Ian were asleep, but Tara still wouldn't wake up, and Nick said I'd better use the other bed in his room.' She took a huge breath. 'I'd have said it was Nick right away, only I thought you might not like it . . .' Her voice tailed off helplessly. 'I'm really sorry, darling. I know it was silly.'

There was a long pause on the other end. 'Daisy, since when do I get jealous over nothing?'

'Hardly ever,' she trembled.

'I was worried sick!' he went on.

'I'm really sorry,' she trembled, nearly in tears.

'And telling silly fibs only makes it sound as if there's something to be guilty about,' he went on.

'I'm sorry, OK? I didn't think! I just didn't like to tell you I'd slept in another man's room, for heaven's sake! I

160

wouldn't like it if you shared a room with another woman!'

'There's no need to shout,' he said patiently.

'Isn't there? A normal man'd be jealous, for heaven's sake!' And she banged the phone down, her eyes filling with tears.

Tara was gaping at her, wide-eyed and vaguely fearful. 'He was only phoning to say Happy Valentine's Day!'

Oh, God, Oh, God, Oh, God, what have I done? Daisy turned her furious misery on Tara. 'See what you've got me into? Because you were too bloody pissed to remember not to put the catch on the door!'

'I'm sorry,' Tara faltered. 'I can't help it if I sleep like a log!'

'Logs don't get pissed! You were in a drunken stupor!'

'I wasn't!'

'You were! And now look what you made me do!'

'I didn't make you lie to Simon! I can't think why you did. He's hardly the rabid jealous type, and it's not as if you were actually up to anything.' Her eyes widened suddenly. 'Were you?'

'Oh, for God's sake, you're disgusting! We're not all like you! I wish you'd never – '

She stopped herself too late. Tara's face crumpled. She yanked on a long T shirt and wrenched the door open.

'Tara, I didn't mean it!' Daisy said desperately.

'Yes, you did.' Tara was in tears, too. 'You only wanted me to come so Simon wouldn't lose his money!'

Daisy grabbed at her, but Tara shook her off. She ran out of the door and disappeared.

Daisy threw herself on to the bed and cried herself sick for two minutes until Ian turned up.

'What on earth's going on?' he gaped, seeing her face. 'First I have Simon on the phone thinking you've been raped and murdered, and now you . . . Where the hell were you? Where's Tara?'

'You can't stay here all day,' Jane said. 'Come to the beach.'

'Like this?' Daisy glanced woefully at the horror-film face in the mirror. 'I look like nothing on earth,' she sniffed, wiping her eyes with the back of her hand. 'I want to go home.'

'Don't be daft!'

'I do. I've got a good mind to phone British Airways and see if there's a seat tonight.'

'It's not that bad,' Jane soothed. 'Try Simon again.'

'I've tried twice! He's always with a wretched client!' She sniffed again. 'It's not just Simon.' Her voice cracked again. 'I feel so bad about Tara.'

'She'll come round,' Jane soothed. 'She knows you didn't mean it.'

'But I did! That's the point.' Tears came to her eyes again and she rolled miserably on the bed. 'She's my oldest friend and she's run to Nick because he's the only one who's been nice to her.'

It was a relief to see the fleeting guilt on Jane's face, too. 'You were provoked,' she pointed out. 'And considering the way she's been behaving, I think we've all been perfectly nice to her.'

'Yes, but she knows we've only been tolerating her.'
She wiped her eyes again. 'Jane, please, go back to the
beach. I'm lousy company and I just feel even more
guilty with you up here, too.'

'I can't leave you like this!'

'Please, Jane. I feel quite bad enough without wreck-
ing your day, too.'

'All right.' Jane paused. 'We're going up the road to
hire another moke. We thought we'd go out somewhere
this afternoon. Will you come?'

'Maybe. If this face wears off. But I've got to see Tara
first.'

When Jane left, she lay miserably on the bed.

I feel so mean and horrible, I hate myself.

*You are mean and horrible. You took it out on Tara
because you were eaten up with guilt. Because even if
nothing whatever happened all night, you wanted it to.*

I did not!

*OK, but you imagined it. You were lying there
under the covers thinking of him lying there under
the covers, and getting all hot and wriggly and thinking hot wriggly thoughts. That's why you lied to
Simon. You were unfaithful to him in thought, if
not in deed.*

She thought of that sharp, dismissive slap and Nick's
curt voice saying she was getting on his nerves, and
tears trickled from her eyes again. And then she thought
of poor Simon ringing for Valentine's Day, and how
she'd shouted at him for not being jealous, and the
trickle turned to a flood.

I hate myself. I wish I was dead.

Somebody tapped at the door again.

163

She wiped her eyes with a soggy tissue. 'Who is it?'

'Nick.'

'Get – lost!'

'Daisy, let me in. Tara's asked me to come and get some things.'

She opened the door instantly. 'Don't tell me she's moving in with you?'

'Of course not. She's upset and doesn't want to wander round the hotel with a face nearly as bad as yours.'

She doesn't want to see me, you mean. And no wonder. Against all her willpower, her wretched eyes starting leaking again. 'I feel awful.'

'So does she, if it's any consolation.'

'Of course she does. I was horrible to her.' Mopping the leaks with the soggy tissue, she sat unsteadily on the bed.

Still limping slightly, he came and sat beside her. 'It's not just that. She feels responsible for your row with Simon.'

'Oh, God.' Daisy put despairing hands to her face.

It was a moment before he spoke. 'Why did you lie to him?'

'I didn't think!' She said it almost angrily. 'I didn't think he'd like it! Would you like it if your girlfriend shared a room with another man?'

'That would depend on the other man.'

Exactly. You said it.

'And on the girlfriend,' he went on.

Exactly. Oh, God, I hate myself.

Her lip trembled all over again. 'I feel so awful. I shouted at him and he hadn't done anything.'

'Come on, Daisy. Turn that tap off.' He put a finger under her chin and turned her face towards him. 'You'll be giving me nightmares with a face like that.'

'Thanks a lot!' Suddenly remembering how he'd behaved earlier, she pushed him away and stood up smartly. 'Just tell me what she wants and get the hell out.'

He caught her arm. 'Daisy – '

'Don't "Daisy" me!' She shook him off.

He stood up. 'Look, I'm sorry about this morning.'

'Like hell!'

'I am. My foot was hurting like – '

'Good. I hope it still is.'

He put on an expression that was supposed to be apologetic, but looked suspiciously like very dry amusement. 'I had to get you out. I wanted to indulge in some really foul, inventive curses in peace and privacy.'

'You didn't have to be so horrible!'

'I know. I'm sorry.'

She was not at all mollified. 'Men are such utter babies. I bet you're one of those pathetic men who pass out when they have to have an injection.'

Feeling slightly better, she folded her arms in a businesslike manner. 'Now will you please tell me what Tara wants?'

'I have a list.' From the pocket of his shorts he took a piece of paper. 'Black bikini,' he read crisply. 'Black T shirt, factor four sun cream, sunglasses, make-up, *Marie Claire*, beach bag.'

It was enough to make her dissolve all over again. *I've upset her so much, she has to send him to get her things. She can't even bear to see me.*

With hands that weren't absolutely steady, she yanked a drawer open, just as somebody else tapped at the door.

'I'll go.' Nick opened it.

'Miss Daisy Rose?' said a voice.

'Yes, thank you. I'll take them.'

As he closed the door, Daisy stared at the basket in his arms. It was huge, filled with ginger lilies, birds of paradise, beautiful tropical flowers . . .

'Looks like somebody loves you,' Nick said.

God knows why. Tears pricked her eyes as she put the basket on the dressing table, but none actually escaped. She gathered the rest of Tara's things, put them in her beach bag, shoved it into Nick's hands and pushed him towards the door. 'Tell her I'll see her later.' She shut the door behind him and picked up the phone.

Forty minutes later she went in search of Tara and found Nick instead. In shorts and a white polo shirt he was heading through the gardens towards reception. He stopped when he saw her. 'Feeling better?'

'Yes, thank you' She eyed the car keys dangling from his fingers. 'Are you going out?'

He nodded. 'I'm getting restless.'

As she looked at him, she thought resentfully that there ought to be a law against certain men wearing white polo shirts. They should be restricted to pink, blubbery men who just looked gross in them. But at least he had sunglasses on, so there was no green-eye effect to contend with. 'Where's Tara? I thought she was with you.'

'She was. I asked if she'd like to come, but she didn't feel like it. She's probably on the beach.' He paused. 'Have you sorted it out with Simon?'

'Yes.' She even felt guilty about that. She had pretended she hadn't got the flowers yet, so he wouldn't think she'd phoned just because of them.

'So it was all a colossal fuss over nothing, he said.

'A bit like your foot,' she said acidly, realizing he was hardly limping any more. 'God help you if you ever break a leg or anything.'

His mouth gave a Sahara-dry twitch. It was really beginning to annoy her how it seemed so impossible to rattle him when she was trying to. He got rattled when she wasn't trying, instead.

'I've just suffered something rather worse,' he said. 'The lime juice and candle treatment, courtesy of one of the watersports boys. The lime juice dissolves the spines and then they drip hot candle wax on it. It was a bit like a Gestapo torture. I had to stuff my shirt in my mouth to keep from screaming and disgracing myself.'

Although she knew he was only winding her up, she couldn't help wincing at the thought of hot candle wax dripped anywhere about her person.

'So take my advice and make damn sure you never sit on an urchin,' he went on. 'It might go down as possibly the worst experience of your entire life.'

'Pity you didn't sit on it, then. That would have given me the best laugh I've had all year.'

'I dare say.' Abruptly, he crisped up. 'I'm off. See you later.'

She watched his departing back and thought, *Why did I say that? It was bitchy.*

Oh, stuff. He deserved it, the way he behaved this morning. She fervently hoped he'd stay out all day, and preferably all night, too, and let her get her assorted emotions under control. The strain of not talking about it to anybody was beginning to tell on her, but if she kept it all to herself, it would eventually go away. It would wear off, as such things always did. Especially when the other party lost interest.

She ran Tara to earth by the pool. Tara had not favoured the pool before; she was a beach baby.

Dressed in the black bikini, she was sitting all by herself in a quiet corner, half surrounded by shrubs, reading a magazine. Hesitantly, Daisy perched on the edge of the sunbed beside her. 'Hi,' she said.

'Hi.' Nobody would have known Tara had been crying. It was only her subdued manner that gave her away.

'I'm really sorry,' Daisy said simply. 'I didn't mean it. I was just upset.'

Tara flicked a page of her magazine. 'It was my fault. You'd never have rowed if not for me.'

'It doesn't matter now. I phoned him and everything's fine. And he sent me some beautiful flowers for Valentine's Day. I didn't let on I'd got them yet, so I've got to phone again later.'

The relief on Tara's face was only partial. 'I bet he was mad with me. I bet he said something.'

'No, he didn't. I just said you'd been fast asleep.'

More lies, more guilt. She'd told Simon more or less everything Tara had had to drink and he'd said, 'Trust her. She'll be in a drying-out clinic soon, the way she's going.'

But Tara was still unusually subdued. 'Cheer up,' Daisy said, patting her knee and putting on her best cheerful voice. 'I could do with a few laughs.'

Tara was still wan. And when she spoke, her voice was wan, too. 'You said I was disgusting.'

Oh, God. I'm still going to be feeling awful about this when I'm ninety. 'I honestly didn't mean it.' Desperately she sought for something that didn't sound like a load of eyewash. Her eyes wandered to the shrubs behind Tara where a bright green lizard watched with a bright black eye.

He was no help at all. 'I'm just jealous,' she said eventually, adding a wink, to make it look good. 'Of you being all fancy-free.'

'Like hell.' Tara flicked another page of the magazine. 'What would you be jealous for? You've got Simon.' Her voice trembled so minutely, only the eagle-est of ears would have picked it up.

It was the first time Tara had ever said anything like this; the first time she had ever let slip any tiny hint of what lay under the mask.

Daisy felt so dreadfully sorry for her, she let her tongue run right away with her. 'I know, but that doesn't stop me feeling a teeny bit jealous now and then.'

Maybe a pinch of truth . . . Lowering her voice conspiratorially, she said, 'I suppose the real reason I lied to Simon is because I can't help fancying Nick just a bit. I felt guilty, I suppose.'

Tara accepted this revelation with mere listlessness. 'I'd be surprised if you didn't. You'd have to be a complete lezzie not to fancy Nick. But it's only an itch, isn't it? It's different. You love Simon.'

169

It was unbelievable how much better this made her feel, as if a huge bag of guilt had been taken off her shoulders and chucked into the sea. 'I was a bit upset with Nick, too. I was fussing about his foot and he got really irritated and slung me out.'

'You can't blame him. Men hate being fussed.'

Daisy hesitated. 'Why didn't you go out with him in the moke?'

She shrugged. 'It was really sweet of him but he was going to the museum or something and I hate things like that.'

She was still so wan, Daisy began to wonder if she was sickening for something, or whether it was just a delayed-action hangover. And while she was wondering how on earth to bring back Tara's bounce, it came back all by itself.

The corners of her mouth lifted, and she un-slumped herself. 'Hi,' she said, much more brightly, over Daisy's shoulder. 'How are you?'

Blair was coming.

'Hi,' he said, with a diffident but rather winning smile. 'I was looking for you on the beach.'

At this, Tara perked up further. 'Pull up a pew. Where's your mother?'

Blair pulled up a tiny drinks table and sat on that. 'Having her hair done.' He hesitated. 'I was thinking of going for a sail and wondered if you'd like to come.'

Tara's perk and bounce were almost back to normal. 'I'd love to,' she said perkily. 'Now?'

'If you don't have anything else to do.'

'Nothing special. Nothing un-special, either, come to that.' She packed her magazine in her beach bag and stood up. 'Let's go, then.' She wiggled her fingers at Daisy. 'See you later, hon.'

'Have fun.'

Phew. Watching them wander down the grassy path to the beach, Daisy thanked Blair from the bottom of her guilt. Feeling utterly relieved on two counts, she returned to her room and phoned Simon again. 'They're so gorgeous, I can't tell you,' she said, eyeing the flowers as she spoke to him. 'They take up half the dressing table. I'll take a photo, to show you.' Her voice trembled slightly. He must have thought of it days ago, got on the phone to Interflora . . . It's so sweet of you, darling. It was such a lovely surprise.'

'It's not much, in the circumstances,' he said ruefully. 'I should be there with you, going for walks on the beach, watching the sunsets . . .'

Oh, if only you were.

She didn't see Nick till dinner, which was a quieter affair than the previous one, except for Tara. She'd bounced right back to normal.

'We've all slobbed on the beach enough,' Nick said crisply, over coffee. 'Tomorrow let's take the mokes and go driveabout.'

'I'd like to see the east coast,' Jane said.

'That's what I was going to suggest. The Atlantic side's very scenic – quite different from here.'

'I won't be coming,' Tara announced. 'Blair's asked me to go deep-sea fishing with him.'

Daisy nearly said, '*That'll be nice*,' but stopped herself, in case Tara thought she was relieved that she wasn't coming. 'You'll hate it if he catches something and you have to watch the poor thing struggling on the end of the line.'

'I won't look. I can't say no – I feel so sorry for him with that awful old hag of a mother.'

'Tara, for heaven's sake!' Jane said, glancing over her shoulder at the candlelit tables.

'They're not here! They went out. And she is an old hag. He was telling me how bossy she is and how she puts all his girlfriends right off.'

'But she won't put you off,' Daisy said.

'Exactly. She's not coming on the boat, anyway. They go right out past the reef where it's rough and she gets seasick. Pity, really. If she'd come I could have chucked her overboard for shark fodder.'

'Tara!' Jane said, but she was half laughing, like everybody else.

Daisy's mind was half elsewhere. They had hired two mokes between them because you could only legally have four in each. If they'd all gone together, Tara would have gone with Nick and she'd have gone with Ian and Jane. She'd had it all worked out in advance.

Now they'd only take one, which meant she'd be sitting next to Nick for hours in a titchy little vehicle that would lurch wildly over potholes and probably lurch her up against him.

Well done, Tara. You've dropped me in it again.

It was even worse, in the end. Ian said they might as well take both mokes since they'd paid for them.

'And you get a much better view from the front seat,' Jane added. 'Besides,' she added wickedly, 'We can't talk about you if you're right behind us.'

172

Knowing Jane, Daisy thought, *this could well be a case of true words spoken in jest.* She could just imagine it.

'I mean, why on earth did she lie to Simon?'

'Damned if I know, love.'

'You don't suppose anything actually happened, do you?'

'Like nookie, you mean?'

'Well, I don't mean a game of Monopoly.'

Guilt was making her absolutely paranoid.

'Let's get going,' Nick said.

The little moke was painted red, its canvas roof in place. 'Right,' he said crisply, as she seated herself. 'How's your map reading?'

'Brilliant, thank you.'

'It'll need to be.' He opened a map and spread it out on her legs. 'We're taking Highway one – '

Anybody would think he was trying to turn her on. He was tracing the route with his finger, which was all very well, except that she was wearing shorts and her bare thigh was underneath. He was leaning right over her shoulder, which was all very well, except that his hair was practically brushing her cheek and a powerful dose of freshly washed and shaved male was assaulting her nostrils.

'. . . and we turn right here, at Speightstown,' he went on, still tracing.

If I were Tara in her best flirt-mode, I'd just love this. 'Would you mind getting your dandruff out of my face?' she enquired mildly.

'I haven't got dandruff. Pay attention, will you?'

'I am. And don't bark at me like some megalomaniac sergeant-major.'

173

'Then stop niggling. We follow the road over the backbone of the island to Cherry Tree Hill. Right?' He looked up, and into her face.

'Right,' she said tonelessly. He was so close, she could distinguish each minute, shaved-off pinpoint under his skin. But at least, like her, he had his sunglasses on.

'Right. If we get lost, I'll blame you.' He started the engine and the moke clattered off down the lane that led to the main road.

There's only one thing for it, she thought. *Self-hypnosis. Keep telling yourself you don't fancy him a bit. There must be a complete turn-off somewhere.*

Unfortunately, she couldn't think of any. His hands were perfect; no fat banana fingers or dirty nails, no flashy rings. His legs were ditto, no skinny white macaroni jobs. She couldn't even console herself with the thought that he probably had a horrible spotty bottom, since she'd seen it twice, and it wasn't.

With this strategy failing so badly, she tried ignoring him altogether. The coast road was narrow and crowded. Little wooden houses, brightly painted in pastel colours, were perched up on concrete blocks, pots of flowers cascading down the steps of nearly every one. On the sea side, plush hotels nestled in their acres of lush gardens, and every now and then the sea shimmered turquoise through the trees. Everywhere greenery grew in such lush abundance, you could almost smell it growing. Flowers were everywhere – bright magenta bougainvillaea, the brilliant scarlet of flamboyant trees; whole hedges of hibiscus.

'Right here,' she said, seeing a sign to Highway four.

'Well done.' He indicated right and turned away from the coast.

Something in his tone irritated her. 'Don't be so patronizing!'

'I'm not being patronizing.'

'Yes, you are. As if you're loftily amazed that I can read a map at all.'

'If I didn't think you could do it, I wouldn't have asked. You're being hyper-touchy.'

'Only because you're being hyper-patronising.'

'Don't be ridiculous.'

'I'm not.'

Jane and Ian were quite a way behind. Glancing in the mirror, he slowed right down and pulled into the side. 'Daisy, if you'd rather go back to the hotel right now, just say so.'

'I wouldn't!'

'Then stop bitching. Or I might be tempted to indulge in some rather more energetic target practice.'

I don't believe this.

Take the mickey. It's the only way with cave-men.

Accordingly she put on an anxious, bimbo lisp. 'Oh, *heaventh*. Now I'm *awfully* thcared. I've made big thtrong man cwoth and if I don't behave mythelf he'th going to thmack my bottom and I'll cwy abtholutely *bucketth* and meth up my mathcara.'

To her great gratification, trying to rile him seemed to work, for once.

'Daisy, for God's sake. It was purely rhetorical.'

'There was nothing rhetorical about yesterday morning!'

He gazed at her a moment. 'Take your sunglasses off.'

'What?'

'I want to check the spark levels. I have a feeling you're doing a welder's blowtorch again and you're a bit close to the petrol tank.'

Ha bloody ha. 'Just drive, will you?' she said crossly. 'Before somebody goes into the back of us.'

Glancing in the mirror, he pulled away. 'I did apologize for yesterday morning, as I recall.'

'You didn't mean it.'

'Please yourself.' He paused minutely. 'You were rather asking for it, anyway. Wandering about in no knickers and a T shirt that advertises the fact – '

'What d'you mean, no knickers? It was a thong! Do you seriously think I'd wander around your room in no knickers?'

'How should I know? It looked like no knickers from where I was standing.'

'You shouldn't have been looking!'

'I couldn't help seeing! Can we please drop the subject?'

She was only too glad to. First, the subject was hardly fit for polite conversation, and second, she was suddenly realizing what a hypocrite she was.

My God, you can talk. Pretending to be asleep while he was whipping his boxer shorts off . . . Talk about double standards.

The road climbed gently through fields of gently waving sugar cane, and slowly the character of the country changed. It became wilder, more rocky, more jungly, with odd creepers clinging to rocks and trees like giant Swiss cheese plants growing everywhere.

The road was remarkably good, with hardly any potholes, and just as well. Apart from the being-thrown-together aspect, there was another reason why she could not do with violent jolting.

She had forgotten to go to the loo before leaving and after rather a lot of passion fruit juice and two cups of coffee for breakfast, she was beginning to be uncomfortably aware of the fact. Still, she could probably last another hour.

They passed the odd little house with a round-eyed child waving from the steps. They passed a rum shop, where men were 'limin' out' round the door. Further up the road, they passed a plump, elderly lady trudging up the hill with a basket on her head. She stood patiently as they went past. Twenty yards further, Nick stopped and reversed back. 'Like a lift?' he called.

'I would, dear. This basket gettin' real heavy.'

She climbed in the back. 'Jus' up the top, dear. By the bus stop.' As he carried on, she began singing softly to herself. Daisy recognized the tune; it was '*Oh, what a friend we have in Jesus.*'

The singing died away. 'Are you enjoyin' this lovely day?' she asked, in lovely, lilting tones. 'Are you praisin' God for it?'

Daisy was too startled to answer.

Nick wasn't. 'We sure are' he said cheerfully.

'That's right, dear. Praise the Lord.' She resumed her singing till they got to the top of the road and a bus stop that said 'Out of City'. Here she got out, replaced her basket on her head, and handed Daisy something. 'Thank you, dear. Enjoy your day.'

It was a mango – a big, rosy, juicy one. 'We will,' Daisy smiled. 'Thank you very much.'

'That was kind of you,' she offered, as he pulled away.

'It was no skin off my nose.'

Oh, please yourself. If I try to make a nice, civilized remark, you could at least accept it graciously.

Obviously she was still getting on his nerves. For quite a few miles, there was a rather tense silence. In a saloon car it would have been oppressive, but in the open-sided moke, with the wind on her face and hair, Daisy bore it well enough.

'We're coming up to the mahogany forest,' he said at last. 'What's left of it.'

The dazzling levels of light dropped dramatically. Through a dense canopy of trees, sunlight played in dappled shafts on the forest floor. It was quiet and cool, like some vast primeval cathedral.

A hundred yards into the forest he pulled up and Jane and Ian parked close behind.

Daisy stepped out, and on to the forest floor. 'Jane, just look at these!' Within a few yards of the moke grew a plant with the most enormous leaves she'd ever seen outside the waterlilies in Kew Gardens.

'They must be four feet long!'

'They're called Elephants' Ears,' Nick said.

As they wandered, Daisy began to curse her choice of footwear. Flimsy, strappy little sandals were not quite the thing here, where roots tried to trip you and the ground was littered with leaves and mossy bits.

Long rope-like lianas hung from the trees, making her wonder whether there were any monkeys to swing on them. As they passed, Nick pulled on one, as if testing it for strength.

'Are you going to play Tarzan?' she asked.

'I'll leave that for Ian.' He had taken his sunglasses off and tucked them in the breast pocket of his shirt; so the fleeting glint did not escape her. 'It's no fun playing Tarzan without a Jane.'

Jane and Ian had wandered further. Ian was actually trying to swing on one, making daft Tarzan noises and Jane was laughing her head off.

A question that had been lurking at the back of her mind pushed its way to the front. 'I'm surprised you didn't bring a "Jane" on this holiday.'

'I don't have a "Jane" at the moment.'

I thought as much, or you'd have mentioned her. She couldn't resist a little dig. 'Maybe you're losing your grip.'

'Now there's a thought.' He swung a liana as they passed. 'Or maybe I'm just getting picky about Janes.'

His softly musing tone unnerved her. Jane and Ian were quite a way ahead, and suddenly she felt a not-so-subtle change in the atmosphere. There was still tension, but of a rather different variety. 'Maybe it's the Janes who are getting picky.'

'Could be,' he mused.

In the quiet, sun-dappled shade, her antennae were suddenly going haywire. A quivering oasis seemed to have descended around them; a tingly, shivery circle of awareness.

It's your imagination. Forget it.

Fortunately, there was a distraction. Various earthy, leafy bits had worked their way between foot and sandal again. She stopped and slipped it off.

179

Unfortunately, Nick was not co-operating. He was close behind her, almost brushing her as she picked and shook bits of forest from her sandal. It was grossly unfair, after all her efforts to keep the shivers at bay. Since she was standing on one foot, it made her go literally wobbly. It made her go so wobbly, she had to put her hand out and rest it on the trunk of a handy tree while she slipped her sandal back on.

That was the plan, anyway. She hadn't counted on Nick screwing it up. And since he was right behind her, she didn't see it coming.

Her hand was no longer on the tree. He had removed it. His fingers were encircling her wrist like a velvet handcuff and his other hand was on her waist.

'Daisy . . .'

Oh, my God. If it was possible to freeze and dissolve both at once, she did.

I don't want this.

Liar. You love it.

Slowly, he turned her to face him.

CHAPTER 9

Her previous wobbles had been mere amateurs. She dissolved in the warm, green river of his eyes.

For about two seconds.

Almost imperceptibly, his mouth started twitching. 'You wouldn't last long in a jungle situation.' He nodded over her shoulder. 'You nearly put your hand on that thing.'

As he let her go, Daisy turned her head sharply. Almost perfectly camouflaged on the bark was a fat brown thing with a segmented body, about the size of his index finger.

By some divine grace, she managed not to screech and jump three feet.

Trembling not so much with revulsion as post-wobble syndrome, she rammed her sandal back on. *What was I doing? Gazing into his eyes like the dizziest bimbo that ever drew breath . . .*

'It was about half a centimetre from your fingers,' he said crisply, thrusting his hands in his pockets.

'And since centipedes can apparently give a very painful bite, I thought a pre-emptive strike was in order.'

Daisy was a mass of confusion. Half of her was convinced he'd done it on purpose just to see whether she dissolved. The other half wasn't so sure. Maybe he'd just been hoping for her to perform the classic female screech and shudder, so he could have a good laugh.

At least she hadn't obliged. 'You could just have told me,' she said, covering her unsteadiness with irritability. 'I wouldn't have passed out like some dopey – '

A massive screech made them both turn sharply.

It was Jane. 'Ugh!' she screeched again. 'I nearly stepped on it! Oh, my God, they're everywhere!'

Instinctively, Daisy looked down. They were, too, once you looked. Big and fat and shiny brown, perfectly camouflaged, they crawled and wriggled on their centipedy business over the forest floor.

Jane and Ian were coming back. 'Let's go,' Jane shuddered. 'This place is heaving with disgusting creepy-crawlies.'

Daisy felt obliged to defend the residents. 'They're not disgusting! They can't help being centipedes. They probably think we're disgusting.'

'Don't be daft – centipedes can't think!'

'Well, that's what they'd think if they could.'

'Let's head back,' Nick said. 'The road carries on straight up Cherry Tree Hill.'

Jane glanced at Daisy as they walked on. 'Are you all right?'

'Of course! Why wouldn't I be?' She didn't mean it to, but it came out faintly snappy.

Looking faintly hurt, Jane went ahead with Ian.

They reached the mokes first. 'See you at the top of the hill,' Nick called, as they pulled away.

All the shock and confusion had produced an uncomfortable side-effect. As they got into the moke, Daisy was very conscious of needing a pit-stop. 'How long before we reach anywhere with civilized facilities?'

He put the key in the ignition. 'If you mean a little girls' room, quite a while. Are you desperate?'

It was ridiculous to feel embarrassed, but she couldn't help it. 'Not quite.'

He turned the engine off again and nodded towards the forest. 'Nip back and take a little walk.'

Oh, help. Why wasn't I born a man? In shorts, it'll mean radical exposure. 'I'd rather not.'

'I won't look.'

He was laughing, she could swear it. 'I'd rather wait,' she said obstinately.

'If it's the centipedes, I'll come and find you a nice, beastie-free zone.'

'It's not the centipedes!' *My God, the last thing I want is an escort.*

'Then what's the problem?'

You, if you want to know. You imagining me squatting inelegantly . . . 'Nothing! Oh, for heaven's sake.' Grabbing her bag she stalked off.

She found a nice little hidey place behind a clump of Elephants' Ears, where nobody passing on the road could possibly see anything. Feeling considerably better, she returned to the moke.

'All right?' he enquired. 'No rear-guard attacks by marauding wildlife?'

His mouth was quivering in a way that made her want to hit him. 'Just drive, will you?'

He turned the key in the ignition, and turned it off again. 'It must be suggestion – you've made me want to go, now. Wait one minute while I find a friendly tree.'

As he strolled off, she began to think it was no wonder he'd laughed. She'd made such a thing of it, like some uptight little prude. If it had been Ian she wouldn't have cared a hoot.

She'd snapped at Jane, too. Being so on edge was making her horrible to everybody. As he strolled back, she made up her mind to be determinedly nice in case they all thought she was suffering from a bad case of PMT.

They came out of the forest into the light, and up a gently winding hill. A little further on it levelled out.

Daisy gave a little gasp.

'Worth a little trip, isn't it?' Nick said. 'Worth dragging yourself off the beach for.'

Before them stretched a panorama of soft green, rolling perhaps two miles down to the coast. Even from here, you could see the mighty Atlantic breakers rolling in. It was so utterly different from the placid Caribbean side, she could hardly believe it was only a few miles away.

Jane and Ian were parked on a grassy verge, taking pictures. 'You've been ages,' Jane said. 'We were beginning to think you'd been eaten by centipedes.'

'I had to make a pit-stop in the forest,' Daisy confessed. 'Too much liquid for breakfast.

Jane made a face. 'What a nightmare. I'd have been terrified of creepy-crawlies biting my bottom.'

'I'd have been right behind you, love,' Ian grinned. 'You can always count on me in a crisis.'

Amid a lot of laughter, they got back into the mokes. 'Map,' Nick said crisply, spreading it on her legs again. 'This bit's slightly more complicated. We follow the coast road to here . . .' – he traced it with his finger – ' . . . and then down past Bathsheba, to St John's church.' He glanced up at her. 'Got that?'

Why can't you be ugly? Why can't you have bad breath or pick your nose or something? Why are you doing this to me? 'Absolutely,' she said brightly.

'The signs were pretty hopeless last time so we'll probably get lost anyway, but do your best.'

'Aye, aye, captain.'

With a sideways glance, he started the engine. 'You're in a bit of a better mood than when we started.'

'I had a headache.'

'So that's what it was.' He reversed the moke off the grass verge. 'I was beginning to think it was me.'

His faintly sardonic tone did not escape her.

And what's that supposed to mean?

Don't think about it, or you really will get a headache. Enjoy the scenery, instead.

Fortunately, this was not difficult. The road descended gently to the coast. Huge breakers crashed relentlessly on a vast white beach utterly different from the other side. There were hardly any trees and it was practically deserted.

And no wonder, when she saw the signs in four languages, saying, '*Do Not Swim Here.*' 'I suppose the currents are lethal.'

185

'I guess so. I wouldn't want to check it out for myself.'

They passed through Bathsheba; a pretty, picturesque little village whose steep, uppy-downy lanes reminded her rather incongruously of Cornish fishing villages. She said as much to Nick.

'It's not so surprising,' he said. 'Coastal fishing villages often have a similar feel.'

She voiced something that had been on her mind for some time. 'Are you from Cornwall?'

'Originally. I used to do a lot of surfing.'

She could just imagine. She recalled that younger Nick, with the longer, wilder hair, and imagined him walking barefoot up a little lane with a surfboard – and the female surf-groupies who inevitably followed wherever there were hunks in wetsuits.

I bet you didn't exactly miss out in that department. 'You must have had some lovely summers.'

'I was a case of making the most of what was on the doorstep,' he said drily. 'We couldn't afford to go anywhere else. Four kids come expensive.'

So does one, when you're a single mother. 'A big family's nice, though.'

'Sometimes.' He glanced at her. 'You're an only child, aren't you?'

'How did you know?'

'Tara mentioned it.'

'I wasn't spoilt rotten, if that's what you're thinking.'

'I wasn't. But all only children are spoilt to some extent. They have to be. All that attention focused on one child who's the centre of the universe . . .'

Although she knew he was right, she couldn't help being irritated. Maybe she had been the centre of the universe, but only because her mother had nobody else.

'Now you're offended,' he said, as the moke puffed up a steep hill. 'I can feel the prickles from here. *Urchina Daisya Longhairya* – a decorative little species and quite harmless, until you touch its tender bits.'

The mere mention of touching her tender bits was enough to unsettle her all over again. But she wasn't going to show it. 'If you're trying to wind me up, you're not going to succeed.'

He glanced at her but said nothing. At the top of the hill they parked on a rocky promontory and watched surfers riding the waves. Some of them were way out, waiting for a big one. Enormous rocks dotted the beach, as if a giant had been lazily tossing stones towards the water.

'I thought the currents were dangerous!' Jane said.

'Not here,' Nick said. 'They only have to worry about the rocks. And the odd passing shark.'

'I thought there weren't any sharks here!' Daisy said.

'Not on the Caribbean side. The reef keeps them out. There's bound to be the odd shark here.'

Jane shuddered as she watched the surfers paddling themselves out. 'They must be absolutely mental.'

'It's the risk that makes you do it,' he said. 'Gets the adrenalin going. Gives you a buzz.'

Daisy watched as someone caught a wave. She watched him twist and skim on the curved wall of water, fall and disappear in a boiling mass of foam.

For what seemed like ages, she couldn't see him.

'Don't fret, Daisy.' With a light hand on the bare nape of her neck, Nick murmured, 'He'll be up like a cork any second.'

Daisy was experiencing a buzz of her own. The very lightness of his touch on a secondary erogenous zone was giving her a king-size buzz. But just as she was about to move away, he moved instead.

Phew.

From Bathsheba her attention was taken by map-reading. There were little roads everywhere, with signs seemingly intended to drive frustrated tourists into the nearest rum shop. Eventually, though, they were climbing a steep, winding hill with a church perched at the top.

'It could almost be England,' Daisy remarked to Jane, as they wandered the churchyard. 'Except for these.' The churchyard was planted with frangipani trees that bore pink flowers, not the usual white variety. Blossoms littered the ground, looking oddly incongruous among twisty old graves and a church that could have been transplanted from an English village.

Nick was hunting out his old Greek. 'I looked him up,' he said, as the others wandered up. 'For some reason best known to himself, the old codger fought for Charles the First in the Civil War and escaped to Barbados afterwards, in case Oliver Cromwell had his head chopped off, too.'

'Why didn't he just go back to Greece?' Daisy wondered.

'Maybe he'd had enough of the ouzo,' Ian grinned. 'Fancied a drop of rum, instead.'

Daisy wandered on. The church was built at the edge of a gently sloping cliff. Far below, beyond rolling swathes of green, the Atlantic crashed on miles of white beach.

It was very quiet, with only the plaintive call of a bird and the warm breeze rustling in the trees. Holding a frangipani blossom to her nose, she inhaled its delicate, lemony scent. 'This has to be the world's most scenic churchyard,' she said, as Nick came to stand beside her. 'Imagine all the people who've come here across that sea. Sugar planters and funny old Greeks . . .'

'And slaves,' he said. 'Poor bastards. Imagine what it must have been like in those ships.'

'Don't,' she shuddered. 'I can't bear to think about it.'

'I don't suppose they were too thrilled with it, either,' he said drily.

She almost flushed, as if he were implying that she were one of those people who say they can't bear to think of dear little lambs being killed and then tuck into a nice Sunday roast with mint sauce. 'I know it was awful. It was barbaric.'

'I wasn't having a go at you.' He gave her waist a little pat. 'I'm going inside.'

Daisy didn't follow. She stayed there, looking at the sea and wondering exactly how many miles of savage ocean lay between here and the coast of Africa, where the slaves had come from. Two thousand? Three? She thought of the friendly, cheerful waiters, the barman who danced as he mixed his cocktails, the beach boys who always had a wicked joke, and the friendly maid who cleaned her room, and wondered how many generations had passed since their ancestors were unloaded from those dreadful ships in chains.

And she wondered why on earth she was getting in such a rattled, edgy stew just because she felt a guilty attraction for a man who was not Simon. She was letting it ruin what many people would consider the holiday of a lifetime.

You know your trouble? she told herself, as they finally headed back to the mokes. *You're getting self-centred and neurotic. If you had something really big to worry about, you wouldn't be agonizing over molehills.*

They stopped for lunch at a charming and utterly unpretentious little hotel that specialized in local food. 'I'm putting on pounds here,' Jane lamented, as they sampled the buffet. 'Candied sweet potatoes and pumpkin fritters . . . I shall have to go on a diet when I get back.'

'You always say that.' Daisy was already on seconds, and wondering if she'd have room for a rather delectable-looking lime pie, too.

She sat diagonally opposite Nick, on a verandah overlooking the sea where little fishing boats bobbed. Their eyes met now and then across the table, but she'd made up her mind how to handle it.

An ex-boyfriend who'd worked in West Africa had once told her about the dreadful heat and humidity and how he'd tried to fight it until he'd realized it was pointless. You just relaxed and accepted it – and waited to get back in the air-conditioning. She'd be back in the air-conditioning soon – back in England, with Simon.

'More wine?' said Ian, brandishing a bottle.

'Yes, please,' she said serenely. 'It's so nice not to have to drive. And such a wonderful chauffeur, too.' She raised her glass to him. 'Cheers, Nick. You're doing a great job'

Her serene-acceptance plan worked wonderfully. Not that she had to test it too much; he never came and sat next to her on the beach or dragged her up to dance after dinner. If he happened to be there when she needed some sun cream rubbed into her shoulders, he never offered to do it. He never came and joined her on the raft. If she happened to collide with him on an early morning walk on the beach, he was always just coming back while she was just going.

At last she began to relax in the way you were supposed to relax in the Caribbean. She began to chill out so thoroughly, it was even an effort to decide what to choose off the lunch menu.

Three more sunsets came and went, three more soft nights of tree frogs singing and tiny bats flitting in the shadows.

Around midday on their ninth day, she lay lazily on her sunbed, reflecting on the unwritten law of holidays. Namely, that the closer you get to departure and the more you're relaxing and enjoying yourself, the faster the days zoom past. She thought lazily about finding the others and wandering off for lunch, but couldn't bring herself to move.

'Daisy!'

She sat up, shading her eyes. 'What?'

It was Nick. Only yards away, he was standing in the edge of the water next to a speedboat. 'Can you spare fifteen minutes?'

'I was just going for lunch!'

'Can it wait? I want to go for a ski but he needs somebody else in the boat.'

'Whatever for?'

'He's not legal otherwise. If the coastguard sees him he'll lose his licence.'

'Oh, all right.' She quite liked sitting in a speedboat with the wind in her hair. Lazily she got up, grabbed her bag and wandered down.

With two hands on her waist and businesslike efficiency, Nick lifted her on to the prow. From here she tiptoed over the hot, gleaming fibreglass to the cockpit, where the driver was extending a hand to help her. 'Hi,' she said.

'How you doin'?' He lifted a lifejacket off the seat beside him. 'He your boyfriend?'

'No, my boyfriend couldn't come.'

'And he let you come here all by yourself?' He tutted gently. 'Dear Lord. I hope he know the risk he takin'.'

Daisy suppressed a smile. Most of the watersports boys were outrageous flirts, but they were so funny, you had to laugh. Like many of the others, he was extraordinarily good-looking, with beautiful white teeth in a face the colour of bitter chocolate and muscles that would give the average male tourist an inferiority complex. He wore a faded T shirt that bore the legend, *Cockspur Rum – The Fighting Cock That Spurs You On,* and a baseball cap.

'I never ski this guy before,' he said. 'He any good?'

She had seen him once or twice. 'Pretty good, not that I'm any great expert.'

192

'I'll soon check him out.' He started the engine and went out a few yards. Nick waded out a bit and the driver tossed him a ski and the line.

'He's going to show off,' he whispered to Daisy, with a grin. 'They always show off when they got a woman in the boat.'

She couldn't help laughing. 'I don't think he's a show-off.'

'You wanna bet?'

He started the engine again and Nick flew up like a spraying cork. Daisy watched for a minute or two as he skimmed back and forth across the wash. 'He is pretty good,' she said to the driver.

He was sitting on the side, steering with his knee and keeping an eye on both the sea ahead and Nick at once. 'He's not bad, but there's too many boats, here, messin' up the water. Maybe we go down by Sandy Lane. Give him a clear run so he can get a rhythm goin'.'

Accordingly, he headed out of the bay and turned south.

Daisy watched Nick for a bit. *If this is what he calls 'not bad'* . . . 'I suppose you're absolutely brilliant,' she said to the driver.

'I'm OK.'

'If you're much better than him, I'd like a demonstration.'

'No way.' He winked at her. 'The other guys'll say I'm showin' off just because I got a beautiful girl in the boat.'

Daisy laughed again. The wind in her face was utterly relaxing and it was a lovely way to see the coast. You could hardly see the hotels – they were all practically buried in their gardens.

'What's your name?' asked the driver.

'Daisy.'

'I'm Troy. The best in the west.' He extended a hand.

She laughed again. 'I won't ask best at what.'

'That, too,' he grinned. 'But first it's the ski-in'. Best on the west coast.'

'Now who's showing off?' she asked, still laughing.

They carried on down the coast and into a beautiful bay with no other boats messin' up the water. After one circuit, the engine seemed to cough a little, the boat juddered, and Nick nearly fell off. Seconds later, it coughed again, and died.

The driver swore softly in the local dialect. Except for a couple of words of good old Anglo-Saxon origin, it sounded like a foreign language. 'What's wrong?' she asked.

He was leaning over the stern, taking the cover off the engine. 'Teethin' trouble.'

Nick swam up, pushing his ski. 'What's the problem?'

'Nothin' I can fix right here.' He didn't seem over-stressed, but that was Bajans for you, Daisy thought. Chilled out to the nth degree.

Another boat was passing quite a distance away. He put his fingers to his lips and let out a piercing whistle. The boat turned and zoomed up and the two drivers held a conversation in utterly incomprehensible Bajan. 'This guy'll give you a lift back,' Troy said. 'And then he'll give me a tow.'

'We can walk,' Daisy said. 'It's not that far.'

'It's very hot,' Nick pointed out, from the water. 'And it's midday. You don't want to get burnt.'

'I won't get burnt! I've got a good enough tan!'

'OK, OK,' he soothed. 'Put those prickles back.'

Since Daisy had her beach bag and couldn't swim for it, the other driver gave them a lift to the beach.

There were no hotels here, just the odd villa hidden in the trees, and hardly anybody on the beach. There was still a little shade from the trees, and a lot of little green fruits littering the sand. 'What are these?' she asked, picking one up.

'Manchineels, and they're poisonous, so put it down. Didn't you read the hotel literature?'

'Most of it.'

'You should have read all of it. That's what they put it in your room for.'

'Don't nag! I'm on holiday!'

'Sorry,' he said drily. 'I didn't mean to sound like your father.'

'I haven't got a father.' She wished at once she hadn't said it. He looked instantly awkward, as people do in such circumstances.

'It's OK, he's not dead,' she went on hastily. 'At least, not that I know of. I never had the pleasure of making his acquaintance.'

They walked a little further in silence. 'That must have been a bit rough,' Nick said at last.

'It wasn't rough at all. You never miss what you've never had.'

She bent to pick up an urchin shell, some of the sun-bleached spines still attached. As they walked, she began picking them off.

195

She couldn't think of any suitable topic of conversation as they strolled on, and neither, apparently, could he. She began get the same feeling she'd had in the mahogany forest. Quivering, uneasy tension, as if something were trembling in the wings.

Don't be daft. Look what happened last time.

'Isn't it amazing how quickly the first week's gone?' she said brightly. 'We'll be back on that plane before you know it.'

'Will you be glad to leave?'

'No way! The thought of that weather, never mind going back to work . . .'

They rounded a corner into the next bay. It was smaller and even more deserted than the last. Not a soul was there.

'Was that guy chatting you up, in the boat?' he asked.

'Not really. He was just funny. He thought you'd be showing off and trying to impress me.' She paused minutely. 'I soon put him straight on that count.'

'I'm sure you did.'

Is it my imagination, or was there something funny in his tone?

They hadn't gone much further before Daisy realized just how she'd been kidding herself the past few days. It had been easy to tell herself the buzz was wearing off, or at least as controllable as the gas under a saucepan. Not once in the past few days had she been alone with him. Not once had she been even within shivering distance, except over dinner, with everybody else diluting the atmosphere. But now, there were just the two of them. Not once did he touch or brush against her, but he didn't have to. All the sensations she'd been trying to ignore had been gently building up, like steam under a valve. She began to walk a little faster.

'What's the hurry?' he asked, in drily amused tones.

'I want my lunch.'

'Then you'll enjoy it all the more. Slow down. It's too hot to rush.'

'I'm starving. I keep thinking of crispy chicken wings and barbecue sauce and – ow!'

'I haven't tried the "ow". Is it a chef's special?'

'Very funny!' She was standing on one foot, detaching a thorny little twig from the other. It had done no damage. 'Thank heaven for that. For a moment I thought it was an urchin.' She glanced up at him. 'And then you'd have had a good laugh.'

'Naturally.' His mouth was quivering minutely. 'I'd have cracked up and said, "serve you right".'

He was very close, far too close for comfort. His eyes were like a warm, African river with the sun on it. 'But I might have been very noble and done my back in giving you a piggy back to the hotel.'

'No, you wouldn't.' Her eyes flickered to the firm muscles of his chest, and the dark, curling hair, still damp from the sea. 'I'd have limped and hopped all the way.'

'Just to be awkward?'

'So you wouldn't sue me for a bad back.' The mere thought of a piggy back reduced her to erogenous jelly.

Just imagine it, my arms around his neck, my legs wrapped around him . . .

Wrapped in the wrong direction, my dear.

Even so . . .

197

'You're quite right, it is hot,' she said brightly. 'I'm going to have a quick cool-off in the sea.'

Dropping her bag and sunglasses in the soft sand, she ran into the water. If anything, the water was even clearer than at the hotel, like turquoise bathwater. A little further out, forests of coral stood out dark against the white sandy bottom.

She waded a little way and stopped, propped on her elbows in calf-deep water. Nearby, a school of tiny fish moved as one, darting and turning just under the surface.

Nick came in after her and swam much further out, threading his way between the clumps of coral. She splashed her face with water, closed her eyes, and tried to think of other things – like crispy chicken wings and barbecue sauce.

She heard the splashing as he came back, but didn't open her eyes. In the circumstances it was preferable not to get a colossal eyeful. There was something about wet male muscle – especially wet brown male muscle, with all those sunlit droplets clinging to it.

'Come on.' He flicked a little water over her. 'You've cooled off enough.'

'You go. I'll stay here for a bit.

'And leave you here on your own?'

'Why not?' she said, pretending to be dozily half asleep 'It's perfectly safe.'

'That's what you think.'

She felt him sit beside her. A little ripple washed over her.

'There are all sorts of marauding beasties waiting to get you,' he went on, in a softly teasing tone.

'Like what?'

'Like the giant flesh-eating urchin that lurks in the coral. If you'd bothered to read the hotel literature you'd know all about it. It slithers out when nobody's looking and engulfs its prey with its gigantic, primeval mouth. It has no teeth, you'll be pleased to hear. It swallows you whole and lets its digestive juices ingest you very slowly. After a day or two it spits out the inedible bits, like hair and bikini.'

Daisy was torn between laughter and shivers as he edged closer. 'Dear me. What else?'

He lowered his voice a little more. 'Or there's the giant marine centipede. Now this is a rather nastier customer. Its squillions of legs have evolved into squillions of tiny paddles, so it swims like a turbo-prop torpedo. It has rows and rows of nasty, sharp little teeth, like a piranha. It watches out for unwary women lying in the water, slithers out of its lair, and before you can say seafood dressing – '

He tweaked her waist so suddenly, she gave a violent jump.

'You rotten devil!' Half laughing, she gave him a violent shove that sent him backwards in the water.

He was up again in a second, grabbing her wrist as she tried to swim away. 'It's particularly partial to rump,' he said, giving her bottom a little tweak.

'Stop it!' Really laughing now, she collapsed in the water.

He wasn't laughing any more. 'You should laugh more often,' he said softly. 'It suits you.'

Oh, help. Her stomach gave a massive, woozy lurch. 'Are you trying to say I'm a misery?'

'No.' For several lurchy seconds, he gazed at her. 'Just that you should laugh more often.'

Get up, Daisy. Any second your wooze is going to show. Pretend your tummy's rumbling and resume that brisk, no-nonsense walk.

She didn't have to. 'Time to go,' he said, much more crisply. 'Before all the crispy chicken wings are gone.'

'Perish the thought,' she said unsteadily.

'On your feet.' He held out a hand. 'If you sit here much longer you'll dissolve.'

I already am dissolving.

She let him take her hand, but somehow, she never made it to her feet. Something happened in between. It wasn't just their wet hands, clasped together, or the eyes that held her like river-green magnets. It was something alive in the air and water between them.

With stomach-lurching clarity it hit her.

It's not just me.

His voice came out in a ragged, barely-there whisper. 'Oh, Daisy . . .'

200

CHAPTER 10

And that was all it took.

They came together in a trembling fusion of salt and wet and heat. It wasn't so much a kiss as an urgent, mutual devouring, as if a dam had suddenly burst.

His mouth was fierce and tender both at once; hard, probing, possessing . . .

His hands moved in a restless fever, from the back of her neck down to the backs of her thighs, and back again. Hers were the same; through his wet hair, over the taut, wet muscles of his shoulders and the soft fuzz on his chest, anywhere she could touch him.

The urgency that possessed her was like her need for oxygen. If she didn't have it, she would die.

Somewhere in the misty depths of her brain, a voice was whispering, '*It was like this before, remember?*'

But it wasn't, quite. She was no untutored novice now, trembling at the unknown. Erotic pathways were established; her body knew the cues and flamed into response almost before they were given. Liquid fingers of fire snaked and darted to every nerve she possessed. They came up for air. Wordlessly he led her, half stumbling, into deeper water. They knelt together on

201

the soft sand, where the water came nearly to her shoulders. As their mouths fused again, she realized why he'd brought her there. Just beneath the crystal surface of the water, he slipped her bikini top down.

She gasped, arching her back as he cupped her little white breasts underwater, teasing their tiny, erect peaks between finger and thumb. Shock waves snaked to the nerve centre between her thighs, while his lips and tongue still set her mouth alight. And suddenly, his mouth left her, and his fingers left her nipples. His hands cupped her bottom and he raised her, lifting her breasts clear of the water. As his mouth fastened on her nipple, Daisy shuddered. She wrapped her legs tight around his waist, squirming as the heat between her thighs pressed against his stomach. His lips left her nipple and travelled in a fevered trail to the other. He teased it with his tongue before taking it in his mouth and sucking it so hard she wanted to scream out loud.

He lowered her again to kneel on the soft sand and their mouths fused once more. His hands fell from her waist to her bottom. He drew her hard against him.

His heat and hardness dug into her stomach, making her gasp aloud. His hands rose again and slid inside the back of her bikini pants.

The feel of his hands, each clasping one little buttock, electrified her.

Go on!

Slowly, like a torture, he slid one hand between wet lycra and skin, over her hip to her stomach.

Go on, go on! In a wordless little plea, she parted her thighs a little more, and he responded. His fingers slid over her untanned skin, through soft, wet curls, until they found the heat he'd created.

Daisy could hardly breathe any more, let alone kiss him. Her mouth left him, her back arching convulsively as he teased and explored.

But it was nothing to what came next. With a swift sudden movement, he thrust his fingers deep inside her.

'Oh, God.' The sensation was almost more than she could bear. He was probing so deep and hard, but not quite deep or hard enough. Somewhere, just out of reach, a throbbing ache was crying out for more. In blind desperation, she groped for the waistband of his shorts and slid her hand inside. In the cool water he was burning hot; hard and powerful enough to fill that ache inside her. She felt his body shudder as her fingers closed around him.

And suddenly he withdrew; put her sharply from him.

Through thudding heartbeats she heard the voices.

'You just can't get away from it,' said a disapproving female voice from about twenty yards away, as Daisy frantically adjusted her bikini top.

'You'd think they'd have the decency to go to their room,' said a crustily disapproving male one. An elderly couple, their English winter pallor still intact, were briskly walking the beach.

'As if there isn't enough of it on the television,' added the female, in pointedly carrying tones, as they passed closer. 'The BBC shows absolutely nothing else these days.'

'And if it's not that, it's homosexuals,' said the crusty male. 'Blasted nation's turning into a race of limp-wristed blasted pansies . . .'

The voices tailed off down the beach.

For a moment they sat silent in the water, in the tense aftermath of cut-off passion. Still trembling with heat and aftershock, Daisy saw him close his eyes in gritted frustration. She saw him put a hand to his shorts, adjusting the uncomfortable evidence.

Her voice was barely steady. 'I can't believe what we just did.'

I can't believe what we might have done.

He opened his eyes. 'At least we gave them something to moan about. Probably made their day.'

It was a brave attempt, but no wry humour could disguise the roughness of his voice.

'It's not funny,' she said unsteadily.

'I know.' He reached across, took her hand.

'Please, Nick, don't.' Keeping her eyes away from him, she withdrew it. Her heart was still racing erratically, and as for that tortured ache between her thighs . . . She swallowed, hard. 'I thought you said I was a passing fancy.'

'I lied.'

She had to turn to him then. 'Why?'

'Why do you think?' His voice was still rough with suppressed passion. 'You'd have been an uptight wreck, thinking I was about to make a move.'

Her heart twisted painfully.

'Why do you think I slung you out of my room the other day?' he went on. 'You were standing right beside me in that bloody T shirt, your hair all over me . . .'

Oh, my God, did I leave all my brains behind at Heathrow?

'I didn't think you were interested,' he went on.

'I thought you knew! I was trying to cover it, but – '

'Then you're a damn good actress.' His eyes were warm, liquid green. 'I thought I caught something now and then, but I put it down to wishful thinking. Until the mahogany forest.'

She swallowed, over an odd lump in her throat. 'But you still didn't – '

'Do you have to sound so surprised? I'm not quite the kind of bastard who sleeps with other people's girl-friends. I can't say Simon's exactly my type, but he seems a nice enough guy. More roughly he added, 'I almost wish he wasn't.'

Simon. The guilt she'd felt until now had been a mere drop in the ocean compared to what was to come. Her voice came out jerky and erratic. 'I don't know what came over me. I love Simon. I really love him. This was just – '

'Lust?'

'I suppose so. I suppose these things happen.'

'Of course they do. Especially in a long-term relationship.' He glanced at her. 'Has it happened before?'

'No! Never!' She felt bitterly hurt that he even asked, until she realized that in the circumstances, it was a reasonable enough question.

'Maybe you've got the two-year itch.' He paused. 'How old are you?'

'Twenty-seven, but I don't see what that's got to do with – '

'It has everything to do with it. I'm thirty-one and I know I'm not ready for commitment. Maybe you're not, either.'

The walkers had passed into the next bay, but another interruption was on its way. A little wooden fishing boat chugged into the bay, a grizzled old man at the helm. He cut the engine and stood with a net, scanning the water.

My God, what came over me? What the hell might I have done, on a public beach?

You were practically underwater. It wouldn't have been that obvious.

She could hardly believe she was even having this mental argument.

A spasm of anguish gripped her. 'He loves me. He's all I ever wanted.'

'Maybe you thought he was.'

'He is!' The enormity of what she'd so nearly done was beginning to hit her, hard. 'I love him! Nothing like this is ever going to happen again! Do you understand? Nothing!' Unsteadily she rose to her feet, half stumbling through the water.

'Oh, Daisy.' He stood up, caught her wrist. 'Listen to me,' he said softly. 'If you've got something good going with Simon, I don't want to wreck it. There'll be nothing else, unless you want it.'

'I don't!' Tears were beginning to course down her cheeks.

'Then nothing's going to happen. Stop crying, for heaven's sake. It's not that bad.'

'It is.' Her voice was close to cracking completely. 'He trusts me. If he ever found out, I'd die. He'd be so hurt . . .'

'He won't find out. Not from me.' He took her hand, raised it to his lips and kissed her fingertips. 'It's not the end of the world.'

After the raw urgency of what they'd just done, such tender restraint caught at her heart. She took her hand away and splashily stumbled back to the sand. Picking up her bag, she started walking towards the hotel.

But as she walked and it sank in, she wasn't just trembling and confused. She began to be angry, too. With both of them. 'Do you always carry on like that? In for the kill after five minutes?'

He was walking right beside her, about two feet between them. 'I got carried away.'

The very fact that he did not reproach her with pots and kettles only made her feel worse. 'I'm sorry,' she said unsteadily. 'I didn't exactly fight you off.'

'No, but I started it. I don't think you'd have made the first move.'

'Does it matter who "started it"?'

'I guess not. Unless you're a couple of kids.' Casting her a wry, sideways glance he put on a whining, high-pitched voice. 'It wasn't *me*, Sir. He started it.'

Despite everything, she managed a very wobbly laugh.

His smile caught at her heart. 'That's better.'

Only on the outside.

For a hundred yards they walked in silence.

I wish I were a Catholic, she thought, in her anguish. *Then I could go to confession and be absolved from this guilt.*

She thought of that night she'd spent in his room, and how she'd pretended to be asleep . . . .

Maybe I can confess this, at least.

She glanced at him. 'Nick,' she said unsteadily, 'I want to tell you something.'

He cast her an enquiring glance. 'Go on.'

'It's really awful. I'm ashamed to say it.'

He looked wryly amused rather than anything else. 'Don't tell me. You kissed someone under the mistletoe while Simon wasn't looking.'

'Please, don't laugh.' Wishing she'd never started, she braced herself. 'I was awake, when you got out of bed the other morning. I saw you. In the mirror.'

'What?' He stopped dead on the sand.

Oh, God, why did I ever say it? 'I was pretending to be asleep.'

His reaction continued to dumbfound her. He wasn't exactly angry or embarrassed or shattered; it was a cocktail of all three. 'I thought you were dreaming!'

'I was pretending.'

'Hell!' He turned away, running a disbelieving hand through his hair. 'Of all the sneaky, devious little . . . How would you like it if I'd done that? Pretended to be asleep and watched you get undressed? I'd never hear the last of it – it'd probably make the tabloids. *'Filthy perve watched me strip'*, says outraged – '

'I'd never have got undressed like that! I'd have gone to the bathroom!'

'That's not the point!' His eyes sparked like green, clashing steel. 'And you had the nerve to come all sanctimonious at me because of one little slap on your backside!'

208

'It hurt!'

'Good! Pity it wasn't a bit harder!'

'I wish I'd never told you! I didn't think you'd be embarrassed!'

'I'm not embarrassed! I just can't believe you did it!'

'I'm sorry, OK?' Wiping the tears with the back of her hands, she carried on.

The sand was hot under her feet and the burning sun only seemed to make the tension worse; cooking it up to boiling point. Fifty yards further on he said rather gruffly, 'Look, I'm sorry I lost my rag. It was just a bit of a shock.'

'Obviously.'

A little further on, he said drily, 'You know something? Today's been an education. I had you pigeonholed under virtually zero for naughtiness. My assessment was way out.'

'After what happened at our first "brief encounter" I'm surprised I rated a zero.'

'I put that down to youthful inexperience. An innocent, caught up in something she couldn't handle.'

'I wasn't that innocent. I wasn't one of those girls determined to save herself for Mr Right.'

'I don't think those girls exist any more. If they do, I haven't met any.'

The sun was beating mercilessly on her head and shoulders, but they were coming up to the last bay before the hotel. It was much busier than the last; dotted with sun umbrellas from the various hotels, sailing boats pulled up on the sand, ski-boats and windsurfers busy in the water. The sand on the corner was thick with manchineel leaves and fruits, and more

209

urchin shells littered the sand. Just as they were rounding it, he caught her wrist. 'Daisy, wait. We might not have a chance to talk like this again.'

'We mustn't.' She returned his gaze as steadily as she could. 'I think we'd better keep out of each other's way as far as possible.'

'I know.' He paused. 'Would you prefer me not to come to your flat in future?'

Her heart twisted again. 'Of course not. You're Ian's friend. If he asks you back, you must come.'

'And we'll pretend this never happened.'

'Exactly.'

He gazed at her a moment longer, his eyes warm and glinting. 'It's going to be a tall order.'

'I know. But it'll wear off.'

'I dare say. Probably a case of us both wanting what we can't have.'

'Probably.' Part of her was dying to get back to the sanctuary of the hotel; part of her couldn't wrench herself away. 'I bet you don't often want what you can't have, in this particular department.'

'I don't often want anything badly enough to care whether I get it or not.'

Her stomach gave a wild, drunken lurch. 'As I said, it'll wear off.'

'I dare say.' He paused. 'But for the record, I've wanted you more badly than I've wanted anything for a hell of a long time. I'd have loved to make love to you.' He paused, nodding his head back down the beach. 'But not like that. I'd have liked locked doors and all night to play with.'

Oh, God, don't, I can't bear it.

His voice was softer, barely there. 'I don't know what it is, but something about you just gets to me.'

Her stomach gave another drunken lurch, but her voice came out lightly enough. 'Don't worry – it'll un-get to you soon enough.'

She turned and resumed a quick, light walk.

If only he'd stop being nice.

Perversely, she'd have loved him to do a classic male sulk and moan about women who get men all worked up and leave them in an agony of frustration, so she could begin to despise him. She recalled a certain Jamie; deceptively mature on the surface. They had been nowhere near actually Doing It, but he'd whinged for ages about how his whatsits were going to ache all night and how he wouldn't be at all surprised if it didn't cause testicular cancer. She had gone off him with miraculous speed.

It would seem that Nick was not going to oblige.

They walked on, past recumbent bodies on sunbeds. In the turquoise water somebody was fooling about on a jet-ski, and a small child screamed as a harassed father dragged it away from the water. 'Emma, stop it. Mummy's waiting. We're going for lunch.'

It was incredibly hot.

As they neared the hotel, she voiced something that had been on her mind. 'Will you tell me something?'

'I might.'

'Did you let Simon beat you on purpose when you had that game with him? So he'd invite you for supper?'

'Hell, I'm not that devious.' He cast her a very sardonic glance. 'You don't think much of me, do you?'

'I'm sorry. I apologize.' It came out taut and brittle, and he caught her arm.

'Daisy, we can't go back like this. There's enough tension coming off you to start a Middle Eastern war.'

He was right. If she went back like this, even Ian would pick something up. Consciously she relaxed her shoulders, forced an unsteady smile. 'Of course I'm tense. I'm cross and bad-tempered because the boat broke down and we had to walk all that way in the sun. I'm hot and irritable and dying for a drink.'

His eyes said, '*Perfect. That's how we'll play it.*' 'Me too. The first beer won't even touch the sides.'

So by the time they reached the beach terrace, that was how they looked. Merely hot, sweaty and parched.

The others were already halfway through lunch. 'Where have you been?' Jane demanded.

'Damn ski boat broke down,' Nick explained. 'We had to walk practically from Sandy Lane. I think I've got sunstroke. I asked Daisy to give me a piggy back but she told me where to get off.'

The laughter that followed made her profoundly grateful to him. It even reduced some of her own tension. 'My actual words were, "Eff off, you wimp",' she said, playing along.

'Dreadfully unladylike,' Nick tutted, pretending to be shocked. 'Gave me quite a turn.'

'I'd have given you a piggy back,' said Tara, predictably enough.

'Then I'll take you next time.' He gave her shoulder a little pat. 'I can't do with these puny women who can't manage thirteen stone over five hundred yards.'

Getting through lunch was easier than she'd expected, although she couldn't help wondering how dumbfounded any of them would be if they knew.

She could never tell either Jane or Tara. She couldn't bear the thought of telling anybody just now, but later she knew she'd be bursting to unburden herself to somebody. Jane would be very sympathetic, but underneath she'd disapprove just a bit. And she'd swear not to tell a soul, but she'd tell Ian. Ian would never tell Simon, but he wouldn't like it. He'd look at her in a different way and thank heaven Jane wasn't like that. He'd think Nick was a complete bastard, and that would be the end of that friendship.

Tara would be entirely sympathetic. She wouldn't judge or disapprove – on the contrary, she'd want all the lurid details. She'd scoff at Daisy's guilt and say everybody did it and not to worry. She'd swear not to tell a soul, but she would. She'd blurt out something one day after a few drinks, and then be terribly apologetic and say she hadn't meant to, it had just slipped out.

Later that afternoon, leaving the others on the beach, she took herself off to the pool. It was cooler here; with lots of shady corners provided by the trees. It was quieter, too; the guests who stuck to the pool were the 'peace and quiet with a good book' type.

Although Daisy had a book, it might as well have been written in Martian. *I've got to do something to take my mind off all this. Something that needs total concentration and wears me out so utterly, I'll fall asleep the minute I hit the pillow.*

She gathered up her things again and went to the watersports shop. It was a little wooden hut at the far end of the beach, crammed with water skis, lifejackets, snorkels and masks. On the sand nearby lay a little catamaran, a Sunfish sailing dinghy, and two sailboards. The wooden door was half open, stable style, and music with a very West Indian beat drifted out.

The person on 'duty' was sitting back with his feet up on the door. He wore mirror sunglasses, chin-length dreadlocks and an utterly chilled-out smile. 'Hi, Daisy. How're you doin'?'

She started. 'How did you know my name?'

'I know everythin',' he grinned. 'What can I do for you?'

'I'd like to do some windsurfing.'

'You do any before?'

'I tried last year, in Turkey, but I couldn't get the hang of it. I'll need some lessons.'

'When you wanna go?'

As soon as possible. 'How about now?'

For the next hour she thought of nothing but trying to balance on that wretched board and pull the sail up without falling off instantly. Determined not to be beaten, she gritted teeth and strained muscles, in between trying not to laugh as her dreadlocked instructor issued helpful instructions with jokes thrown in, and tried to persuade her into a wild night out at the Harbour Lights, in Bridgetown.

'No!' she yelled, half laughing as she struggled to get the sail up. 'I told you – I'm being faithful to my boyfriend.'

With a chilled-out smile, he gave in. 'That's what I like to see. A woman faithful to her man, even if he stupid enough to let her loose in Barbados.'

214

God, what a hypocrite I am. 'I think my lesson time's up,' she told him, trying to sound brisk and no-non-sens-ish. 'I'll practise on my own for a bit.'

'OK, but not too far out. The wind stronger, out of the bay.'

'I'll be fine,' she assured him.

'Not too far, OK?' He was still holding on to the board. 'Know what my granny used to tell me? The sea have no back door.'

It was salutary to see a healthy respect for the sea under that chilled-out exterior. 'Don't worry; I'm the last person to get over-confident.'

'I'll be watchin' anyway.'

For another forty minutes she worked at it, going a little further each time, turning, coming back with the wind, and starting again. And somehow, all that virtuous exercise seemed to be blotting out her guilt. By the time she dragged the board up the beach, exhausted, it almost seemed that she'd imagined the earlier incident; a naughty, illicit fantasy borne of too much sun-warmed idleness.

Before the feeling wore off, she went to ring Simon. She had exhausted herself so thoroughly, it was a job not to fall asleep on her sunbed afterwards. It was even more of a job not to fall asleep later in between shower and dinner.

'I didn't see Nick all afternoon,' Tara said. Sitting at the dressing table, she was taming her hair with a hot brush. 'I wonder what he was up to?'

'I haven't a clue.' Daisy said drowsily, from the bed. She had been well aware of his conspicuous absence, but had been trying not to notice.

Tara changed the subject. 'Will you come with me to the wildlife reserve? I'd love to see the monkeys.'

'If you like. We can take the moke.' Since she was paying a third of the cost, she had got herself added to the insurance. Tara had forgotten to bring her driving licence, predictably enough.

'I asked Blair, but it's not really his scene,' Tara went on. 'They're leaving the day after tomorrow, anyway.'

'Yes, I gathered.' Trying hard to wake up, Daisy sat up and covered a yawn.

'So that only gives me two nights,' Tara went on, in demurely wicked tones.

I might have known. Tara had been with Blair a lot; sailing, snorkelling, never mind dancing after dinner. She hadn't been flirting the way she had with Nick, possibly because she had the sense to realize Blair would not be able to handle it like Nick.

'We're going to some club in Bridgetown after dinner,' Tara went on. 'And afterwards, what better than a nice little stroll down the beach? It'll be absolutely deserted at that time in the morning. Just him, me, and the Caribbean moon, tra-la . . .'

Daisy couldn't help thinking of another beach that had seemed absolutely deserted, at the time. 'Let's just hope some maniac insomniac jogger doesn't trip over you.'

'It's not that I want to do it in the sand,' Tara said, rather huffily. 'If you ask me, there should be a law against a man of that age having to share a room with his mother.'

I wish to heaven I was sharing with my mother. Then I wouldn't have to listen to you planning a roll in the sand

216

when I'm so desperately trying to put all such things out of my mind. 'I wouldn't have thought Blair was exactly your type. He's too quiet.'

'He's not that quiet when you get him on his own. I think he's rather sweet. And he's got lovely eyes.'

'You'll probably never see him again!'

'I might. Lincolnshire's not exactly the end of the world.' Tara released the last shining wave from the hot brush and started brushing it out. 'Not that I particularly care one way or the other.'

Suddenly, Daisy had to probe further. 'How can you not care? How can you just sleep with somebody once, and not care whether you ever see him again?'

'Quite easily.' Tara began applying the first of many coats of mascara. 'It's sometimes a disappointment anyway, so you don't want to see him. And if it's not, you've had the thrill without having time to get emotionally involved. Saves an awful lot of trouble, believe me. Besides, once I've bonked somebody the itch very often wears off. You sort of get them out of your system.'

The thought that sprang instantly to Daisy's mind appalled her so much, she banished it instantly. She gazed at Tara's darkly shining hair. 'I thought it was Nick you were after, a few days ago.'

'Daisy, do give me credit!' Tara put her mascara down and swivelled slightly on her chair. 'I'd hardly make a play for a friend of Ian's!'

'You were flirting like mad!'

'That was just mucking about. Just a laugh.' She returned to her make-up.

Daisy felt awful for assuming the worst. She had misjudged her, and why? Because of dog in the manger jealousy.

Bitch in the manger, you mean.

Feeling stiff from the unaccustomed strain on her muscles, she forced herself from the bed and dressed for dinner.

It was barbecue night; everything from suckling pig to the local spicy chicken stew. The white-clothed tables were strewn with cullings from the gardens; pink and red hibiscus with their shiny leaves, and red hot cats' tails like big furry catkins.

A chef in immaculate whites was searing steaks at a barbecue hot enough for Hades. Daisy joined the queue and found Nick right behind her.

'Sorry,' he murmured. 'I'm not following you on purpose.'

She already knew that. 'Where did you go, this afternoon?'

'Up to North Point. I watched the waves crashing and tried to think good and noble thoughts.'

Perversely, she felt more relaxed with him now it was all out in the open. The attraction was acknowledged, but nothing was going to happen. It was just one of those things you had to live with.

But even so, it wasn't easy to have him standing right behind her. He was wearing light beigey trousers and some olivey, lineny open-necked shirt that only intensified his eyes. *If* Cosmopolitan *ever ran a feature on 'Our Ideal Holiday Fling'* she thought, *he'd be the double-page spread*.

Especially when he did that funny little smile that did things to her insides. 'You're looking very fetching,' he

218

said, but in the tones he might have used to his granny. 'If you're not careful the chef'll have you up on the buffet too, with an apple in your mouth.'

She was wearing a halter-necked white dress, virtually backless, with a swirly skirt; her hair swept up in a loose knot, because of the heat.

But rather than acknowledge the compliment, she winced. 'Poor little thing,' she said, glancing at the little roasted piglet. 'I couldn't bring myself to have any.'

'I'm afraid I'm not so tender-hearted.' He glanced ruefully at his already-laden plate. 'I couldn't let it die in vain.'

'How on earth will you manage a massive steak on top of that lot?'

'I'll do my damnedest.' He gave a very wry, almost imperceptible wink. 'The general idea is to stuff myself so full of food, I have no appetite for anything else.'

How on earth can he joke about it?

What would you prefer? Tense, brooding resentment? Frustration as thick in the air as barbecue smoke?

She managed a rather wobbly smile. 'I just hope you won't be rolling around in agony tonight, with indigestion.'

'I hope I will. A good dose of gut-ache takes your mind off everything else.'

This was getting uncomfortably close to the bone, but before it could affect her, Marion breezed up behind him. Like the past few evenings, she and Blair were joining them for dinner. The first time had been at Tara's invitation; after that it had just seemed silly to let them eat alone when it was painfully clear that they were dying for company.

Over the meal it was soon obvious that Marion was none too keen on her son swanning off with Tara after dinner. She dropped heavy hints about them all going clubbing, until it looked as if Tara was about to say something very rude about mutton prancing about like lamb. Jane and Ian said tactfully that clubbing wasn't quite their scene any more, but they wouldn't mind a drink somewhere. Marion perked up, and Nick suggested a trip to St Lawrence Gap, where there was a picturesque little harbour to stroll around.

Blair's relief was obvious.

Daisy was glad of an excuse not to join them. 'I'm really shattered,' she said, with perfect truth, when they were all about to depart. 'I was hours on that windsurfer. I'm ready for bed.'

She avoided Nick's eye as she said it, but knew he understood perfectly.

Tara came up with her, to get the key. 'Why don't you go with them?' she demanded. 'It's so boring, going to bed so early and now Nick'll be landed with Marion all evening. She fancies him, if you ask me. Did you see her over dinner?'

'For heaven's sake, Tara, it wasn't exactly blatant. She just finds him attractive. Anybody would. Do you think you'll suddenly stop finding men attractive when you hit fifty? There are plenty of really old ladies who still drool over Sean Connery. My granny used to say she still felt eighteen.'

'She still ought to pick someone her own age. I wouldn't be a bit surprised if she doesn't start fluttering her eyelashes at poor Nick tonight and jiggling her silicone tits at him.'

'Tara!' She couldn't help laughing. 'Of course she won't!'

'I wouldn't put it past her. Poor Blair – I'd die if my mum carried on like that.'

Daisy was still laughing, albeit very wryly. 'I'm sure you'll console him very nicely.'

'You bet I will.' Tara gave a monumentally wicked wink. 'Give him one lovely memory to take home, poor boy. I have a feeling about Blair. Still waters, and all that . . .'

'Just don't eat him alive, that's all.'

As she finally got into bed, Daisy tried not to think about Tara's plans for the latter part of the evening. She thought about Simon, lying fast asleep with his alarm set for six-fifteen, and wondered if he'd ever do what she'd done, and if so, whether he'd tell her. And if he did, would she confess in her turn, or just be nobly forgiving and guiltily relieved that they were quits?

She thought about her mother lying fast asleep with Barney at the end of her bed, and couldn't help comparing her to Marion. Her mother never had that vaguely predatory gleam in her eye. There was a softness about her, a vulnerability, which was no doubt why she got hurt over and over again.

Poor Mum. At least Barney will never tell her he needs his 'personal space'.

And although she was trying hard not to, she thought of Nick.

'I know I'm not ready for commitment . . .'

I was right, wasn't I? He's a butterfly. Flitting from one blossom to another.

221

Yes, but at least he tried to keep a lid on it. He might even have succeeded, if you hadn't insisted on that long walk back down the beach.

Why ever did I?

You were thinking of your tan. Walking's the best way to get a good, even tan.

Was it really that? Or did I subconsciously just want to be alone with him for a bit?

Still wondering, she fell asleep.

The bedside clock said ten past three when Tara finally came back. 'You don't have to creep around in the dark – I'm awake,' she called, groping sleepily for the bedside light. 'Did you have a wild time?'

'Don't – even – ask!' With a voice like Thor the god of thunder on one of his grumpier days, Tara flung her bag on a chair and stomped into the bathroom.

Daisy was instantly wide awake. 'What happened?'

'I said, don't – ask!'

For a few minutes there was the sound of toothbrushes and bottles of cleanser being abused, taps being rammed on and off.

Daisy waited patiently. She knew Tara would spill the beans eventually, and probably before two more minutes had passed on the digital clock.

Eventually she emerged from the bathroom, ripped off all her clothes, threw them on the floor, and slipped on a short black nightie. Then she got into bed, but didn't lie down. She sat up, arms folded, her face a curious mixture of crossness and woe.

Daisy waited patiently.

'I ask you,' said Tara. 'I mean, I *ask* you.'

Oh, dear. 'Don't tell me – Marion had it all sussed. She was lurking down the beach to save her son from your predatory clutches.'

'Guess again.'

She thought. 'A terminal case of brewer's droop?'

'Worse.'

What could be worse, if you were Tara? 'Don't tell me he's gay and still hiding in the closet?'

'Not even that!' Tara's face was a mixture of shock and disbelief. 'He's a *Christian*! A born-again *Christian* who doesn't believe in sex before marriage! He's twenty-nine and he's never bloody *done* it! Not bloody *once*! Can you believe it?'

CHAPTER 11

Daisy couldn't help it – she started laughing hysterically.

'It's not funny!' Tara was on the verge of tears. 'I wouldn't have minded so much if he'd told me before. I mean, we were nearly there, and then suddenly he got cold feet and told me he was terribly sorry, he really wanted to, but he'd made a vow or something . . .'

Daisy wasn't laughing any more. How could she, when a certain scene of 'nearly there' was still so vivid? Whatever it was in her stomach that normally lurched, it was going one better with a vertical take-off worthy of a Harrier jump-jet. 'If he really was a virgin, it'd have been a disaster anyway.'

It wouldn't have been a disaster with Nick.

Stop it!

'That's not the point!' Tara sniffed, wiping her eyes. 'I really liked him, and he made me feel like some dirty old slapper from King's Cross.'

For an incredulous moment, Daisy wondered whether Tara was about to do a St Paulette on the road to Damascus; suddenly announce that she had

Seen The Light. 'He didn't start preaching at you, did he? About lusts of the flesh and – '

'Of course not,' Tara said irritably. 'If he had I'd just have laughed and thought he was a complete prat.'

Phew. Much as she'd like her to tone it down a bit, a born-again Tara was more than she could cope with.

'But he was so sweet and apologetic, I started feeling sorry for him, instead,' Tara went on. 'He said he hoped I didn't think he was pathetic, but he wanted to marry a virgin and they'd learn about sex together.' She made a brave attempt at a couldn't-care-less shrug. 'Makes you laugh, doesn't it?'

Poor Tara. Probably for the first time in her entire life she'd been turned down on moral grounds. The shock must have stunned her – like being told that she actually *had* been found under a gooseberry bush and all this stuff about pregnancy was just a gigantic con to scare girls into Not Doing It. 'It's his loss,' she said, rather too heartily. 'Doesn't know what he's missing.'

'Trust me,' Tara sniffed. 'Of all the blokes on the island, I have to pick the only born-again celibate. His mother hates all this religious stuff,' she went on. 'He was telling me on the way back. She pokes fun at him and tells him he's not normal. And the girls he goes out with are usually born-agains too – all sweet and virginal, I suppose – so she hates them on sight and puts them all off.'

'You'd have thought she'd be glad he went out with you, then.'

'She was. She just wanted to come, too. He said she just can't accept that she's not young any more. She spends a fortune on face-lifts and bum-lifts and tit-lifts.

She flirts with his friends and embarrasses the hell out of him. He won't bring them home, any more. I said why doesn't he leave home but he says he can't, she hasn't got anybody else. She's been through three husbands and the last one left her four years ago. For a younger woman, of course.'

'It's terribly sad.'

'I don't feel sorry for her a bit. Beastly, muttony old tart. She always had affairs, he told me. No wonder he's born-again. Kids always react against their parents.'

Like me, Daisy thought, with a pang of anguished guilt. *How awful to be determined not to be like your mother. She's not a muttony old tart – she's just one of those women fated to fall for the wrong man again and again.*

Tara sighed and slipped between the sheets. 'Poor Blair. I just hope it'll be worth it – all this saving himself. Can you imagine anything worse than two virgins on their wedding night?'

'I suppose it used to happen all the time.'

'A bit late to find out he's useless, isn't it? Mind you, you wouldn't know any different. Not that I can talk. I thought I knew Marcus.'

She turned on her side on the pillow. 'I knew there was something wrong after the first month or so. He never wanted to do it as much as I did. I began to think I was a nympho. I didn't realize he was having it off with half a dozen boyfriends on the side.'

Under the flippancy, Daisy knew it still hurt far more than she would ever admit. 'You've got to forget Marcus. You'll find somebody a million times better.'

'I don't want anybody. Not a permanent fixture, anyway. It's better like this, believe me. Unless you're really lucky, the bastards only screw you up or let you down. Look at your mother. Some people are just jinxed.' She turned the bedside light off. 'Night, Daise.'

'Night. Sorry I laughed.'

'It's OK.' After a moment she added, 'Don't tell anybody, will you? Jane'd just think it serves me right.'

Her voice was muffled, as if she was crying and trying not to show it. Daisy's heart went out to her. 'She wouldn't.'

'She would. I haven't told you anything, right? We just went out and had a brilliant laugh.'

'I won't say a word. Promise.'

Daisy ate hardly any breakfast. She saved all her toast, wrapped it in a plastic bag and a couple of hours later swam out to the raft.

Lying on her stomach, she broke it into tiny bits and dropped it in the water. Little blue and yellow fish swarmed in a boiling mass to the surface; gobbling and darting greedily at every morsel.

How nice to be a fish, she thought. *So uncomplicated. Just eat and make little fishes and try not to get eaten yourself. No worrying about your mother, or whether your mate will care if you had your eye on another fish. I really don't know why we've spent trillions of years evolving from things like you to have all these problems.*

The raft rocked gently as somebody climbed the steps. 'What are you doing?'

Oh, help.

It was Nick. She moved up a little bit, and dropped more toast in the water. 'Just thinking how nice it'd be to be a fish.'

He sat sideways, about three feet away. 'It'd be pretty boring.'

'Not necessarily. I read somewhere that fish only have a seven second memory.' *I wish I did. You'd never feel guilty about anything.* 'Every seven seconds, the whole world's new. Imagine that.'

He shook his head. 'That can't be right. Some fish have their own lair. Moray eels, for a start. How would they remember how to find it?'

'I don't know. Why do you have to complicate my nice uncomplicated theory?'

'Sorry.' His eyes were catching sun-glints off the water. 'Shall I go away and start again?'

No, just go away. You're too much too cope with at this time in the morning. 'I thought we were supposed to be keeping out of each other's way.' She wished instantly she hadn't said it. It was petty – as if she couldn't bear him near her. 'I'm sorry,' she added hastily. 'I suppose we can sit and natter for five minutes.' Injecting her voice with brightness, she changed the subject. 'So how was last night?'

'Fine. We wandered round the harbour, had a drink, and came back. I hope you didn't chicken out because of me,' he added.

'It wasn't you. I really overdid it on that windsurfer yesterday. I'm aching like mad today.' She was, too. 'It's like when you go ski-ing after a whole year – it kills you at first.'

Seeming satisfied with this, he changed the subject. 'What's up with Tara?'

'How do you mean?'

'She's not quite her usual self.' He nodded toward the beach, where Tara was just disappearing into the gardens. 'She was talking to Blair five minutes ago. He was about to take the Hobie Cat out, without her. She looked a bit upset.'

She followed his gaze. Blair was alone on the little catamaran, picking up speed as he caught the wind outside the shelter of the bay.

Oh, Lord. I hope it's not a case of 'Get thee behind me, Eve, and take thy beastly apple back to the greengrocer's.'

'Have they fallen out?' he went on.

She shrugged. 'I wouldn't know.'

'Did she have a good time last night?'

'Oh, yes. They had a brilliant laugh.'

'Well, it looks like something's happened.'

'You're a bit of a nosy old woman, aren't you?' she said lightly.

'I just don't like to see her looking upset.'

Spilling the beans just wasn't on, not after she'd promised. 'It's probably nothing. Knowing Tara, she's probably just found out he likes pulling the wings off daddy-long-legs. Or he's told her he's got to spend his last night with his mother.'

'Their last night's already arranged. We're all going to some *alfresco* place down the beach. She wouldn't take no for an answer.'

He lowered his voice a fraction. 'But I didn't come here to talk about Tara.'

Oh, Lord, I knew it. 'Nick, *please*. I really don't want to talk about it.'

229

The raft rocked gently as a speedboat passed nearby. It was Troy – waving as he went.

They both waved back, with happy-as-Larry smiles, as if they were chilled-out as a fresh lime sorbet.

'I know you don't,' Nick said. 'But we must.'

'Then that's where you're wrong. We mustn't.'

He turned to her. 'Let me translate that for you. What you really mean is, If we don't talk about it we can pretend it never happened and then maybe I'll actually believe it never happened and I can go back to my nice, cosy little relationship with Simon and keep on pretending I don't want anybody else.'

It hit the bullseye dead centre. She stood up jerkily.

'No, Daisy.' His hand on her wrist was as firm as his voice. 'You're going to sit down and hear me out.'

'Let – go!' She tried to wrench herself away. 'You have no right to – '

'I don't care.' His grip felt like a velvet-covered handcuff.

What was she to do? Fight him and have the whole beach witness it? Unsteadily, she sat. 'You can talk all you like. I'm not listening.'

'Then I'll talk to myself.' He relaxed his grip, but did not let her go. 'It's no use trying to kid yourself. You know what would have happened yesterday if that pair of Ancient Brits hadn't chosen that precise moment to go for their route-march. You were no more capable of slamming the brakes on than those fish were capable of refusing that bread.'

Do you have to remind me?

Willpower was no use against the dizzying sensations that came rushing back. As he no doubt knew all too well. 'It was toast.'

'Whatever it was, they couldn't get enough of it.'

Somehow she kept her voice cool, her eyes on the beach. 'How very gentlemanly of you to rub my nose in it.'

'I don't pretend to be a "gentleman". I'm just stating the facts you're trying to hide from.'

He paused. 'You want me as much as I want you.' His fingers on her wrist suddenly felt more like a whispered caress, and his voice wasn't much better. Or worse, depending on how you looked at it. 'So what are we going to do about it?'

Her stomach did another vertical take-off and crashed into her voicebox. The sounds that came out wobbled dreadfully. 'I seem to recall you saying that you're not the kind of bastard who sleeps with other people's girlfriends.'

'And I meant it. So I repeat, what are we going to do about it?'

It took a moment for the enormity of this to hit her. It hit her so hard, she half expected to see shock waves rippling from the raft. 'I thought you said you didn't want to wreck my current relationship.'

'And I meant it, at the time. I've been thinking a lot, since then.'

Keep calm. Don't let him see what a state you're in.

He knows, anyway.

Maybe not. He didn't know before. What did he say about you being a good actress? Bluff it out.

She turned to him, with what she hoped was a casually dismissive tone. 'Look, Nick, I think you've got the wrong idea somewhere. Yes, I find you attractive. I find a lot of men attractive, as it happens. What was the term you used? Passing fancies? I get a lot of passing fancies, but that's all they are, so don't get the idea that you're anything special. I've been away from Simon too long, that's all. I was thinking about him and wishing he was with me. I was sitting in that water thinking about what we'd be doing if we were together. As a man would so delicately put it, I was desperate for a really good seeing-to. And lo, there you were.'

For several seconds his eyes held her like twin green magnets. 'You know something?' he said at last, very softly. 'You're a liar. And a pretty hopeless one, at that.'

'Think that, if it makes you happy.'

A gentle splashing made her turn. Until they were nearly there, neither of them had noticed the elderly couple swimming up to the raft. They were both about seventy – the woman doing a nervous, head-up breast-stroke, to keep her hair dry – the man doing a side-to-side head-up crawl.

'All right, dear?' called the man, as the woman approached the steps.

'Just about, dear. It's further than it looks, isn't it?'

Nick stood up, took the woman's hand as she clambered up the steps.

'Thank you so much,' she panted. 'I didn't realize it was so far. I'm terribly puffed.'

Giving heartfelt thanks for the interruption, Daisy got up. With a casual, 'See you later', and barely a splash, she dived in.

It was on the way back that the aftershocks really hit her.

God, how I lied to him.

And all for nothing. He's not that stupid.

What do you mean, 'that' stupid? He's not stupid at all.

She even began to wonder whether she'd misunderstood. It would have been easy enough, the state she'd been in.

No, I didn't. He was telling me quite plainly I've got no business carrying on a supposedly monogamous relationship with Simon when I was barely a shiver away from rampant nookie with somebody else.

If it hadn't been for those Ancient Brits . . .

Like some dreadful virtual-reality in her head, the images zoomed back.

She swam faster, as if she could escape them, but they bore down on her like sharks scenting blood. Kneeling in that warm, silky water, his mouth, his hands . . .

Something lurched so violently, it made her gasp, swallow water, and start to choke. But it didn't stop the virtual-reality. Like a video tape, it moved on, to what might have been.

As her feet touched bottom, she half stumbled from knee-deep water.

Calm down.

She headed for the shower, just between the garden and the sand, and let the clear cool water wash over her. Jane and Ian were lying about ten yards away, in the shade, where she'd been lying half an hour ago.

'You were swimming like a bat out of a watery hell,' Ian said as she picked up her towel.

'I need the exercise,' she said, blotting her face and hair.

'No, you don't.' Jane yawned loudly. 'It's us that need the exercise but this place is making me lazier than ever. I really ought to go shopping – I've got so many wretched presents to buy. But I can't be bothered to get off the beach.'

'Buy them at the airport, love,' Ian said comfortably. 'There's bound to be shops full of everything.'

Jane yawned again. 'God, I must go for a swim or something. I'm exhausted already and it's only eleven o'clock. Where's Tara?'

'I'm just going to find her.' Daisy wrapped her sarong around her waist. 'See you later.'

I can't believe Jane hasn't noticed anything.

That's because she's not looking. If she suspected anything, she'd notice fast enough.

Trying to settle herself, she walked deliberately slowly through the gardens, barefoot over the coarse tropical grass. A pair of doves walked jerkily together, pecking at something in the grass. She thought for a poignant moment how her mother would have loved it here. The gardens were crammed with the kind of plants you only saw in greenhouses at home or as houseplants, only ten times bigger and lusher, making you feel sorry for their poor little relations crammed into pots at home. Round a shrub with red, bell-like flowers, a hummingbird hovered and darted on invisible wings, its body iridescent green.

Tara was not at the pool, nor was she at the shop, buying chocolate. And just as she was about to check their room, Daisy glanced up and saw her sitting on their balcony.

'What are you doing up there?' she called.

234

'Eating worms.'

She hadn't heard Tara say this for ages, but it had been familiar enough, years ago. *'Nobody loves me, everybody hates me, going down the garden to eat worms . . .'*

'I'm coming up.'

Their door was open, a pink-uniformed maid cleaning the room, which explained why Tara was sitting on the balcony.

Daisy went out, sliding the glass doors shut behind her. 'What is it?'

Tara did her best to smile. 'Just Blair being a prat. Anybody'd think I was about to rip his shorts off and rape him, the way he carried on. I only went up to say hi, and he'd hardly even look at me. He said he was just about to take the Hobie Cat out, and I said, "Can I come?" and he went all nervous and wouldn't look me in the eye and said maybe it'd be better if I didn't.' Although she was doing her best, her eyes misted with tears. 'I was only being friendly and he acted as if I was some she-devil sent to tempt him.'

For the moment, everything else was forgotten. Although she felt considerable sympathy for Blair, who had evidently seen Tara in her best man-eating mode and was expecting her to pounce again, she was cross with him, too. He should have realized that even Tara would never push it once she'd seen a red light. Removing a damp towel, she sat in the other rattan armchair. 'Like you said, he was just being a prat. Take no notice.'

'That's what I keep telling myself, but it's not very nice.'

When Tara was upset, there was only one way to get her out of it. 'Pious little prig. I hope he gets willy-rot. It's probably a shrivelled acorn, anyway.'

'It wasn't,' Tara said, but an embryonic giggle escaped her.

'I bet he has done it before. Only he was probably absolutely useless and the girl told him and that's why he's waiting to get married first. So it'll be too late for the poor cow to change her mind.'

Tara was beginning to erupt like her old self. 'He'll stick to the missionary position, of course.'

'Oh, of course. As Simon's father once said to him, "My boy, a gentleman always supports himself on his elbows".'

Tara choked. 'He didn't!'

'He did.'

They both collapsed into fits.

The maid slid the door open. 'Can I sweep the balcony?' she asked, in lovely, lilting tones, with a smile to match.

'Of course.'

Still in fits, they went inside and collapsed on the newly-made beds, instead.

As they gradually recovered, Tara said, 'I could murder some Fruit and Nut. Do you know, if it weren't for the calories, I think I'd almost rather have a bar of chocolate than a bonk.'

Daisy exploded all over again. 'Much less trouble. No wet patch.'

'And no worrying about little bars of chocolate coming along later.'

'More's the pity. You'd love that – stuff yourself with

half a pound of chocolate and a few months later you've got a litter of little mini-bars.'

'Brilliant. And at least you know what you're getting. You don't get a bar of Fruit and Nut telling you to sod off, it's saving itself.'

They went into another wave of fits, just as the maid came back with her duster and broom. 'I finish now,' she said, giving them rather dubious looks.

'Thanks very much,' they said together, and once the door had shut behind her, they exploded again. 'I hope she didn't think we were laughing at her,' Tara said guiltily.

'I doubt it. Probably just thinks we're mental. Never mind – we'll leave her a good tip.' Suddenly realizing that Tara had banished Nick from her mind for five whole minutes, Daisy stood up. 'Let's get out of here. Why don't we go to the wildlife reserve?'

'What, now?'

'Why not?'

It took them a mere five minutes to change into shorts and T shirts, and another five for Tara to pop to the shop for some fortifying chocoholic's delight.

Having left her plain baseball cap in their room, Daisy bought a pink one, saying 'I love Barbados', and threaded her swiftly plaited pony-tail through the hole at the back. 'Now I feel like a proper tourist,' she said with satisfaction.

'We have to eat it now, or it'll melt.' Tara passed her two already-softening squares as they wandered back to the beach. 'I hate to say it, but that's one department where men are better than chocolate. They can be hot and hard at the same time.'

They doubled up again, like a pair of schoolgirls sharing a smutty joke in the street. Daisy knew there was a hysterical edge to her laughter, but she didn't care. She laughed so much, she almost choked on a piece of hazelnut.

She was still laughing when they arrived at the little clutch of wooden sunbeds under the little thatched hut, and there her laughter abruptly died.

Ian was still exactly where she'd left him twenty minutes before. But Jane was gone, Nick sitting in her place.

Tensing right up inside, Daisy avoided Nick's eye altogether. 'Can I have the keys to the moke?' she asked Ian. 'We're thinking of popping over to the wildlife reserve.'

'Lord, I'm sorry, love.' Ian's face was as apologetic as his voice. 'Jane just took it. Went to look for presents at Sunset Crest.'

Oh, damn. 'Any idea how long she'll be?'

'She didn't say, but you know Jane. Could be hours, once she's started. I'm sorry, love. We had no idea you were planning anything.'

'It's my fault – we only just decided. We should have checked first.'

'What about a taxi?' Tara asked.

Old economies died hard. 'It'll cost a fortune. He'll be waiting hours. We could get the bus. It's only a dollar, anywhere on the island.'

'Bus?' Tara echoed, as if she'd suggested they go by penny-farthing. 'It'll take forever, all round the houses, stopping every five minutes . . .' She glanced at Nick. 'Can we borrow your moke?'

238

'For heaven's sake, Tara,' Daisy said irritably. I'm not insured for Nick's.'

Nick stood up and stretched slightly. 'I'm not doing anything special. I'll drive you over.'

Daisy gaped as if he'd suggested running over a few old ladies for a laugh. 'We want to go on our own!'

'Daisy!' Tara sounded almost shocked; a most unusual state of affairs. 'It's extremely sweet of you,' she said, standing on tiptoe to plant a kiss on his cheek. 'Take no notice of my ratbag friend. We accept your offer with a grateful thanks. Don't we, ratbag?'

Daisy was torn in half. She could hardly act like some sulky six-year-old and say she didn't want to go any more. But she felt like it. She'd been really looking forward to a girls' only trip with Tara. It was ages since they'd had a laugh like that, almost like the old days, and heaven alone knew she needed some light relief.

'It's very noble of him,' she said, with only a minute trace of tartness.

She might as well not have bothered, because nobody seemed to notice. Except Nick, of course – in a minute but telling flicker of his eyes. 'Give me five minutes to get changed – I'll see you in reception.' He added a little pat on the seat of Tara's shorts. 'Work out the route while you're waiting.'

At least she didn't have to sit in front with him. Tara was only too happy to have that dubious honour.

She wasn't so keen on the navigating bit. 'Daisy, you do it,' she said, after a couple of miles. 'The writing's so titchy, I can't see a thing. I think I need glasses.'

'Since when?'

'A few months now, only I'm too vain to get any.'

'Pass it over, then.'

Daisy was almost glad of something to take her mind off things, not that it worked very well. In between directing Nick through the myriad lanes that criss-crossed the island, she was thinking very uncomfortable thoughts.

You're being grossly unfair, getting mad with him. You just don't like hearing the truth.

But I don't want it to go any further, and he does.

Are you sure you don't?

She concentrated on the map, and the evocative names. Depressing, too, bringing back snippets from her guide books. Indian Pond, where a girl had drowned herself out of love. Hackleton's Cliff, where said Hackleton had committed suicide by riding his horse at full gallop over said cliff.

Bastard. Poor horse.

And Mount Misery. What had happened there? A few poor slaves hanged for trying to run away?

Not some stupid tourist hanging herself, anyway, because she's consumed with guilt. You really must get this thing in proportion. As human problems go, it's not even a fleabite. Think of all you've got going for you. A great job, enough money, a man who loves you and is working his guts out because he couldn't bring himself to let his colleagues down.

They climbed up over the backbone of the island again, into more rugged country, rocky gullies filled with a riot of vegetation.

'What are those trees?' Tara asked. 'They look a bit like a plant my mum's got in the conservatory.'

240

'I haven't a clue,' Nick said. 'Not bananas, anyway. Could be mangoes.'

'They're breadfruit,' Daisy said. 'They were brought here from the South Pacific as cheap food for the slaves. That's what the *Bounty* was carrying when they mutinied.'

Nick glanced over his shoulder. 'How did you know that?'

'I'm a mine of useless information.' In the interests of veracity she added, 'I've been reading a guidebook or two. I like to know a little bit about where I'm staying, apart from the price of a rum punch.'

That was one reason, anyway. Trying to distract myself from you was the other.

The country changed again, to rolling, windswept fields where cows grazed. The reserve was miraculously clearly signposted, so directions were hardly necessary. He parked; Daisy hung back a little as he and Tara strolled towards the rustic wooden entrance, and then wished she hadn't.

'Three adults, please,' Nick was saying, as she caught them up.

She whipped her purse out. 'I'll pay for myself, thanks.'

'Daisy, don't complicate matters.'

'I'm not complicating anything – I'd just rather pay for myself.'

'Then you're too late,' he said, pocketing his change. 'That's what comes of dawdling.'

'Lucky guy,' grinned a member of staff as they went through the turnstile. 'One girl not enough for you?'

What with one thing and another, Daisy was just in the mood for getting her own back. 'Don't tell anybody, but he's our grandfather,' she said, with a confiding smile. 'He's on these miracle monkey hormones. Nobody ever guesses unless they see him without his teeth in.'

The man broke into a rolling velvety chuckle, and Tara erupted into giggles. How Nick reacted she couldn't see, since she purposely wasn't looking.

'Come along, Grandpa.' Still giggling, Tara took his arm and lowered her voice to a hissy whisper. 'Let me know in plenty of time if you need to *go*, won't you?'

Just to be awkward, he showed not the slightest signs of irritation. 'I want me tea,' he quavered, in a crotchety old voice. 'I don't want to see no piddling monkeys. I want me tea and a biscuit. I can feel one of me turns coming on.'

Tara exploded, and despite her best, cross efforts, Daisy found herself forming a cross, reluctant smile.

The sun was very hot, but twisty little paths wove between shade-giving trees and shrubs. The first resident they saw was a large and very purposeful-looking tortoise with red markings on its shell. Moving faster than any tortoise Daisy had ever seen, it was heading for the undergrowth, its leathery, reptilian neck stretched to its fullest extent. It looked for all the world like a ninety-year-old desperate to get to the pub before closing time.

'Looks a bit like you, Grandpa,' Tara giggled, still hanging on to Nick's arm. 'Before you had your monkey treatment, that is.'

242

'No respect,' he quavered. 'In my day, young trollops who cheeked their elders got a good old-fashioned – '

'What's that noise?' Tara stopped on the path, frowning. 'Listen!' An odd, clacking noise was coming from the undergrowth.

Together they peered through the tangled branches.

My God, Daisy thought. *Even here, you just can't get away from it.*

Tara exploded into fits.

Quite unconcerned with their audience, a pair of tortoises was energetically ensuring the patter of tiny tortoise feet for future generations.

'As if there isn't enough of it on the television,' said Nick, quite deliberately mimicking the Ancient Brits who'd interrupted them the day before.

Daisy flushed furiously, and Tara erupted again.

'And they call this wholesome family entertainment,' Nick tutted. 'Dear me.' Sandwiched between them, he put a hand round each of their shoulders and over their eyes. 'I can't have my grand-daughters corrupted. I'll have you know I take my responsibilities very seriously.'

Volcano Tara was still erupting helplessly.

Daisy wriggled free of his arm. 'I really don't know what we were gawping at. If a pair of tortoises can't do what comes naturally with without a load of moronic humans sniggering . . .'

'It was just the shock!' Tara said, sounding hurt. 'I wonder if there are any babies? I'd love to see some babies.'

They carried on down the twisty path, belatedly realizing that midday was not a good time to come. Most of the residents seemed to be taking siestas.

Tortoises were everywhere, however; some charging around like the first, others munching at the odd bit of grass that lined the path.

Tara befriended one, tickling it under its chin until it stretched out its wrinkly old neck in obvious ecstasy.

Daisy stood back a little in the shade, watching. And after a moment or two, Nick strolled back to stand beside her. 'I didn't come just to annoy you.'

'I didn't think you did.'

He cast her a sideways glance, one hand thrust in the pocket of his shorts. 'Like I said, you're a hopeless liar.'

'All right, so I did. Can you blame me? You're not exactly sticking to the rules.'

'I'm not sure I understand your rules. That was what I was trying to work out before you ran away.'

'I swam. And I don't want to discuss it any more. There's nothing to discuss.'

'Why do you keep saying that? His voice was very low, almost inaudible. 'Because you think you'll eventually believe it?' Although he wasn't touching her, he was so close he might as well have been. The tension was palpable, like a restless, erotic ghost hovering between them.

'What are you afraid of?' he asked, very softly.

Her eyes were still on Tara. 'Nothing,' she said. 'Especially not you, so don't flatter yourself.'

'You know what I think?' he mused, more softly still. 'I think it's yourself you're afraid of. Or rather, your alter ego. She's a shockingly naughty girl, that other

244

Daisy. She wants to say "what the hell" and do shockingly naughty things. And you're just terrified of letting her out again.'

Although her heart was beating like Afro drums, she wasn't going to show it. She turned to him, thanking heaven for the person who invented sunglasses. 'If we're talking egos, let's talk about yours. It's a super-deluxe king-size, isn't it? And like most men's egos, connected directly to your dangly bits. And it just can't bear being turned down.'

CHAPTER 12

It was a moment before he spoke. 'What do you want me to say? That sex has nothing to do with it?'

She said nothing.

'Do you want me to tell you I'm in love with you?'

Her heart gave a savage little twist. 'I wouldn't believe you if you did.'

'I'm not going to lie to you. I've told you how I feel. Something about you just gets to me. And yes, I want you. I want you like mad.'

He was doing it on purpose, she could swear. As if he knew that merely hearing it made her stomach lurch for England.

I'd rather you lied. I'd rather you employed all the rotten, sleazy lies men have used ever since Ug lured Og back to his cave. I can despise a liar.

Oh, if only Jane hadn't taken the other moke.

Everything was conspiring against her, even the warm, humid air was sapping her defences. Ever since they'd left the hotel she'd been trying not to look at him; trying not to see the chest so carelessly exposed by his unbuttoned shirt, the strong, tanned arms and legs . . .

'Speak to me, Daisy.'

In the still, birdsonged air the scent of him wafted to her – nothing from a bottle this time, just warm, clean male and freshly washed shirt . . .

'What's the point?' Somehow she kept her voice steady, her eyes on Tara. 'You don't listen. I've told you I don't want to talk about it, but you keep on and on . . .'

'What do you expect me to do? I can't turn this thing off, not now. I'm not a bloody machine.'

'Try,' she said unsteadily. 'Have a cold shower.'

Just as she was about to move away, the tension was broken for her. An American family with two little children was coming up the path. They stopped barely two yards away, where another tortoise was attacking a little clump of grass with patient deliberation; opening its toothless jaws wide, taking aim, and snapping them shut over its lunch.

'Wow, look at the turtle!' exclaimed the mother. 'Isn't he cute? Just like ET.'

The children descended on the tortoise, who did not, however, want to share a warm, interactive experience with two under-fives. He withdrew all extremities forthwith and prepared to sit out the assault. So they bounced up to Tara's shelly friend instead, who apparently felt just the same about dear little children.

'Poor kids,' Tara sighed, coming to join them. 'He doesn't want to play. He liked me, though. I think I found his G spot.'

Must you talk about G spots?

Tara linked arms with Nick again, and they strolled on. The path wasn't wide enough for three abreast, and just as well.

Daisy's mind was a tortured mass of guilt. It was no use kidding herself she'd been wholeheartedly thankful for the interruption. Part of her, she knew, had been revelling in the illicit thrill of being close to him, hearing him say he wanted her like mad. Part of her had almost wished they were alone again, with only the animals to see them. Part of her had even wished for more.

In the torrid heat, her imagination soared into steamy stratospheres. He would take her roughly in his arms and tell her he was sick of her hypocritical pretence. He would fling aside her protests as easily as her clothes, which he would fling into the bushes, and –

My God, what's happening to me? Practically fantasising about being 'taken'? Am I turning into one of those women who like a bit of rough?

To realize that that was exactly what she did want shook her rigid. No ritual; no deliciously teasing eye contact over a candlelit dinner, no twenty minutes' foreplay, just swift, devastating –

'Daisy, are you listening?'

She crash-landed instantly. 'Sorry?'

'I was saying that tortoise reminded me of poor old Percy,' Tara said, over her shoulder. 'Percy used to like his chin tickled, remember?'

Nick glanced back at her. 'Percy?'

'His full name was Percy Bysshe Shelley,' she replied, just as if tortoises were the only things in her head.

'After the poet,' Tara added unnecessarily.

'*Ode to the West Wind*, and all that. Daisy and her mum sort of inherited Percy from the old lady who'd

248

lived in the cottage before. She'd had him for yonks – found him scoffing weeds in her garden in 1962 or something and couldn't very well take him since she was moving to an old people's home. I really don't see why not. I'm sure he'd have been a lot less trouble than the human residents. Just a bit of lettuce now and then.'

'He didn't like lettuce much.' Daisy had scarcely thought of poor old Percy in ages. 'He preferred dandelions and dead pansies and tomatoes. He loved tomatoes. The juice used to dribble down his chin.'

'But he died,' Tara went on. 'Daisy used to hibernate him in a box of hay in the shed, all snuggled up, and one spring we went to see if he'd woken up and he was dead. Very dead,' she went on, in her own spade-calling way. 'And the rats had been at him. Daisy cried buckets. We gave him a full funeral in the garden. We sang *All Things Bright and Beautiful, All Creatures Great and Small*, and my beastly brother Tom sang All Reptiles Vile and Foul, and she was so upset she kicked him in the whatsits.' She started giggling. 'And that wiped the grin off his face, I can tell you. It was a rather disorderly funeral, after that.'

Ducking under an overhanging branch, Daisy thanked heaven after all for Tara's daft conversation. As a distraction, it could scarcely be beaten.

Nick cast her another over-the-shoulder glance. 'I wouldn't have thought you had violent tendencies.'

'Now and then,' she said casually. 'When required.'

Blithely oblivious, Tara went on, 'She actually meant to kick him in the stomach but she missed. Served him right, if you ask me. He was writhing around on the grass yelling, 'Me nuts! Me nuts!' and Daisy kept saying, 'What does he mean, nuts?' She was only ten, poor old Daise, and what with no male family members, if you'll pardon the pun, her education was a tad hazy in some departments.'

One thing about Tara, Daisy thought despairingly, was that you could always absolutely rely on her to dredge up the most embarrassing moments of your life in front of the very last person you wished to hear them. Never mind always managing to draw the conversation round to something vaguely connected to nookie. Who else would manage to get from tortoises to nuts in one easy step?

But Tara hadn't finished. 'So I set about educating her,' she giggled, as they followed the path through the shrubby undergrowth. 'I drew a lovely little picture – I was really good at art, you know – and I labelled it beautifully, saying "willy" with "penis" in brackets, and "nuts" with "testicles" in brackets – I was frightfully proud of knowing the proper words, only I think I spelt it test*a*cles. Anyway, it would have been a wonderful biology lesson only unfortunately it was in the middle of a history lesson and we started giggling and Miss Grove – a right old hag, she was – said, "Tara Wentworth, what are you doing?" And I said, "Nothing, Miss Grove", and of course her beady little eyes lit right up and she came and snatched it up and nearly had heart failure.'

She was cracking up by now, and so, by the look of his shoulders, was Nick. And despite everything, Daisy found herself rather desperately joining in. If nothing else, it eased her tension. They rounded a corner in the path and found themselves by a little pond. There was a little bench there, and on this she and Tara collapsed in fits.

Still laughing, Nick tossed a tiny pebble into the pond. 'Any teacher who had to cope with you two has my profound sympathy.'

Something stirred in the still green water, poking out a very reptilian snout. Tara jumped. 'My God, it's an alligator!'

'It's a cayman,' Daisy said, having glanced at the leaflet-guide. 'Looks a bit like Miss Grove, don't you think?'

They erupted all over again.

Miss Grove stared disapprovingly for a moment or two and sank again, leaving only her nostrils showing.

'You didn't finish the saga,' Nick said. 'I'm on tenterhooks. Did you have to sit on the naughty seat for a week?'

Tara exploded.

Daisy had to hand it to him. Only a psychic would ever have suspected the previous conversation. *And if you can do it* . . . 'It was ridiculous,' she said lightly. 'We were made to feel like a pair of dirty little beasts and our parents were called in. It more or less blew over after my mother explained that Tara was only trying to fill me in on certain things, but they never looked at us quite the same after that.'

'And Samantha Cartwright wasn't allowed to play with us,' Tara reminded her. 'Her parents thought we were bad influences.'

'We never liked her anyway. She used to pinch and tell tales.'

251

Tara consulted her guide. 'Where are the monkeys? I'm dying to see them.' She stood up and marched on.

From behind, Daisy noticed that her white cut-offs barely covered her squidgy bits, and how unbelievably brown her legs were. With them she wore a shocking pink crop-top – shocking pink was Tara's favourite colour, appropriately enough. Why is there no shocking blue? she wondered. Or shocking green?

She felt colourless by comparison; in practical, navy shorts, beautifully cut though they were. With them she wore a short-sleeved white shirt, tied at the midriff. And after the mahogany forest, sturdy trainers with socks.

As they came to the end of the leafy paths, past huge aviaries where parrots screeched, and into the sun, Daisy was suddenly very aware of several things. First, it was unbelievably hot. Second, she'd had only a glass of mango juice and a coffee for breakfast, third, that her fleeting fantasy had left very trembly aftershocks, and fourth, that these combined factors were making her feel she might very well pass out.

Don't be ridiculous. You've never passed out in your life. You're doing the wallyette bit again – wanting to swoon delicately so he can sweep you up in his strong, muscly etc. etc. . . . .

God forbid. She recalled a friend at work who had fainted at a very hot, crowded airport in Greece. And sure enough, she had found herself in the arms of some incredible, tanned hunk with eyes like black olives and a smile to die for.

'Would have been the best bit of the entire holiday,' she'd sighed. 'Only unfortunately, I'd wet myself.'

What a nightmare. To distract herself from this and everything else, Daisy read the leaflet she'd picked up at the entrance. The monkeys had their own area; a grove of large trees with a path around them. 'They're descended from the African Green monkey,' she read aloud. 'But in a few hundred years they have evolved into a distinct species and are considered a pest by farmers.'

Several dark, cheeky faces peered at them from the branches; a large male, several juvenile delinquents and a mother with a baby clinging to her chest.

Tara whipped a packet of peanuts in their shells from her bag. 'I bought these from an old lady on the beach. I'm not really that keen, but I bet they will be.'

'I'm sure you're not supposed to feed them!' Daisy pointed out.

'Oh, stuff. It's not as if I'm giving them chewing gum.'

'Yes, but – '

'Daisy, don't fuss,' Nick cut in. 'If anybody says anything, we'll plead ignorance. Rules are made to be broken,' he added, with deceptive casualness. 'Of such is the spice of life. The salt on the egg. The Worcester sauce in the Bloody Mary.'

Never mind the nearly-nookie in the sea . . .

Sweetly oblivious, Tara held up some nuts on her outstretched palm and before long, a bolder monkey darted down and snatched them. From the safety of the tree, he ate greedily, scattering shells everywhere. As soon as they were gone, he returned for more.

Emboldened by this, the baby-toting mother followed suit. Her infant's eyes were huge and sad in a wizened little face, making Daisy long to cuddle it.

At Tara's request she took several photos, but eventually realized that her wilt-sensations were not just due to a subconscious desire to faint and be swept up, etc. etc. 'I've got to get out of the sun,' she said, handing the Nikon to Nick.

She made her way back towards the entrance, where a round, thatched, African-style roofs kept the sun from gift shop and cafe. She chose a few postcards, bought a cola, ordered a toasted sandwich, and sat in the blissful shade.

She wrote 'Dear Simon,' and stopped. Putting her her fingers to her temples, she felt suddenly weak, and not just from heat and lack of food.

She stared at the blank postcard again, imagining for one awful minute writing the awful truth.

'Dear Simon, It's all very well being noble and self-sacrificing, but if you'd put us first I wouldn't be in this mess. I have to tell you that I was very nearly unfaithful to you the other day, with Nick. There's some colossal electricity between us and I'm not sure I can resist it much longer. Would you mind awfully if I did it with him, just once? You can fax me at the hotel, yes or no. I still really love you, but quite frankly, I'm beginning to think it's the only way to get him out of my system. I'll absolutely hate myself afterwards, and I'll probably hate him, too, but . . .'

She laid her pen down, leaned her elbows on the wooden table and put trembling fingers back to her temples.

My God, how can I even think it?

'You OK, dear?' asked a lilting voice.

It was the waitress, with her sandwich. 'More or less,' she said lightly, forcing a smile. 'Just the heat and no breakfast.'

'Why no breakfast?'

It wasn't the waitress this time.

Daisy tensed up instantly, but said nothing until the waitress had departed. There was nobody else near, only a party of Germans a couple of tables away. 'Will you please go away?' she asked, in a low, tense voice.

'You're not OK, are you?'

No, and I never will be while you're around. 'I'm fine. Please, go back to Tara.'

'Tara's quite happy. She's nattering to an equally monkey-loving couple from Yorkshire. Apart from which, you're not the only one in need of rehydration.'

He went to the counter, bought a mineral water and came back. He sat opposite, sucking noiselessly through a straw.

Daisy started to eat her sandwich.

He was watching her all the time. Even under the sunglasses she could feel it and tension turned her sandwich to wood chips in her mouth. Eventually she said, 'If you've just come to start all over again you can forget it.'

'I came to see if you were all right.'

Yeah, right. 'Of course I'm all right.'

She finished the first half of the sandwich and pushed the rest away. Although it was perfectly nice, she just wasn't hungry any more. She took a suck of her cola and started scribbling a postcard.

'Who are you writing to?' he asked.

'My mother.'

'Why wouldn't she come?'

'She didn't want to leave the dog. She's only just got him and she thought it'd unsettle him.'

'*Dear Mum*,' she wrote. '*You'd love it here – if I ever come back I'm going to bring you. The flowers are just gorgeous – I'll get you some hibiscus cuttings from the gardens. We're at the wildlife reserve and Tara's feeding peanuts to the monkeys. I'm having a brilliant time, except –* '

She looked up. 'Will you please stop looking at me?'

'There's nothing else I want to look at.'

'Go and look at the monkeys.' She carried on writing. '*– except for Simon not being here, of course – sometimes I think he's a workaholic –* '

'Maybe I should have brought my mother,' he said, in a sarcastic tone she'd never heard him use. 'If we'd both brought our mothers this whole thing might have stayed at the recipe stage; just the ingredients assembled on the kitchen table, instead of every pan burnt and an awful mess all over the kitchen.'

With monumental self control, she didn't even look up. 'Speak for yourself. I clear up my mess as I go along.' '*. . . Give Barney a cuddle for me –* '

'You'd like to clear me up, wouldn't you?' he went on. 'A good squirt of that stuff that kills all known messes stone dead and bingo, the kitchen's all sparkly clean enough for Simon to eat his dinner off the floor.'

'*. . . love, Daisy, XXXX*.' She started furiously scribbling the address. 'I never wanted you in the kitchen in the first place. I wish you'd get the hell out.'

With unsteady fingers she fumbled in her purse for stamps and stuck one on. She began writing another card, not even knowing who it was going to. It was either that, or look him in the eye.

'If I thought you really meant that, I'd back off now,' he said.

Her heart and stomach twisted painfully. She put her pen down. And unless she put her foot down too, he was going to go on and on for ever. If not now, somewhere, sometime later.

It was easier here, in a relatively public place. With the solid wooden table between them, the waitress not far away and the Germans talking cheerfully, she felt more secure, more controlled than before. 'Will you get one simple fact into your thick head? Whatever happened yesterday, it was a one-off. I was caught off guard. There's more to a relationship than sex, and I'm not going to jeopardise what I've got for some fleeting excitement. Because that's all it would be. I've never wanted that kind of relationship. I can't handle them, and I certainly couldn't handle a fling. I couldn't cope with the guilt.'

He said nothing.

Feeling more confident, she went on, 'I know we can't forget what happened, but I'd be profoundly grateful if you don't refer to it ever again.'

It was ages before he spoke. 'Is that what you really want?'

'How many times do I have to say it? Do you want it in writing?' On an impulse she did just that. took up a postcard, scribbled,

'*Dear Nick,*
FORGET IT!
Daisy.'

and shoved it across the table. 'OK?'

As he took it, his mouth gave a tiny, sardonic twist. 'No kiss?'

She snatched it back, scrawled a huge 'X' and shoved it back at him. 'Satisfied?'

For a long time he was silent. She could have sworn he was about to say something like, 'Take those sunglasses off, look me in the eye, and say it again.' She was so certain he was going to say it, she was girding her eyes up for the coolest impassive grey they could muster.

And all for nothing.

He tucked the postcard in his breast pocket. 'Aren't you going to eat that sandwich?'

Slightly shaken, she shook her head. 'No.'

'Pass it over, then. I hate to see good food go to waste.'

In the late afternoon, Daisy removed the daggerboard from her windsurfer and dragged it up the beach, exhausted. The wind had picked up and it had needed all her concentration and muscle power to stay on board, never mind turning and coming back. But she felt exhilarated by her efforts. She had gone much further, and had actually started to feel a modicum of confidence.

Dreadlocks came to help her. 'You be in the Olympics soon,' he grinned. 'You comin' on great.'

'I'm a little less hopeless,' she agreed. 'I'll go again tomorrow.'

She went straight to the beach bar for two lime squashes, drank one at once, and took the other to the beach beds where Jane was lying. Jane seemed to be surgically attached to that beach bed. If she even swam to the raft, it was a miracle.

'It made me tired just watching you,' she yawned. 'All these people with manic energy – Nick's another one, out on the Hobie Cat like a demon . . .'

Daisy had seen him go, with Ian. He had whipped out of the bay, picking up speed with the wind, and raced north with one hull out of the water.

'I didn't know Nick could sail,' she said.

'Oh, yes. He used to do a lot in Cornwall, apparently. I hope he brings Ian back in one piece.' She sat up and adjusted the back of the slatted wooden bed. 'So how was the wildlife thingy?'

'Oh, fine. Masses of monkeys, so Tara was pleased. And then we went for lunch to a hotel at Crane Beach – it was beautiful, like a Roman villa.' She wished to heaven she'd been in a better frame of mind to enjoy it. It had been a nightmare – trying to seem casually relaxed while her insides were a mass of guilty confusion.

'Tara's found some more company,' Jane observed, scanning the beach. 'She seems to have gone off Blair. I suppose he's a bit quiet, for her.'

'Just a bit.'

Tara was on the raft, with two or three men Daisy had not noticed before. There was a lot of noise wafting across the water, and not just Tara's giggles, either. There was male laughter, too.

'They're Italian,' Jane said. 'Only arrived today. They look really good fun.'

Things are looking up for Tara, then. Daisy sat back on the sunbed Ian had vacated, and let her eye take in a wide-angle view of the scene. The days were going so fast, she wanted to imprint it on her brain for the miserable winter days still to come.

I could have had such a lovely time here, she thought. She gazed at the beach that curved gently to the right, and the bay after that, curving into the distance. She would remember the feathery casuarinas that trimmed the beach. She'd remember the placid turquoise sea, the little waves lapping, the coo of doves in the trees, and the whistling cry of the cheeky black birds that hovered beadily around the beach terrace, waiting to steal leftovers the minute you got up. She would remember the glorious riot of flowers, the tiny hummingbirds, and the bats that flitted in the dusk. She would remember that unbelievable sunset, the liquid gold on the water, the chirps of tree frogs and the lilt of soft steel bands. She would remember the soft, caressing night breeze, the heat of midday, and the bliss of getting into the air-conditioning. She would remember the monkeys and tortoises and Dreadlocks, and the beach barman who danced as he mixed a cocktail to blow your head off.

And Nick.

Very apt name, when you think about it. I wonder if the devil was called Young Nick when he was young?

He was a fallen angel, so he must have been nice once. I can just see how it might have started.

For heaven's sake. Father Christmas is a Nick, too, only with Saint added.

Nick's no saint.

Neither are you.

She thought about the fleeting fantasy she'd had at the wildlife reserve. Now she could think more rationally, it was easily explained.

*It was your subconscious, wanting him to force you.
Then you could say to your conscience, 'It wasn't me. He
made me do it.'*

*Gosh, I'm wasted in marketing. I should have been a
shrink.*

She turned over and lay on her stomach. The sun was
lovely now, not too hot, just right for dozing in.

Vaguely she heard Marion come and sit for a while,
talking about dinner and what time she'd booked the table
for, and had Jane tried the beauty parlour, they'd just done
her a great pedicure. Vaguely she heard Tara come and say
she was going to some scuba diving centre with the Italians
and to tell Daisy she'd be back in plenty of time for dinner.

The next thing she knew, Jane was tapping her on the
shoulder, saying, 'Wake up, Daisy, you can't miss the
sunset. I've got you a little reviver.'

Feeling almost drugged, her face damp and hot from
lying on the towel, Daisy struggled to sit up. Nearly
everybody was gone from the beach; there was just Jane
and two or three couples sitting in the sand.

She sipped the rum thing Jane had given her. The
alcohol kick-started her immediately, but there was
plenty of lime juice, too, and sugar to balance it.

The sea was liquid gold, the sky burning orange, a
few clouds black on the horizon. A ski boat whizzed
past, the skier silhouetted back against the water. And
drifting into the bay on a breeze like a whisper, came a
Hobie Cat, its sails dark against the sky.

'And about time too,' Jane said. 'I was beginning to
wonder where on earth they'd got to.'

They watched as Nick steered it on to the sand. He
stepped from the canvas deck to one white hull and

261

thence to the beach. Together with Ian, he pulled it up on to the dry sand.

'Must weigh a ton,' Jane commented. 'That's the best exercise Ian's had since we've been here.'

Ian strolled up cheerfully. 'Quite a wind, further out,' he said. 'Nick had it going at practically ninety degrees to the vertical. I nearly needed a change of shorts.'

'Don't be disgusting,' Jane tutted. 'If you're going to the bar, get me another rum thingy, will you?'

Daisy sat back, sipping her reviver through a straw, and watching Nick furl the sails. In the failing light, he looked as dark as one of the locals. One or two tree frogs were waking up; chirping to their lazier brethren to get moving. Tiny waves lapped on the shore.

The 'paradise' epithet was not overdone, she thought. No wonder people came here to get married. She thought of Simon, and how she'd thought he'd planned to propose on Valentine's Day, and how Valentine's Day had actually turned out.

Something tugged painfully at her heart.

Ian came from the bar with the drinks and perched on the end of Jane's sunbed. The beach guard had taken the cushions off all the unoccupied ones, leaving hard wooden slats.

Nick strolled up, said 'Cheers' as Ian handed him a beer, and tapped Daisy's calf. 'Move up.'

She drew her knees up, giving him enough room to sit on the end.

For a while they sat just watching the dying sun.

Nick half turned to her. 'I saw you, on the windsurfer. You were going well.'

'She went miles out,' Jane said. 'I was getting in a bit of a tizz. She went so far you couldn't see her at all when she fell off. I went and told Dreadlocks, but he was keeping an eye on her.'

'I was perfectly all right,' Daisy said. 'There was nothing to get in a tizz about.'

'Yes, but what if you hadn't been? What if he'd forgotten?'

'Then it would have been a nice cheap way to get to Antigua.'

'They don't want to lose tourists,' Nick said. 'These watersports guys have all got eyes in their backsides.' He half turned to Daisy again. 'I don't suppose we could lose you even if we wanted to.'

'Thanks a lot!'

'What a very unchivalrous remark,' Jane tutted. 'You'll have to make up for it tonight. I don't think I've seen you dance with Daisy once since we've been here. I realize you're probably terrified of Simon thrashing you to death when we get back, but I absolutely insist that you dance with her at least once tonight. Marion permitting,' she added wickedly.

Jane, please . . .

'I wouldn't dare,' he said, lazily enough to fool anybody. 'I've always had a thing about long silky hair. I can even get turned on by an Afghan hound.'

Jane was cracking up.

'Add the Caribbean moon factor and a few beers and I'm liable to go seriously out of control,' he went on. 'Turn into a raging mass of lust and forget she's spoken for.' He took another suck at his beer. 'I don't want to get my face slapped. I can't stand pain.'

'He's a terrible baby,' Daisy retorted, trying to ignore the havoc-wreaking images he had created. 'You should have seen the fuss he made when he stepped on that titchy little urchin.'

'Watch it.' Just as if she were Tara in her best flirt-mode, he grabbed her ankle and started tickling the sole of her foot.

If he thought he was going to get his own back by making her do a giggly bimbo, he was disappointed. She hated having her feet tickled – it made her think of the more subtle kind of torture. 'Stop it!' She aimed a sharp, toe-first kick at his ribs. It was a lot sharper than she intended.

With a muttered curse, he let her go. 'You vicious little . . .'

'That'll larn yer.' Jane was giggling in a way that made Daisy wonder how many sundowners she'd got through since Happy Hour started. 'She's secretly miffed that you spurn her and dance with Marion, instead. Isn't that right, Daisy?'

'Heartbroken. I cry myself to sleep every night.'

With her mischievous wooden spoon, Jane carried on stirring. 'So you must remedy that tonight, Nicholas Heartbreak Trevelyan. Would you not agree with me, dearest Ian?'

'Absolutely, love.' Ian was leaning comfortably against her knees. 'Blokes like us – all heaving with the answer to every maiden's prayer – have a duty to spread ourselves around. I shall do my bit by dancing with not only Daisy, but Tara and Marion and any other deprived creature who catches my noble and self-sacrificing eye. And if any of them forget themselves

264

and grope me during the smoochy ones, I shall stiffen my upper lip and take it like a man.'

With Jane giggling like an elderly aunt who's been at the cooking sherry and Nick chuckling like brown velvet, Daisy found herself joining in.

Jane's hands crept around to his lower stomach. 'If you're very good, I'll grope you during the smoochy ones.'

'Jane, behave yourself.' Pretending to be shocked, he pushed her hands away.

She responded with a wicked grin, her fingers tiptoeing down over his stomach like naughty spiders. 'I'm coming to get you, big boy . . .'

Ian made a grab, Jane shrieked, and two drinks went flying into the sand. A mock fight ensued, ending with Ian throwing Jane over his shoulder and running down to the sea. There was a massive splash, and a lot of shrieky laughter as various unseen liberties were obviously taken underwater.

Gradually the laughter died away. In the dark, rippling water they stood locked in a chest-deep clinch.

Daisy looked away, not just because she suddenly felt like a Peeping Tomette, but because something had caught at her heart. They were so in tune with each other, so perfectly at ease . . .

She felt suddenly isolated, and terribly lonely.

It was suddenly very dark, very quiet, with only the lap of waves and the tree frogs. From somewhere in the distance came an echo of laughter. On the horizon, the lights of a massive cruise ship winked as it headed for islands new.

Nick was not touching her, though if he'd moved back four inches, he would have been. He was still gazing at the water.

'I'm sorry I kicked you,' she said unsteadily. 'I just hate having my feet tickled.'

'I'll live.' He didn't turn or even move his head.

She sucked the last, melted-ice dregs of her drink. 'I'd better go. Shower and wash my hair . . .'

'You can drop these at the bar on the way.' He retrieved Jane's and Ian's glasses from the sand. 'Make yourself useful.'

She slung her beach bag over her shoulder and took the sandy glasses. 'See you later.'

'Bye.'

As she left the beach, she turned her head fleetingly. Jane and Ian were coming back, arm in arm, laughing as they strolled up the sand. Nick had moved into the space she'd vacated. Hands linked behind his head, he was facing the shimmering water.

Of one thing she was sure. Certain matters were now so thoroughly closed, the files might as well go in the shredder.

And I should, therefore, be rejoicing. And I am. But not half as much as I should be.

CHAPTER 13

After the warmth outside, her room felt like a freezer. Feeling guilty for wasting electricity by leaving the air-conditioner on, she switched it off and ran a bath, adding Invigorating Essence of Seaweed bubbles.

The image of Jane and Ian was still vivid in her mind. She wondered what Jane would do in her place, and suddenly knew that Jane would never have got into this situation in the first place. She'd have told Ian from the word go, on New Year's Eve. On the way home she'd have said, 'You know that Nick chap? I was nearly very naughty with him once. Aeons before I met you, of course.'

She'd have described it very farcically and eventually he'd have laughed – maybe rather wryly – and said something like, 'Randy little sod. Mind you, I'd probably have done exactly the same.'

Daisy lathered her hair with Pink Grapefruit shampoo. *Why didn't I tell Simon? It's not as if he's the ludicrously jealous type.*

You know why, so stop kidding yourself. Even from that very first moment when you saw him on the dance floor, you knew the vibes were still there. If it had been Rob

Carter, who now affects you about as erotically as York-shire pudding . . .

She let the water out and stood under the shower, rinsing both body and hair. And just as she was unscrewing the conditioner, somebody banged on the door. 'Daise, it's me.'

Trust you. Just when my hair's half-washed.

Wrapping herself in a towel, she opened the door.

Tara was bright of eye, bushy of tail, and looking very pleased with herself. 'We went down to see about diving,' she explained, as Daisy applied peach oil conditioner. 'They're all going to do a complete course but it's terribly expensive and takes five days so I wouldn't have time anyway – still, I'm going to do a dive with them the day after tomorrow but we have to do all the beginners' stuff first – in the pool with all the gear so we know all about regulators and stuff – just wait till I tell you about this Alessandro – I wouldn't mind twiddling his regulator, I can tell you – he's from Napoli, and – '

Here we go again.

Rinsing her hair over the side of the bath, Daisy tried not to listen. Here she was, doing her damnedest to be faithful in the face of colossal temptation, and the only thing in Tara's head was the size of the Italian salami.

'They're all coming to this *alfresco* place after dinner,' Tara giggled. 'There's a bar – you don't have to eat there – Alessandro said we could go on somewhere really ravey afterwards.'

'Well, don't just eat and charge off,' Daisy said irritably. 'It'd be terribly rude – it's Marion and Blair's last night and they've invited – '

'Nobody asked if I wanted to go!' Tara rounded on her indignantly. 'I don't even like Marion, and Blair thinks I'm the worst thing since HIV – why the hell should I sit there being nice? Anyone'd think I was with my parents, having to eat with a load of boring people just because they all had a nice game of golf together and Mrs So and So knows somebody who used to live down the road from Auntie Jean's flaming mother-in-law!'

'All right, all right,' Daisy muttered, wrapping her hair in a towel. 'Sorry I spoke.'

'You know your trouble?' Tara demanded, folding her arms. 'You're getting boring. You're getting so boring and middle-aged, you'll soon be worrying about being "regular" and sorting out your pension.'

'I'd rather be worrying about my pension than obsessed with where my next slice of nookie's coming from!'

'What the hell do you care? Unless you actually *are* jealous, of course.'

Daisy knew it was a sarcastic joke, but Tara's sarcastic jokes often hit nerves. Looking determinedly in the huge mirror that ran above twin basins set in marble, she yanked a comb through her tangles.

'I wouldn't be surprised if you were.' Tara was warming up nicely. 'I've been too polite to say this before, but I think Simon's just a tad boring. And I don't feel a bit bad about saying it. I know he doesn't like me.'

'Don't be ridiculous,' Daisy snapped, yanking at a tangle the size of a small bird's nest.

'I'm not stupid, Daisy, although you all seem to think I am sometimes. I know exactly what Simon thinks of me. And you know what? I couldn't give a stuff.' She flounced out and almost slammed the door.

As soon as she left the bathroom, Tara went in. Daisy wished to heaven she'd kept her mouth shut. And it upset her to hear Tara say Simon didn't like her. He didn't dislike her. He just didn't exactly approve of her. He thought her indiscreet and over the top. And he was right. Simon was almost invariably right about everything.

When Tara emerged she had half-dried her hair, and was applying a couple of coats of clear polish to her nails.

They got ready in tense silence, broken only by the ramming shut of drawers and cupboards. 'If you must borrow my cleanser, will you please at least put the top on afterwards?' said Tara crossly.

'I haven't touched it! You must have left the top off yourself.'

Tara grumped off to do her make-up in the bathroom. Wondering what on earth to do with it, Daisy brushed her hair. Up? No way, she couldn't be bothered with the kind of fiddling a really sleek up-job required. Down? Maybe not. Quite apart from Nick's 'Afghan hound' remark, the last thing you needed in Barbados was a fur coat round your neck.

Up, then.

When she'd finished, the effect wasn't quite what she'd intended. Instead of looking as if it'd been thrown up in couldn't-give-a-damn haste, the golden-brown masses looked rather as if she'd contrived a carelessly sexy disorder. A look that whispered flirtily, '*All you've got to do is take one pin out . . .*'

Well, too bad. If anybody's going to be thinking about taking pins out, I don't think it's going to be you-know-who.

Once her thoughts had drifted to a certain person, they would not be diverted. '*Something about you just gets to me . . .*'

Her stomach gave a wild, involuntary lurch.

She almost wished he'd given her a load of smoothie bull about how ravishingly beautiful she was.

He's not that stupid. I'm not ravishingly beautiful.

No, but you don't exactly look like a pig's bottom, either.

She gazed at her reflection. Ages ago, an ex-boyfriend had said, 'I don't know what it is about you. You're not exactly beautiful but there's a certain haunting *je ne sais quoi* . . .'

Even Simon had never told her she was beautiful. On the odd occasion when his emotions had been about to go right over the un-British top, he'd stopped himself and said, 'Come here, Funny Face.' Or Shrimp, or Piglet. She liked it. It was just Simon.

A pang shot through her, a cocktail of loneliness and guilt.

'*They'd have managed. Nobody's indispensable.*'

Nobody else had said it. Only Nick had pointed out the simple truth she had not wanted to acknowledge.

Oh, Simon, why didn't you come with me?

'Should I wear my black dress or my pink one?' Tara called.

'How the hell should I know?'

'All right, ratbag. Pardon me for breathing.'

Daisy put on the white, halter-neck, swirly-skirt dress. It was the coolest thing she possessed and its total lack of back showed her golden tan off like nothing else. Its demurely high neck concealed her lack of front like nothing else, too.

Tara put on a short black dress that showed a goodish flash of cleavage without letting anybody actually fall into it, and a pair of spiky black heels.

Daisy put on a pair of gold leather sandals that were neither high nor spiky, but gave her an extra couple of inches.

She added enough make-up to turn her eyes smoky dark grey, some barely-there rose lipstick, and a good squirt of Jean-Paul Gaultier.

Tara was ready first. 'See you in the bar. Don't forget the key.'

When she'd gone, Daisy felt even worse. She'd been working up to saying something conciliatory, and had left it too late.

She wandered down a few minutes later. The bar was adjacent to reception, and like all the public areas, sturdily roofed against the rain, but open to the soft air. There wasn't even a front door to the place, just an open, welcoming archway into a main building that had been there long before Atlantic-hopping jets had even been thought of.

More like a large lounge, clusters of comfortably upholstered rattan chairs were grouped round little glass tables, somebody was playing the piano softly, and fans whirred overhead. Beds of tropical plants divided it from the gardens, making you feel you were outside even when you weren't.

She heard them before she saw them. Tara's giggles travelled far, and no wonder. Two groups of chairs had been pushed together for her Italians to join the party.

Just to be awkward, Nick was the first to see her coming. And just to be even more awkward and prove that he had manners too, he rose to his feet just as Simon would, and said, 'Sit here, Daisy,' and went to find another chair.

She sat between Jane and Marion, and was introduced to Alessandro & Co. They were all about twenty-seven or eight, all handsome as the devil – although she had to agree that Alessandro perhaps had the edge – and uniformly charming. She smiled, asked appropriately chatty questions, ordered a gin and tonic and nibbled toasted coconut, dishes of which adorned the table.

Nick was sitting at the end of the group, where she didn't have to look at him unless she wanted. However, she soon became aware of a pair of women only yards away, who did want to, and were.

They were about thirty; very smart, very assured, very groomed. One was very fair, with short hair in a shining cap, the other was dark, with ditto. And they kept giving Nick the eye. Not overtly, but it was obvious they were talking about him.

Although she knew it was ridiculously bitch-in-the-manger, Daisy started hating them thoroughly. And just as she was about to say she was starving and wasn't it time they went, the fair woman came over.

'It's Nick, isn't it? Nick Trevelyan?'

From his reaction, it was obvious he hadn't noticed her before.

'Fiona James,' the woman smiled. 'I used to work at Schell and Browning – it must be a good five years ago but you were on the same floor, and – '

'Good Lord, Fiona!' With a smile any woman could drown in, he had already stood up. 'How are you?'

'Fine. Small world, isn't it?' An almost imperceptible pinky softness came over her face. Her voice was low and husky, not the crisp, rather brittle type Daisy had expected. She also had an incredibly attractive smile.

Daisy hated her instantly.

'Shrinking all the time.' He bent down, kissed her on the cheek. 'You're looking great. Come and join us.'

Did he bonk her, I wonder?

He went for more chairs, and Fiona brought her friend. There were introductions and Marion said brightly, 'Why don't you two join us? We're going to a little *alfresco* place just down the beach.'

'We'd love to, but we're booked for dinner at Carambola,' Fiona explained. 'In fact, we have to go very soon.'

Daisy wished she didn't feel so pleased.

They left soon afterwards. 'Maybe we'll see you on the beach,' Fiona said to Nick.

'I hope so. Have fun tonight.'

'You too.'

Daisy watched them go, and watched Nick watching them before he sat down again.

'One of your old flames?' asked Marion, very archly.

With a distinctly wry expression, he lowered his voice. 'If she were, I wouldn't have been frantically wondering who the hell she was.'

274

Daisy was distinctly shaken. He had covered so well, nobody would ever have known; certainly not Fiona, who had clearly gone off in a basky-pink glow.

Nick glanced at his watch. 'If we're going to get any dinner tonight, it's time we went.'

Marion duly invited the Italians, but they had pre-paid their hotel dinners and were going to get their money's worth and follow later.

Eventually they all piled into two taxis, since nobody wanted to have to stick to one miserable drink.

It wasn't far. They passed many of the hotels they'd dithered over at the brochure stage. All the names had been so evocatively Caribbean, all the pictures so equally enticing, choosing had almost come down to sticking a pin in. Discovery Bay, Tamarind Cove, Treasure Beach, Coconut Creek . . .

When they arrived, Tara looked vaguely, uncharacteristically uncomfortable. 'I feel a bit overdressed,' she whispered. 'My cut-offs might have been more appropriate.'

'Tara, you can wear whatever you like.' Daisy added a making-up smile. 'You look really nice.'

Tara smiled back. 'You're not really boring, you old hag.'

'I am a bit, but thanks anyway.'

The place was built up on stilts; on a wooden platform at the edge of the beach, and utterly informal. Many people were in shorts, and the clientele was as diverse as the United Nations. Faces ranged from just-off-the-plane white, through varying stages of pink to the deepest chocolate of the locals.

Since Marion was nominally leading the party, it was she who asked for a table for seven, and was shown to something right away from the sea. Her protestations were loud, but cut short. Nick took over and twenty seconds later tables were being rearranged right by the railing that overlooked the beach. There had been no fuss, no obvious argument.

As she took her seat, Daisy realized that however laid back he seemed, Nick possessed the X factor. A certain indefinable authority had slipped over him like a silk tie that he wore only when necessary. He preferred the open-necked shirt; he would not throw his weight about just to impress, but he would never be palmed off with second best.

The table was at right angles to the sea, and Daisy was at the sea end, opposite Marion. Nick was next to Marion, Ian on Daisy's left.

It was pleasantly noisy, lots of chat and laughter coming from nearby tables and their own. In the adjacent garden, a band with steel pans and electric guitars was playing, the odd couple already dancing under the trees.

Service was quick and pleasant. As she munched her way through spicy crab backs and swordfish and gazed out at the breeze-rippled water, Daisy thought what a good choice Marion had made. She infinitely preferred the casual to the grand, and the food was excellent.

'You must be missing your boyfriend,' Marion said, as Daisy tucked into coconut cream pie.

'I am, but I can't say I want to go home.'

'Me neither,' Marion said, with feeling, and turned to Nick. 'How about you?'

'It's been great, but I've had enough,' he said. 'I'll give BA a ring in the morning. Check on seats for tomorrow night.'

Daisy's coconut pie suddenly stuck in her throat. 'Why?'

In the moment before he answered, his eyes seemed to say, '*Why do you think?*' 'I've chilled out enough. I'm getting restless. And quite apart from a job I've scarcely had time to get my teeth into, the estate agents just faxed me details of a flat on the river. It's just what I want and these things go quickly.'

She shot him a suitably bright smile. 'Good luck. Don't let anybody beat you to it.'

'I don't intend to.' His eyes held her a moment longer. 'When I find something I want, I go for it.'

'And I bet you always get it,' Marion said.

'Not always.' His eyes were still on Daisy. 'Very occasionally I have to admit defeat.'

The coconut cream pie was tasting like budgie seed. 'Can't win 'em all,' she said lightly.

'No. But I always have a damn good try.' He raised a beer to his lips. 'Cheers.'

Desperate to change the subject, Daisy turned to Marion. 'What time's your flight tomorrow? You're having a few days in Florida, I gather.'

'Too early.' Marion made a face. 'We won't even make breakfast. I haven't started packing yet.'

'Then you'll be up half the night.'

'Mum's always up half the night,' put in Blair, from down the table. 'She goes swimming at two o'clock in the morning.'

'Only once, Blair, don't exaggerate. I sit on the balcony and read. And I'm not the only insomniac.'

277

She turned to Nick. 'Your room's more or less opposite ours. I've seen you, out on the balcony or wandering down the beach at Lord knows what hour. You must be one of those people who don't need a lot of sleep. A lot of high achievers are like that. Too much nervous energy.'

'No, just my guilty conscience.' He winked at Marion, and very fleetingly caught Daisy's eye.

She looked away. Finishing her coffee, she gazed at the sea. It was quicksilvered with moonlight and the wretched tree frogs were providing a heartaching back-up group to the steel band. They were playing one of those West Indian songs that sound incredibly corny till you're actually there. She watched a young couple walk hand in hand on the soft sand below, and envied them their happiness.

'Honeymooners,' Marion said. 'The place is full of honeymooners and senior citizens.'

Ancient Brits . . .

Abruptly, Nick pushed his chair back. 'If you've finished your coffee, Marion, come and dance.'

She didn't need asking twice. And before long, everybody was dancing. The music livened up, reggae, calypso, all with a beat to get even a corpse moving.

She danced with Blair, with Ian, and with one of Tara's Italians, whose name was Giuliano. He was an outrageous, charming flirt who told her in tones of profound, satin-accented shock that her boyfriend must be crazy to let her out of his sight.

Yes, you're dead right there. But she enjoyed the flirtation. It meant nothing to either of them – he would have said the same to anybody. He danced with Jane straight afterwards, and Daisy collapsed back in her seat, thanking heaven she hadn't left her hair down. Despite the little breeze, it was very humid.

Fanning herself with the cocktail menu, she looked around for a waiter to bring her a drink.

'What is it you want?' Nick was suddenly there, about to resume his seat.

'Oh – ' she hesitated. 'Just a lime squash.'

He glanced around, beckoned, and somebody came.

'One lime squash and a beer, please,' he said.

'Yes, sir.'

Instead of taking his own seat, he took Marion's, right opposite her.

Now what? We have surely exhausted a certain topic, and there can't be anything else he wants to talk about.

So she opened another. 'What's this flat like?'

'It's right by Tower Bridge. On a marina with a boat space.'

'Sounds lovely. I bet they go like hot cakes.'

'I like that part of London. And I'm sick of renting. I want my own place.'

She thought fleetingly of the rent she was paying each month. Simon had given up now, but until a few months back he'd been increasingly on at her about the futility of putting money in a landlord's pocket when you could be investing in your own bricks and mortar. And he was right, but there was more to a place to live than wise investment strategy.

She liked Richmond, the view from the hill over the river, the deer in the park. London was so ridiculously expensive, anything she could afford to buy in a halfway decent area would not be a quarter as nice. She liked sharing with Jane and Tara. There was the odd argument, but they had a lot of laughs. At least it was never boring.

Rather than look him in the eye, she gazed over the sea and pretended to be drinking in the atmosphere.

Even while not looking, she was painfully aware, out of the corner of her eye, of everything about him. The flickering scrutiny of those onyx-green eyes. One arm, lying on the table. His shirt, of olivey-green cotton and a cut that whispered 'expensive'. His hair, not as tidy as it had been when they'd arrived, but dishevelled from a lot of dancing. His tangy, elusive scent drifted across the table, mingling with warm male . . .

'Before I leave, I simply must go for a midnight swim,' she said brightly, and cursed herself instantly, in case he thought she meant skinnydipping and was trying in some perverse way to tease him. 'So's Tara. It'll be just like when we were kids, sneaking out for a midnight feast.'

When he spoke, his voice was warmer than she'd expected, but very slightly roughened, like melted chocolate with bits in it. 'Watch those beasties, won't you?'

She gave a quick, light smile to cover the memories such beastie-talk evoked. 'We'll take our beastie-repellent.'

She was leaning forward on the table, her arms folded as she gazed over the water. Suddenly he leaned forwards too, folding his arms exactly the same, as he followed her gaze.

'It must be very fascinating, whatever you're looking at,' he mused. *You're afraid to look me in the eye, aren't you?*

He didn't have to say it out loud, not that anybody would have heard if he had. Tara had just come back to the table with Alessandro, but since she was talking and laughing at the speed of light and focusing on only him, she'd never have picked it up.

'I want to remember it,' she said lightly. 'Replay it like a video when I'm driving to work in the rain.'

For some daft reason, the proximity of his arms to her own was unnerving her. The contrast made something quiver at the back of her neck. It was obvious, of course, that his were about twice the girth and several shades more tanned, that their fuzz of dark hair contrasted so sharply with her own, almost invisible golden down. It would have been a bit odd if they didn't.

Male and female created He them. Daft, wallyette flutterings attacked her again, so politically incorrect they would very likely be banned when the government eventually brought in a Minister for Women. It would be a criminal offence to feel like this; all dithery at the thought of being scooped up in strong, muscly, etc. etc. You would be obliged to reverse-fantasise about getting so iron-pumped at the gym that you'd think nothing of scooping up the nearest New Man who took your fancy and carting him home before having your energetic, multi-orgasmic way with him.

'I wouldn't have thought you'd want to replay this holiday,' he said, very quietly. 'I was rather under the impression that I'd wrecked it for you.'

'Oh, Nick.' Her heart and stomach lurched together like two drunks. At that moment, she knew it would have taken next to nothing for her to give in. He would only have to gaze into her eyes, say softly, 'Come on, let's dance,' and –

She felt his eyes, questioning, waiting.

'Have I?'

She swallowed, hard. 'Please, Nick . . .'

Please, Nick, what? Please, Nick, shut up? Please Nick, just grab me? Please, Nick, just take this decision out of my tortured, wavering hands?

The change in him was subtle, but instantaneous. 'I'm sorry. The subject is closed.' His tone crisped up, and he sat back. It was as if a cool, invisible curtain had come between them.

He glanced around, as if looking for someone. 'Excuse me.' With the kind of smile he might have given his secretary – polite and appropriate – he left the table.

The feeling in Daisy's stomach took her back years. It reminded her of the ghastly feeling she'd had at seventeen, sitting by the phone waiting for Rob Carter to ring, while knowing he wasn't going to ever again.

Their drinks came, and she was heartily glad of the distraction. Tara was still oblivious to everybody but Alessandro, and the others were apparently still squandering calories on the dance floor.

Minutes later, Jane and Blair came back, with Ian and Marion close behind. And right behind them was Nick. He sat in his original seat and cast her barely a glance.

'God, I'm shattered,' Jane sighed, flopping into her chair. 'It's more exhausting than the Cindy Crawford workout.'

'You've only done that once,' Daisy reminded her.

'Yes, because it's so shattering. Ian, darling, do find a waiter before I die of dehydration.'

She picked up the drinks menu, fanned herself, and stopped abruptly. 'Nick! You're at it again! Shirking your responsibilities!'

Jane, please . . .

'Tell him, Ian.' Mischievously Jane turned to her other half. 'Just look at poor Daisy, sitting there like a wallflower just because he's afraid of getting his face slapped . . .'

Jane, please . . .

'Disgraceful behaviour.' Ian sat heavily beside her. 'Nick, my son, be a man. Gird up thy lethal hip-wiggle and hit that floor. Unless you want Jane on at you all night, that is.'

His performance could have won him an Oscar. With a wry, you've-got-me smile, he glanced diagonally across at Daisy. 'Looks like it's give-in-gracefully time.' He raised one dark eyebrow. 'Shall we dance?'

He didn't grab her wrist, like he had on New Year's Eve. There was just a feather-light hand on her waist, the proprietary touch of a man who knows he has possession for the next ten minutes.

The band was playing some incredibly catchy number she had heard several times before, in the hotel. The beat was that unmistakable West Indian rhythm she'd heard belting from the Jolly Roger; the kind that made you itch to dance in a way you wouldn't at home. There was something earthily sexual about it, as anybody with even a drop of Caribbean blood showed all too clearly. They danced differently, using their hips in a fluidly suggestive way. Most of the tourists looked awkward and shuffly by comparison.

But not Nick. As if he'd taken in the rhythm with his mother's milk, he moulded his body to the beat; nothing over the top, but just at ease with it.

The music was so intoxicating, she could only relax and do the same. It was like floating in the music, rather than swimming frantically.

And gradually, he moved closer, took her by the waist for a few seconds, swung her in a little circle, and moved away again. He did it again, a little circle, moving away . . .

The heartbeat rhythm was getting into her blood. When the music stopped, she could only think, '*I could have danced all night . . .*'

'Well, you've done your duty,' she said lightly. 'Thank you so much, and all that.'

He touched her arm, guiding her away as somebody pushed past. 'We're not off the hook yet,' he said drily. 'Since we missed the first half, it won't count as a proper go. Maybe one more, to be on the safe side?'

'If you say so. I wouldn't want to get you into any more trouble with Jane.'

There was no pulsing beat this time, just the lilting softness of the steel band, and a velvety male voice singing. Quite casually, Nick put the statutory arm round her waist and took her hand in the required manner.

And in the required manner, she allowed him to take her hand, and rested the other against his shoulder. Like this, they began to drift very slowly around the tiny floor. It was all incredibly restrained, incredibly civilized. There was no roaming of hands, no warm breath on neck or hair.

He kept about three inches always between them, no more. His hand on her waist did not rove either up or down; it stayed like a whisper, his thumb just brushing the bare skin above the skirt of her dress.

Her eyes were just level with the top of his shoulder, her hand resting lightly on his chest. The scent of him wafted warm into her nostrils.

She had never heard the song before, but it possessed a haunting quality that shivered the hairs at the back of her neck. The voice was deep, dark brown, melting like velvet into the night.

'Gosh, it's hot, isn't it?' With a bright smile, she pulled back a little.

For an instant, his eyes dropped from her face and came right back. 'Maybe you should take that swim, later.'

'I don't think so, not tonight.'

'Why not?'

'Well, I think Tara's going clubbing with the Italians, and I'd never go on my own – in any case I've gone off the idea – it's all lovely in theory but in practice it's chillier than you think.'

'Chilly? In Barbados?' He drew back and raised an eyebrow. 'You need toughening up,' he murmured, and the ritual drift continued.

The music stopped at last, and he didn't suggest another. 'That should keep Jane quiet for a bit,' she said, as they left the floor. 'And if you're leaving tomorrow night, you won't be called upon again.'

She tripped brightly up the wooden steps to the restaurant area, as if she'd just been at a Scottish country dancing lesson.

They stayed another hour, more drinks, more dancing, although not from Daisy. She chatted instead, to Marion, to Jane, to anybody.

When they left, Tara went the other way, towards Bridgetown with her consorts. She was not the only female member of the party. Sitting at the bar had been a couple of Manchester girls, not long off the plane and obviously dying for fun. Daisy had seen them doing the classic two-girls-out bit; pretending they were perfectly happy with their own company, but casting longing glances at the dancing, hoping to heaven for a couple of at least passable men to come and chat them up. And lo, Giuliano and friend had obliged. With much combined hilarity, the entire party loaded itself into taxis.

Daisy almost wished she was going with them.

She ended up in the taxi with Marion and Blair, and listened with half an ear to Marion's chatter. Until she said, 'I'm really mad with Nick, you know.'

Daisy turned to her, startled. '*Mad*? With *Nick*?'

'It was supposed to be my treat. And when I asked for the bill, they told me it was already paid. He'd sneaked off and done the dirty. I could have walloped him; I really could. I said, 'Nick, I'm practically old enough to be your mother, so do as you're told.'

She turned to Daisy with a very rueful smile. 'But he just smiled at me and said, 'Marion, give in gracefully.' She sighed. 'What could I do?'

'Not a lot,' Daisy agreed.

'Used to getting his own way, I dare say.'

'I dare say.'

They all piled out at the other end. There were protracted farewells in the gardens as they strolled room-wards – the usual chorus of 'Goodbye' and 'Have a good flight' and 'Lovely to meet you'.

Goodnight, Marion, goodnight, Blair, goodnight, Jane, goodnight, Ian.

'Goodnight, Nick.'

'Goodnight, Daisy. Sweet dreams.'

'You too.' With a bright smile, she walked quickly through the night-scented gardens to her room.

Only when she was inside did she toss away the mask she'd been wearing ever since that slow, restrained drift under the trees.

She sat trembling on the bed.

My God, what is happening to me?

He had done nothing. He had barely touched her. He hadn't so much as pecked her on the cheek.

Yet never in her entire life . . .

I want him. I want him so desperately I could die.

CHAPTER 14

She closed her eyes. An action replay was running in her head and she couldn't find the stop button.

He had known, she was sure. He must have sensed it through her skin, through her quivering fingertips. It was as if he'd been saying, '*You told me to back off, and that's exactly what I'm doing. If you're having second thoughts, that's your problem.*'

She hadn't needed to be clamped to him for desire to explode through her like a mind-bending drug. Dizzy with it, she had drawn back a little, and realized too late that under the white silk jersey of that no-bra dress, her body was giving her away.

He must have seen, but there had not been so much as an eyelash-flicker. She could just imagine what another type of man would have said.

'*Either you've got a couple of outsize goosepimples there, luv, or my luck's changed.*'

As if he were still there, still holding her a tantalising three inches away, she felt a resurgence of that overpowering urge to melt into him. To surrender.

She pulled the curtains open, slid open the doors. Leaning over the balcony, she took deep, calming breaths of scented air, but they did nothing to calm the fever inside her.

There was no precise moment when the idea came to her. It was as if it had been lying dormant all along, only waiting its chance.

Just this once, she told herself, like a thief planning the raid that was going to make him rich for ever. *Just this once, and I swear I'll never do it again.*

What if he's not there? He might have gone straight to bed.

He will be.

He might not. Just because Marion said –

He will be. I just know it.

She waited half an hour, desire and anticipation building like some lethal drug. She took a quick, cool shower, brushed her teeth. She sprayed herself with a whisper of Jean-Paul Gaultier, put her white dress back on and messed her hair a little, so that it would look as if she had done none of these things.

When she finally slipped out of the door and down the wooden steps, her heart was pounding like race-horse hooves. But she would not make it too obvious. She would not walk right under his nose, right under his balcony.

She walked diagonally across the gardens, heading for the far end of the beach. She walked quickly, so it wouldn't look as if she were hoping to catch his eye. If he were there, he could not fail to see her. The dress would stand out like a candle in the dark.

There was nobody on the beach. Removing her sandals, she stepped on to the soft sand. It was very quiet, with barely even a rustle of the leaves in the breeze and the tree frogs chirping. It wasn't quite dark; at intervals along the beach lamps were hung high in the trees, giving just enough light to see by.

The moon was well up, casting liquid silver on the water. She walked slowly, feeling the soft sand under her feet, dangling her sandals from her fingers. She passed the gardens of a villa you would scarcely know was there. Frangipani trees edged the beach; she picked up a fallen blossom and inhaled its scent before tossing it away.

She walked a hundred yards before stopping to sit in the sand. She sat with her knees drawn up, gazing at the dark shivering water, as if all she wanted was to drink in the tropical night.

Gradually, as the minutes passed and her racing heartbeat slowed, the fever that had been raging in her brain abated.

My God, what am I doing?

Sitting in the sand, my dear, playing an elaborate game of come-and-get-me. And it looks like you're going to be sitting here all night.

She put her hands to her face, blushing at her own stupidity.

Whatever came over me?

Lust, my dear. It makes fools of the best of us. Go back to your room and just be thankful nobody else is ever going to find out what an idiot you've been.

She stood up smartly and started walking back a good deal more quickly than she'd come.

Prat, dope, idiot, you want locking up, you're not safe to be let –

'Hello, Daisy.'

She stopped dead on the sand. 'Nick!'

Her heartbeat zoomed straight back into orbit. About six feet away, he had stolen so softly out of the darkness, she had neither seen nor heard him. 'What are you doing here?'

'Looking for you.'

Oh, my God. The fever surged back, more overpowering than ever.

'I saw you, wandering down the beach,' he went on.

Heaven help me. 'Good heavens, I should have thought you'd be tucked up in bed by now.'

'I wasn't tired.'

'Nor me,' she said lightly. 'I just couldn't resist a little walk – after all, this time next week I won't have a beach to walk down – seems a shame to waste it, doesn't it?' Even to her own ears her voice sounded too rapid, too brightly forced.

Folding his arms, he leaned against the trunk of a tree. 'I thought you might be going for that swim, after all.'

She gave a wonderfully airy laugh. 'Heavens, no.'

'And I thought I'd better come and save you from the beasties.'

His softly mocking tone did dreadful things to her insides. 'Well, it's terribly kind of you, but I've only seen one little crab, nothing to worry about, so you're a trifle redundant, I'm afraid.'

'So it would seem.'

He was watching her, but he made no move. She knew she ought to say something bright and brisk, something like, 'Well, better get back,' and start a brisk, no-nonsense, nothing-but-walks-even-crossed-my-mind march back to the hotel. The spirit was willing, but the flesh . . .

Turning from him, she gazed out at the quicksilvered sea. 'It's so beautiful,' she said brightly.

'Yes,' he said. 'It is.'

'I just couldn't bear to lie in bed reading a stupid book when there's all this outside, I mean, how often do you get something like this on your doorstep?'

He made no reply.

Daisy, for God's sake, go. 'I suppose I'd better be getting back,' she went on. 'Can't stay here all night, can I?'

Although he made no reply, he was still watching her. Over six feet or so of gentle night air, she could feel his eyes. Her every nerve quivered with tortured anticipation.

Her body shivered on a knife-edge of ecstasy. Any second now, he would take a couple of steps towards her. Like a whisper, he would put his hands on her waist. Her eyes closed just at the thought; her insides dissolving like wet tissues . . .

She heard him move. He came to stand not quite behind her, but a little to the side.

For several, endless seconds, the earth seemed to pause in its spinning. She could scarcely breathe.

'You know something?' he said.

With those three words, her anticipation began to crumble. His voice was wrong. There was no softness, no roughened-velvet huskiness . . .

She turned her head. His face was thrown into shadow, his eyes as dark and unfathomable as the sea. She moistened her lips. 'No. Tell me.'

'It's time to go. You don't need all night to file it in your memory bank.'

If she'd still been in any doubt, his tone would have put her straight. Crisp, cool, matter-of-fact – 'And it wasn't very clever, wandering the beach on your own at this time of night,' he went on.

For God's sake, don't let him see how you feel. 'Nick, this isn't the Bronx.'

His eyes were still shadowed; as unreadable as a Sanskrit poem. 'No. But it's hardly circumspect behaviour. It could be . . .' He paused. '. . . misconstrued.'

In that ghastly moment, it dawned on her exactly what he was saying. *Don't take me for a fool. I know exactly why you're here.*

She wanted to throw up.

Even more crisply, he nodded towards the hotel. 'Shall we go?'

'Of course.' She said it casually, to cover that sick black hole in her stomach.

They walked quickly, several feet apart, and neither spoke a word. It was too late to wish to heaven she'd never given into temptation, but that didn't stop her.

So why did he come? Just to make me feel an abject fool? She longed to ask him, but silence would at least preserve the shreds of her dignity.

When they stepped at last from the soft sand to the hotel gardens, she paused to put her sandals back on. 'You needn't wait. I think I can make it back to my room without mishap.'

She straightened up. He was watching her, his hands thrust in his pockets. When he spoke the cynicism in his voice was marked. 'You know what? I'd have a lot more

293

respect for you if you'd been honest. If you'd said, 'Look, Nick, I don't want a relationship, but I'd like to sleep with you anyway. Instead of virtuously pretending you wanted nothing to do with me and arranging a "chance" little meeting on the side.'

She felt suddenly as if she were in one of her own nightmares; stripped naked, ridiculed, scorned. But even then, she sought desperately to cover herself. 'I went for a walk! W - A - L - K! If you thought anything else, you're sadly – '

'Don't lie to me, Daisy. Please.'

She couldn't give in. She couldn't admit it and drown in a shameful mire of her own making. With suitable scorn, she said, 'My God, your ego really takes the cake. Have you somehow got it into your head that I toddled down the beach with the express purpose of somehow – '

'Yes,' he said. 'That's exactly what I think. You were desperate for some excitement, but terrified of the attendant guilt. You thought that like this, it would just "happen" and you needn't feel too bad about it.'

If he had taken a whip to her face he could not have hurt her more. Without thinking, she swung her arm and dealt him a colossal slap on the cheek. She had never done such a thing before, and the stinging in her palm shocked her.

'Hurts, doesn't it?' He had not flinched or even moved. 'I'm not going to hit you back, although I know you'd like me to. Then you could cast me as the villain of the piece. And not for the first time, either.'

Feeling sick with emotions she could not name, Daisy walked quickly on, desperate for the sanctuary of her room.

'You'll thank me, when you've calmed down,' he went on sardonically, his long stride more than keeping up with her own.

Her voice came out like broken icicles. 'You have a very lively imagination, I'll say that for you.'

'I don't think so.' His tone was biting in its cynicism. 'Do forgive me if I say that slap was uncalled for. I have not only saved you from the agonies of post-hanky-panky guilt, I've saved Simon from being a hapless cuckold. In my own humble opinion, I have behaved like the perfect gentleman.'

Her voice trembled with anger and misery. 'You're no gentleman.'

'And you Daisy, are no lady.' He paused, nodded down the path. 'I won't come any further. Go to bed and dream of Simon. As you said, he's all you ever wanted.'

An hour and a half later she was still longing for sleep that would not come.

Why?

To punish you. For not falling at his feet from the first. I bet he's not used to being turned down.

Maybe he wasn't sure. Maybe he had his suspicions, but had to follow me to be sure. And I gave myself away.

She thought back to how she'd stood with her back to him, just longing for him to make the first move.

Like an asking-for-it bimbo.

For the nth time, a wash of burning shame made her bury her face in the pillow. She longed to cry, but once she started she'd never stop. Then there would be long drawn-out shudders, and Tara would come back and hear them, and how would she explain? Never mind her face, still blotched and red-eyed in the morning.

I feel so sick. How will I ever face him tomorrow?

With bluff, like tonight.

She was still awake an hour later when Tara came back. She had left the door unlocked, not wanting to face her.

'Are you awake?' Tara whispered.

She made no reply.

'Oh, well.' Tara hiccupped, giggled softly to herself, and went to the bathroom.

Daisy closed her eyes tight, longing for oblivion.

Tara came out, rummaged softly in a drawer, and spent a minute or two doing something. She tiptoed to the door, opened it, and shut it again. She turned the bathroom light off, and slipped into bed with a deep, satisfied sigh.

Daisy came out of a drugged sleep to hear somebody banging on the door. The clock said nine-fifteen.

She padded comatose to the door. A waiter with a laden tray held at shoulder level stood outside. 'We didn't order . . .' she began, and stopped. Of course, that was what Tara had been doing last night. 'Yes, we did. Sorry. Come in.'

She opened the balcony doors for him, and he started laying the table. Daisy went into the bathroom, and by the time she emerged, he was gone.

Tara was coming to life.

'Why did you order breakfast in the room?' Daisy demanded.

'I thought it'd be a nice little treat! We've never remembered to fill the cards in before!'

And they hadn't. Filling in a breakfast card and hanging it on your doorknob every night had seemed like too much effort.

Daisy had never felt less like eating, let alone enjoying the paw paw, pancakes and toast Tara had ordered. She still felt sick, with the ghastly feeling you get when you realize that what you thought was a nightmare was nothing of the kind.

Thank God Simon didn't ring this morning. I couldn't have faced it.

'You'll be pleased to know,' Tara giggled as she poured coffee, 'that I have not yet had carnal knowledge of a certain person. I believe that un-happy situation might be rectified this afternoon, however.'

Please, please, not sex. I can't take it.

She felt as if she'd never, ever want sex again. She felt as if she'd been to some sort of aversion therapy session, designed to put you off for life.

'The others are taking a trip round the island,' Tara went on. 'And he's staying here. Which means there'll be a nice empty room.'

'Wonderful.' Daisy gazed listlessly at the pool, where a man with a net was fishing out leaves. On the balcony walls, tiny brown, sparrow-like birds were gathering, clinging by their claws to the rough coral stone as they waited for pickings.

Tara put the sugar bowl on the top of the railing. They descended like flies, dipping their tiny beaks and looking nervously all around. A tiny, black and yellow bird with a slender curved beak hung back, hesitant.

Leaving half her paw paw, Daisy put it on the wall with the sugar. More birds descended at once, pecking greedily at the yellow flesh.

I might as well give them all my breakfast right now. I can't eat it.

'You look awful,' Tara commented.

I'm not surprised. 'I didn't sleep very well.'

'You were snoring like a pig when I came in.'

It was no use contradicting her. 'Did you have a good time last night?'

'Brilliant. Danced our socks off.' She giggled. 'And we had a quick goodnight snog. Well, not that quick. He's a lovely kisser.'

Will you shut up?

My God, look who's talking.

Tara finished her breakfast, showered, and went to the beach. Daisy was still sitting there at half past ten. She sat motionless, letting the birds swarm all over the table.

The maid came and she had to go. Since Nick never went there, she went to the pool. She stayed there all morning, but felt compelled to join the others for lunch, or they'd think something was amiss. To her immense relief, Nick was conspicuous by his absence. Nobody seemed to notice a thing, although her sunglasses helped to hide her dull eyes.

'Nick's got a seat on BA tonight,' Ian said, over lunch. 'Wants to go and look at this flat before somebody else get an offer in.'

'Where is he, anyway?' Jane asked. 'I haven't seen him all morning.'

'Dunno, love. He said something about North Point.'

His previous words came rushing back. '*I sat watching the waves crashing in, and tried to think good and noble thoughts.*'

'I hope we're going to see him before he goes,' Tara pouted. 'I hope he's not just going to sneak off.'

'Of course not. He said he'll see us all in the bar around six-thirty, if not before.'

He wasn't with Fiona and friend, anyway, Daisy thought wanly. She had seen them at the pool, anointing themselves carefully, timing their grilling to the minute.

I wish it was tonight already. I wish he was gone. I hate him.

No, you don't. You hate yourself.

I hate him, too.

In the late afternoon, when the heat of the sun was waning, she went to do battle with the windsurfer again. The wind was fresher, taking her by surprise as she went out of the bay. She fell several times, and it took all her new-found skill to stay on board. The time passed more quickly than she realized, and just as she was twenty yards from the beach on her final run back, Dreadlocks zoomed up in the hotel ski boat. 'I had to close the shop – it's gone five already and I got another job to go to.'

The mere interruption had made her fall in. 'I'm so sorry – I forgot the time.'

'No problem. Just leave it on the beach, but take out the daggerboard so nobody can sail it away. You can take it to your room till the mornin'.'

'OK,' she smiled. 'Don't worry.'

He zoomed off, and she hauled herself up again, and carried on to the beach. Tara was frolicking in the shallows, waiting for her. She swam up, grabbed the board, and made her fall again.

'*Must* you?' Daisy pushed her wet hair from her face.

Tara giggled and flicked water over her. 'All this healthy exercise – I'm getting really worried about you, Daisy.'

There was no point getting up again, hauling that heavy sail up again for a few more yards. She swam with one arm, towing it in. 'You could do with some healthy exercise, if you ask me.'

'I've just had some. I don't know about healthy, exactly, but it used up quite a few calories, I can tell you.'

Oh, God, if she's going to give me every lip-smacking detail, I can't take it.

Tara swam alongside, giggling in a way that said she had put away a fair amount of alcohol either before or after, or both. 'He's fast asleep, poor boy, but it always has the reverse effect on me. Gives me loads of energy.'

'Go for a run, then.'

'Stuff that. I'll have a go on this.'

'Don't be ridiculous. You haven't a clue.'

'I have! I'll have you know there was an *extremely* hunky windsurfing instructor in Skiathos – he was called Kyriacos or something – and he said I was a natural.' From the other side of the board, she stuck her tongue out. 'So there.'

'A natural at what?'

Tara giggled again. 'Go on, let me have a go. I'm just in the mood.'

Daisy gave an inward sigh. Why not? If not, she'd only have to endure lurid details of another activity for the next half hour. 'All right. I'll go and get a drink before the bar closes. I'm parched.' She cast a quick glance towards the beach bar and her heart sank. About twenty yards away, between her and it, was a tall dark figure in shorts. Arms folded, he was looking at the precise spot where she stood.

Oh, hell. Hurriedly she said, 'Look, Tara, I think I'll go up to the room instead and order some tea from room service. The watersports shop's closed, so when you've finished you have to take the dagger-board out in case somebody pinches it. Bring it up to the room.'

'Yeah, yeah.'

'Tara, are you listening? He'll go mad if it gets lost. He'll get into trouble.'

'OK, OK. Get off, will you?'

Daisy unbuckled her lifejacket. 'And put this on.'

'I hate lifejackets. They flatten my boobs.'

'Put it on! What if you crack your head on the mast?'

'OK, OK, keep your knickers on.'

'See you later, then.'

'Bysie bye.'

There was no avoiding him. He was standing right by her sunbed, which he would no doubt have identified by her navy and white striped beach bag. She walked up stiffly, picked up her sunglasses and put them on, grabbed her towel and bag.

'Daisy – '

Ignoring him, she turned up the beach.

He caught her arm. 'That's right, run away again. You always run away, don't you? Bury your head in the sand like some tunnel-vision bloody ostrich.'

His voice was low and rough, almost angry, and stirred her anger and misery in return. It was no use pretending any more. Compounding her lies would only make him despise her more. 'Why did you do it? You were the one who wouldn't let this thing go. You wanted me.'

'Not like that, I didn't.'

'So why did you follow me? Just to humiliate me?'

'No, believe it or not.' His voice was still rough, still angry. 'What was I supposed to do? You disappeared down the beach and didn't come back. I thought maybe something had happened to you.'

'Like hell.'

'My God.' His eyes burned over her face, green and scathing. 'Of all the cynical little bitches . . .'

'Why shouldn't I be a bitch?' Her voice rose slightly, unsteadily. 'You were the bastard to end them all last night. Nobody has ever . . .' She paused, steadying herself. 'Nobody has ever made me feel so cheap and dirty as you did last night.'

'What about me?' His voice was rougher, green glints of anger in his eyes. 'How d'you think I felt? Shall I tell you?' He paused. 'Like some sleazy bloody gigolo, that's how. Summoned to service a bored housewife who wants a bit on the side.'

It felt like a whip on her face; a heavy-duty rhino-whip, intended to scar for life.

'You and your bloody double standards,' he went on. 'How would you feel if I had a long-term girlfriend at home and came sniffing around you for a quick thrill? You'd be denouncing me as the archetypal playing-around bastard.'

She could not take any more. Fighting tears, she ran through the gardens to the sanctuary of her room.

She threw herself on the bed and let the suppressed sobs out at last. For ages they racked her till at last they gave way to long, gasping shudders. She had never, ever felt so sick, so ashamed, so miserable in her life. Still wet and salty from the sea, she shivered in the air-conditioning. She slipped under the bedspread and still shuddering, fell asleep. When the phone woke her, it was dark. For a moment she didn't know what time of day it was. 'Hello?'

'Hi, Daisy, it's me. Ian and I are just off to the bar for that drink with Nick. You hadn't forgotten, had you?'

Daisy battled with her fogged brain. 'No, but – '

'When you come, could you ask Tara to bring my gold pen? She borrowed it yesterday morning to write a postcard. I hope to heaven she hasn't lost it.'

'She's not here at the moment, but I'll tell her when she – ' She broke off, gaping round the empty room.

Tara. Where was Tara?

CHAPTER 15

'Daisy, are you there?'

'Jane – I've got to go – see you later – ' She banged the phone down, grabbed her key and ran.

Don't panic. She's probably on the beach, having a drink with somebody. Or by the pool.

She checked the pool first, but there was no Tara. The beach bar was long closed, but she checked the bar, ignoring the slightly askance looks from people already dressed for dinner, who evidently thought bare feet, bikini and hair like a haystack was not quite appropriate for the cocktail hour.

She raced through the gardens, past the watersports shop, over the soft sand to the place where the wind-surfer should be.

And wasn't.

Oh, my God. She scanned the horizon, but it was dark now, there was nothing to see.

She can't be out there.

She can. She'd been drinking. She wasn't in control. Nobody was watching her.

Panic rose in her. She raced back through the gardens to reception, where Nick was paying his bill. 'Can you

304

call me a cab in about – ' he glanced at his watch, '– forty-five – '

'Excuse me,' Daisy said rapidly to the receptionist. 'I can't find my friend – I think she might be – '

Nick's hand had frozen just above his credit card slip. 'Daisy, what's wrong?'

'I can't find Tara.' Clad in only her bikini, her bare feet leaving sand on the tiled floor, she panted it out. 'She was on that windsurfer and she hasn't come back and – '

'Daisy, calm down.'

His soothing tone made her want to hit him. She turned to the receptionist instead; a serenely beautiful girl with elegantly coiled braids, whose serene smile was slowly fading. With deliberate, un-hysterical calm, she said, 'I think my friend's still out on a windsurfer. I've looked everywhere I can think of. I let her take my board just after the watersports shop closed – nobody was watching her and she'd had a few drinks – '

'She might be with Alessandro,' Nick cut in. 'Have you checked?'

Hope leapt in her, and died as quickly. 'But the windsurfer's not on the beach! She'd hardly have carried it anywhere – it weighs a – '

'We'll check, anyway. Do you know the room number?'

'No! How would I know?'

He turned to the receptionist. 'There are three Italians who arrived yesterday. I think they're sharing a room.'

The girl checked. 'Two one one,' she said, dialled the number, and handed the receiver to Daisy.

'Hello? Is that Alessandro?'

'Is Giuliano.'

'Guiliano, it's Daisy. Is Tara there?'

'Sorry, she not here.'

'Is Alessandro there?'

'Si, he in the *doccia*. You want him?'

'Guiliano, this is very important.' Deliberately she kept her English slow and simple. 'Was Alessandro with Tara; before he go in the *doccia*? Was he on the beach with her? Or in the bar?'

'No, he sleeping.' He was half laughing as he said it. 'Dario and me, we come ten minutes ago and the lazy son of beetch, he sleeping. You want him?'

'No, it's OK. *Grazie*.'

Sick with fear, she hung up. 'She's not there. Alessandro was asleep till ten minutes ago.'

Nick crisped up instantly. 'Then we'll inform the emergency services.' He turned to the receptionist. 'Can you – '

She had already picked up the phone.

The next few minutes were a nightmare of helpless inactivity; repeating the same information for the coast-guard – she went at about five o'clock – yes, she was wearing a lifejacket – ' She stood shivering in her bikini, talking like an automaton.

At last Nick took her arm. 'We can't wait here doing nothing. We'll find a boat and get out there.'

It was as if last night had never happened. They practically ran to the beach. 'There aren't any boats,' she said, trying to subdue her rising panic. 'They've all gone home.'

About twenty yards away, a group of Bajan boys were sitting on the edge of the sand by the water, laughing and pushing each other around. Daisy went running up. 'We need a boat,' she said rapidly. 'My friend went out on a windsurfer and she hasn't come back and I'm terrified she's – '

They cracked to attention. 'You tell the coastguard?'

'The hotel's informed them,' Nick said. 'But we need to get out there now.'

'OK, man.' The boys conferred rapidly in Bajan, and one of them uttered a piercing whistle.

From out of the shadows further down the beach came another figure. He yelled something in Bajan, and the boy yelled back. He turned to them. 'Wait here – we go to find some of the guys.'

Waiting was an agony, but it was less than ten minutes before a beat-up old Land Rover reversed on to the sand, a trailer and boat behind it. Three or four willing hands un-hooked the trailer, rolled it into the sea, launched the boat, and did it all in reverse.

Troy got out and said something incomprehensible to one of the others, who drove it back up the beach. This time, he wasn't laughing. 'Who you lose?' he asked,

'Tara,' Daisy said. 'The dark one.'

'I know she. What time she go?'

Sick with dread, she repeated the information, but they wasted no time while she did it. Nick was whipping his shoes and socks off and chucking them on to the sand. He whisked Daisy into the boat, gave it a massive shove, and climbed in.

'I guess she'll have drifted north-west,' he said.

Just hearing him say it made the cold lump in her stomach spread its fingers everywhere.

'Yeah, but the wind very light, and if she tryin' to get back, she maybe not gone too far,' Troy said.

He nodded back towards the beach. 'The guys go to find another boat. We get more eyes out there.'

'It's very good of you,' Daisy said, and thought instantly how daft it sounded.

'No problem.' They headed out of the bay.

Apart from the odd cloud, the sky was clear. The boat's lights were woefully inadequate, but the stars were diamond-bright. The water shimmered placidly, but for the first time it terrified her. You knew where you were with northern seas. Rough and cold, you messed with them at your peril.

This sea was different. It was warm and smiling, beckoning you to lie in its limpid arms . . .

Six little words echoed endlessly in her head.

'*The sea have no back door.*'

Not far behind them, two other boats were following. Troy slowed down, yelled something, and a conversation carried across the water.

'We fan out,' he said.

North-west. Away from the island. Sick with fear, Daisy recalled the map she'd looked at on the plane. A mass of blue, with a few tiny specks . . .

'You check the starboard side, I'll take port,' Nick said crisply.

Their eyes were on desperate stalks, searching for any flash of white board in the water. The soft night air echoed with shouts of 'Tara! Tara!'

Before long, the grey, naval-looking vessels of the coastguard passed in the distance. It gave her comfort to know the emergency services were already out, but even with a hundred boats, it was like looking for a needle in a watery haystack.

After half an hour, Daisy was hoarse with yelling, her eyes so strained from searching, she began to see things that were not there. Every silvered ripple, every white plastic buoy that had broken free from a fishing net made her heart leap with hope, only to crash again into despair.

She began to shiver, both from the cool night breeze and from fear. Remorse was eating into her like a cancer.

How could I have left her there, with no-one to watch her? I know what she's like. Over-confident after a few drinks. She'll have gone too far out, tried to get back, fallen again and again, got exhausted . . .

Oh, Tara. What are you thinking now?

'Tara!' Desperation entered her voice. 'Tara!'

It echoed on the still air.

She was sitting in front, next to the driver, where she could stand up, holding on the windscreen, and get a better view. Nick was behind her. She was glad he didn't come out with soothing platitudes. None of them spoke an unnecessary word.

'Tara!'

She and Nick yelled in turn, straining their ears for a call in reply. And each time, there was nothing but the engine, and the water slapping against the hull.

How long had they been out there now? Forty minutes? An hour? And with each minute . . .

She began to think the most nightmarish thoughts of her life. She began to think of steeling herself to make a dreadful phone call to Tara's parents. She thought of guilt following her for the rest of her life. Everybody would say, 'You mustn't reproach yourself,' as people always did. But she would, for ever. Obsessed with Nick, she had deliberately set out to be unfaithful to Simon and this was the result.

She must be so exhausted, so frightened.

The lights of the island were barely visible any more. Maybe she was already too far out to see them.

'Tara!'

The wind was fresher now, a little swell undulating the surface. She shivered. Nick was standing now, holding on to the back of her seat. 'Tara!'

Suddenly the engine coughed and spluttered like tubercular tramp. She gaped, horrified, at Troy.

For the first time, he smiled, his teeth very white in the dark. 'Relax. I just change the gas tank.'

The boat bobbed gently as he disconnected the hose, and re-attached it to another tank. And as he did so, Daisy thought she heard something. 'Listen!'

They all stiffened. It sounded like a piercing whistle, from far away.

They strained to see. And almost at once, they saw it together. The pinprick light of a small boat, coming towards them flat out.

Until it was almost upon them, and she saw the windsurfer being towed behind, she did not dare allow herself to hope. Both boats rocked wildly as a shivering bundle was handed arm to arm over the side.

Her mouth was so dessicated, the words would barely come out. 'Thank you so much, I'm so grateful – '

'No problem.'

The boat zoomed off, as if it were an everyday occurrence. Nick had taken Tara. Shivering with cold and exhaustion, she sat on his lap.

'Really, Tara,' he tutted. 'If you didn't want to come for a farewell drink with me, you only had to say so.'

Daisy's heart twisted. Under the jokey tone was a roughness he couldn't quite hide.

Tara could barely speak, but she tried. 'You know me. Anything to avoid buying a round of drinks.'

Troy was all smiles again. 'You catch any fish?' he asked, over his shoulder.

Her teeth were chattering. It was almost impossible to think anybody could get so cold in such relatively friendly temperatures. 'Sorry. I didn't bring my net.'

'Dear Lord.' Tutting gently, he turned the boat around. 'I come all this way and she don't even got a fish for me.'

Daisy turned around, reached for Tara's hand.

Tara held it so tight it hurt. 'Sorry if I gave you a fright, you old hag,' she whispered.

Daisy's eyes filled with tears. 'Don't you "old hag" me, you old hag.'

Tara's voice was a trembling ghost of its usual self. 'I was beginning to think I'd never taste Fruit and Nut again.' A half-choked sob came from her throat.

'Hush, love.' Nick held her close, rocking her like a baby. 'It's over.'

Silently, she shivered all the way back to the hotel beach. Daisy ran through the gardens to the room. Leaving the door open, she turned the bath taps on and by the time Nick arrived, Tara shivering in his arms, it was half full. They stripped off her lifejacket and dumped her in the warm water, bikini and all.

Nick turned to Daisy. 'She'll be fine now. I'll get some food sent up.'

She hadn't even thought about food. 'Jane and Ian will be wondering where on earth we are.'

'I dare say they'll have heard. I'll go and put them out of their misery.'

His clothes were wet from Tara, the bottoms of his trousers soaked from getting in and out of boats. 'You might still make that plane.'

He shook his head. 'I'll give them a ring – I could do with that drink after all.' His lowered his voice. 'She was bloody lucky.'

Her heart turned over, to think of what might have been. 'I know. Thank you for coming with me.'

'What the hell did you think I'd do?' An odd, almost angry expression came into his eyes. 'Shrug my shoulders and say it wasn't my problem?' Without waiting for a reply, he nodded towards the bathroom. 'Don't leave her. I'm going to reception. Somebody'll need to radio the coastguard or they'll be out there all night.'

Tara slept like a corpse. Daisy had to wake her when the breakfast arrived. She had ordered everything Tara loved; Rice Krispies with sliced bananas, pancakes with maple syrup, hot chocolate as well as coffee.

Apart from her subdued manner, Tara seemed none the worse for her ordeal. 'I feel such a fool,' she said, almost in tears as she drank her chocolate. 'Putting everybody to all that trouble . . .'

312

'Oh, Tara. It could happen to anybody.'

'No, it couldn't. I'd had about four rum punches and I was half hammered. I kept falling off and got exhausted pulling the sail up over and over again and by the time I realized I couldn't sail it back and started trying to paddle it in, I was miles out. I yelled and yelled, but it was getting dark and there was hardly anybody on the beach.'

Her eyes filled with tears. 'I started feeling sick, from the rum. And then it was dark, and I was paddling like fury, but I knew I wasn't making any headway. I should have started swimming, but I'd left it too late, it was too far . . .'

Her voice broke off. Steadying herself, she said, 'I kept wondering where I'd get washed up, and how everybody in the hotel'd be saying, 'Who was it?' 'Oh, you know, that dark girl in the pink bikini, the one who's always pissed and throwing herself at anything in trousers.' She put her hands to her face.

Daisy shot around the table, put her arms around her. 'Don't be daft. They'd say, 'You know, the dark one with the incredible figure.'

'You lying cow.' Through her tears, Tara went on, 'I kept thinking of post-mortems, and wondering if they'd find out I'd just had sex, and whether Mum and Dad would have to find out I'd only just met him – '

By the time she got herself under control, the coffee was going cold.

Despite everything, Tara did justice to her breakfast. She had been too exhausted last night to eat. Suddenly she put her knife and fork down. 'You looked awful last night. As if you'd been crying. Was it because of me?'

Daisy shook her head. 'You don't cry when you're as frantic as I was. It was before.' She braced herself and lied. 'I was feeling all hormonal and missing Simon like mad. I tried to phone but he had the wretched answerphone on. And I had this daft notion that he was out with somebody else.'

'Not much chance of that.'

'I know. I was just being daft.'

Tara poured the last of the maple syrup over her pancake and put the pot on the rail for the birds. Rather shamefaced, she said, 'I didn't really mean it, what I said about Simon. I was just being ratty.'

'So was I.'

'I know. But I'd be a ratty cow if I had to put up with me, too.'

'Oh, Tara.' They laughed together.

'I feel awful about making Nick miss his flight,' Tara said, finishing her pancakes.

'He didn't seem exactly bothered.'

'Even if he was, he'd never say. He's so nice.'

Thinking of how kind he'd been to Tara, Daisy was torn in half. 'Yes,' she said.

'You don't know how nice.'

Daisy looked up. There was an odd, almost ashamed look on Tara's face. 'What is it?'

In the silence, a little brown bird hopped daringly on to the table, perched on a mini pot of raspberry jam and began tucking into it.

Keeping quite still, Tara said, 'I told you a whopper the other night. I did come on to him.'

Daisy gaped at her. 'When?'

'That morning when we had the row. He was so nice, I went right off my stupid head and started trying to kiss him.' She put her hands to her face, and the little bird took fright and flew away. 'God, what he must have thought . . .'

Daisy still could not believe it. 'How did he react?'

'How d'you think?' Tara recovered slightly. 'He said he was very flattered, it wasn't that he didn't find me attractive, but he'd rather we were just friends. He was so nice, I didn't even feel that much of a fool.' Her voice cracked. 'I do now. I feel so awful . . .'

Not half as awful as I feel. Tara had at least been honest about it. There had been no hypocritical pretence, no sneaking about under cover of darkness.

She thought back to that morning, after the row. She would only just have left him, and there was no doubt what sort of state he'd been in. And lo, along had come luscious brown Tara ten minutes later, throwing herself into his arms. It would have been so easy for him, so tempting . . .

There was a knock at the door. 'I'll go.'

She found Nick outside, in shorts and an unbuttoned denim shirt. 'How is she?'

'Fine. Come in.'

He followed her to the balcony, where Tara was dropping bits of bacon over the balcony to a cat in the shrubs beneath.

'How's the castaway?' He handed her a brown paper bag. 'I got you some emergency rations.'

Tara took out half a dozen bars of assorted chocolate.

'Oh, Nick.' In tears, but smiling too, she threw her arms around his neck.

Daisy left them and went for a shower. Seeing them together was more than she could bear, and she couldn't quite understand why. There was nothing between them, and probably never would be.

Gradually, during the morning, she psyched herself up to speak to him, but it was impossible. He was never alone. Tara and Alessandro were with him on the raft. Ian and Giuliano were with him at the beach bar. Jane was nattering to him in the shade. He was talking local politics to a beach vendor, in between buying coral necklaces for his assorted sisters.

He was leaving that night, on the same flight he should have taken the night before. Around four-thirty he left the beach to shower and re-pack the few things he'd needed to get out again.

For five minutes after he'd gone, Daisy braced herself. If she left it too long, he'd be in the shower. She had a reason to see him, and not a trumped up pretext, either. Quite deliberately, she went in her best beach-messy mode — salty-wet hair screwed back into a pony tail, a scruffy old T shirt and crumpled beige shorts.

Sick with apprehension, she tapped on his door.

He seemed startled to see her.

'I know you're busy, but I need to talk to you a minute,' she said rapidly. 'May I come in?'

'Be my guest.' He stood aside to let her pass and showed her on to the balcony.

It was much bigger than their own, practically within spitting distance of the sea. A palm tree waved its fronds so close, you could practically touch them. She sat on the rattan armchair he indicated.

'I was wondering about Troy and the other drivers – I know we thanked them and all that, but they must have used quite a bit of fuel and I was thinking I should give them something, only I'm not sure how much. What do you think?'

'It's taken care of,' he said. 'I saw them this morning.'

I might have known. 'How much did you give them? It's not fair for you to have to – '

'I said, it's taken care of.'

Her voice was cracking slightly. 'They were so good. They all seem so laid-back, but in a situation like that . . .' With an effort, she got her voice under control. 'It was my fault they had to go in the first place. I should never have left her. I knew nobody was watching her.'

He crossed his legs, one ankle resting on his knee. 'It was no more your fault than it was mine. If I hadn't upset you, you wouldn't have left her in the first place.'

She could not look at him. 'It was only the truth. Everything you said was true.' She swallowed, hard. 'I went down to that beach with only one purpose in mind. I thought if we . . .' She could not bring herself to say 'made love'. '. . . if we . . . did it, just once, I'd get you out of my system.'

When he finally spoke, there was more than a trace of cynicism in his voice. 'Then maybe we should have.'

'No. You were right, I could never have lived with the guilt. And besides . . .' She took a deep breath. 'I think what actually happened was infinitely more effective.'

'At getting me out of your system?'

At getting anybody out of my system. Just now, I feel as if my sex drive's been surgically removed. 'At the risk of sounding over-dramatic, it was a kind of fever.' She hesitated. 'And it's gone.'

It was ages before he spoke. He didn't look at her. He barely moved a muscle. The sounds of the beach seemed very far away; the whine of a boat, somebody laughing . . . 'None of it should have happened. I should just have walked you back and said good-night.'

Her heart twisted. 'I think it was better the way it was. It was the penicillin I needed.'

For the first time, she looked him in the eye, and it wasn't as difficult as she'd thought. He wasn't angry or resentful. He almost smiled; albeit a very dry effort. 'I've been called a lot of things, but penicillin's a new one.'

Somehow, she managed a little smile in return. 'Actually, I shouldn't have said penicillin. I'm allergic to it.'

'You don't say.' His eyebrows gave a drily rueful lift. 'I certainly produced an adverse reaction.'

He added another almost-smile, and a pang caught at her heart. She suddenly thought how lovely it would be to be friends with him, but like the man said, you could never really be friends with someone you were attracted to. The sex bit always got in the way.

'I won't keep you.' She stood up. 'I'll see you in the bar before you go. And if I don't have a chance to say it later, I hope I haven't wrecked your holiday, too.'

318

'I'll get over it.' He took the hand she offered and added a light kiss on her cheek. 'Be happy.'

'You, too.' With a bright smile, she left him.

Ten days after she got home, the nightmares started. The first time, she was alone. The second, Simon was beside her.

She awoke sweating and terrified.

Simon roused at once. 'Daisy, what on earth . . .'

Oh, the relief of waking up. Her heartbeat slowing, she lay back against the pillow. 'It was so horrible . . .' Her voice broke off in tears.

'Darling, tell me.'

She could hardly bring herself to describe it. 'I dreamt we found Tara too late. She was still lying on the windsurfer, but . . .' Where she had got the images from, she could not imagine. Dead blue flesh, dead, staring eyes, her dangling feet half eaten by fish . . .

Simon put the bedside light on. 'You're still blaming yourself. I can't think why.'

'Because I should have been watching her. And I wasn't.'

'Daisy, why should you watch her? She's not a three-year-old.'

They had had this conversation before, shortly after her return. 'If she drinks too much and takes stupid risks, it's hardly your problem,' he went on.

He had said this before, too, and something inside her snapped. 'Have you never done anything stupid? Have you never done anything stupid or reckless in your entire life?'

He looked taken aback. 'Of course I have, but – '

'Then don't be so damned smug and uncharitable! You're like the rest of all your damned family – so smug and perfect – everybody's misfortunes are always their own fault, aren't they? AIDS victims, single mothers – and if your father ever goes banging on about single mothers again like he did last Sunday, I swear to God I'm going to tell him to stop insulting my mother, and I don't care if the damned lady captain of the golf club's there – dreadful old hag – ' She put on an exaggerated cut-glass voice – '*Quite right, Edward, couldn't agree more* – why haven't you *told* them? Are you ashamed of me?'

'How can you say that?' Simon looked as if she'd hit him. 'You know I hardly ever see them without you – I'm hardly popping in every five minutes – and as for the old man, I know he goes on a bit, but he doesn't really mean any of it. It's just his way.'

Already she was feeling bad.

'I don't know what's got into you lately,' he went on. 'If it's this Tara business, maybe you should see a counsellor.'

'A counsellor?' She could hardly believe he'd said it. 'You loathe counsellors! You're always saying they're psycho-babbling charlatans who just can't get proper jobs!'

'Well, you should see somebody. If it's giving you nightmares, you've got a problem.'

He switched the light off, snuggled under the duvet with his back to her. ''Night.'

Daisy was nearly in tears. She knew she had upset him. His parents had always been kind to her – she had no right to attack them.

The nightmares continued. Every few nights she woke in a lather of fear. And she didn't need a counsellor to tell her it was guilt, and the only way out was to confess everything to Simon.

She preferred the nightmares.

She saw nothing of Nick. A few weeks after they got home, Jane said one evening, 'Ian, did you manage to speak to Nick about supper next Saturday?'

'I got hold of him at the office, but he can't make it.'

Jane looked put out. 'That's the third time we've asked him!'

Ian shrugged, but he looked a bit like a dog you've told to go away, he smells. 'Probably busy, love.'

When he'd gone, Jane spat blood on his behalf. 'Damn Nick – he was glad enough to come on holiday with us! I suppose he can't be bothered now he's got some super-powered job. Ian's really upset but he'll never admit it. Well, stuff him. Who needs friends like that?'

All this compounded Daisy's guilt. She hated seeing Ian hurt and Jane thinking ill of him. If it was because of her that he was staying away . . .

It's probably nothing to do with you. He's just busy. A new job, new acquaintances . . .

Things with Simon were not exactly brilliant, either. She felt irritated with him, flared up over tiny things.

One Saturday morning, when he was staying over and it was raining like the wrath of God, Tara came wailing that her car battery was flat because she'd left her lights on. Simon had just got up, and was tucking into scrambled eggs at the kitchen table.

'Simon, you couldn't give me a hand, could you?' Tara pleaded. 'I've got some jump leads but the car's parked front first and I need to push it out to get at the battery.'

Simon tutted, not loudly, but enough. 'Tara, how many times have you left your lights on?'

Daisy snapped. 'Oh, stay there. I'll help her.' She flounced into the hall, pulled on a raincoat over her nightie and shoved her feet in to some old trainers.

Simon came right after her. 'Darling, you stay here. I'm dressed – I'll go.'

'No, Simon,' she snapped. 'Go back to your breakfast. I'd hate it to go cold.'

He followed her down anyway, and they had a flaming row in the pouring rain; her pushing him away as she helped Tara heave her car out of its space, and bringing her own round to meet it bonnet to bonnet.

'Go – *away*! We don't – need – you!'

His mouth set, he went back inside. They got the car started, but Tara was nearly in tears. 'I feel awful. If I'd known it was going to cause all this trouble, I'd have called the AA.'

'He was just being a pain,' Daisy said irritably, the rain pouring down the back of her neck. 'Ignore him.' She went inside, wet and cross, and yelled that he was a miserable pain in the bum and not to worry, neither she nor Tara would ever ask him to help with anything ever again.

Simon duly refused to row, and she yelled at him again on that count. He asked mildly if it was PMT, and she yelled no, it was PITBS, short for pain-in-the-bum

Simon, and he put his eggy plate in the dish-washer, said he'd give her a ring later when she'd calmed down, and left.

Daisy lay on her bed and cried. Everything was horrible; her pleasant, ordered certainties crumbling all around her. However she tried to pretend, nothing was the same as before. She felt a little as she had when Tara's beastly Tom had told her at the age of eight that Father Christmas did not exist.

She spent the morning ironing, watching the rain outside, and feeling so miserable she could die. She tried to think of ghastly civil wars, famines, and people with troubles a million times worse than her own. She ironed mechanically, telling herself she was neurotic and self-centred. And suddenly, she realized she had ironed a silk-lookalike shirt on a cotton setting and burnt an iron-shaped V right on the front. Nearly in tears, she threw it in the bin, on top of coffee grounds and the broken shells from Simon's eggs.

The bottom of the iron was coated with burnt-on synthetic, and she had nothing to get it off with. Cursing, she turned it off and put the kettle on for a cup of coffee. She yanked the fridge door open for milk, but there was only skimmed, which she hated in coffee. In the fridge door, next to the milk, was a bottle Jane had bought at the duty-free in Barbados. It was ready-made rum punch, just add ice and water.

On an impulse, she opened it.

The smell knocked her for six. Not the alcohol, although just the concentrated fumes could have almost have made her tipsy. It was the evocative warmth of it; rum and sugar, lime and nutmeg and sunshine; the essence of Barbados in a bottle.

She closed her eyes. The smell took her right back to the beach bar, the sun on her back, the sounds of boats on the water, calypso wafting from the barman's radio, the soft cooing of doves in the gardens. It took her back to gentle nights, the chirp of tree frogs, liquid gold sunsets, and tiny waves lapping on the sand.

And to the one person she had been trying to forget.

It was no use pretending. She sat desolate at the kitchen table.

What am I going to do?

She recalled his last words to her in his room. *'I'll get over it.'*

And you can bet your sweet life he has.

'Be happy.'

I've never been so miserable in my life.

She poured a tiny shot from the bottle, and the taste was even more evocative than the smell. If she closed her eyes she could almost imagine she was back there, drifting with him under the stars . . .

A poignant longing washed over her, but not like before. That had been a physical longing, an inflamed, desperate arousal.

This was different. She just longed to see him, to talk to him, to hear his voice.

What am I going to do?

She took another mouthful.

I wish I could get blind drunk and oblivious, but I never do. A couple of these and I'd just throw up and feel even worse than I do now.

I couldn't feel any worse than I do now.

The phone rang.

She gave it a guilty glance. *Simon. Being all patient and forgiving, as usual.*

Guilt washed over her. *I've been vile to him, snapping and bitching over such little things* . . .

It wasn't Simon.

Five minutes later she scribbled a note, threw a few things in a bag, and ran from the flat.

The traffic was dreadful. Every little old man in a hat who thought twenty-eight miles an hour quite fast enough, thank you, was taking his little old wife to the shops. Cursing and muttering, she made her way to the nearest shops and parked on yellow lines.

First she dashed to the florist on the corner, bought six bunches of freesias; then she dashed back to a bookshop, dithered over the latest bestsellers, chose two, paid, and ran.

Her car was just outside, a blasted traffic warden already dispensing a ticket. 'Get on with it!' she snapped. 'I haven't got all day!'

And then the nightmare really started.

CHAPTER 16

'I don't think you've paid for that, Madam.'

Daisy whirled around. An unsmiling middle-aged man put a hand on her arm. 'I think you'd better come with me.'

'What?' She gaped at him. 'Of course I've paid! Look!' She indicated the bag with the shop's name on it. 'I can show you the receipt!'

'Not those, Madam. That.' He pointed, to somewhere under her left arm.

Daisy went numb. Held there, almost obscured by her thick jacket, was a small paperback she had dithered over. 'I was going to buy it, but I changed my mind,' she said rapidly. 'I meant to put it back but my hands were full of flowers – I'm on my way to my mother's, you see, she's got to go into hospital, and – ' Passing shoppers were looking, whispering as they went. Beginning to panic, she tried to shake him off. 'I'm not a thief!'

'That's what they all say.' He pointed at a sign in the window. 'SHOPLIFTERS – WE ALWAYS PROSECUTE.' 'Come inside, please, Madam. We don't want any unnecessary unpleasantness.'

* * *

Four hours later, Daisy arrived at her mother's. The pots outside were full of scented narcissi, turning creamy heads to the rain. 'Sorry I'm late,' she said brightly, as Barney bounded up to meet her, tongue and tail flying. 'The wretched car wouldn't start – I'd left my lights on again. I had to wait for the AA to come and start it.'

'You shouldn't have rushed down. It really wasn't necessary.' Her mother was paler than usual, but doing her best to look cheerful.

Daisy hugged her and handed over the flowers and books. 'Something to read while you're in there. If you get a chance, that is. I just hope you don't get some old dear in the next bed who natters non-stop.' How she forced such brightness into her tone she would never know.

'It's sweet of you, darling.' She hesitated, and said apologetically, 'I'd never have worried you, but you might have rung and wondered where I was.'

'I expect you'll be out in no time. I'll take a few days off and come and look after Barney.'

'You'll do no such thing – I don't want you taking time off. In any case, Mrs Lewis has offered to have him. It'll probably only be a day or two, anyway.'

Please God, only a day or two.

A log fire was burning in the little sitting room, something her mother rarely bothered with except on the most miserable days, or if guests were coming.

Barney put his nose under her hand, asking for a stroke. She scratched his rough woolly head and he gazed at her with liquid brown adoration.

'How's Simon?' her mother asked.

'Oh, fine. Sends his love.'

That night, in her old room, under the patchwork quilt her mother had made so many years before, she rang him on her mobile. 'Simon?' Her voice was trembling more than her hands.

'Daisy! I phoned earlier and got some message from Jane about you having to rush down to your mother's. Is she all right?'

'I hope so.' She kept her voice very low, in case her mother overheard. 'She's got a lump. It came up on a mammogram and needs investigative surgery. She's not saying much, but she's absolutely terrified. She's going to have to sign a consent form for a mastectomy, in case.'

'Oh, Christ,' he said.

'It's not just that.' Her voice hovered on the brink of tears. 'I stopped to buy her a couple of books to take into hospital and I was in such a state I forgot to pay for one of them and I got arrested for shoplifting.'

'What?'

She choked back a tear. 'I haven't told her – I couldn't worry her any more – they just wouldn't believe me – I got carted off to the police station and everything – I tried to ring you but you weren't in – I explained that I'd been in a terrible hurry and worried about my mother and the police were quite nice, but the fact is I was outside the shop with something I hadn't paid for. I'm going to have to go to court.' Her voice cracked at last. 'Oh, Simon, what am I going to do?'

The line seemed to have gone dead. 'Simon?'

'Hell.' He sounded as if a rugby ball had hit him in the guts. 'I'm still trying to take it in.'

'You'll represent me, won't you?'

There was an awful silence. 'Darling, I can't.'

She was stunned. 'What do you mean, you can't?'

'I mean it's not possible. Firstly it wouldn't be ethical, and secondly, we just don't do criminal law. I'll find you a – '

'You just don't want to, do you?' Her voice broke at last. 'You're terrified of your damned partners finding out your girlfriend's accused of shop-lifting!' Trembling with anger and misery, she switched the phone off.

She gazed around the room; old school photos, a picture of Tara's old pony Jasper, ballet certificates, several scruffy old teddies sitting on a cane armchair – she had never had the heart to get rid of them. Simon had slept here several times, crammed into her single bed. He had laughed gently at her old photos, teased her about the teddies. In return she had teased him about being embarrassed because the bed creaked when they made love.

She had been so happy, then. He had seemed like a rock, always there for her.

And just when I need him most, he deserts me.

When she got home on Sunday night, she told Jane and Ian. 'I know you feel let down, love, but he's right, you know,' Ian said. 'Most legal practices specialize in something – divorce or conveyancing or whatever. Simon's lot just don't do this kind of thing. You'd be much better off with somebody experienced.'

'I know.' Already she felt guilty for being unreasonable. 'They told me it's probably better to plead guilty since it's a first offence – I'll probably just get off with a fine or something.' Her lip trembled. 'How am I going to bear it? Standing in the dock like a criminal?'

'We'll come with you,' Jane said.

'But why should I plead guilty when I'm not? It'll be admitting guilt and I never meant to steal the wretched thing!'

Jane came and put her arm around her. 'We know that, even if they don't.'

Later Ian said, 'By the way, I had a phone call from Nick last night. He's having a bash to christen the flat and we're all invited.'

Twenty-four hours ago she knew the mere thought of seeing him would have made her stomach lurch for England. Now it seemed more like just another crisis, adding to the well of fear and anxiety in her stomach.

'Simon too, of course,' he added.

Of course he'd invite her as half of a couple. What if he was half of a couple, too?

I won't go. There's bound to be some ravishing Amanda-lookalike on his arm, playing hostess.

'When is it?' she asked casually.

'About three weeks. A Friday night, and he said to take taxis because parking's a bit of a nightmare.'

Three weeks. She'd still have the court case hanging over her, never mind her mother. Her stomach contracted. She was having the operation on the Tuesday. By Tuesday night, at least she would know.

On Monday night, she came home very late after going straight from work to the hospital.

Tara was still up, lying on the sofa watching an old Christopher Lee *Dracula*. 'How is she?'

330

Daisy flopped in one of the navy cord armchairs. 'Terrified, and trying not to show it.' She tried to smile. 'We won't know anything till tomorrow afternoon. Fingers crossed.'

'I'll cross everything.' Tara got up. 'Like a hot chocolate?'

'I'd love one.' She felt too tired even to go to bed.

When Tara returned with two mugs, her mouth was twitching mischievously. 'You'll never guess where they sent me today.'

Daisy already knew. 'You told me – that accountant's you've been to before – the one with the ghastly old bloke who's got ginger hairs in his ears and calls you poppet.'

'No, they phoned just before I left this morning and swopped me. Guess where?'

'Kensington Palace? To be Princess Di's social secretary?'

Tara made a face. 'Nope. To Thingy and Whatsit Investment Bank – you know, where Nick works. I'm staying there the whole week.'

Her mouth was suddenly dry. 'Did you see him?'

'You bet. I'm working for an Imogen Parker – and she works for *him*. She's a bit of a bitch – one of those uppity cows who look down on mere secretaries. I found Nick's office – very flash too – he was in a meeting so I left a note with his secretary – she was about fifty, one of those battleaxey types who protect their boss like a tigress with a wounded cub. And around ten to one, guess what?'

'What?'

'He came to my office! And Imogen Whatshername went all preeny and smirky – I could tell a mile off she fancies him – and he'd come to see *me*!' She hooted with laughter. 'He came and kissed me and said, 'Grab your bag, Tara, we're going for lunch.' You should just have seen Imogen Whatsit's face!' She hooted again. 'One of the other girls was telling me he's the youngest director they've ever had – I said it was weird, really, he seems so laid back, but she said not at work he's not.' She giggled. 'She said they call him God – not just as in top chap, but as in Greek – not that he's Greek of course, but because of his colossal fanciability.'

Daisy didn't exactly need it spelt out.

'I gave him everybody's love,' Tara went on. 'And he sent his back, and said he's looking forward to seeing us all at this do.' She sighed. 'But he's going away tomorrow, to Frankfurt and Zurich, so we won't be doing lunch again. Pity, really. That Imogen's face was the best tonic I've had all year.'

Daisy finished her chocolate, dragged herself to bed, but still lay awake till well past two.

Simon was with her when she phoned the hospital next day. Sick with apprehension, she could not bring herself to pick up the phone.

'It's probably nothing,' he said. 'My mother had a lump once. Most of them are benign.'

'Yes, but what about the others?'

'Darling, don't get yourself in a state before you even know.'

She turned on him. 'How can I help being in a state? Would you be so damned calm if you thought your mother had cancer?'

'It's no good yelling at me,' he said, with a trace of irritation. 'Ring the hospital.'

She was so wound up, she hardly knew what she was saying. 'I told you it was tempting fate when you lied to the Parkers and said she was ill!'

He looked as if she'd hit him.

'I'm sorry,' she said unsteadily. 'I didn't mean it – I know it had absolutely nothing to do with it, but I'm just so terrified . . .'

His expression resembled noble patience just hanging on by a whisker. 'I'll ring, if you're too nervous to do it.'

'No. I'll do it.' Her hands had such a bad case of the DTs, she dialled wrong the first time. And when she was eventually put through to the right department and had to wait, she felt positively ill. Two minutes later, sick with relief, she put the phone down. 'It was OK. She's clear.'

'What did I tell you?' He picked up the newspaper and turned to the financial pages. 'You got all in a stew for nothing. Masses of women have lumps. My mother took hers in her stride.'

'Your mother would!' Her dizzying relief erupted into anger. 'She's so damned *sensible*, isn't she? Like all the rest of your damned family! Sensible and stiff-upper-bloody lipped!'

Practically for the first time since she'd known him, Simon raised his voice. 'Will you stop going on about my family? Why have you got it in for them all of a sudden? What the hell has got into you lately?'

She turned away. 'Nothing,' she trembled. 'I was just worried, what with the court case and everything . . .'

He flung the paper aside. 'It's not just that! You've been like this for weeks! Jumping down my throat, attacking me practically every time I open my mouth! I've had it up to here! If you don't sort yourself out . . .'

He stopped short.

'What?' she said.

He would not look at her.

She took a deep breath. 'Simon, are you having second thoughts about this relationship?'

He ran an exasperated hand through his hair, but did not answer.

'Are you?' she repeated.

With a heavy sigh, he turned to her. 'Yes, if you want to know. I'm beginning to think we're not . . . well . . . compatible. You're so irrational sometimes, and I try to be patient, but . . .'

His voice tailed off.

'Is there someone else?'

'No!' He sounded both hurt and angry. 'Do you think I'd two-time you?'

No. You'd never do that.

As she looked at him, it seemed as if a fog that had been round her head for ever was clearing. 'Were you feeling like this before I went to Barbados? Was that another reason you didn't come?'

He would not look her in the eye. 'It was maybe a part of it. I could have got away if I'd really wanted. But I thought maybe if we had a couple of weeks apart . . .'

My God, what a fool I've been. How could I ever have imagined he was going to propose? 'Why didn't you tell me?'

He turned to her at last, his eyes like a hurt spaniel. 'I thought you needed me.'

'Oh, Simon, if only you'd said.' Her eyes filled with tears. 'I've been having second thoughts, too.'

Under his stunned expression was a relief he couldn't quite hide.

They talked for a long time, but she said nothing about Nick. That would really hurt him, and she wanted desperately for them to stay friends.

'I'm sorry I've been such a cow lately,' she said. 'It wasn't you. I've just been wound up.'

'I knew there was something.' He took her hand. 'I'll always be there if you need a friend.'

For the second time, her eyes filled with tears. 'Me, too. If you need any buttons sewn on . . .'

'I wouldn't dare.' He gave her a hug and stood up. 'I'd better go. Give my love to your mother. I'm really glad she's all right.'

'I know.' She swallowed. 'I didn't mean it, about your parents. Give them my love, won't you?'

'I will. And if you need any advice about this court case, you've only got to ask.' He kissed her goodbye at the door, and she shut it behind him.

Two years of her life gone, just like that. Part of her was desperately sad. The rest of her knew it was right. She thought back to so many little things, even the way he'd talked about shares at the New Year's Eve Ball.

He was getting bored with me even then, and I was too stupid to see it.

But when she went to bed that night, a burden had gone from her shoulders. The guilt was gone at last.

Three days before Nick's party, she was having a really bad day at work. Just when they were all ready to go with a hair-care special, a rival chain had beaten them to it and undercut their prices, too. It was their worst nightmare, and the product manager was going ballistic.

In the midst of this chaos, the phone rang again. When she put it down a minute later, Daisy was blank with shock. 'Now what?' asked Trish, at the next desk. 'If anything else goes wrong today . . .'

'It wasn't work.' With a dazed smile, Daisy slipped out and rang Simon on her mobile. She had spoken to him several times since the break-up, mainly about the case. 'Simon, I just had my solicitor on the phone. They've dropped the charges!'

'What?'

'You may well say "what". I wrote to them with a doctor's note to prove I hadn't just made it all up, but I never thought . . .'

'Neither would I. A chain like that's usually got a very hard-headed policy in such matters. But maybe somebody has a heart, after all.'

'I can't believe it.' Hair-care campaign or no, she was floating on pink champagne. 'I'm going to write and offer a donation to a charity of their choosing. What do you think?'

'It's up to you. Can't do any harm.'

She hesitated. 'You're still invited to Nick's do on Friday. Will you come?'

'I don't think so – I've got a hell of a lot of work on, but tell him thanks anyway.' He paused.

'I've been offered a salaried partnership.'

'Oh, Simon! I'm so glad.'

'I'd have preferred an equity partnership, of course, but I can't afford it without borrowing from the old man. Still, the way my investments are going, it shouldn't be too long.'

'Congratulations, Simon. You deserve it.'

I've only got one thing to worry about now. How to smile and pretend I don't care if Nick's got some ravishing cow hanging on to him.

Since four in a taxi was a bit of a squash, they ordered one of those stretch limo jobs which only cost a few quid extra. Jane said it made her feel like a Saudi princess being taken to Harrods, and Ian said in that case, he'd have to be the statutory guardian eunuch, so she'd better not expect too much of a performance, later on.

Tara said it made her feel like the Queen Mother; she practised doing Royal Waves out of the window and smiling kindly at the peasants.

Daisy laughed at all of them, and tried to pretend she was looking forward to a really good party, instead of wishing they could divert down a side street so she could throw up.

Ian and Jane had brought two bottles of Veuve Clicquot. Tara had brought a mug saying, 'Nick's Mug' with a dopey face, because she said it was so naff, she just couldn't resist it. She had also brought a paperback entitled, *Everything You Always Wanted To Know About Pulling The Birds But Were Afraid To Ask*.

Daisy had gone blank where presents were concerned. In desperation she had bought a pewter hip flask bearing the KGB insignia from someone at work who had just been to St Petersburg and brought half a dozen back, and it had seemed like a good idea at the time.

What a stupid present. Why didn't I just get a plant or a bottle of single malt?

337

She'd been expecting one of those rather stark warehouse conversions, but the driver dropped them off at a waterside haven that could almost have been in some seaside village. Cottage-style houses and flats were grouped on three sides of a marina, sleek yachts lying quiet on its darkly shimmering water.

'Look,' said Jane, pointing to a gap in the buildings beyond. 'Tower Bridge, right in his back yard. It can't be more than two minutes walk away.'

However magnificent the setting, Daisy was too sick with nerves to take it in. She noticed nothing till they found themselves outside his door.

The person who opened it said, 'Hi, come in, you can dump your coats in there.'

'There' was a large bedroom with one low, double bed and not much else. It was already piled with coats. Through an open door an *en suite* bathroom was visible.

Thank heaven. Daisy's nerves were making a pit-stop a priority. 'Don't wait for me – I'll see you in there.'

The bathroom was all white, gleaming with newness. She automatically inspected her face, automatically renewed her lipstick, automatically blotted it and automatically smoothed a wisp or two of escaping hair.

Trying to steady her nerves, she left the bedroom and followed the noise across a large hall floored with blond wood and oriental rugs.

She found herself in a huge room, reminding her of one of those New York penthouses you see in the movies; acres of blond wood and massive windows running practically its entire length. It was packed with people and party-noise, and Nick was nowhere to be seen.

She oozed through to the window. The curtains were open. Yachts gleamed on the water below, and not far distant rose Tower Bridge across the river.

A familiar squeal of laughter made her look round. Through various clusters of glass-wielding partygoers, she saw him. He wasn't looking in her direction. Jane, Ian and Tara were with him. And standing right next to him was a woman. He was smiling, introducing her to everybody, and she was smiling back. She was young; probably younger than Daisy, smooth light brown hair drawn smoothly back and eyes like dark blue beacons.

She had steeled herself, of course. She had known exactly what to expect. Somebody eye-catchingly attractive with a set, honeyed smile and the kind of narrowed eyes that say, 'I only like women if they're old or ugly. Preferably both.' You could spot them a mile off, though men never could. You honey-smiled back and felt perfectly justified in loathing them and talking about them the next day. 'My God, what a cow! Did you see her looking daggers because I just talked to him?'

The trouble was, the girl next to Nick was not like this at all. She looked nice.

I hate her.

She turned away, and looked at the river.

'Nice view,' said a voice beside her.

'Spectacular,' she smiled. He was tallish, thirty-five-ish medium build-ish, and rather scruffy, with un-designer stubble and a nondescript old T shirt.

She had guessed that Nick's dress code would be, 'Wear what you damn well like', and they were. People were wearing everything from the kind of glitz appropriate for smartest club, to the kind of thing you might walk the dog in. Daisy had chosen slinky chocolate satin trousers, with a cream silk shirt, and no jewellery but gold twists in her ears.

'You haven't got a drink,' said Scruff, who had a rather nice, musical voice, however. 'Let me get you one.' He held out a hand. 'I'm Ben.'

'Daisy,' she smiled, and duly shook.

'You've beaten me to it,' said a familiar voice at her elbow. 'I was just about to introduce you.'

'Oh, hello Nick!' She made a good show of suitably taken-off-guard surprise. At least he was alone, so she didn't have to smile sweetly at whoever the wretched girl was and pretend to be delighted to meet her. 'I didn't see you when I came in – I was just admiring your view.'

'I'll get you that drink,' said Ben. 'White wine? Kir? Gin? He's got just about everything.'

'A Kir would be lovely, thank you.' He disappeared, and she was left with Nick.

After so long, it was like a kick in the stomach. Her assorted systems were going haywire. The tan had faded, but he still had that residual olivey tone – he would never look winter-white. He wore an olive needlecord shirt, open at the neck, and dark brown cord jeans.

And his eyes were just the same, reducing her to a quivering wreck. 'How are you?' he said.

'Fine.' she managed a bright smile. 'It's a lovely flat.'

'It will be, when I finally get some furniture. I'm still

more or less camping out, but at least there's room for all these people.'

'You've got enough.'

For several seconds, he gazed at her. 'Ian just told me you split up with Simon.'

Her heart leapt violently. 'You mean you've only just heard?'

'How would I hear? It wasn't on the *Ten O'clock News*.'

I must have been mad to assume he'd have heard on the jungle telegraph. And as for letting my heart take off every time the phone rang . . .

'Any particular reason?' he asked.

She tried desperately to do a casual shrug. 'We'd just come to the end of that particular road.'

A blonde girl tapped his arm. 'Sorry, Nick – Natalie says to get your butt in the kitchen this instant – your oven timer's defeating her.'

'The *oven timer*? I don't know how to work the damn thing!' But he was half laughing, in a tolerant male way. He dropped a little pat on Daisy's waist. 'I'd better go, or I'll be in trouble. See you later.'

He left, and the Ben person returned with a glass.

'Thank you,' she smiled.

Natalie. Her stomach was curdling like mayonnaise that's gone wrong. '*Get your butt in the kitchen*.' *If she talks to him like that already, they must be very intimate. I hope she comes out in horrendous acne, the cow.*

She sipped her Kir and felt sick, as the Ben person nattered about the river; had she ever thought about the Vikings sailing three hundred warships up it, and did she know 'Thames' was actually a Celtic word?

She listened politely – it would have been interesting if she hadn't felt curdled inside – made the odd intelligent comment, and longed to go home.

For half an hour she went through the motions; Jane and Ian wandered up with a couple called Sarah and Felix, the group expanded, she finished her Kir and had two more, and felt not only curdled but well on the way to being half cut, too.

Eventually Tara came up, looking moderately flushed, but not over the top. She pulled Daisy aside and half-whispered. 'That Ben chap in the tatty T shirt, you'll never guess who he is.'

'Go on, amaze me.'

'Well, he's not actually anybody you've heard of, but – ' She leaned closer and whispered, 'When his Dad snuffs it, he's going to be a Lord. Can you believe it? He looks like a bag-man!'

Only mildly surprised, Daisy eyed him again. 'People like that don't give a damn what they look like.'

'Still, he's quite nice looking. I might chat him up later.' She turned and scanned the rest of the party. 'Good, food at last. I'm starving.' At the far end, people were already hovering hungrily near the kind of antique pine table that could have done for a family of twenty. 'She looks a bit like him, don't you think?'

'Sorry?' Daisy frowned.

'Nick's sister, you dope.'

'His *sister*?'

'Oh – I forgot. You didn't meet her when we came in, did you? You were in the loo. That girl in black, with her hair up.'

Daisy's legs had suddenly developed minds of their own. One was saying to the other, 'I do a good jelly impression. Can you do wet cotton wool?'

With a frown of concentration, the girl in black was busily arranging dishes on the table.

'She's a cook,' Tara explained. 'Runs a catering business with that fair girl, so he got her to do the eats. She said he's the easiest client they've ever had – he said do what you like as long as there's plenty of it.' She turned to her. 'Coming to eat?'

'I'm not hungry yet. You go.' The mayonnaise in her stomach had un-curdled itself wonderfully, but as always, once she got rid of one curdled mess, another was right behind it.

Now what do I do? Let him do the running, and maybe realize he's not going to flog a dead horse twice?

Half an hour later, when she'd put away enough exotic nibbles to counteract the Kir, Nick was suddenly right beside her.

'Oh, hi,' she said brightly. 'The food was lovely. Your sister did you proud.'

'Yes,' he said. 'I might even give her a bonus.'

'I must get the recipe for those little ricotta thingies,' she went on brightly. 'And those prawn things were gorgeous – and as for that nutty meringue thing, I made an absolute pig of myself.'

His eyes had never left her face. 'Nuts can be dangerous. Some people are allergic to them.'

His eyes were melting her like snow in May. As if a computer virus had got into her system, every nerve ending she possessed was going wild. Her voice was still just about working, however. 'Yes, but she'd labelled it, so nobody could possibly be in any doubt, as long as they can read, of course . . .'

His voice was nearly normal, too. Only a faintly husky edge suggested the virus might possibly be contagious. 'I was wondering,' he said, 'about that allergy you were suffering from in Barbados. As I recall, something produced a violently adverse reaction. Are you still suffering?'

Her heart and stomach lurched together like two drunks. 'I wasn't exactly allergic to it. I didn't quite realize at the time, but there was another ingredient causing the reaction.'

'And you identified it.'

Oh, help. She nodded.

'And eliminated it.'

Her voice was packing up. 'Not exactly. It sort of went of its own accord.'

'In which case, contact with the original substance will no longer be dangerous.'

That depends on your definition of dangerous.

She swallowed, hard. 'I think maybe it could be attempted.'

His eyes flowed into her like warm, green rivers. 'But the ambient conditions must be right. An atmosphere like this . . .' – he glanced around at the cheerful, noisy crowd – '. . . would never do.'

'Not exactly,' she croaked.

'But maybe later . . .' He touched her arm as somebody pushed past saying, '. . . *and she'd put my mobile in the bloody freezer – I didn't find it for three days – I went right off my head –* '

Daisy hardly knew what she was saying. 'Jane's ordered a taxi for one o'clock – they've got a wedding to go to tomorrow, you see, in Sussex or somewhere – and they have to make an early start, but – '

'But you don't.' His eyes held her like twin green magnets. 'So unless you're going to change into a pumpkin – '

'Nick!' A jovial voice interrupted him. 'You'll never believe what I just heard about John Sergeant from Platt and Gardiner! He's jacked it all in and gone to some Shetland croft to *paint*! Mind you, I always did think he was a trifle odd . . .'

How she got through the rest of the evening, Daisy would never know. She was like a schizophrenic; half on anticipatory fire, the other half chatting animatedly, even listening to bores with equanimity, not that there were many of those.

Now and then, Nick caught her eye across the room, and she could have sworn the air crackled.

When one o'clock loomed, it was easy enough to get herself deep in conversation with a Helen somebody whose husband worked for Nick and was having terrible trouble with her six-month-old twins' *au pair*.

It was easy to say, 'Heavens, one o'clock already?' when Jane tapped her arm and said, 'Are you coming?'

'I'm not a bit tired – you go – I'll get a cab later.'

Tara was engrossed with a Jonathan somebody – but rather to Daisy's surprise she left with Jane and Ian, having bestowed her phone number first, of course. On the way out she winked at Daisy and whispered, 'He wanted to take me home, but I'm playing hard to get.'

345

After they'd left, Nick came and sat on the arm of the sofa beside her. Helen was now telling somebody else about the *au pair's* complete inability to understand washing machines. 'Tara's calmed down a bit,' he said.

He had slid his arm along the back of the sofa, where it just touched her hair. And even that contact was reducing her to a woozy jelly. 'She's still Tara, but she's getting her act back together.'

'I guess an experience like that does something to you. Must concentrate the mind, when you think you've got a fair chance of not making it.'

Somebody else was taking their leave; he got up to see them off. Gradually, nearly everyone had gone but his sister and her colleague. Daisy had spoken to her, and even got the recipe for the ricotta thingies.

It was well past two when the last guests left and Natalie and friend were still piling their equipment into boxes. Although she knew it was crazy, Daisy felt ridiculously self-conscious about being the last to go, as if everybody knew why she was doing it. 'Heavens, I had no idea it was so late,' she said brightly, as Nick waited to help them cart it all downstairs. 'I really must call a cab.'

'Wait till I get back,' he said casually. 'There's a reliable company I use all the time. Are you ready?' he added, to his sister.

Absolutely, Mr Trevelyan,' she said, tongue in cheek. 'I left the bill on the kitchen table and prompt payment would be appreciated.'

With half a very dry smile he took a wodge of notes from his trouser pocket. 'That prompt enough for you?'

346

'Ooh, cash!' she squeaked. 'We won't have to declare it!'

'I didn't hear that,' he said drily. 'Come on – let's get that van loaded.'

During the minutes that she was on her own, Daisy raced to the loo, frantically wished she had a toothbrush, and ate half an apple, instead. When she came out, the place seemed unbelievably quiet and empty, just some of the more melodious kind of jazz wafting softly from the CD player.

There was a fair amount of debris left; glasses, coffee cups, plates left in corners. Natalie and friend had still been clearing when he'd told them to leave it; it was high time they got off home.

She began collecting it all up, took it to the kitchen. It was as big as she'd expected, a window overlooking the marina. The units were wood, dragged in sunny yellow. There was an island unit large enough to seat six and state-of-the art everything, but it all looked comfortable rather than colour-supplement perfect, with a clearly lived-in sofa against one wall. She dumped everything on the worktop, went for more. And while she was collecting glasses, she heard the door open.

Trembling adrenalin shot through her.

He came in. He shut the door. And for a moment, he just stood there, his back against it.

'I was just tidying up,' she said unsteadily. 'It's an awful – '

'Leave it. I have someone coming in the morning.'

Unsteadily she replaced the plates on a tiled coffee table.

It was about fifteen feet, eye to eye. A thin, fifteen-foot line of common-or-garden London air, suddenly conducting electricity like premium quality copper wire.

'I thought they'd never go,' he said.

CHAPTER 17

She was never quite sure afterwards who made the first move; maybe it was him by a millisecond. It was as if some profound new law of physics had been created, viz. *'When two bodies of equal attraction have been kept apart by extraneous factors, such bodies will, when these factors are eliminated, come together at the speed of light 10^2.'*

There were no preliminaries; no lazy rituals for the sake of form. As if they'd been starved, mouths fastened on each other, hands trembled, touching everywhere they could, heartbeats going like tribal drums.

As they came up for air, he fumbled at the tiny, pearl buttons of her shirt with fingers too desperate to cope with them. 'How many of these damn things – '

'Let me . . .' Her fingers were smaller, quicker, and while she disposed of them one by fevered one, his fingers fell to the zip of her trousers. As the last pearl slipped from its buttonhole, the satin trousers slithered to her ankles.

With warm, firm hands he slipped the shirt from her shoulders as she undid the cuffs. It slithered to the floor. But however fevered his fingers, he had no trouble with her bra. In half a second he released the fastening, his lips running a hot trail over the side of her neck as he cupped her breasts. 'Oh, Daisy, Daisy . . .'

She gasped aloud as his fingertips teased her nipples, almost falling over herself in her haste to kick herself out of her trousers.

Somehow, they managed a trembling-heartbeat little laugh. 'Don't break an ankle, for God's sake – not now –' He half lifted her out of them, his lips trailing hot over her stomach as he peeled her tights down. One by one she lifted her feet, and he tossed them aside.

She was pulling at his shirt, desperate to get it off him. He lifted his arms, she pulled it over his head and threw it aside. He wore nothing underneath; their hot skins fused together like molten metal.

He knelt, slipping her tiny lace knickers to her ankles, his lips moving agonizingly over her stomach, down over the soft curling hair. And as she kicked them off, the tip of his tongue snaked in between her thighs.

Daisy gasped. It wasn't just desire that overpowered her; it was something raw and primeval, something that would not wait.

She groped at his zip but he stopped her. Scooping her up like thistledown, he carried her away. Through the red mist of desire and a pounding heartbeat, she saw nothing until he laid her on a huge, white bed. Through a red mist she saw him kick off his shoes, yank off his socks, and undo his zip. Boxer shorts and trousers were yanked down together.

She had seen him like this before, but this was different. There was no guilt, nobody to interrupt them.

He came to her and their mouths fused again. But after a second, he tore himself away. Reaching for the bedside table, he yanked a drawer open.

'No, Nick.' Her voice was husky as she pulled him back. 'It's all right. You don't have to – '

There was nothing more to stop them.

As their mouths fused again, she felt for him, trembling as her fingers closed around his burning hardness. His body shuddered; his hand slid between her thighs.

A strangled gasp came from her throat. She could wait no longer and he didn't ask her to. He didn't tell her to slow down, as her trembling fingers guided him. Like steel into satin, he slid into her.

Just for a moment he paused, his body shuddering, poised just above her.

Although she wanted to wait, to savour the first ecstasy, already an explosion was building, out of her control. And with his first deep thrusts, it was upon her. From somewhere far away, she heard her own sharp cries as her body jerked and convulsed beneath him. Oblivious to everything, she was tossed from one screaming peak to another, until at last she lay limp beneath him. Opening her eyes, she found him gazing down at her, his eyes as warm as African rivers. 'Oh, Daisy,' he whispered, brushing her face with his fingers. 'You drive me wild . . .'

Her only reply was to pull him close, squeezing him inside, urging him on to the peaks she had just left. She held him tight, revelling in the rising tide of his possession as he thrust harder, deeper, faster, until his body tensed and quivered and a low, gasping shudder came from his lips.

For a long time they lay side by side, still locked, their heartbeats drifting back to earth.

Lazily he stroked her hair, dropped a soft kiss on her forehead. 'We wait all this time, and all I can manage is a two-minute performance.'

A little laugh shook her. 'Do you hear me complaining? I couldn't have waited.'

Under her hand, his chest quivered in return. 'Just as well, or you'd have sacked me already.'

She squeezed the limp, tender thing inside her, like a kiss.

'That was nice,' he murmured, so she did it again. Chuckling softly, he ran a hand down her back and gently squeezed her squidgy bits. 'I think I've wanted you ever since you were trying to change that wheel and desperately trying to stay decent so I wouldn't see your peachy little bottom.'

'I knew you were looking, you beast.'

'Of course I was. It was the most entrancing sight I'd seen in years.'

Their laughter melted together, like their bodies. 'But it wasn't just that,' he went on. 'The clincher was when you –' He pulled away, slipping out of her at last. 'I knew there was something missing. Your hair. Let it down.'

Slowly she sat up. Seductively, she took out the pins one by one, untwisted the silk-covered band, and let it tumble around her shoulders.

Gently he lifted it, pushed it back from one breast, bent and kissed her nipple. He lay on his back, his arm around her as she lay on her side, her arm across his chest. Snuggling her even closer, he drew her left thigh to lie across his stomach.

For a while they lay quiet, his fingers gently winding in her hair. 'What happened with Simon?'

'It had just turned into a comfortable habit. For both of us. And I just hadn't realized.'

'That's what I was hoping. Only I was beginning to think it was wishful thinking. I couldn't push any more. It had to be your decision.'

And you were right. She tried to remember the precise moment when she'd known. It was the electricity that had confused her. Electric sex would never have been enough. Slowly she'd realized that she *liked* Nick more than Simon. Slowly she had realized just how Simon's occasional self-righteous intolerance irked her, and equally, that he would never change. Nick did not judge and disapprove, as Simon did. Simon would have spent all night looking for Tara when she was lost; he would have swum shark-infested waters if necessary, but later, he would have despaired at her irresponsible stupidity. He would have matched her to his own exacting standards and found her wanting.

And slowly, she had come to realize that what she had wanted from Simon was more than any man could ever give. Out of the blue, something had triggered a long-forgotten childish fantasy. She opened her mouth to tell him, and stopped herself.

For God's sake, do you want to put him off already?

With a little shiver, she nestled closer.

'You're cold,' he murmured. 'We should be under the covers, not on them.'

They wriggled underneath and re-nestled. And just as she was drifting off, he said drowsily, 'Something's

353

eluding me. The title of a book, or a film . . . He paused. '*Stay With Me Till Morning*. That was it.'

Her heart gave an odd little twist.

'But it's still wrong,' he murmured, into her hair. 'Stay with me till Monday morning. Or Sunday night, at least.'

Something warm and delicious stole through her. 'I haven't even got a toothbrush,' she whispered.

'I think that can be arranged.' He dropped a soft kiss on her hair and they drifted into sleep.

When she awoke she lay for a dozy moment wondering where on earth she was.

It came back pretty fast. He was no longer beside her, but the sounds of running taps from the bathroom told her he wasn't far away.

She stretched deliciously. Oh, the heaven of realizing that what you'd thought was only a delicious dream was nothing of the kind.

After a minute he emerged from the bathroom, a towel around his waist. 'Did I wake you up?' With a smile that made her heart turn over, he sat on the edge of the bed, dropped a soft kiss on her lips and brushed a wisp of hair from her forehead.

'No,' she smiled. His face was damp and the smell of toothpaste brought a tiny thread of anxiety into her lovely pink glow. *Oh, help. I don't want him kissing me properly before I've even brushed my teeth.*

'Like some coffee?' he asked.

'I'd love some.'

He dropped another kiss on her hair and stood up.

And as he was halfway out another anxious thought struck her. 'What time's your cleaning lady coming? I don't want her finding a trail of bras and knickers on the floor.'

Choking back a laugh, he came back. 'Daisy, I really will have to sort you out. You can't go through life worrying what people are going to think.' Still laughing, he kissed her again. 'But don't fret – I'll hide the evidence.'

Once he was gone she nipped to the bathroom. There was a huge bath, a separate shower and a bidet, all in gleaming white with gold fittings. But of course, no spare toothbrush. She wondered whether he'd mind if she borrowed his, decided he wouldn't, and gave her teeth a really good clean.

Behind the door she found a navy towelling bathrobe, slipped it on, and padded on bare feet to the room they'd partied in.

Bright sunshine gleamed on the boats in the marina. A large, orange-beaked seagull perched on the chrome rail of a yacht, and dropped a mess on the deck.

Daisy laughed to herself. 'You're going to be popular.' A toasty-brown coffee smell was already wafting from the kitchen, and he was pouring fresh orange juice into a couple of glasses.

She tiptoed up behind him and slid her arms around his waist.

He turned at once and slid his arms around her waist, instead. 'You were supposed to stay in bed,' he said, in mock-cross tones, dropping a soft kiss on her hair. 'I was going to bring you breakfast.'

'I had to get up and brush my teeth,' she confessed: 'I borrowed your toothbrush – I hope you don't mind. I gave it a good wash afterwards.'

'I don't mind your little germs.' Gently he tweaked her waist. 'Humour me and go back to bed.'

Well, if you insist . . .

She lay in a haze of dreamy contentment, waiting.

When he came, there was only coffee and orange juice after all. 'I've rather screwed up the catering,' he confessed. 'There isn't even an egg.'

A ripple of laughter shook her. 'Dear me. Maybe I'd better go home right now.'

'I'll be taking you home in a couple of hours anyway.'

Her face crashed.

'To get some clothes,' he teased. 'It wouldn't be proper for you to stay the entire weekend without even your pyjamas.'

Oh, the relief. 'Can I have a shower first?'

'You can, but . . .' A dangerous glint danced at the back of his eyes. 'I was rather hoping you'd christen that bath. It's been sitting there all lonely and unloved ever since I moved in and I'm sure you could do with a really good soaping.'

Although her assorted systems were going haywire, she put up a wonderful pretence. 'It'd be a terrible waste of water. That bath's big enough for two.'

'Is it?' he mused, playing along wonderfully. 'Such a notion had never even occurred to me.'

Daisy valiantly repressed her warm, woozy laughter. 'Maybe I'll just have a lick and a promise.'

'Then I promise I'll give you a good soaping.' The

spark glinted wickedly as he drew the covers back to just below her nipples. 'And as for licks . . .'

He drove her home an hour and a half later. Jane and Ian were long gone, and to her relief, Tara was still in bed. She didn't want to have to tell anybody yet – it was still too heady to share. She changed into jeans and a sweater, rammed more things into a bag – scribbled a note saying, *'Gone away for the weekend, Love Daisy, XX,'* and laughed to think what they'd make of it.

He was waiting for her, but not in the E-type. 'It wasn't very practical,' he'd said, opening the garage door to reveal a new, state of the art saloon car with lovely leather seats. 'And a magnet for specialized thieves.'

He drove back to the City in lovely spring sunshine, and they spent the morning wandering round his backyard. It was only a short walk to both Tower Bridge and William the Conqueror's Tower, but they left those for the tourists. Instead he showed her the backwaters he loved; streets that looked almost Dickensian, cobbles and old dark buildings that could have stepped out of Fagin's London. They walked past the site of the Clink, a medieval prison, where a museum now stood. He showed her the remains of the thirteenth century Palace of the Bishop of Winchester, next to the Clink. They followed the grassy embankment, bought huge ice-creams with chocolate flakes in them, and wandered along the river to Shakespeare's New Globe Theatre where more tourists milled with cameras.

'I thought it'd look odd, when they were building it,' she said, as they surveyed the Tudor timbers, the round thatched roof. 'But it looks quite happy. Maybe the ghosts of the old Globe have come to make it feel at home.'

'Maybe.' He dropped a kiss on her hair. 'There must be enough ghosts in this part of London. If they ever do *Julius Caesar*, there'll probably be a few Romans arguing the toss about whether Cassius looks "lean and hungry" enough.'

It was clouding over, getting chilly, so they stopped for coffee and cognac at a pub where Dr Samuel Johnson used to sup his port, came out into a downpour, and ran back.

He sent out for pizza and they talked for hours as the rain poured down outside. They sprawled on a sofa together, watched a corny old film, laughed and talked until it was dark. They went out to a supermarket for steaks, oysters, smoked salmon, salad, sticky toffee pudding and cream, and Daisy cooked for him. And they talked more, and made love again.

The following morning, after a lazy bathrobed breakfast of scrambled eggs with smoked salmon, coffee and Buck's Fizz, while April showers fell on the yachts outside, Nick said there were only two things you could do on a rainy Sunday morning: read the papers or go back to bed. And since he hadn't been for the papers . . .

Half an hour later, when he was proving beyond all possible doubt that he could keep her trembling on the edge of ecstasy for longer than she'd ever dreamed possible, the phone rang.

'Who the hell . . .' With gritted frustration, Nick reached to the bedside table. 'Trevelyan,' he said impatiently.

Of all the lousy timing . . .

Daisy lay back, one arm flung behind her on the pillow. Waiting was a torment.

'Oh, Lord,' Nick was saying. 'No, don't worry. Is she . . .?'

He was listening again, but with only half his brain. The other half, she could see from the way the sheet stood up like a mini-tent, was elsewhere.

Whoever was on the other end, they were clearly not going to shut up in a hurry. Nick's face was a picture; desperate to get off the phone, but unable to manage it without being abrupt to the point of rudeness.

Well, why not a return favour while she waited? Keeping her face a picture of long-suffering patience, her fingers stole under the sheet to the tent pole.

'*Stop it!*' He mouthed it, trying not to laugh.

I've hardly even started. Her fingers slithered and massaged in a lazy orgy of erotica.

His face creased in agony. 'Don't worry about it,' he was saying, his crisp, businesslike tones making her want to crack up. 'No, it's really no problem – '

Her fingers were still at it, like a seasoned courtesan.

'Cut it out!' This time he said it aloud, trying not to laugh as he pushed her away. 'Sorry,' he added into the receiver. 'I'm looking after a friend's dog and the damn thing's not house-trained. As you were saying . . .'

Time to move up a notch . . . Wriggling right under the sheet; she began a more throughly erotic treatment.

'No, Mike, don't worry about a thing, I'll see to – *stop it*!' Torn between frustration and laughter, he aimed a slap at her, and missed. 'Sorry,' he said, crisply into the phone. 'That animal's heading for trouble. Yes, Mike, I'm sure. Don't worry. Yes – OK Bye.'

And he slammed the phone down.

He ripped the sheet away. And after a brief mock fight, which Daisy did not try very hard to win, he pinned her down, holding her wrists on either side of her shoulders. 'Before we go any further, I have to acquaint you with couple of ground rules regarding dirty weekends in this establishment.'

For a man torn between savage arousal and laughter, he did a fair job of sounding mad.

And for a woman equally torn, Daisy surpassed herself, too; putting on a Cockney twang worthy of Eliza Doolittle. 'Sorry, guv. I fort gents liked that sort of fing.'

Manfully he suppressed a choke of laughter. 'Silence, you shameless baggage, or I'll turn you over and wallop you. When I have a guy who works for me on the phone, telling me his wife has just gone into labour and he won't be in tomorrow, I do not want to be heavy breathing down the phone. Right?'

Womanfully, she choked too. 'Right, guv. When you're on the blower, I won't never touch your lusty spear again.'

He did choke. 'My *what*?'

'Your lusty spear, guv. That fing wot – '

Further choking was beyond both of them. And after their mutual hysterics had subsided, he pinned her down again. His voice was as warm as his eyes, roughened with desire, but still mock-mad. 'And now, you shameless baggage, I'm going to get my own back.'

His melting kiss was only the start. His lips blazed a tantalizing, erotic trail south.

Although she was dissolving, Daisy somehow kept the act up. 'Gawd 'elp us, whatever is 'e a doin' of?' She clamped her knees together. 'Muvver! Save me from a fate worse than deff!'

'Nobody's going to save you.' He brushed his lips against the soft, curling hair. 'Open your legs, you trollop. I'm going to make you beg for mercy.'

Jane, Ian and Tara all gaped at her.

'With *Nick*?' Jane echoed.

'Well, stone me,' said Ian.

'You sneaky cow!' said Tara.

'This wouldn't have started in Barbados, would it?' Jane asked with dawning suspicion.

Daisy was prepared for this. They had agreed that in the circumstances . . . 'No,' she said, with perfect truth, since strictly speaking it had started a good deal earlier. 'We both knew there was something, but nothing actually happened.'

'Not even when you spent the night with him?' Tara demanded.

'Especially not then.'

Light was dawning on Tara's face. 'My God, no wonder you were in such a foul mood all the time.'

'She's not now,' Ian grinned. 'Just look at her face. Like the cat that's had the goldfish.'

* * *

Daisy had that smile on her face for weeks. For over two months, she spent every weekend with him, and during the week she'd see him at least once.

It was around the middle of May that her first euphoria began to fade.

'I have to go away this weekend,' he told her, one Wednesday evening. 'To Cornwall. It's a family thing.'

Her tone did not betray the shadow that fell on her heart. 'In that case, I'll go to my mother's. I've been neglecting her.'

The following evening, she confided in Jane. 'I know it's silly, but I just felt so hurt that he didn't invite me. I'd invite him, if I had a family do. It's as if he doesn't want me to meet them.'

'Daisy, family dos can be a complete pain. Maybe he didn't want to inflict it on you.'

'Maybe. And maybe he didn't want his assorted female relatives nudging each other and whispering, 'Do you think it's serious?'

'Oh, rubbish,' Jane scoffed, rather too heartily.

Daisy's lip trembled. 'I'm crackers about him. I've never felt like this about anyone. I want to tell him, but I can't. He's never said he loves me. Not once.'

'Maybe you've been too "available",' Jane said rather awkwardly. 'I hate to say it, but every time he lifts his little finger, you jump. You even ducked out of something else the other week, to see him. Maybe you should be a bit more elusive. Keep him guessing.'

She forced a smile. 'All very easy in theory . . .'

Until then, she had lived for the moment, milking every heady drop out of just being with him. Any tiny fears about losing him had been ignored. No man comes with a guarantee. No man says, 'Look, this is going to last exactly six weeks, or six months, or until you want it to end.' If you weren't prepared to take the risk, you would never have a relationship worth a damn.

But perhaps she had been too 'available'. The following week, when he phoned and suggested a French film and dinner, she said she was terribly sorry, but someone at work was having a hen night and she couldn't get out of it.

'Fine,' he said, quite cheerfully. 'Have fun.'

Great.

Just to make it worse, Ian brought Simon back from the squash club the following night. He already knew about Nick, of course.

'I did wonder,' he confessed. 'I had a feeling he had his eye on you.'

She felt compelled to fib. 'Nothing happened, Simon. Not until we'd split up.'

'Not from want of trying on his part, I bet.'

If only you knew.

He hesitated. 'Maybe I'm prejudiced, but be careful, Daisy. He struck me as the archetypal serial heart-breaker and I'd hate to see you get hurt.'

Thanks a bunch. 'I don't have any claim on him, Simon. We're just having fun.'

Over the next few days she agonized over her relationship with Nick; looking for any little sign that she was more to him than fun and good sex.

He could be very tender, of course, but did it mean anything? Simon had been tender, even till shortly before the end.

And look what happened there. I was so blithely sure of him.

The less secure she felt, the more it came out in an increasingly assumed casualness with Nick. Only when they were in bed did she drop the act; it was easy to let go and let passion mask her increasing love for him. She began to be paranoid about the fact that he never said he loved her. He said he loved her hair or the soft little screams she made when she climaxed, but it wasn't the same.

One Sunday night, only an hour after they'd made love, he drove her home after yet another weekend together. Daisy was fighting tears, because he hadn't said it yet again.

'Are you all right?' he asked, as he drove through Richmond Park. He always went through the park, where the leaves were new, tender green on the trees, creamy candles of chestnut blossom were breaking, and a herd of fallow deer grazed on the emerald grass.

'I'm fine,' she said brightly.

He glanced across at her. 'You seemed a bit edgy today.'

'I'm fine!' she snapped, and wished to heaven she hadn't.

'All right, all right,' he soothed. 'I know a bad case of hormones when I see it.'

He sounded almost like Simon, who had prided himself on his noble tolerance of PMT. It did affect her. She did get snappy; tearful and more than usually vulnerable . . .

She went suddenly cold.

Oh, God.

When he dropped her off, her goodbye kiss was rushed and distracted. She ran inside, shut her bedroom door, and leafed frantically through her diary.

Heaven help me. Why don't I mark these things so that I know? She tried desperately to put dates to events, but things were jumbled up in her mind. It was a couple of days after she'd lied to him about the party. Six weeks ago.

For some reason, her brain veered to something else, a couple of weeks later. A takeaway lunch, grabbed in a rush from a supermarket. A sandwich, prawn and mayonnaise.

Why did I think of that?

Almost before she'd asked it, she knew. Her brain had not been idly wandering; it had merely short-circuited the usual thought processes.

She felt sick. Far sicker than she'd felt after eating that sandwich. She hadn't been desperately ill; just ill enough that leaving the flat had seemed highly unwise for thirty-six hours.

My God. My pills.

The following day, in her lunch hour, she slipped out to the chemist and bought a home test kit. The instructions told her that although a false positive result was almost impossible, a false negative was not.

So even if it comes up negative, I'll still be in agonies.

She did not have that agony, at least. It came up clear as the Caribbean sea.

CHAPTER 18

The sickness she felt had nothing to do with 'morning'.

'What are you going to do?' Jane asked.

'I don't know.'

'You have to tell him.'

'I can't!' The tears she'd been trying to suppress welled up at last. 'What if he thinks I did it on purpose? To trap him?'

'Daisy, he has a right to know.'

'I know, but – ' She put her hands to her face. 'If he'd just said once that he loves me . . .'

'Men say that all the time. It doesn't necessarily mean anything.'

'Jane, he said he "wasn't ready for commitment". Those were his very words.'

Keeping the secret was dreadful. It affected her relationship with him. When they made love, she could not respond in quite the same uninhibited way. When he asked what was wrong, she said lightly that it was just work-related stress.

She agonized endlessly. One option was unthinkable, the other almost as bad. He was about to take delivery of a yacht. He was planning to sail it to Jersey, and that was just for starters. Responsibilities such as this were just not on his agenda.

She lost sleep from worrying. People began to say she looked tired – a polite euphemism for awful. When even Nick said it, she told him she wasn't sleeping very well. Endlessly she told herself to take her courage in both hands and tell him, and every time she saw him she chickened out.

She had told nobody but Jane. She even put off phoning her mother, whose almost psychic voice-reading would tell her something was wrong.

When her mother phoned ten days after the test, wondering if everything was all right, Daisy felt dreadfully guilty. 'I was just about to phone you,' she fibbed. 'I was thinking of coming down the Sunday after next, if that's OK.'

'That'll be lovely.' Her mother hesitated. 'I might invite somebody for lunch, if you don't mind.'

From her tone, Daisy knew it wasn't old Mrs So-and-so from down the lane. 'You've got a new man, I take it.' She tried to sound pleased and sounded like a disapproving elder sister, instead.

'I won't ask him, if you'd prefer,' her mother went on, 'but I've seen him a few times and I thought it'd be nice if – '

'Of course, Mum.' She forced an enthusiasm she was far from feeling. 'I'd love to meet him.'

That weekend, while collecting her things from Nick's bathroom, she called, 'I'm going to my mother's next Sunday.'

He was in the bedroom, pulling a sweater over his

shirt. Drily he said, 'You said that in a certain tone. A "you're not invited" tone.'

'I didn't think you'd want to come! You didn't invite me when you went home!'

'That wasn't purely a social visit. There were problems to sort out.'

'Like what?'

'If you really want to know, my sister's ex was making trouble.'

She felt both guilty and angry with him at the same time. 'Then why didn't you say so before?'

'I'm sorry,' he said simply. 'I just didn't want to bore you with family problems.'

If only you'd said . . . 'If you'd really like to come, I could do with some moral support. She's got a new man and I know I'm going to hate him on sight.'

'Why do you say that?'

'Why d'you think? They're either useless spongers who think a woman on her own must so desperate she'd just love to support them, or else they're not spongers who think it'd be amusing to string her along for a few months. I hate the lot of them.'

'Daisy.' Tutting gently, he slid an arm around her waist. 'Don't pre-judge the poor guy. He might not actually have horns and a tail.'

His smile, the glint in his eyes made her heart turn over. For a moment, she imagined three little words shattering them for ever.

'Nick, I'm pregnant.'

His reactions would stare her in the face. First disbelief, followed seconds later by a dawning, *'Oh, hell, what have I got myself into?'* She went home without telling him, and cursed herself for a coward.

Three days before they went to her mother's she awoke feeling dreadful. It was only ten past six, but pain had brought her from sleep; familiar, cramping pains that were somehow much worse than usual.

Suddenly she was wide awake. Gripped with pain and panic, she ran to the bathroom.

She took the day off, cried for most of it, and longed for Jane to come home.

'I'd have thought you'd be relieved,' Jane said, when she finally got her alone.

'I should be, but . . .' The tears came again. 'We made a little life together, and it's gone, just like that. What if I'm one of those women who miscarry all the time?'

Jane did her best to comfort her. 'One in seven pregnancies ends in miscarriage. My sister had one, and she's got two perfectly healthy little monsters. It was probably just Mother Nature getting rid of a bad job.'

Daisy flooded with tears. She couldn't bear to think of any tiny life they'd created being a 'bad job'. But that wasn't the only reason. She knew she was crying for something she'd hardly dared to dream.

And still she didn't tell Nick. She drove him to her mother's and wanted to tell him all the way, but what was the point now? He still might think she had done it to entrap him. He wouldn't trust her any more.

Pale and tense, she desperately tried to cover it, but knew the cracks were showing. The cottage was picture-postcard pretty; the garden crammed with flowers.

369

It was warm and sunny, early roses scented the garden and bees hummed buzzily. Her mother looked lovely and took to Nick at once, and he to her.

She tried desperately to like the new man. He was perhaps a little older than her mother, but not by much. He was still very good-looking, barely grey, with the kind of beard that ought to belong to a sea captain and eyes that glinted with intelligence and humour.

'We met at an antiques fair, a few weeks ago,' her mother explained. 'I was looking for a little pine mirror for the bathroom and we sort of collided over the porcelain.'

'It was rather a contrived collision,' confessed the man, whose name was Charles. 'I'd had my eye on Isabel from the moment she walked in the door.'

Daisy felt the old, familiar antipathy rise in her. The spark in his eyes was suddenly looking like something else she knew all too well. Another smoothie. Another practised operator who saw her mother coming. Dislike rose in her every time she saw him look at her; every time she saw him touch her hand or brush her shoulder as he went past.

At least he lived a couple of hundred miles away; he had only come down for the weekend, just as he had come for the antiques fair. He was a collector of antique porcelain, and that put her off, too. Another arty type who loved acquiring beautiful things, like women with vulnerable eyes who were longing for love.

They sat outside in the little garden, where her mother's tubs were already cascading with the kind of flowers nobody else had in their summer tubs. Blue, star-like flowers, and little pink things she'd never seen before. They ate pasta with delicate Mediterranean vegetables in a creamy, delicious cheese sauce. There was *ciabatta* bread, salad, lots of Italian wine to wash it down with, and a meringue afterwards, with masses of cream and the first strawberries picked from a farm that grew proper strawberries; the kind with flavour.

Nick loved it all and said so, and her mother smiled and flushed, and Charles kissed her cheek and told her she was wonderful, and Daisy looked away. She fondled Barney, who was dying for a lick of cream and had never given anyone bullshit in his life.

Seeming to sense her antipathy, Charles tried to draw her out, asking about her job, her interests, and the more he tried, the more she felt her replies becoming shorter. She knew her mother was noticing, but she couldn't help it. She felt he was trying to ingratiate himself with her.

Just as she'd given a last finger-ful of cream to Barney, Nick turned to her. 'I think we should take that animal for a quick walk and let him work off all that cream.'

Barney's ears could pick up 'walk' at fifty miles. He went loopy, barking and bounding up and down, his tail going in erratic circles.

'Yes, you go,' said her mother brightly. 'By the time you're back, I'll have the coffee ready.'

Daisy clipped Barney to lead and they set forth. The hedge was new and green, the creamy heads of cow parsley still fresh on the verges. 'You must have read my mind,' she said to Nick, as Barney strained on the leash. 'I was dying to – '

'That wasn't the reason.' He led her into a meadow where no sheep grazed, and let Barney off. 'I was ashamed of you, if you want to know. Did you have to be so childish?'

'What?' She gaped at him.

His voice was curt, his mouth set firm. 'The poor guy was doing his best to be pleasant and you behaved like a spoilt brat. Your mother had gone to all that trouble and you made not the slightest effort. She was cringing. Couldn't you see it?'

She felt as if he'd beaten her; thrown her against the wall.

'You know what I think?' he went on. 'I think you're jealous. She's still relatively young, still attractive, but you're so used to being the centre of her universe, you just don't want to share her.'

'*What*?' Anger rose in her, so white and furious she could barely contain it. 'How dare you say that? You don't know what she's been through! They all start off like him, all telling her she's wonderful and smarming enough to make you sick! Do you really think I don't want her to be happy? I want it more than anything in the world!'

'You made up your mind to dislike him. You said so yourself.'

She could not deny it, but he would never understand. He had not seen the heartbreak, heard her mother crying softly at night. 'Of course you'll take his side. You're a man. You're all the same.' She walked stiffly on, but he grabbed her arm.

'What the hell's that supposed to mean?' He was really angry now, she could see it in his eyes, and the tense fingers on her arm.

Daisy was close to tears. It was Simon all over again; her miserable inner edginess spilling over into totally irrational attacks. 'I'm sorry, I didn't mean *you*,' she said unsteadily. 'I just can't help mistrusting him. You just don't know what she's been through and I just can't bear to see it happen again.'

Afraid she was about to break down, she avoided his eye, called Barney, and re-attached him to his lead. 'We'd better get back.' She walked quickly, avoiding his eye, but very conscious of his semi-exasperated gaze. She knew exactly what he was thinking. *'Damned women – I give up.'*

On their return she made a massive effort for her mother's sake. Pretending she'd had a headache, she did her best to be pleasant to Charles.

The atmosphere relaxed. They sat for a long time over coffee, talking about everything from Barbados to Georgian silver and eventually her mother produced tea, with home-made Florentines, chocolate cake, and tea in her non-matching delicate cups.

At six-thirty, Daisy thought she could begin to make noises about leaving without being premature.

Charles kissed her on the cheek, said he hoped very much to see her again and shook hands with Nick. Nick kissed her mother on both cheeks, said it had been a lovely day, and hoped to see her again. Daisy kissed her mother, said it had been lovely and she'd be down again very soon, kissed Barney's head, and waved brightly as she drove away.

Nick was very quiet in the car. A tense, heavy silence hung like a brooding curtain between them.

'What's wrong?' she asked eventually.

'Nothing.' He made an effort at desultory chat, but the tension was still there.

The westering sun cast golden light on the fields, but she saw nothing. A horrible fear was building in her and the closer they got to Richmond, the worse it got. He seemed to be miles away.

She pulled up outside the flat, three spaces from his own car. Forcing brightness, she asked, 'Are you coming in, or will you go straight home?'

He turned to her, an odd, foreboding expression in his eyes. 'Daisy, I have to talk to you.'

Something pierced her with anguish. 'Oh, really? What about?'

He hesitated, looked away. 'Oh, hell. I just don't know how to say it.'

Oh, God. Every ghastly detail of the day was replaying in her head. She had behaved like a spoilt brat, yelled, sworn at him . . . If he no longer wanted anything to do with this unpredictable emotional nightmare, who could blame him?

She felt like a prisoner waiting for the firing squad; desperate to get it over, but at the same time praying for the last-minute reprieve that was never going to come.

She could feel the tension coming off him. He must have been psyching himself up for this ever since they'd left.

Whatever you do, don't cry. Acting for her life, she said airily, 'Tell me, then. We can't sit here all night.'

He ran a tense, exasperated hand over his hair. 'I wish I'd never said it. I'm probably way out – it's just a shot in the dark, my intuition . . .'

After her first intense relief, her eyes widened with bewilderment. 'I don't understand.'

'I'm probably way out,' he repeated, as if trying to convince himself. 'It's ridiculous, for heaven's sake . . .'

'What?' Her voice was suddenly urgent, demanding.

'It's Charles.'

'What about him?' For a wild moment, she wondered whether he'd seen him on *Crimewatch*, but Nick never watched such things.

For ages he paused. 'I think he might be your father.'

'What?' After the first, stunned disbelief, she all but laughed. 'Nick, you can't be serious!'

'I should never have said it.' Restlessly he turned in his seat. 'It was just something in his expression, some vague likeness, some mannerism or other . . . It didn't hit me at first, but he was so desperate for you to like him, never mind your mother. I saw them exchanging glances, and there was something I couldn't put my finger on at first, but suddenly, just as we were leaving. . .'

Dumbfounded, she was unable to take it in.

'I'm probably quite wrong,' he went on. 'I should have kept my mouth shut.'

Slowly, it was making unbelievable sense. Her mother had been so desperate for everything to go well, desperate for her to like him. And his intuition had been right before, when he'd said Simon was not right for her.

Her voice came out like a zombie's. 'His name was Chas – my father's name, I mean. It's short for Charles.'

'That's no evidence. It's a common enough name.'

The more he back-pedalled, the more she was certain he was right. 'She wanted me to meet him before she told me. She wanted to see how we got on.'

'Then I should have let her tell you. Even if I'm right, I should have let her say it.'

But he couldn't un-say it now. Slowly, something swelled in her chest like a tight, black balloon. 'Where has he been?' Her voice rose, shaking with anger and emotion. 'Where has the bastard been all these years? How dare he come back now?'

She turned the key in the ignition. 'You go home. I'm going back. I've got to know.'

'You can't go like this!'

Before she'd realized what was happening, he'd reached across and removed her keys from the ignition. 'If you must go, let me drive you. The state you're in, you'll have an accident.'

'I won't!' She made a grab for the keys, but he held them out of reach.

'I mean it, Daisy. I'm not letting you go like this.'

'What do you mean, let me? You can't stop me!'

'Just watch me.'

By now she knew him well enough to know he'd never give in. Although he showed it rarely, a streak of granite lurked under that laid-back facade. 'But we'll be hours, there and back! And you've got to get up in the morning!'

'So have you.'

They decanted to his car. On the way down he talked little, but she more than made up for it. Things she'd never told anyone came welling out. 'I used to have this fantasy, when I was about seven. I'd come home from school one day and there would suddenly be a Daddy there, like everybody else's. A nice, smiley Daddy with nice blue eyes, like Tara's. I loved Tara's father. He was always there at sports day, in the fathers' race, at the nativity play and the ballet concerts. We used to make Fathers' Day cards at school, and the teacher used to smile brightly and say, 'You could make one for your granddad, if you like.'

He said nothing, but his silence was warm and sympathetic. 'I used to fantasize about what they'd all say when he turned up at last. Something terrible would have happened to him; he'd have been captured by pirates or something ridiculous. I used to see these TV daddies in the advertisements, all smiley and jokey and think he'd be just like that. He'd have a shiny car and a briefcase and wear lovely white shirts for work and a checked shirt for mowing the lawn and want man-appeal beefy gravy on his dinners. He'd come home at six o'clock, and my mother would kiss him in the hall and say, 'What sort of a day have you had, dear?' like Tara's mother, and he'd say, 'Oh, not bad, is supper ready?' And he'd test me on my spellings, like Tara's father did, and give me fifty pence if I got them all right . . .'

Her voice trembled. 'I must be so screwed up. I think maybe that was partly what attracted me to Simon; he seemed so safe and reliable and had all the answers to everything. I never realized at the time, but maybe in some daft way . . .'

Her voice tailed off. 'You can laugh, if you want.'

'Oh, Daisy. I'm not laughing.' He reached across, took her hand and squeezed it.

His voice was so warm, her eyes filled with tears. 'I stopped asking Mum what had happened very early on. I could tell it upset her. She didn't even have a photo. She'd told me that she loved him very much, but she just couldn't find him and he didn't know about me but he'd really love me if he knew.'

She took a deep breath and went on, 'It wasn't till I was about seventeen that she told me. They met in Florence when she was eighteen, on the *Ponte Vecchio*. She fell like a ton of bricks. They had three days, in some little *pensione*, and up in the Tuscan hills. And then he had to go to Brindisi, to catch a ferry to Greece. They swopped addresses, and both promised to write. She did, of course, and eventually her third letter came back saying, 'Not known at this address.' She went three hundred miles to see him, and the woman at the house was very nice, but told her she was very sorry, she must have got the wrong address.'

She talked nearly all the way, and all the way he held her hand. Even when he had to change gear, he still held it; and she did it for him. When they arrived at the cottage it was dark, but she could see Charles' car still parked outside. Before she could get out, Nick caught her. 'Wait for me. And take it gently.'

But she couldn't. She had to ring the bell three times and Barney was barking frantically before her mother opened the door in her dressing gown. Her face was flushed, her hair tumbled in a way that meant only one thing.

Daisy felt sick. 'Is he my father?'

Her mother's face said it all. Guilt, shock, and anguish washed it all at once.

Daisy pushed past her into the house. 'Where is he? Tell him to get down here!'

Barney was still barking frantically. Almost immediately, Charles descended the stairs, in what were obviously hastily pulled-on trousers. 'Isabel? What on – '

Daisy lost it, completely. 'You bastard!' She flew at him, punching his chest, his stomach, anywhere she could reach. 'You damned, filthy, rotten bastard! Where were you? I hate you, you lousy, filthy – '

It was Nick who pulled her off, held her arms at her sides, restraining her. She fought him too, trying to twist away from him, tears streaming down her cheeks. Vaguely, as he half carried her out, she heard her mother crying, Charles trying to soothe her. Outside, in the dark and silence with the door shut, she collapsed against Nick. They stood still in the dark, and she cried a river down his shirt.

When he eventually got her into the car, she was racked with shudders. She assumed they were going home, but fifteen minutes later, he pulled into the car park of a modern hotel. He took the keys out and turned to her. 'Daisy, listen to me. If they've got a room, we're going to stay here the night. I understand why you reacted like that, but tomorrow you have to talk to your mother calmly.'

She nodded, like an exhausted child.

He came back minutes later and they were taken up to the soulless kind of room you get in certain business hotels. Beige twin beds, beige carpet, trouser press, tea and coffee tray.

She lay limp on the bed.

He picked up the phone, ordered two brandies and made her sit and drink one. He sat beside her on the bed, his arm around her. 'I don't want to see him,' she said, over and over again. 'I just don't want to see him.'

He smoothed the hair from her tear-stained face. 'Daisy, whatever happened, it's not your life. You must let her make her own decisions.'

While he was in the bathroom she undressed and slipped into one of the single beds. Shivering in the cold starchy sheets, she watched him undress and switch the light off. But instead of getting into the other twin, he slipped in beside her.

For a moment she was paralyzed with indecision. She could hardly say, 'Nick, we can't *do* anything, I'm on the tail-end of a miscarriage.'

She moistened her lips. 'Nick, we can't sleep together – I've got my – '

'We can sleep. We don't have to make love.'

With his arms folded around her, his breath on her hair, she fell asleep almost at once.

She awoke to find him dressed in trousers but no shirt, pouring boiling water into cups. 'It's pretty awful coffee, but better than nothing.' He sat on the edge of the bed, dropped a soft kiss on her lips. 'How are you feeling?'

It had all come back instantly, every last, nightmarish detail of it. She pushed her tumbled hair back and shivered. 'I don't think I can even face Mum. I certainly can't face him. If he's still there, I'm not going.'

'I'll ring her. Tell her you want to see her alone.'

She sipped her coffee; it wasn't so bad, after all.

He pulled on his shirt. 'I'm going out to find tooth-brushes and shaving stuff – I can't go anywhere like this.' He turned to her. 'Is there anything special you need?'

'No, I'm fine.' She knew he meant 'women's things' and that if she did, he would not be a bit embarrassed about buying them. The very fact of his thoughtfulness made something well up inside her.

'I won't be long.' He came and kissed her and it welled up almost to the point of no return.

Just as he was at the door, she called, 'Nick!'

He turned. 'Yes?'

She just could not do it. 'If you see a bottle of Nivea . . .'

'Will do.' With a smile, he left her.

She lay alone in the beige bedroom, wondering how on earth she would have got through last night without him. How on earth was she going to get through the day? Even with him beside her, it was going to be a nightmare.

'Your *father*?' Tara squeaked. 'You're kidding!'

Still suffering after-shocks, Daisy braced herself for a long session. 'It wasn't altogether his fault,' she explained, five minutes later, 'but he was engaged to somebody else at the time and never told Mum, of course. He got his jacket stolen on the ferry, with her address in it, so he couldn't write. And when her first letters turned up he was away at college and his mother opened them. She opened the first by mistake, or so she said. She was terrified of him breaking it off with this other girl, because she was so sweet and "suitable", so she sent the next couple back. And when Mum turned up on the doorstep, she just said he didn't live there. She was very convincing, Mum said. She just thought he'd given her the wrong address on purpose. She thought it was her own fault for being too keen. She thought she'd frightened him off.'

Jane gave an incredulous whistle. 'The poisonous old – '

'So how did he find out?' Tara topped up three glasses with Macon Blanc.

'His mother told him. She'd become ill; not desperately, but she panicked and thought she was going to die. Felt guilty, I suppose. She still had the letters. This was about five months ago. He still had no idea about me – Mum hadn't said a word. But he wrote to her, and of course it was the wrong address so it took him a while to trace her, but they met, and, well . . .'

'Strewth,' said Tara. 'How weird to meet your dad after all this time. What's he like?'

Daisy shrugged. 'Nice enough, but he's a stranger. I couldn't suddenly be all lovey-dovey with him. We met him later, for lunch; he'd moved to a pub down the road. I was so glad to have Nick there, I can't tell you. I felt really awkward.'

She sighed. 'But Mum's really happy, I can tell. If he messes her about, God help him. But at least he's solvent. Reasonably flush, I think, so at least he won't be sponging off her like Miles.'

'Did he marry this other girl?' Jane asked.

'Yes, but they got divorced a few years ago. Amicably, apparently. She's re-married. He said they were both just far too young.' She paused. 'He's got two sons, James and Oliver.'

'Crumbs!' Tara's eyes widened. 'Two half brothers! I hope they're not like Tom.'

'Nobody could be as bad as Tom,' Daisy joked.

'Damn cheek!' Tara chucked a cushion at her, and in the subsequent laughter, the remains of Daisy's tension eased. 'I made Nick miss nearly a whole day at work. He never said a word, but I feel so bad.'

'Oh, stuff it,' Tara said comfortably. 'You needed somebody with you at a time like that.'

You can say that again.

When Tara had gone to bed, Jane emptied the last of the Macon into their glasses. 'You still haven't told him, have you?'

'What's the point, now?' Daisy gave a despairing sigh. 'But I wanted to. I nearly did, but it wouldn't come out. What with everything else, it hardly seemed the right time. And I could hardly throw it at him in the middle of the M4; the traffic was diabolical. Besides, he had to get to work for at least a couple of hours and I thought he'd had quite enough to cope with already. It was just about the worst shock of my life and he was so supportive . . .' Her voice choked over a massive lump in her throat. 'All the way back I wanted to tell him I loved him but it just wouldn't come out.'

'Because he hasn't said it first.'

Daisy nodded, and put her head in her hands.

'Anyone can say it, Daisy. Ian hardly ever says it, but I still know. It's what they do.'

'I know, but – '

Jane looked oddly guilty. 'Look, I know we promised to keep it quiet, but Ian told Nick about the shop-lifting thing. Ages ago. I wasn't supposed to tell you, but it was Nick who got the charges dropped.'

Daisy gaped at her. 'Nick? How?'

'He knew somebody. The grandson of the man who owns the chain works for him. He had a quiet word, and that was it.'

The lump in her throat was like Mount Everest. She had told him about it in every nightmarish detail, right down to her euphoria when her solicitor had phoned and lifted that dreadful cloud from her shoulders at last. And he had said not one word.

Sleep refused to come that night. At a quarter past two, she got dressed, grabbed her car keys and slipped out. The roads were empty. She put the radio on; late night mood music. The City was even quieter than the rest of London, sleeping under a bright moon, the river flowing placidly under bridges that sparkled with a million lights.

She was no longer unsure. Not even one tiny butterfly fluttered in her stomach.

His chest made a lovely pillow. 'I feel so bad, dragging you from your nice warm bed,' she said sleepily. 'I should have waited till tomorrow.'

'It is tomorrow. And it was an emergency, after all. Crossed wires need sorting out sharpish, and ours were in a hell of a mess. The way you were carrying on lately, I thought it was you looking for a way out.' He dropped a soft kiss on her hair. 'You should have told me,' he said for the fourteenth time.

'I thought you'd hit the roof. You said you weren't into commitment.'

'Oh, Daisy.' He turned on to his side, stroked a finger down her cheek. 'That was months ago. I didn't want to say it till I was sure. Sure that I meant it for good, not for just a couple of months or a couple of years.'

But he had said it now. They both had. Filled with woozy contentment, Daisy was really looking forward to waking up in the morning and realizing that what she had thought was just a delicious dream was nothing of the kind.

'All I knew then was that I wanted you,' he went on.

She thought back to that dreadful night on the beach. 'You could have had me. But you turned me down.'

'And you'll never know how I wished I hadn't.' Like a whisper, his fingers stroked the bare skin of her shoulder. 'But I didn't want you on those terms. A quick fling, with someone else's woman . . .'

She ran her fingers over his chest. 'I still can't believe I did it. But you always did have that effect on me.' A little ripple shook her body. 'Right from the word go you turned me into a shameless hussy . . .'

'Shameless my backside.' He reached down and tweaked her squidgy bits. 'A really shameless hussy would have waited till Juliet had gone upstairs, whipped her knickers off again and said, "Well, what are you standing there for? Get on with it!"'

His shameless-hussy-voice started her giggling helplessly.

His chest shook in return. 'Instead of which you charged off, thanking heaven you'd escaped that den of iniquity . . .'

As their laughter died away he mused, 'You know something? I went looking for you, that night. I

385

borrowed a motorbike and went all over Wandsworth, looking for that beat-up old car.'

'You what?' She raised her head, astonished.

'For hours. In the rain, with an *A to Z*. And could I find you?'

'We'd gone! Tara's father came up unexpectedly and found Tom stoned out of his head and cannabis plants growing all over the kitchen windowsill. Tom told him they were tomatoes, the idiot. We were packed off home before you could say Old Bill.'

'Poor little Daisy.' He chuckled, like warm brown velvet. 'From one den of sin to another . . .'

She lay back, wondering what would have happened if Tara's father had decided to play golf, instead. 'It was better, like this. We were terribly young. And you needed to sow your wild oats. We both did.'

'I was no saint,' he confessed.

'That was part of the attraction. That wicked glint in your eye.' She couldn't help thinking about what she'd lost, and a wave of sadness washed over her. 'I hope it wasn't me, that little lost oat. I hope I'm not "stony ground".'

His arm tightened around her. 'It was just bad luck. There's plenty of time.'

She wasn't going to let it cloud her happiness.

Already the room was filling with the light of dawn. 'I hate to say it, but there's sod all for breakfast,' he said drowsily. 'I don't think there's even an egg.'

Warm, sleepy laughter quivered through her. 'Maybe I'd better go home now, then.'

'You can't.'

'Why not?'

'Because,' he said sleepily, 'my arms are clamped around you in *rigor exhaustedis*. You'd need a crowbar to get them off.'

She hoped they'd stay *rigored* till Kingdom Come.

'I must say, she makes a beautiful bride,' Jane sighed. 'All misty-eyed and radiant.'

'Gorgeous.' Tara sipped her champagne. 'And talking of gorgeous, I think I might go and indulge in some mildly outrageous flirtation with the best man.' With a wink, she strolled off.

Ten yards away, Tara's mother said to Daisy's mother, 'They make such a lovely couple, Isabel. So *right*, somehow. And Daisy looks so happy. I don't know whether it's my imagination, but she seems to have filled out a bit. Fuller in the face, if you know what I mean.' She lowered her voice. 'She's not, well, *expecting*, is she?'

'Good heavens.' Isabel peered through the crush to give her daughter a closer look. 'She hasn't said anything.'

'I can always tell.' Tara's mother allowed herself a placid smile. 'I always think it shows in the face first, long before the waist begins to thicken. I suppose it's the hormones.'

In the corner, next to a lavish arrangement of cream flowers, Daisy's great-aunts Eileen and Dorothy were peering through the crush. 'How can you be sure?' asked Great-aunt Eileen dubiously.

'I can't, dear. It's just a look they get.'

'I can't see anything,' said Great-aunt Eileen.

'Of course you can't, dear. You haven't got your distance glasses on.'

Ian oozed through the crush and slipped an arm around Jane's waist. 'Far be it from me to gossip, my love, but I just overheard some old biddy telling another old biddy she thought Daisy looked pregnant.'

'Dear me,' Jane tutted. 'I can't think where she got that idea from.'

'Exactly,' said Ian. 'I nearly tapped her on the shoulder and said, 'Excuse me, but if Daisy were in an "interesting condition" I'd know all about it because she'd have told my beloved – in strict confidence, of course – and my beloved would have told me.'

Jane smiled serenely and gave him a peck on the cheek. 'Of course I would, darling. Hold your tummy in.'

En route to the best man, Tara was waylaid by her mother. 'Daisy's looking very well, dear. Better than I've seen her in ages.'

'Of course she is, Mum. She's in love.'

Tara's mother lowered her voice. 'I didn't quite mean that, dear. I meant "well" well. As in "happy event" well.'

'Really, Mother.' Tara assumed suitably wide-eyed shock. 'Are you suggesting that Nick and Daisy have been indulging in naughty dalliance before – '

'Tara, do stop taking the mickey, dear. I do know what goes on nowadays. Isabel told me they've been practically living together for months.'

'I think you've had too much champagne, Mother,' Tara said severely. 'I shall ask one of the waitresses to make you a nice cup of tea.'

Five yards away, Daisy smiled across at her Great-aunts Dorothy and Eileen. 'I keep getting Looks from people,' she whispered to Nick. 'Do you suppose somebody's let a certain cat out of the bag?'

'More than likely,' he said. 'Maybe it's time we made a certain announcement.'

'But we said we'd wait!'

'Oh, what the hell,' he winked. 'While they're all in a party mood . . .' Taking her hand, he forged a path through to the end buffet table, where he tapped the best man's gavel on the table. 'Ladies and gentlemen . . .'

The room gradually fell into an expectant hush.

'We weren't going to announce this just yet,' he said, 'But you'll know soon enough, so why not?'

A little ripple ran around the room.

'Daisy didn't want to steal her mother's thunder,' he went on, 'but I'm very happy to tell you that after much bended-knee pleading on the part of this no-good reprobate, she has finally consented to make an honest man of me. So if any of you have recovered sufficiently from Charles and Isabel's wedding to come to another in five weeks, the invitations will be hitting the mats very shortly.'

The ripple turned to a Mexican wave of buzz and Ian banged the gavel again. 'If you've got anything left in your glasses, folks, let's have a toast to the next happy couple. Nick and Daisy.'

Amid the surrounding cheers, Nick gazed down at his bride-to-be. 'You can't wriggle out of it now.'

The glint in his eye still made her heart turn over. 'You dope,' she said, nearly as misty-eyed as her mother. 'Wriggling out of it's positively the last thing I – '

389

The photographer was caught on the hop, but the kiss went on long enough for him to get some really good shots.

Ian glanced at Jane, who had a certain little smile on her face, and light dawned. 'She is, isn't she?'

'Yes,' she whispered. 'But keep it quiet for a bit.'

The best man, who also happened to be Charles' son Oliver, grinned at Tara. 'Not only a sister, but a brother-in-law, too. I think this calls for a celebratory night out, don't you?'

Tara most certainly did.

'Well, how very nice,' said Great-aunt Eileen to Great-aunt Dorothy. 'It wouldn't have been quite seemly for her father to give her away before he'd even married her mother.'

Great-aunt Dorothy wore a very satisfied smile. 'Now I really *am* sure,' she whispered. 'I shall pop to the wool shop on Monday and find a pattern for a really lovely shawl.' She tapped a passing waiter on the shoulder. 'I'd like some more champagne, please.'

'Really, Dorothy, you'll be tipsy,' said her sister.

'I hope so, dear. I'm just in the mood.'

**THE EXCITING NEW NAME
IN WOMEN'S FICTION!**

PLEASE HELP ME TO HELP YOU!

Dear *Scarlet* Reader,

Last month we began our super Prize Draw, which means
that **you could win 6 months' worth of free Scarlets!**
Just return your completed questionnaire to us (see addresses at end of questionnaire) before 31 July 1997 and you
will automatically be entered in the draw that takes place on
that day. If you are lucky enough to be one of the first two
names out of the hat we will send you four new Scarlet
romances every month for six months, and for each of
twenty runners up there will be a sassy *Scarlet* T-shirt.

So don't delay – return your form straight away!*

Sally Cooper

Editor-in-Chief, *Scarlet*

QUESTIONNAIRE

Please tick the appropriate boxes to indicate your answers

1 Where did you get this Scarlet title?
Bought in supermarket ☐
Bought at my local bookstore ☐ Bought at chain bookstore ☐
Bought at book exchange or used bookstore ☐
Borrowed from a friend ☐
Other (please indicate) _____

2 Did you enjoy reading it?
A lot ☐   A little ☐   Not at all ☐

3 What did you particularly like about this book?
Believable characters ☐   Easy to read ☐
Good value for money ☐   Enjoyable locations ☐
Interesting story ☐   Modern setting ☐
Other _____

4 What did you particularly dislike about this book?
_____

5 Would you buy another Scarlet book?
Yes ☐   No ☐

6 What other kinds of book do you enjoy reading?
Horror ☐   Puzzle books ☐   Historical fiction ☐
General fiction ☐   Crime/Detective ☐   Cookery ☐
Other (please indicate) _____

7 Which magazines do you enjoy reading?
  1. _____
  2. _____
  3. _____

And now a little about you –
8 How old are you?
  Under 25 ☐   25–34 ☐   35–44 ☐
  45–54 ☐   55–64 ☐   over 65 ☐

cont.

9 What is your marital status?
Single ☐ Married/living with partner ☐
Widowed ☐ Separated/divorced ☐

10 What is your current occupation?
Employed full-time ☐ Employed part-time ☐
Student ☐ Housewife full-time ☐
Unemployed ☐ Retired ☐

11 Do you have children? If so, how many and how old are they?
_____
_____

12 What is your annual household income?

under $15,000	☐ or	£10,000	☐
$15–25,000	☐ or	£10–20,000	☐
$25–35,000	☐ or	£20–30,000	☐
$35–50,000	☐ or	£30–40,000	☐
over $50,000	☐ or	£40,000	☐

Miss/Mrs/Ms _____
Address _____
_____
_____

Thank you for completing this questionnaire. Now tear it out – put it in an envelope and send it to:

Sally Cooper, Editor-in-Chief

USA/Can. address
SCARLET c/o London Bridge
85 River Rock Drive
Suite 202
Buffalo
NY 14207
USA

UK address/No stamp required
SCARLET
FREEPOST LON 3335
LONDON W8 4BR
Please use block capitals for address

NOGEN/4/97

Scarlet **titles coming next month:**

CAROUSEL   Michelle Reynolds
When Penny Farthing takes a job as housekeeper/nanny to Ben Carmichael and his sons, she's looking for a quiet life. Penny thinks she'll quite like living in the country and she knows she'll love the little boys she's caring for . . . what she doesn't expect is to fall in love with her boss!

BLACK VELVET   Patricia Wilson
Another *Scarlet* novel from this best-selling author! Helen Stewart is *not* impressed when she meets Dan Forrest – she's sure he's drunk, so she dumps him unceremoniously at his hotel! Dan isn't drunk, he has flu, so their relationship doesn't get off to the best start. Dan, though, soon wants Helen more than he's ever wanted any other woman . . . but is she involved in *murder?*

CHANGE OF HEART   Julie Garratt
Ten years ago headstrong Serena Corder was involved with Holt Blackwood, but she left home because she resented her father's attempts to control her life. Now a very different Serena is back and the attraction she feels for Holt is as strong as ever. But do they have a future together . . . especially as she wears another man's ring!

A CIRCLE IN TIME   Jean Walton
Margie Seymour is about to lose her beloved ranch, when she finds an injured man on her property. He tells her not only that he is from the 1800s, but that *he*, not she, owns the ranch! It's not long before feisty Margie Seymour is playing havoc with Jake's good intentions of returning to his own time as soon as he can!